Keep it simple. Secure the spaceport. Hold until relieved.

Nothing new there.

Remember your training.

The question was whether the landings would be enough. Alighan was a heavily populated world in the Theocracy of Islam, with over two billion people in the ocean-girdled world's teeming cities. The Marine assault force consisted of the four companies of the 55th Marine Aerospace Regimental Strikeforce, a total of five hundred eighty men and women . . . against an entire world.

True, they were exceptionally well armed and armored men and women, and they seemed—for the moment at least—to have the element of surprise. Even so, fewer than six hundred Marines against a population of two billion who would fight to the death and take as many Marines with them as they could.

Impossible.

Ridiculously impossible.

But the United Star Marines specialized in the impossible, as they and their predecessors had done for the past eleven hundred years . . .

STAR STRIKE

BOOK ONE OF **THE INHERITANCE TRILOGY**

IAN DOUGLAS

An Imprint of HarperCollinsPublishers

EOS
An Imprint of HarperCollins*Publishers*
10 East 53rd Street
New York, New York 10022-5299

First Eos paperback printing: February 2008

HarperCollins® and Eos® are registered trademarks of HarperCollins Publishers.

Printed in the U.S.A.

10 9 8 7 6 5 4 3 2 1

To CJ and Garin, good friends who saw me through rough times. And, as always, for Brea.

Acknowledgments

My special thanks to David Plottel, friend, programmer, mathematician, and ubergeek, for his insights into Leonhard Euler and the God-equation known as Euler's Identity.

STAR
STRIKE

Prologue

Deep within the star clouds of the Second Galactic Spiral Arm, a sentient machine detected the blue-white shriek of tortured hydrogen atoms, and a program hundreds of thousands of years ancient switched from stand-by to active. Something *was out there . . . something massive, something moving at very nearly the speed of light.*

*Even the hardest interstellar vacuum contains isolated flecks of matter—hydrogen atoms, mostly, perhaps one per cubic centimeter or so. The object's high-speed passage plowed through these atoms, ionizing many, leaving a boiling hiss in its wake easily detectable by appropriately sensitive instrumentation. The disturbance was a kind of wake, created by a mass of some hundreds of millions of tons plowing through the tenuous matter of the interstellar void at near-*c.

The sentry machine had taken up its lonely vigil half a million years before, during the desperate and no-quarter war of extermination against the Associative, a war that had laid waste to ten thousand suns and countless worlds scattered across a third of the Galaxy. Occasionally, it conversed with others of its kind—a means of staying sane through the millennia—but for most of its existence it had been asleep, dreaming the eldritch dreams of a being neither wholly mechanism, nor wholly biological.

The builders of the Sentry called themselves something that might have translated, very approximately, as "We Who Are." Other species across light centuries of space and hundreds of millennia called them many other things. The

*inhabitants of Earth, once, had called them "Xul," a name
that in ancient Sumeria had come to mean "demon."*

*A far older civilization had called them the Hunters of
the Dawn.*

*However they were known to themselves or to others,
how they were identified was less important for their view
of themselves than was their evolutionary imperative, the
drive, refined over millions of years, that made them what
they were. For the Xul, existence—more,* survival—*was an
absolute, the defining characteristic of their universe. In
their worldview, survival meant eliminating* all *potential
competition. Their culture did not have anything like
religion, but if it had, their religion would have been a kind
of Darwinian dogmatism, with the fact that they had so
far survived serving as proof that they were, indeed, the
fittest.*

*For the Xul, the first requirement for continued survival
was the detection and identification of potential threats to
existence. An object with the mass of a fair-sized asteroid
traveling through the Galaxy at near-*c *velocities indicated
both sentience and a technology that might represent a
serious threat.*

*With an analytical detachment more characteristic
of the computers in its ancestry than of organic beings,
the Sentry tracked the disturbance through local space.
A ripple twisted the fabric of space/time, and the Sentry
shifted across light-years, emerging alongside the massive
object, traveling at precisely the object's velocity.*

*At this speed, a hair's breadth short of the speed of light
itself, the universe appeared weirdly and beautifully compressed, a ring of solid starlight encircling the heavens
slightly ahead of the hurtling vessels. With the patient calm
of a lifespan measured in millennia, the Sentry reached out
with myriad senses, tasting the anomalous traveler.*

*Outwardly, the object was an ordinary asteroid, a car-
bonaceous chondrite of fairly typical composition, with a
dusty, pocked surface of such a dark gray color as to be
nearly coal black. Outwardly, there was no indication of
intelligent design—no lights, no artificial structures on the*

surface, no thruster venturis or other obvious clues to the object's propulsive system. Even the high velocity might be an artifact . . . a souvenir of a long-ago close-passage of a black hole or neutron star, with the resultant slingshot effect whipping a random, dead rock to within one percent of c.

But the Sentry's gentle probings elicited other evidence, proof that the fast-moving object was both the product of technology and inhabited. A steady trickle of neutrinos proved the presence of hydrogen fusion plants, providing power for life-support and secondary systems. The tick and flux of even more subtle, virtual particles revealed the operation of a quantum effect power system, tapping the base state of space itself for the energies necessary to move that much mass at that high a speed. The drive was quiescent now, but the potential remained, a subtle aura of shifting energies representing fields and forces that might engage at any moment. Perhaps most telling of all, a powerful shield composed of interplaying gravitic and magnetic fields swept space far ahead of the starship—for starship is what the object was—clearing its path of stray subatomic particles lest they strike rock and cascade into deadly secondary radiation, frying the ship's passengers as they slept away the objective decades.

For passengers there were—some fifty thousand of them, stored in a cybernetic hibernation that let them pass decades of subjective time without the need for millions of tons of food, water, and other expendables. At the moment, the only member of the starship's crew that was actually awake was a being far more closely related, in its basic nature, to the Sentry than it was to the slumbering beings in its care, a sentient computer program named Perseus.

For over five hundred years, Perseus had overseen the routine operation of the asteroid starship and her refugee passengers, monitoring drive systems and power plant, life support and cybe-hibe stasis capsules. The ship, christened Argo, had fled distant Earth a few years after the devastating attack on that world by the Xul; her destination was another galaxy entirely, M-31, in Andromeda, something over two million light-years distant.

The voyage as planned would take almost 2.3 million years objective, but on board the clocks would record the passage of barely thirty years. Argo's sleeping passengers, for the most part, were members of Earth's political and economic elite. Many were representatives of the governments of the United States and of the American Union who'd felt Humankind's only hope of survival lay in avoiding all-out war with the technologically advanced Xul, in escaping the enemy's notice, in fleeing to another galaxy entirely and beginning anew.

Their decision proved to be a supreme exercise in wishful thinking. The Xul sentry engaged Perseus as the sentient program was still shifting to full operational mode. It had time to engage a single emergency comm channel before the Xul group-mind overwhelmed it in an electronic cascade of incoming data.

Parts of Perseus were hijacked by the alien operating system; others were wiped away, or simply stored for later exploration.

And within the Argo-planetoid's heart, fifty thousand human minds cried out as one as they were patterned and replicated by the intruder. Moments later, the asteroid's immense kinetic energy was instantly transformed into heat and light, bathing the Xul Sentry in the actinic glare of a tiny nova.

By the Xul way of thinking, the asteroid starship represented both a threat and unfinished business.

Neither could be tolerated.

1

0407.1102

The Specters descended over the Southern Sea, slicing north through turbulent air, their hulls phase-shifted so that they were not entirely within the embrace of normal space. Shifted, they were all but invisible to radar, and little more than shadows to human eyes, shadows flickering across a star-clotted night.

On board Specter One-one Bravo, Gunnery Sergeant Charel Ramsey sat huddled pauldron-to-pauldron with the Marines locked in to either side of him. The squad bay was red lit and crowded, a narrow space barely large enough to accommodate a platoon of forty-eight Marines in full Mark 660 assault battlesuits. He tried once again to access the tacnet, and bit off a curse when all that showed within the open mindwindow was static. They were going in blind, hot and blind, and he didn't like the feeling. If the Muzzies got twitchy and started painting their southern sky with plasma bolts or A.M. needlers, phase-shifting would not protect them in the least.

"They're holding off on the drones," Master Sergeant Adellen said over the tac channel, almost as if she were reading his mind. Likely she was as nervous as the rest of the Marines in the Specter's belly. She just hid it better than most. "They don't want to tip the grounders off that we're on final."

"Yeah, but it would be nice to see where the hell we're going," Corporal Takamura observed. "We can't see shit through the LV's optics."

That was not entirely true, of course. Ramsey had a window open in his mind linked through to the feed from the Specter's cockpit. Menu selections gave him a choice of views—through cameras forward or aft, in visible light, low-light, or infrared, or a computer-generated map of the planet that showed twelve green triangles in a double-chevron formation moving toward the still-distant coastline. Ramsey had settled on the map view, since the various optical feeds showed little now but water, clouds, and stars.

The MLV-44 Specter Marine Landing Vehicles were large and slow, with gull wings and fusion thrusters that gave them somewhat more maneuverability than a falling brick, but not much. Each mounted a pair of AI-controlled high-speed cannon firing contained micro-antimatter rounds as defense against incoming missiles, but they relied on stealth and surprise for survival, not firepower, and certainly not armor. A Specter's hull could shield those on board from the searing heat of atmospheric entry, but a mag-driven needle or even a stray chunk of high-energy shrapnel could puncture its variform shell with shocking ease. Ramsey had seen the results of shrapnel impact on a grounded Specter before, on Shamsheer and on New Tariq.

The Specter jolted hard, suddenly and unexpectedly, and someone vented a sharp curse. They were falling into denser air, passing through the cloud deck, and things were getting rougher.

"One more of those," Sergeant Vallida said, her voice bitter, "and Private Dowers gets jettisoned."

"Hey, Sarge! I didn't do anything!"

"Don't pick on Dowers," Adellen said. "He didn't know."

"Yeah, but he *should* have. Fucking nectricots. . . ."

It was rank superstition, of course. Even if it went back over a thousand years. Maybe it was the sheer age of the tradition that gave it so much power. But somehow, back in the twentieth or twenty-first century, it had become an article of faith that if a Marine ate the apricots in his ration pack before boarding an alligator or other armored transport, the vehicle *would* break down. Over the centuries, the focus of the curse had gradually shifted from apricots to genegineered nectricots, but the principle remained the same.

And Ela Vallida had walked in on Dowers back on board the *Kelley* just before the platoon had saddled up that morning, to find him happily slurping down the last of the nectricots in his drop rats. Dowers was a fungie, fresh out of RTC, and not yet fully conversant with the bewildering labyrinth of tradition and history within which every Marine walked.

"Fucking *fungie*," Vallida added.

"Belay that, Sergeant," Lieutenant Jones growled. First Platoon's CO wasn't evenly physically present on the squad bay deck; the eltee was topside somewhere, plugged into the C^3 suite behind the Specter's cockpit, but she obviously was staying linked in on the platoon chat line. "Chew on him after One-one Bravo craps out, and you have something to bitch about."

"Aye, aye, sir," Vallida replied. But Ramsey still heard the anger in her voice.

Likely, he thought, it was just the stress. This was always the roughest part of a Marine landing, the long, agonizing wait, sealed into a tin can that was flying or swimming toward God-knew what kind of defenses. Did the Alighani Muzzies know the Marines were coming? What was waiting for them at the objective?

How many of the men and women sealed into this Specter were going to be alive an hour from now? . . .

Don't even think about that, Ramsey told himself. *It's bad ju-ju. . . .*

Not that he actually *believed* in luck, of course . . . or in the power of nectricot curses. But he didn't know anyone who'd survived the hell of modern combat who didn't engage in at least a few minor superstitious behaviors, and that included Ramsey himself. He never went into combat without a neumenal image of his Marine father watching from a minimized mindwindow. Totally irrational, he knew.

His mental gaze shifted to the tiny, mental image of Marine Master Sergeant Danel Jostin Ramsey, resplendent in his dress blacks . . . an image recorded just days before the landings on Torakara.

The Specter gave another hard lurch. According to the feed from the cockpit, it was raining outside now, and lightning flared behind the clouds ahead. The mission planners had chosen to insert through a large, tropical storm, taking advantage of lightning and rain to shield the assault group's approach for a precious few seconds longer.

"Listen up, people," Lieutenant Jones' voice said over the platoon net. "We're three minutes out, and about to drop below the cloud deck. Remember your training, remember your mission downloads. Keep it simple! We secure the spaceport, and we hold until relieved. Ooh-rah?"

"Ooh-rah!" the platoon chorused back at her.

Seconds later, a loud thump announced the release of the battlezone sensor pods, and the main tactical feed came on-line as thousands of thumb-sized microfliers were shotgunned into the skies ahead of the assault group. Ramsey opened a mental window, and entered a computer-generated panorama of ocean, and the coastline to the north. Red pinpoints illuminated the coast, marking generators, vehicles, and other power-producing facilities or units. The spaceport was marked in orange, the Fortress in white, with sullen red patterns submerged within the graphics, indicating the main power plants.

As he watched, more power sources winked on. That might be an illusion generated by the fact that more and more BZ pods were entering the combat area, but it also might mean the enemy had been alerted and was waking up.

But so far, the skies were quiet, save for the flash of lightning and the sweeping curtains of rain.

Remember your training. Yeah . . . as if that were a problem. *Remember your downloads.* Their mission parameters had been hard-loaded into their cephlink RAM. It wasn't like you could freaking *forget.* . . .

Keep it simple. Secure the spaceport. Hold until relieved.

Nothing new there, either.

The question was whether the landings would be enough. Alighan was a heavily populated world in the Theocracy of Islam, with over two billion people in the ocean-girdled world's teeming cities. The Marine assault force codenamed Green 1 consisted of the four companies of the 55th Marine Aerospace Regimental Strikeforce, a total of 580 men and women . . . against an entire world.

True, they were exceptionally well armed and armored men and women, and they seemed—for the moment at least— to have kept the element of surprise. Even so, fewer than six hundred Marines against a population of two billion . . .

Impossible.

Ridiculously impossible.

But the United Star Marines, once the United *States* Marines, specialized in the impossible, as they and their predecessors had done for the past eleven hundred years.

Alighan. The name was derived from the Arabic term for "God is Guardian," and the name suited the place. The system of five rocky planets orbiting a K0 star was strategically positioned along the New Dubai trade route, a channel for ninety percent of the interstellar shipping between the Heart Worlds and the Theocracy. Control Alighan, and you controlled access to the Islamic state . . . or to the Heart Worlds, depending on which way your battlefleet was headed. Scuttlebutt had it that the Terran Military Command wanted Alighan as an advance base for deeper strikes into Theocratic space.

The key, of course, was the planetary starport, Al Meneh, "The Port," which doubled as the system capital. The battleops plan called for the Marines to seize and hold the starport. Within a standard day—two at the most—the Navy transports would arrive from Kresgan, bringing with them the Army's 104th Planetary Assault Division, the 43rd Heavy Armored Division, and elements of the 153rd Star Artillery Brigade and the 19th Interstellar Logistical Support Group.

And the Marines, those who'd survived, would be off to their next planethead.

Five hundred planetary assault Marines against two billion Muslim fanatics. . . .

Ramsey shook his head, a gesture unseen within the massive helmet of his 660-ABS. In fact, the vast majority of the local population would *not* be fanatics. Most of the population down there would be ordinary folks who wanted nothing more than to be left alone, especially by their own government.

But experience gained so far in the present war—and in other wars fought against the Theocracy and similar governments over the past eleven centuries—taught that the ones who *did* fight would do so with all their heart and soul, with no thought of quarter, and with no mind for the usual rules of war.

They would fight to the death, and they would take as many Marines with them as they could.

So far as the Marines of the 55th MARS were concerned, they would be happy to help the Muzzies find their longed-for medieval paradise.

Without going with them.

USMC Recruit Training Center
Noctis Labyrinthus, Mars
0455/24:20 local time, 1513 hrs GMT

"Gods and goddesses, Jesus, Buddha, and fucking Lao *Tse*! Those fat-assed bastards up in Ring City are trying to fucking destroy *my* Corps! . . ."

Gunnery Sergeant Michel Warhurst stopped his pacing in front of the ragged line of recruit trainees and shook his head sadly. "*You* maggots are trying to fucking destroy my Corps! My *beloved* Corps! And I am here this morning to let you know that I will *not* stand for that!"

Recruit Private Aiden Garroway stood at a civilian's approximation of attention, staring past the glowering drill instructor's shoulder and off into the velvet, star-riddled blackness of the Martian night. After a brief flight down from the Arean Ring, he and his fellow recruits had been unceremoniously hustled off the shuttle, herded into line by screaming assistant DIs, and were now being formally inducted into Recruit Company 4102 by the man who would rule their lives for the next sixteen weeks.

He was actually enjoying the show, as the drill instructor paraded back and forth in front of the line of recruits. Three assistant DIs stood a few meters away, two glowering, one grinning with what could only be described as evil anticipation.

He'd been expecting this speech, of course, or something very close to it. For the past two years, ever since he'd decided to escape a dead-end jack-in and shallow friends by enlisting in the United Star Marines, he'd lived and breathed the Corps. Boot camp, he knew, would be rough, and it would begin with exactly this kind of heavy-handed polemics, a strategy honed over the centuries to break down the attitudes and preconceptions of a hundred-odd kids with civilian outlooks and build them back up into *Marines*. It was part of a tradition extending back over a thousand years . . . and it self-evidently worked.

And getting through boot camp, he'd decided, wouldn't be all that tough, not for *him*. After all, he knew what it was all about. He knew . . .

"What the fuck are you daydreaming about, maggot!?"

The DI's face had appeared centimeters in front of his own as if out of nowhere, contorted by rage, eyes staring, mouth wide open, blasting into Garroway's face with hurricane force. The sheer suddenness and volume forced him to take a step back. . . .

"And *where* the fuck do you think you're going, you *slimy* excuse for an Ishtaran mudworm? Get back here and toe that line! I am *not* done with you, maggot, not by ten thousand fucking light-years, and when I am done you will know it! Drop to the sand! Give me fifty, right here*!"*

Startled, Garroway swallowed, looked at Warhurst, and stammered out a "S-sorry, sir!"

The senior drill instructor's face blended fury with thunderstruck. *"What* did you say?"

"I'm sorry, sir!"

"What did you just call me? Gods and goddesses of the Eternal Void, I can't *believe* what I just heard!" Warhurst brought one blunt finger up a hair's breadth away from Garroway's nose. *"First* of all, maggot, I did *not* give you per-

mission to squeak! None of you will squeak unless I or one of the assistant drill instructors here gives your *sorry* ass permission to squeak! *Is* that understood?"

Garroway wasn't sure whether a response was called for, but suspected this was one of those cases where he would get into trouble whether he replied or not. He remained mute, eyes focused somewhere beyond Warhurst's left shoulder.

"Give me an answer, recruit!" Warhurst bellowed. *"Is* that understood?"

"Yes, sir!"

"What?"

"Yes, sir!"

"Second of all, for your information my name is *not* 'Sorry.' So far as you putrid escapees from a toilet bowl are concerned, I am *sir*!" He turned away from Garroway and strode up the line, bellowing. "In fact, so far as you mudworms are concerned, I am *God*, but you will *always* address me as *'sir!' If* you have permission to address me or any of the other drill instructors behind me, the first word *and* the last word out of your miserable, sorry shithole mouths *will* be *'sir!'* All of you! *Do* I make myself abundantly clear?"

Several in the line of recruits chorused back with, "Sir, yes, sir!" A few, however, forgot to start with the honorific, and most said nothing at all, or else mumbled along.

"What was that? I couldn't hear that!"

"Sir, yes, sir!"

"What?!"

"Sir, yes, sir!"

Warhurst turned again to glower into Garroway's face. "Third! Recruits will *not* refer to themselves as 'I'! You are not an *I*! *None* of you rates an *I*! If for *any* reason you are required to refer to your miserable selves, you will *not* use the first person, but you *will* instead say 'this recruit!' That goes for all of you! *Is that clear?"*

"Sir, yes, sir!"

"Fourth! *If* I give you an order, you will *not* say 'sir, yes, sir!' You will reply with the correct Marine response, and say *'Sir*, aye, aye, *sir!'* You are *not* Marines and you may never be Marines, but by all the gods of the Corps you will *sound* like Marines! *Is* that clear?"

"*Sir, yes, sir!*" came back, though it was made ragged by a few shouted "Sir, aye, aye, sirs." The recruits were all looking a bit wild-eyed now, as confusion and sensory overload began to overwhelm them.

Garroway thought Warhurst was going to explode at the company for using the wrong response. Reaching the left end of the line, he spun sharply and charged back to the right. "*Idiots*! I ask for recruits and they give me deaf, dumb, and blind *idiots*!" Turning again, he charged back to the left, raw power and fury embodied in a spotlessly crisp Marine dress black-C uniform. "*Get* the shit out of your ears! *If* I ask a question requiring a response of either 'yes' or 'no,' you *will* say 'sir,' then give me a 'yes' or a 'no,' as required, and then you will again say 'sir!'" Stopping suddenly at the center of the line, he turned and bellowed, "*Is that clear?*"

"Sir, yes, sir!"

"And *when* I give you an order, you *will* respond with 'sir, aye, aye, sir!' Remember that! 'Aye, aye' means 'I understand and I will obey!' *Is* that understood?"

"*Sir, yes, sir!*"

Garroway was impressed. Under the DI's unrelenting barrage, the line of recruits, until moments ago a chaotic mélange of individually mumbled responses, was actually starting to chorus together, and with considerable feeling . . . but then the DI was back in his face once again, eye to eye, screaming at him. "*What the hell are you doing on your feet, maggot? I gave you a direct order! I told you to give me fifty! That's fifty push-ups!*"

Damn! Garroway had been as confused as the rest, stunned into unthinking immobility by the DI's performance. He dropped to the ground, legs back, arms holding his body stiffly above the sand, and started to perform the first push-up, but then Warhurst was hauling him upright by the scruff of his neck, dangling him one-handed above the sand, still screaming. "I did *not* hear you acknowledge the order I gave you, mudworm!"

"Sir, yes, sir! Uh, I mean, aye, aye, sir!"

"*What was that?*"

"Sir! Aye, aye, sir!"

Warhurst released him. "*Gimme those fifty goddamn push-ups!*"

"Sir! Aye, aye, sir!"

Garroway dropped again and began cranking out the push-ups. He'd worked out a lot over the past couple of years, knowing that this sort of thing would be routine. He'd also spent a lot of time recently working in the Recovery Projects back on Earth. There he massed a full 85 kilos, so he had a bit of an advantage of some of the other kids in the line. On Mars, he only weighed 32 kilos, compared to the 60 kilos he carried at his home level in the Ring.

So right now he weighed half what he normally did, and was feeling pretty strong, even competent. The push-ups came swiftly and easily as Warhurst continued to parade up and down the line of recruits, finding fault everywhere, screaming invectives at the other recruits. Before long, Garroway wasn't the only one doing push-ups. He completed his count and stood at attention once more, surprised to find he was breathing harder, now. In fact, his chest was burning.

The Martian air was painfully thin, despite the nano-chelates in his lungs that increased the efficiency of his breathing. The terraformers had been reshaping Mars for almost four centuries, now, hammering it with icebergs to begin with, but more recently using massive infusions of nanodecouplers to free oxygen from the planet-wide rust and restore the ancient Martian atmosphere. For the past two centuries, the air had been breathable, at least with nanotechnic augmentation, but it was still thin, cold, and carried a harsh taste of sand and chemicals.

Abruptly, as if at the throw of a switch, Gunnery Sergeant Warhurst's fury was gone. Instead, he seemed relaxed, almost paternal. "Very well, children," he said, standing before them with his hands on his hips. "You have just had your first fifteen minutes of Marine indoctrination and training . . . an ancient and hallowed tradition we refer to as 'boot camp.' Each of you has volunteered for this. Presumably, that means each of you *wants* to be here. I certainly understand that desire. The Marines are the best there are, no question about it.

"However, I want each and every one of you to take a moment and think very hard about this decision you've made. Behind you is the shuttle that brought you down from the Arean Ring. If for any reason you are having second thoughts, I want you to turn around right now and plant your ass back on board that shuttle. You will be flown back up to the Arean Ring, where you can retrieve your civilian clothing, have a nice hot meal, and make arrangements to go home. No questions asked. No one will think the less of you." He paused. "How about it? Any takers?"

Out of the corner of his eye, Garroway sensed movement down the line to his left. Someone was wavering . . . and then he heard the sound of footsteps in the sand, moving toward the rear. He didn't dare look, however. The formation was still at attention, and he had a feeling that if he turned his head to look, Warhurst's sudden nice-guy persona would vanish as abruptly as it had begun.

"Smart boy," Warhurst said, nodding. "Anybody else? This will be your last chance. If you miss that shuttle . . . then for the next sixteen weeks you *will* be *mine*."

Garroway thought he heard someone else leave the line, but he wasn't sure. He knew *he* wasn't going to quit, not now. He was going to be a Marine. . . .

"Handley!" Warhurst snapped, addressing one of the recruits. "Eyes front!"

"Sir! Aye, aye, sir!"

A long silence passed. Warhurst stood before them, his head down, as if he were listening to something. Then he looked up. "I want each of you to open your primary inputs. Full immersion."

Garroway did so. His neurocranial link implants opened to a local feed coming down from the Martian Ring. It was coded, but each had received the appropriate clearances up at the receiving station.

There was a moment's mental static, followed by the always odd feeling of standing in two places at once . . .

. . . and then Garroway was standing on another world.

It was night there, as it was at Noctis Labyrinthus. It was also raining, though the link was not transmitting the feel of the rain on his skin, or the bluster of the wind.

He could see, however, a formation of Marine landing vehicles skimming in a few meters above the surf and spray of a beach, their black hulls shimmering as they phased into full solidity, their variform shells unfolding into landing configuration. Lightning flared . . . or perhaps it was a plasma bolt fired from the shore. It was tough sorting out exactly what was happening, because there was a great deal of noise and movement.

One of the landing vehicles crumpled with nightmare suddenness in midair, flame engulfing its gull-winged form, the wreckage tumbling out of the sky and slamming into the surf in a crashing fountain of spray and steam. *Plasma bolt*, Garroway thought. An instant later, a beam of dazzling incandescence struck down out of the black overcast, a white flash starkly illuminating the beach and the incoming formation as it lanced the squat building from which the plasma bolt had been fired. The explosion further lit the night, as the first of the shape-shifting landing craft began touching down.

In his mind, Garroway turned, watching as other craft passed overhead. There was a city behind the beach . . . and what looked like a large and sprawling spaceport. Beams of light continued to spear out of the angry heavens, vaporizing enemy hardpoints.

And now, individual Marines were appearing in their cumbersome combat armor, bounding through flame and smoldering wreckage and sand dunes to close with the enemy.

"This," Warhurst's voice said in Garroway's head, "is taking place on a world called Alighan, about four hundred light-years from where you're standing right now. There's a slight delay in the feed, but, within the uncertainties imposed by the physics of FTL simultaneity and the time lag down from the Arean Ring, it is happening more or less as you see it. The image is being relayed from our battlefleet straight back to HQ USMC. Colonel Peters thought you should see this."

More Marines surged across the beach, sweeping toward the outer Alighan beach defenses. Other landing craft had passed over those bunkers and gun emplacements and were settling to ground on the spaceport itself. Fire continued to lance out of the sky, pinpoint bombardments called down by Marine spotters. Garroway found he could hear some of the chatter in the background, a babble of call signs, orders, and acknowledgments.

"The Islamic Theocracy," Warhurst went on, "has blocked several key trade routes into their territory. Worse, they have supported terrorist incursions into Commonwealth Space, seized Commonwealth vessels, and are suspected of holding Commonwealth citizens as slaves.

"As you should know by now, the sole purpose of the U.S. Marine Corps is to protect Commonwealth worlds and Commonwealth citizens. To that end, a naval battlefleet and a Marine Expeditionary Force have been dispatched to effect a change in the Theocrat government. Their first step is to capture the spaceport you see in the distance, so that Army troops can land and occupy the planet.

"The politics of the situation are unimportant, however. Marines go where they're sent. They do what they're told to do. They do so at the behest of the United Star Commonwealth, and the Commonwealth Command Authority. All very nice, neat, and clean. . . .

"But *this*, children, is what modern combat really is."

The scene around Garroway was rapidly becoming a burning nightmare out of some primitive religion's hell. With a mental command, his point of view drifted up from the beach toward the spaceport, where the heaviest fighting was now taking place. The landing craft all were down now—those that had survived the approach. Upon touching down, their fuselages had broken into sections, becoming automated mobile gun platforms; the wing, cockpit, and spine assemblies then each had lifted off once more, becoming airborne gunships that darted across the scene like immense, spindly insects, spewing plasma bolts and blazing streams of autocannon fire. And individual Marines, forty-eight to each LV, fanned out across the flame-tortured landscape, hunting down the enemy one gun position or hardpoint at a time. Overhead, Marine A-90 Cutlass sky-support attack craft darted and swooped like hideously visaged black hornets, locking in on ground targets and blasting them with devastating fire.

Clouds of gray fog swept over the landscape from different directions—combat nano and counternano, waging their submicroscopic battles in the air and on the ground. Disassemblers released by the Muzzies were seeking out Marines and vehicles, while the counter-clouds roiling off Marine armor and vehicles sought to neutralize them. The result was a deadly balance; in places, the ground was melting, the rain hissing into steam.

Almost in front of him, a Marine bounded in for a landing, his combat suit making him seem bulky and awkward, but the impression was belied by the grace of movement on the suit's agrav packs. The Marine touched down lightly, aimed at an unseen target with the massive field-pulse rifle mounted beneath his right arm, then bounded again.

The armor itself, Garroway saw, was mostly black, but the surface had a shimmering, illusive effect that rendered it nearly invisible, an illusion due to the nanoflage coating which continually adapted to incoming light. In places, he saw blue sparks and flashes where enemy nano-D was trying to eat into the suit's defenses, but was—so far—being successfully blocked by the suit's counters.

Neither near-invisibility nor nanotechnic defenses could help this Marine, however. As he grounded again, something flashed nearby, and the man's midsection vanished in a flare of blue-white light. Legs collapsed to one side, head and torso to the others, the arms still, horribly, moving. Garroway thought he heard a spine-chilling shriek over the link, mercifully cut off as the armored suit died. Rain continued to drench the hot ruin of the combat suit, steaming in the flare-lit night, and the armor itself, exposed to the relentless embrace of airborne nanodisassemblers, began to soften, curdle, and dissolve.

The arms had stopped moving. There was a great deal

of blood on the ground, however, and slowly dissolving wet chunks of what might be . . .

Gods. . . .

Garroway struggled not to be sick. He would *not* be sick. He wrenched his mental gaze away from the feed, and stood once more in the Martian night.

"Being a Marine is one of the greatest honors, one of the greatest *responsibilities* available to the Commonwealth citizenry," Warhurst said, his voice still speaking in his mind over the implant link. "But it is not for everyone. It requires the ultimate commitment. Fortitude. Courage. Character. Commitment to duty and to fellow Marines. Sometimes, it requires the ultimate sacrifice . . . for the Commonwealth. For your brother and sister Marines. For the *Corps*.

"You've all just seen what modern combat is like . . . what it's *really* like, not what the entertainment feeds would have you believe. Do any of you want to see this thing through?"

Garroway heard others leaving the line; he didn't know how many. He also heard someone retching off to his left.

After a long pause, Warhurst nodded. "Okay," he said. "Get 'em out of here."

With a whine, the agrav shuttle at Garroway's back lifted into the Martian night. He felt the flutter of wind as it passed overhead, and he watched its drive field grow brighter as it accelerated back to orbit, back to the Arean Rings that stretched now across the zenith like a slender, taut-pulled thread of pure silver.

"You maggots," Warhurst growled, his former tough-DI persona slowly re-emerging, "you *mudworms* are even more stupid than I was led to believe. All right. Show's over. Like I said earlier, from this point on, you are *mine*. I personally am going to eat you alive, chew you up, and spit your worthless carcasses out on these sands.

"But maybe, *maybe*, a few of you will have what it takes to be Marines." Turning, he addressed one of the assistants—the evil-grinning one. "Sergeant Corrolly!"

"Yes, Drill Instructor Warhurst!"

"We need to find out what these worms are really made of. Let's take them on a little run before breakfast!"

The evil grin grew wider. "*Yes*, Drill Instructor!"

"Move out!"

"Aye, aye, Drill Instructor!" The assistant DI turned to face the waiting survivors of the morning's muster. "You *heard* the Drill Instructor! Recruit platoon . . . lef' *face*! For'ard, *harch*! And . . . double time! *Hut! Hut! Hut!* . . ."

Garroway began to *hut*.

And within twenty minutes, as he dragged screaming leg muscles through the fine, clinging, ankle-deep sand of the Martian desert, he was wondering if he was going to be up for this after all.

What the *hell* had he been thinking when he'd volunteered? . . .

2

Green 1
Meneh, Alighan
0512/38:20 hours, local time

Ramsey kicked off, his 660-ABS armor amplifying his push and sending him in a low, flat trajectory across bubbling ground. Maneuvers like this always carried a damned-if-you-do, damned-if-you-don't risk. Jump too high and your hang time made you an ideal target; jump too low and flat and a miscalculation could slam you into an obstacle.

He came down next to a ferrocrete wall, his momentum carrying him into the half-collapsed structure with force enough to bring more of it down on top of him, but he was unhurt. A quick check around—he was a kilometer from the city's central plaza. All around him, the skeletal frameworks of skyscrapers rose like a ragged forest, a clean, modern city reduced in minutes to ruin and chaos. Some of the damage was due to the Marine bombardment, certainly, and to the firefight raging now through the enemy capital, but much, too, had been self-inflicted by Muzzie nano-D.

In fact, Ramsey's biggest tactical concern at the moment were the nano-D clouds, which were highlighted by his helmet display as ugly purple masses drifting low across the battlefield. Where they touched the ground or surviving fragments of building, rock, earth, and ferrocrete began dissolving in moments, as the submicroscopic disassemblers in the death clouds began pulling atom from atom and letting it all melt into a boiling and homogenous gray paste.

Where the cloud hit counter-nano, sparks flashed and snapped in miniature displays of lightning. Nano-D, much of it, possessed intelligence enough to attempt to avoid most countermeasures; victory generally went to the cloud with both the most numbers and the most sophisticated programming.

A Muzzie field-pulse gun opened up from a ferrocrete bunker two hundred meters ahead, sending a stream of dazzling flashes above his head. Almost automatically, Ramsey tagged the structure with a mental shift of icons on his noumenal display, which hung inside his thoughts like a glowing movie screen. His suit AI melded data from a wide range of sensory input into a coherent image. In his mind's eye, he could see the bunker overlaid by the ghostly images of human figures inside, and the malevolent red glow of active power systems.

"Skyfire, I have a target," he said, and he mentally keyed the display skyward, tagged with precise coordinates.

Seconds later, a voice in his head whispered what he'd been waiting to hear. "Target confirmed. Sniper round on the way."

Several seconds more slipped past, and then the cloud deck overhead flared sun-bright, and a beam of light so brilliant it appeared to be made of solid, mirror-bright metal snapped on, connecting clouds with the bunker.

At the beam's touch, the bunker exploded, ferrocrete and field-pulse gun and Theocrat soldiers all converted to fast-expanding vapor, blue-white heat, and a sharp surge of gamma radiation. The ground-support gunners out in Alighan orbit had just driven a sliver of mag-stabilized uranium-cladded antimatter into that gun emplacement at half the speed of light. The resulting explosion had vaporized an area half the size of a city block, leaving very little behind but hard radiation and a smoking hole in the ground.

Unfortunately, the enemy had weapons just as powerful, and as minute followed bloody minute, more and more of them were coming on-line. He needed to move . . . but first, this looked like a good place to leave one of his mobile weapons.

Working quickly, Ramsey pulled a KR-48 pack out of a storage compartment on his hip, extended its tripod legs with a thought, and placed the device atop what was left of the wall. Through its optics, the image relayed through his helmet AI to his brain, he checked its field of fire, giving it a clear view toward the city's central plaza.

His 660-ABS had more than once been compared to a one-man tank, but so shallow an image wildly missed the point, and in fact was insulting to the battlesuit. In fact, tanks had become obsolete centuries ago thanks primarily to the rise of battlesuit technology. Wearing an ABS, a Marine could walk, run, or soar for distances of up to a kilometer, could engage a wide range of targets on the ground and in the air with a small but powerful arsenal of varied weaponry, and could link with every other ABS in the battle zone to coordinate attacks and share intelligence. An ABS allowed its wearer to shrug off the detonation of a small tactical nuke less than a hundred meters away, to survive everything from shrapnel to radiation to heavy-caliber projectiles to clouds of nano-D, and to function in any environment from hard vacuum to the bottom of the sea to the boiling hell-cauldron of modern combat.

In fact, *any* contest between a lone Marine in a 660 battlesuit and a whole platoon of archaic heavy tanks could have only one possible outcome.

What was important, however, was why, after a thousand years, individual and small-unit tactics were still of vital importance in combat. For centuries, virtual-sim generals had been predicting the end of the rifleman as the centerpiece of combat. The energies employed by even small-scale weapons were simply too deadly, too powerful, and too indiscriminate in their scope to permit something as vulnerable as a human being to survive more than seconds in a firefight.

Somehow, though, the venerable rifleman had survived, his technology advancing to extend his effectiveness and his chances of survival. The truth was, a planetary ground-assault unit like the 55th MARS could drop out of orbit, seize the starport, and *hold* it, where larger, faster, and more powerful AI-directed weaponry would simply have vaporized it.

Of course, by the time the Muzzies were through defending the port, most of it would be vaporized, wrecked, or otherwise rendered unusable anyway. That was the problem with war. It was so damned destructive . . . of personnel, of property, of entire cultures and societies. . . .

He completed setting up the KR-48 and keyed it to his helmet display. He switched on the weapon's power shields, to keep it from being directly targeted by roving enemy combat drones or smart hunters, then bounded clear, making his way around the perimeter of the city plaza. Gunfire continued to crack and spit from the surrounding buildings, those that hadn't been demolished yet, but the accuracy of the Marines' orbital sniper fire seemed to be having a telling effect on the defenses. The instant a Marine came under fire, the attack was noted by Skyfire command and control, and the attacker would in moments be brought under counterfire, either by high-velocity rounds chucked from orbit, or from the A-90 ground-support aerospace craft now crisscrossing the skies above the port complex, or from other Marines on the ground linked into the combat net.

"Bravo one-one-five," a voice whispered in his mind. His AI identified the speaker as Captain Baltis, his platoon commander, but he recognized the dry tones without his suit's comm ID function. "Hostile gun position at six-one-three-Sierra. Can you neutralize it, Ram?"

He zoomed in on the indicated coordinates on his map window. The enemy fire was coming from the top of a forty-story structure two kilometers ahead. A drone feed showed the Muzzie gunners, clustered on a rooftop overlooking the plaza, clustered around a tripod-mounted high-velocity sliver gun.

"I'll see what I can do," Ramsey replied. "Why can't we leave it to Sniper?"

"Because that would bring that whole tower down," Baltis replied, "and we have civilians in there."

Shit. The Muzzies didn't seem to care whether their own civilians were caught in the line of fire or not. But the Marines were under standing orders to minimize collateral damage, and that meant civilian casualties.

"Okay. I'm on it."

Rising, he bounded forward, covering the ground in long, low, gliding strides that carried him both toward the objective building and around toward the right. He was trying to take advantage of the cover provided by some smaller buildings between him and the target. As he drew closer, someone on the rooftop spotted him and swung the heavy-barreled weapon around to bear on him. He felt the snap of hivel rounds slashing through the air above his head, felt the impacts as they punched into the pavement nearby with bone-jarring hammerings and raised a dense cloud of powdered ferrocrete.

Dropping behind a plasteel wall, he connected with the KR-48 he'd left behind, using his suit's link with the weapon to pivot and elevate the blunt snout toward the target building. On the window inset in his mind, he saw the KR-48's crosshairs center over the top of the building; a mental command triggered a burst, sending a stream of thumb-sized missiles shrieking toward the rooftop gun emplacement.

The missiles vaporized chunks of cast stone, but the Muzzies' armor damped out the blast effects. He'd been expecting it; he was using the weapon as a diversion, not for the kill.

Instantly, the Muzzie gunners swung their weapon back to the south, searching for the source of incoming fire. Ramsey watched the shift in their attention, and chose that moment to leap high into the air.

A mental command cut in his jump jets in midair, and he soared skyward, clearing the upper ramparts of the building, cutting the jets, and dropping onto a broad, open rooftop.

He used the flamer connected to his left wrist to spew liquid fire into the gun emplacement. The enemy troops were shielded against tactical heat, of course, but the suddenness of his appearance, arcing down out of the sky, surprised and startled them, and the torch blast melted the plastic mountings of the hivel gun and toppled it over onto its side.

Shifting his aim, he torched the floor of the rooftop enclosure, cutting open a gaping crater. Two of the Muzzie infantrymen were caught in the collapse of the roof, falling through in a shower of flaming debris; Ramsey shifted to the mag-pulse rifle mounted on his right arm and hammered away at five more Theocrat soldiers who were busily crowding back and away from his landing point.

One of the hostiles managed to open fire with a sliver gun at Ramsey, and the Marine felt the hammer of high-speed rounds thudding into his chest and helmet armor, but he held his ground and completed his targeting sweep with the pulse rifle, watching the barrage smash through enemy armor like a rapid-fire pile driver, shredding, rending, turning titanium laminate carballoy into bloody scrap.

The last of the hostiles collapsed on the blazing rooftop, or toppled through the gaping hole in front of them. The entire engagement had taken perhaps three seconds.

"Bravo one, Bravo one-one-five," he reported. "Target neutralized."

"Good deal," Baltis replied. "Now get your ass forward! You're behind sched!"

"On my way."

Another leap, and he sailed off the burning building's upper story, using his jump jets to brake his fall.

His suit AI was flagging another gun position just ahead. . . .

USMC Recruit Training Center
Noctis Labyrinthus, Mars
0720/24:20 local time, 1738 hrs GMT

"Fall in! *Fall in!*"

Panting hard, Garroway stumbled up to the yellow line painted on the pavement. The run, which Warhurst had lightly declared to be a shake-down cruise, had lasted two hours and, according to his implant, had covered nearly 14 kilometers. A number of the recruits hadn't made it; at least, they'd not kept up with the main body. Presumably, they were still straggling along out in the desert someplace, unless Warhurst had sent a transport out to pick them up.

Garroway had assumed that the meager third-G of Mars' surface gravity would make calisthenics—no, *PT*, in the Marine vernacular—easy. He'd been wrong. *Gods,* he'd been wrong. The run across the rugged highlands of the Noctis Labyrinthus had left him at the trembling edge of collapse. His skinsuit, newly grown for him when he'd checked in at the Arean Ring receiving station, was saturated with sweat, the weave of microtubules straining to absorb the moisture and chemicals now pouring from his body. His leg muscles were aching, his lungs burning. He'd thought the implants he'd purchased two weeks ago would have handled the extra stress.

This was *not* going to be easy.

The worst of it was, Gunnery Sergeant Warhurst had accompanied them on that run, and so far as Garroway could tell, the guy wasn't breathing hard, hadn't even broken a sweat. His uniform was still crisp, the flat-brimmed "Smokey Bear" hat of ancient Corps tradition still precisely squared above those hard, cold eyes.

"Okay, children," he said, planting his hands on his hips. "Now that we've warmed up a bit, it's time we got down to work. Hit the deck, push-up position! And *one!* And *two!* . . ."

By now, the sun was up, though much of the run had been through the foggy, pre-dawn darkness. Mars was a tangle of mismatched terrain, rendered both beautiful and twisted by the centuries of terraforming. The sky was a hard, deep, almost violet-blue, the sun shrunken and cold compared to back home. The ground was mostly sand, though patches of gene-tailored mosses and coldleaf added startling accents of green and blue. The run had brought them in a broad circle back to Marine RTC Noctis Labyrinthus, a lonely huddle of domes and quick-grown habs in a rocky desert. East, the tortured terrain of the Vallis Marineris glowed banded red and orange beneath the morning sun, and open water gleamed where the Mariner Sea had so far taken hold.

Damn it, he couldn't *breathe*. . . .

"Come on, kiddies!" Warhurst shouted. "You can give me more than that! There's *plenty* of oh-two in the air! Suck it down!"

What sadist, Garroway wondered, had decided that *this* was where Marine recruits would come to train? Centuries ago, of course, RTC had been on Earth . . . at a place called Camp Pendleton, and at another place called Camp Lejeune. Those places were no more, of course. The Xul Apocalypse had wrecked both bases, when tidal waves from the oceanic asteroid strikes had come smashing ashore. For a time, Marines had been trained on Luna, and then at one of the new LaGrange orbital bases, but almost two centuries ago, with the completion of the Arean Ring, the Corps had transferred much of its training command to Mars. The first recruits on the surface at Noctis Labyrinthus, Garroway had heard, had done their PT wearing coldsuits and oxygen masks. He was beginning to think someone had jumped the gun in deciding to forego the support technology.

"Okay! Okay! On your feet!" Warhurst clapped his hands. "How are we doing, kids? Eyes bright? Hearts pumping? Good! We have a very special treat in store for you now." He pointed. "See that building? Fall in, single file, in front of that door! *Move it! Move it!*"

The platoon scrambled to obey, running fifty meters across the 'crete pavement and lining up outside the door. A sign beside the doorframe read sickbay.

That puzzled Garroway. They'd pumped him full of medinano at the receiving station, enough, he'd thought, to kill everything in his system that wasn't nailed down. He'd already had several thorough physicals, back on Earth Ring, and in Mars orbit. What were they going to . . .

Realization hit him just as Warhurst began addressing the formation.

"This, children, is where we separate the *real* men and women from the sheep. You were all informed that this would be part of your recruit training, and you all agreed when you thumbed your enlistment contract. However . . . if any of you, for any reason, feel you cannot go through with this, you will fall out and line up over there." He pointed across the grinder at one of the assistant DIs, who was standing in front of a transport skimmer. "You will be returned to the receiving station, and there you may make arrangements for going home. No one will think the less of you. You will simply have proven what everybody knows—that the Marine Corps is *not* for everyone. Do I have any takers?"

Again, Garroway thought he felt some of the recruits in line around him wavering. The terror was almost palpable.

"If you file through that door," Warhurst continued, a tone of warning giving his edge a voice, "you will be given a shot of decoupling nano. It won't hurt . . . not physically, at any rate. But after the shot takes effect, you will be unable to access your personal cerebral implants. Right now, each of you needs to think about what that means, and decide if being a Marine is worth the cost."

The decoupler shot. Yeah, they'd told him about it, but he'd already known about it, of course. It was one of the things that set the Marines and a few other highly specialized elite military units apart from the Army, Navy, or the High Guard. Wonderingly, Garroway looked down at his right hand, catching the glint of gold and silver wires imbedded in the skin at the base of his thumb and running in rectilinear patterns across his palm.

He was going to lose his implants.

The vast majority of humans had cereblink implants, including palm interface hardware, quantum-phase neurocircuitry, and a complex mesh of Micronics grown layer by layer throughout the brain, especially in the cerebral sulci and around the hypothalamus. The first nano injections generally were given to the fetus while it was still in womb or in vitro, so that the initial base linkages could begin chelating out within the cerebral cortex before birth. Further injections were given to children in stages, at birth, when they were about two standard years old, and again when they were three. By the time they were four, they already possessed the hardware to let them palm-interface with a bewildering variety of computers, input feeds, e-pedias, and machines. Most basic education came in the form of electronic downloads fed directly into the student's cerebral hardware. Adults depended utterly on hardware links for everything from flying skimmers to paying bills to experiencing the news to opening doors to talking to friends more than a few meters distant. The cereblink was one of the absolutely basic elements of modern society, the ultimate piece of technology that allowed humans to interface with their world, and interact with their tools.

And now, the recruits of Company 4102 were about to lose that technology and, for the first time in their lives, would face the world without it.

The thought was terrifying.

"Okay, recruits! First five in line! Through the hatch, on the double!"

The first five recruits stumbled up the steps as the door cycled open for them and vanished into the building. Garroway watched them go.

He thought about quitting.

This was the one part of recruit training that he'd wondered about, wondered whether or not he could make it through. Oh, he knew he would *survive*, certainly. Millions did, and most went on to be U.S. Marines. And if he could get through these next few weeks, his old hardware would be reconnected and he would get new implants as well. Marines were hardwired with internal gadgetry and high-tech enhancements that most civilians didn't even know existed.

But the thought of being cut off like that . . .

Many of the humans now living on Earth, he understood, were pre-tech . . . meaning they went through their lives, from birth to grave, as completely organic beings. No technological chelates cradling their brains and brain stems, no nanocircuitry growing through their neural pathways.

No EM telepathy, so no way to talk to those around you unless you were actually in their presence or you happened to have a portable comm unit with you. No translator software; if your friend didn't happen to speak your language, you were out of luck. No e-conferencing in noumenal or virtual space. No e-Net linking you with every other person and every electronic service across the Solar System.

No way to access news, or weather—assuming you were on Earth which actually *had* weather—or med access, or e-pedia information feeds, or travel directions, or life journals, or any of the hundreds of other data downloads necessary in today's fast-paced life.

No sims. No download entertainment. No way to interact with either the stored or broadcast simvids that let you take the role of hero or villain or both.

No way to buy the most basic necessities. Or to find them, since most shops now were on-line.

No driving ground cars, piloting mag skimmers, or accessing public transit.

No books, unless you could find the old-fashioned printed variety . . . and that was assuming you could read them. No more educational feeds . . . and no access to personal e-memory. Gods, how was he going to remember *anything*? . . .

And there was Aide. For Garroway, that felt like the worst . . . losing access to Aide, the AI mentor, secretary, and personal electronic assistant he'd had since he was a kid.

Without his hardware, the world was suddenly going to be a much smaller, much more difficult, much narrower place . . . and knowing that he would survive that narrowing did not make the prospect any more bearable.

Cut off from technological civilization, from society, from everything that made life worth the living. . . .

"I know it seems extreme, kids," Warhurst said, using a telepathic feed to whisper inside their minds. "You feel like we're cutting you off from the universe. In boot camp we call it *the empty time*."

Garroway wondered whether the DIs had some secret means of accessing their implants and hearing their thoughts . . . or if he just knew and understood what the recruits would be thinking now. Probably the latter. It was against the law to sneak into another's private thoughts and eavesdrop, wasn't it?

"The thing is," Warhurst went on, "there will be times as a Marine when you won't have the Net to rely on. Imagine if you're on a combat drop and something goes wrong. You end up a thousand kilometers behind enemy lines. You don't have the local Net access codes. Worse, if you try to link in, the local authorities will spot you. Somehow, you have to survive without the Net until you can make contact with your sibling Marines.

"Or maybe you just have to go into a hot DZ on a planet with no Net at all, and there's a screw-up and the battlefleet Net isn't up and running for, oh, a standard day or two or ten. Believe me, it happens. What *can* go wrong *will* go wrong. What are you going to do then?

"The answer, of course, is that you will be Marines, and you will *act* like Marines. You will be able to draw upon your own resources, your training, your experience, and you will survive. More than survive, you will kick ass and emerge victorious, because *victory* is the tradition of the Corps!"

Garroway felt a little better after Warhurst's speech. Not *good* . . . but better. He gave a mental click to increase neural serotonin levels and help lift his mood. Hell, that was another thing he'd be missing in the next few weeks—the ability to alter his own emotional state as necessary. He felt a tiny, sharp stab of fear, and instantly suppressed it.

How did Marines control the fear if they didn't have access to neural monitoring software or the ability to deliberately tailor their emotional state? Or were the wild stories true, stories to the effect that Marine combat feeds eliminated fear and boosted such emotions as rage and hatred for the enemy? He'd always assumed those tales were nonsense, the product of civilian ignorance. Still . . .

"If you children want to be Marines," Warhurst's whisper continued, "we have to know who and what you are. How you react under stress. We need to know your *character*. And we need to take you, *all* of you, down to your most basic, most elementary level and build you up, one painful layer at a time. At the end of these sixteen weeks, you will not be the men and women you were. You *will* be Marines . . . *if* you make it through."

It made sense, of course, what Warhurst was saying. Boot camp always had required an initial breaking down, so that the drill instructors could mold recruits into Marines. And there were other factors besides . . . like cutting the recruits off from outside sources of information so that they were utterly dependent on their instructors. Like taking away anything that would distract them from the grueling physical and intellectual training ahead.

Like getting them to rely upon themselves.

"Believe me," Warhurst added, and Garroway swore he could hear a grin in the man's inner voice, "for the next few weeks you children won't need your tech-toys, and you'll be *way* too busy to miss 'em! Besides, you'll have me to tell you what you need to know! Next five in line! Through the hatch!"

Garroway thought one last time about quitting, and shoved the thought aside.

"Don't worry, Aiden," his inner AI whispered in his mind. *"I'll be back. You'll see."*

Together with four other recruits, he bounded up the steps and into the unknown.

3

Green 1, 1-1 Bravo
Meneh, Alighan
0824/38:22 hours, local time

"Okay, Marines. How are we going to do this?"

Ramsey considered the question. Staff Sergeant Thea Howell rarely asked for advice. When she did, the problem was certain to be a certified bitch.

With the vantage point of the gods, he looked down on the city. In the noumenon, the imaginal inner space of his mind's eye, he was hovering above the city center and starport as if from a giant's towering perspective. Physically, in fact, he was crouched in what had been a basement, shielded from view by several tons of rubble, and the closest Marine to his current position was nearly five hundred meters away, but he was only distantly aware of any of that. His cereblink and the fleet's SkyNet, however, allowed them to share a noumenal conference space, complete with tiny red icons marking the position of each known Muzzie soldier, gun, and vehicle, green for Marines, white for civilians or unknowns.

The tacsit was clear enough. Theocrat riflemen had holed up in another skyscraper, an eighty-three-floor tower at the edge of the central plaza, and they'd turned the place into a fortress, with portable rocket launchers and at least one light plasma cannon. Life scans had revealed a heavy concentration of civilians in the smaller buildings clustered about the tower's base; smash the tower with close-air ground support or orbital fire, and several hundred civilians would die.

So rather than standing off and bombing the Theocrats, the Marines would have to do this the old-fashioned away, with a direct CQB assault.

And it was going to get damned messy.

"From the top down," Ramsey said after a moment, answering Howell's question. Under his control, green lines of light flicked across the imaginal landscape, taking advantage of available cover, then vaulting into the sky to converge on the tower roof from four directions. "*Has* to be. Otherwise we fight our way up that tower one floor at a time."

"Agreed," Howell said. "But that rooftop is over 250 meters straight up. Too far for jumpjets."

"Then we'll need to ride Specter guns," Sergeant Chu pointed out. "And we'll need to move straight up and *fast*."

"Roger that," Corporal Ran Allison said. "Looks like a lucky two-fiver."

The slang referred to twenty-five percent casualties . . . *if* they were lucky. It was a grim and chillingly sobering assessment.

"Ten of us," Howell said, noting the green icons surrounding the tower, a kilometer distant. The icons flashed, one after another, as she ran through the names. "Me, Beck, and Santiago on one. Hearst and Daley on two. Rodriguez and Gertz on three. Ramsey, Allison, and Chu on four. Coordinate on me. I've put the call out, and our rides will be here in two mikes. Everyone get set."

Ramsey dropped out of the noumenal link and began shouldering upward through the layer of debris above him, his combat suit's paramusculature allowing him to move aside several tons of debris as he climbed. Heaving aside a 3-meter chunk of ferrocrete, he emerged again into the smoke-stained light of the Alighan morning.

The pace of the battle had slowed considerably, now that the defenders had been reduced to a few isolated pockets of resistance scattered across a ruined city. In less than the promised two minutes, a Specter gun hissed overhead, an awkward-looking fragment of one of the landing vehicles that had brought the Marines down to the planet's surface hours before. Piloted by an independent AI, kept aloft by agrav pods and protected by a ball-turret plasma gun, the flier looked like a black insect, complete with gangly, slender legs equipped with powerful grapples. Reaching up, he grabbed hold of one of those legs and locked on; the jointed member retracted partially, pulling him clear of the wreckage and into the air.

Corporal Allison and Sergeant Chu were already on board the tactical carrier, grappled to the aircraft's other legs and retracted up into the partial shelter of the machine's body. The rubble dropped away as the vehicle swiftly ascended, rotating and banking toward the distant tower.

The helplessness and the sense of being exposed were sharper now than during the landing craft descent earlier. The gun was sharply maneuverable, however, and the artificial intelligence piloting it possessed inhumanly fast reflexes. It was easier on the stomach not to watch. Ramsey closed his eyes and merged with the assault team gestalt, watching again from the gods' perspective as four green icons representing the fast-moving Specter guns converged on the objective.

All four aircraft street-skimmed in toward the tower, zig-zagging all the way to take every possible advantage of buildings, trees, and rubble. Hivel rounds snapped past the flier, and once Ramsey felt the solid shock of a heavy detonation close by. His helmet readout warned of a gamma pulse; someone was firing antimatter rounds at them. He felt another thump as the gun's plasma weapon fired, knocking down an incoming rocket that had targeted them.

He saw a sudden flare as one of the incoming Specter guns took a direct hit despite its evasive maneuvering. According to his link, both Daley and Hearst jumped clear as the aircraft crumpled and slammed into the rubble-clogged street below.

The remaining three tactical carriers reached the base of the skyscraper at the same instant, changing vectors to travel straight up the sides of the tower in a stomach-wrenching maneuver that was only partly eased by the inertial dampers in Ramsey's armor.

Three seconds, the pilot AI whispered in his mind, and he opened his eyes in time to see of blur of ferrocrete and structural ornamentation flashing past.

Two seconds . . . one second . . .

Another gut-twisting shift in vector, and the Specter gun slipped over the rampart encircling the top of the tower. A mental command, and he was released from the craft's unfolding leg, dropping onto the roof, striking, rolling, coming up with his mag-pulse rifle raised, his helmet electronics already tracking the nearest threat. The weapon was set to AI control, and he let his suit guide him; the weapon triggered as soon as it had a solid targeting lock.

The first Muzzie rifleman went down, his armor hammered by a rapid-fire barrage of magnetic pulses. The top of the building became a bewildering and rapidly unfolding blur of motion and weapons fire, as two of the other Specter guns came up over the ramparts and released their payloads of Marines.

The Specter gun carrying Howell, Beck, and Santiago took a direct hit as it hovered above the rampart, an antimatter blast flashing with deadly brilliance at the edge of the tower. Ramsey overrode his weapon control and shifted aim to the Muzzie gunner—a low threat because he was facing away from Ramsey as he manhandled the massive A.M. accelerator for a second shot, but he was trying to target the three Marines on that side of the tower as they fell from the burning transport. Ramsey triggered his weapon, and the enemy soldier folded backward around the kinetic impulse slamming into his spine, his weapon cartwheeling across the roof with the impact.

A warning went off in his mind; gunners were targeting him. He cut in his jumpjets and sailed across the roof, pivoting in midair to target one of the Muzzie gunners who was standing up behind a waist-high ferrocrete barrier, tracking Ramsey as he sailed through the air.

The stricken Specter gun slammed into the edge of the tower, metal burning furiously, catching and holding for a moment before rocking back and off the roof, crashing to the street eighty-four-stories below. The remaining two guns hovered above opposite sides of the building, ninety meters apart, coordinating their plasma weaponry with the fire from the eight Marines now fanning out across the roof.

A transparent wall overlooked the rooftop, a penthouse or upper story of some sort, enveloped in hanging plants, and with a sunken interior that formed a well-protected redoubt. The transparency—plastic and shatterproof—melted as someone inside detonated a thermal charge. An instant later, a swarm of APerMs emerged and arced into the sky before descending on hissing contrails—antipersonnel missiles, each the size of a man's forefinger, each with an on-board AI smart enough to identify an enemy's armor signature and home on it relentlessly, each with a dust-speck's worth of antimatter in magnetic containment. Ramsey's armor fired a countermeasures charge, and flashes of actinic brilliance from the hovering guns picked individual missiles out of the air with hivel kinetic-kill rounds each the size of a grain of sand. The sky turned to white fire. . . .

At first he thought the threat had been neutralized, and he started moving forward once more. In the next instant, his helmet display flashed warning; there were still APerMs in the air.

He triggered another countermeasure burst . . . but it was too little, too late, and he couldn't get them all. APerMs slashed into Howell and Beck, who was bounding along-side her, blasting gouts of molten laminate from their armor, knocking the two Marines backward.

"Thea!" Ramsey screamed, and then he was standing twenty meters from the open penthouse, hosing the low, cavern-like opening in front of him with his flamer. One of the hovering Specter guns with a good line of sight added lance after flaring lance of plasma energy to his fire; Ramsey could see figures writhing and incinerating within the flames.

Turning, he bounded across the rooftop to the two fallen Marines. Corporal Gerry Beck was dead, his helmet punctured, then exploded from within. There was a *lot* of blood, and only smoking, blackened shards remained of helmet and skull.

Staff Sergeant Thea Howell, however, was still alive. The AP round had struck her in the chest, shattering ribs, rupturing a lung, flooding her torso with hard radiation, but her diagnostic feed showed she was still alive as her armor struggled to control the damage. She was already deep in medical support stasis.

Thea. . . .

Crouching above her body, he turned his fire against a last remaining clump of Muzzie gunners behind a ferrocrete wall. One of the Specter guns burned down the last of them, and the firefight came to an abrupt end.

But Ramsey continued to hold the broken body of Thea Howell, letting his own armor make automatic feed connections and linkages so that he could bolster her suit's damaged support systems.

Besides being a fellow Marine and the platoon's senior NCO, Thea was an old friend, and frequently his lover.

She was *family.*

And he didn't want to see her die. . . .

USMC Recruit Training Center
Noctis Labyrinthus, Mars
1045/24:20 local time, 2003 hrs GMT

Garroway felt . . . alone. Alone and utterly empty.

And he couldn't even mind-click himself a serotonin jolt to lift the settling black mist of depression . . . or ask Aide for help.

"I know you're all feeling a bit low right now," Gunnery Sergeant Warhurst said, smiling. "But I have *just* the ticket! We're going to run. *Comp*'ney, lef' *face*! For'ard *harch*! Double time, *harch*! . . ."

Garroway still felt dazed and lost. After his ten-minute session with the Navy corpsmen in the sickbay, he'd been led back out into the weak sunshine of the Martian morning and marched to chow.

He'd barely tasted the food, and ate it automatically. After that there'd been an indoctrination class, with an assistant DI lecturing the company on Corps tradition, and on what it meant to be a Marine.

And now, they were out in the cold once more, running. Who the hell was he trying to kid? His first six hours in the Corps, and already he wanted to quit.

Something, though, was keeping him going . . . one tired foot after the other.

Aiden Garroway had been born and raised in the 7-Ring orbital complex in Earth orbit, a son of an extended line marriage, the Giangrecos; on his Naming Day, he'd taken his name from Estelle Garroway, the woman who'd also passed on to him his fascination with the Corps.

It had been Estelle who'd told him about other Garroways who'd been Marines. There was one, a real character who'd fought in the UN War of the mid-twenty-first century, who was still remembered in Marine histories. "Sands of Mars Garroway," he was known as, and he'd led a grueling march up the Vallis Marineris only a couple of thousand kilometers from this spot to attack a French invasion force.

And later there'd been John Garroway, a gunnery sergeant who'd made first contact with the N'mah, an alien civilization at the Sirius Stargate a century later . . . and General Clinton Vincent Garroway who'd fought and won the critical Battle of Night's Edge against the Xul in 2323. And other Garroways had served in the Corps with distinction ever since, first in the old United States Marines, then, with the gradual assimilation of the old U.S. into the United Star Commonwealth, in the old Corps' modern successor, the United *Star* Marine Corps.

It had been Estelle who'd suggested he join the Corps. She'd known how unhappy he was at home.

Not that home life had been abusive or anything like that. Most of his mothers and fathers were okay, and he deeply loved his birth mother. But with twenty-five spouses and one hundred eighty-three children and grandchildren underfoot, along with numerous aunts, uncles, in-laws, and cousins, the living quarters allotted to the Giangreco line family, though spacious enough, tended to be something of a zoo. There was always someone to put him down, tell him what to do, or shove him out of the way. His job in the aquaculture farms was boring and dead-end. There were no better options for educational downloads until he specialized in a career, and farming water hyacinths for the Ring filtration matrices decidedly was *not* what he intended to do for the next century or two. Hell, life at home with that many parents and sibs was like life in a barracks, anyway; the Marines seemed a logical option.

The problem was Delano Giangreco, the patriarch of the line, and a committed pacifist. A member of the Reformed Church of the Ascended Pleiadean Masters, he didn't quite insist that everyone in the family follow Church doctrine regarding diet, luminous tattoos, or ritual nudity, but he *did* insist on observance of the Masters' Pax. No mention of war within the house, no downloads touching on military history, battles, or martial arts. Garroway had been twelve before he'd even heard of the Marines, and then only because of the electronic emancipation laws. Once you were twelve and had chosen your name, no one else could censor your thoughts or your data feeds, even for religious purposes.

But those feeds could be monitored by parents or guardians until a person was eighteen, and Garroway had received almost weekly lectures on the evils of war and the falsity of such historical lies as military glory, honor, or duty.

Somehow, though, the lectures had only increased his determination to learn about the Corps, and about all those other Garroways who'd served country and, later, Commonwealth. By the time he was sixteen, he'd picked up some semi-intelligent software, with Aide's help, which let him partition his personal memory storage, and keep parts of it secret from even the most determined morals-censoring probes.

But the need to do so, to keep his guard up against his senior father's intrusions, had been a powerful incentive to get himself out of the home and off on his own.

His senior father had disowned him when he learned Garroway had enlisted. No matter. He had a new family now. . . .

If he could keep up with it. If he quit, if he gave up, he would be right back in the Rings looking for work—probably in one of the environmental control complexes or, possibly, the nanufactories.

Hell, he'd rather run himself to death.

"Christ," Mustafa Jellal muttered at Garroway's side. "Is the bastard gonna run us all the way up Olympus?"

The recruit company had been running steadily west for almost an hour, now, slogging uphill almost all the way. Somewhere over the western horizon was the staggering mass of Olympus Mons, the largest volcano in the Solar System, though its peak was still far over the curve of the Martian horizon. Jellal's mutterings were purely fictional, of course. The mountain known as Olympus Mons was five hundred kilometers across at the base, and reached twenty-one kilometers above the surrounding terrain; the raw, new, artificially generated atmosphere on Mars was still only a step removed from hard vacuum at the summit.

The Noctis Labyrinthus lay at the eastern rim of the Tharsis Bulge, the vast, volcano-crested dome marking a cataclysmic upwelling of the Martian mantle 3.5 billion years before. The broken, canyon-laced terrain of the Noctis Labyrinthus—the "Labyrinth of Night"—was the result of floods released by the sudden melting of permafrost during that long-ago event. The ground, as a result, was a difficult tangle of rocks and channels that made footing treacherous and the climb exhausting.

"Save your . . . wind . . . for running," Garroway muttered between pants for breath. His side was starting to shriek pain at him, and the thinness of the incompletely terraformed atmosphere was dragging at his lungs and his endurance. How much farther? . . .

Jellal suddenly fell out of the formation, stepping to the side, hands on his knees as he started to vomit. Garroway maintained his pace, staring straight ahead. Behind him, he could hear one of the assistant DIs talking to Jellal, though he couldn't hear what was being said. In a moment, the column had continued up a dusty hill covered in patches of gene-tailored dunegrass, and passed well beyond earshot of what was being said.

A minute or two later, however, just over the crest of that hill, Warhurst bellowed for the company to halt. The recruits had become strung out over a half kilometer of ground, and it took minutes more for the trailing runners to catch up with the main body. Garroway stood at attention as more and more recruits fell in to either side, breathing hard, savoring the chance to suck down cold gulps of air and try to will his racing heart to slow.

After a few heavy-breathing minutes, he was glad to see Jellal jog past and take a place farther up the line. He'd met the young Ganymedean Arab at the receiving station up in the Arean Ring. Mustafa Jellal had been friendly, cheerful, and outgoing, and seemed like a good guy. Garroway had started talking with him at chow last night, partly out of a sense of isolation kinship. There was a lot of anti-Muslim sentiment throughout the Sol System right now, had been ever since the outbreak of hostilities against the Theocracy, and during the conversation Garroway had had the sense that Jellal was feeling lonely, a bit cut off.

Garroway had been wrestling with loneliness as well—he wasn't prepared to call it *homesickness* just yet—and felt a certain kinship with the dark-skinned Ganymedean recruit. After chow, they'd gone back to the center's temporary barracks, and there they'd opened a noumenal link and shared bits of home with each other—Jellal taking him on a virtual tour of the Jellal freestead complex at Galileo, on Ganymede, with Jupiter looming banded and vast just above the horizon, and Garroway showing him Sevenring, with Earth huge and blue and white-storm-swirled through the arc of the Main Gallery's overhead transparency.

He wondered how the guy was feeling now, with his implants switched off.

It was actually a pleasant respite, a chance to simply stand and breathe. Warhurst waited a few minutes more, until the last tail-end Charlie straggled over the top of the ridge and took his place in line.

"Glad you could join us, Dodson," the DI said with a sour growl to his voice. "Okay, recruits, listen up. A few hours ago, we let you see a Marine action now taking place on Alighan, a few hundred light-years from here. We've just received a feed from USMC Homeport. The Marines on Alighan report both the starport and planet's capital city are secure. Army troops are now deploying to the surface to take over the perimeter.

"Lieutenant General Alexander, in command of the Marine Interstellar Expeditionary Force, has reported that the op went down according to plan and by the book. He singled out the 55th Marine Aerospace Regimental Strikeforce, which spearheaded the assault on the planethead, saying that despite heavy casualties, they distinguished themselves in the very best traditions of the Corps.

"So let's give a Marine Corps war-yell for the Fighting Fifty-fifth! *Ooh-ra!*"

"Ooh-ra!" the company yelled back, but the response was ragged and weak, the recruits still panting and out of breath.

"What the *hell* kind of war-yell is that?" Warhurst demanded. "The Marines fight! They overcome! They improvise! And they fucking kick ass! Let me hear your war-yell!"

"Ooh-ra!"

"A good war-yell focuses your energy and terrifies your opponent! Again!"

"Ooh-ra!"

"Again!"

"Ooh-ra!"

"Oh, I am so terrified." He sighed, shaking his head. "Children, I can tell we have a *lot* of work to do. Down on the deck! One hundred push-ups! *Now!*"

The respite was over.

Green 1, 1-1 Bravo
Meneh Spaceport, Alighan
1158/38:22 hours, local time

An enemy sniper round cracked overhead, striking the side of a building a hundred meters away with a brilliant flash and a puff of white smoke. Ramsey looked up without breaking stride, then glanced at Chu. "Five," he said. "Four . . . three . . . two . . ."

Before he could reach "one," a blue-white bar of light flashed

out of the heavily overcast sky and speared a building nearly
two kilometers away. Six seconds passed . . . and then another,
much louder crack sounded, a thunderous boom with a time
delay. By this time, remote drones and battlefield sensors had
scattered across some hundreds of square kilometers, and any
hostile fire or movement was instantly pinpointed, tracked, and
dealt with—usually with a high-velocity KK round from orbit.

"You're a little off on your timing," Chu told him. "Count
faster."

"Ah, the guys in orbit just want to make liars out of us."

"Not guys," Chu said, correcting him. "AIs. That response was too fast for organics."

"Even worse. We're into the game-sim phase of the op,
now. No combat. Just electronic gaming. The bad guys poke
a nose out of hiding, the AIs in orbit draw a bead and lop it
off."

"You sound bitter."

"Nah. I just wonder how long it'll be before they don't
need us down here on the ground at all. Just park a task force
in orbit and pop bad guys from space, one nose at a time."

"Never happen," Chu said. "*Someone's* gotta take and
hold the high ground, y'know?"

"That's what they taught us in boot camp," Ramsey
agreed. "But that doesn't mean things won't change."

Despite the scattered sniper fire, the worst of the fighting
appeared to be over, and the Marines of the 55th MARS had
emerged victorious. Not that there'd been doubt about the
outcome, of course. The enemy's technological inferiority,
tactical and logistical restrictions, surprise, and morale all
had been factored into the initial ops planning. The only real
question had been what the butcher's bill would be—how
many Marines would be lost in the assault.

The two Marines were walking across the ferrocrete
in front of one of the shuttle hangars at the spaceport, still
buttoned up in their 660 combat cans. Off in the distance,
an enormous APA drifted slowly toward the captured starport, hovering on shrill agravs. Another APA had already
touched down; columns of soldiers were still filing down the
huge transport's ramps.

Smoke billowed into the sky from a dozen fires. The damage throughout this area was severe, and they had to be careful picking their way past piles of rubble and smoldering holes melted into the pavement. Nano-D clouds had drifted through on the wind hours before, leaving ragged, half-molten gaps in the curving walls and ceiling, and the shuttle itself had been reduced to junk. A large area of the floor had been cleared away, however, and the structure was being used as a temporary field hospital, a gathering point for casualties awaiting medevac to orbit. Several naval corpsmen were working in the hangar's shadowed interior, trying to stabilize the more seriously injured.

Staff Sergeant Thea Howell was in there someplace. After that last firefight atop the tower, Ramsey had crouched beside his wounded friend until a combat medevac shuttle had arrived, then helped load her aboard. That had been three hours ago. As soon as Army troops had started filtering in from the starport, Ramsey and the others from 1-1 Bravo had hiked back to the port. Ramsey had located Howell on the platoon Net, and was hoping to see her.

"Ram! Chu! What the hell are you guys doing here?"

The two Marines turned, startled. Captain Baltis had a way of appearing out of nowhere. "Sir!" Ramsey said. Neither he nor Chu saluted, or even came to attention; standard Marine doctrine forbade ritual in the field that might identify officers to enemy snipers. "One of our buddies, sir. Howell. We'd like to know if—"

"Haul your ass clear of here and let the docs do their work," Baltis snapped. "We'll post the status of the wounded when we get back to the ship."

"Yes, sir, but—"

"We will post their status when we get back aboard ship."

Ramsey sagged. "Aye, aye, sir."

"Get your asses over to the Fortress. We'll be disembarking from there."

"Aye, aye, sir!"

The Fortress—what was left of it—loomed above the skyline of Meneh not far from the ocean. It was called El Kalah, which in the creole-Arabic spoken throughout the Theocracy meant "fortress." Originally a vast dome half a kilometer across bristling with ball turrets, each turret mounting plasma, A.M., or hivel accelerator weapons, El Kalah had been the first target in the pinpoint orbital bombardment of the planet, and there was little left of the complex now save the shattered, jagged fragments of dome enclosing a smoking ruin open to the sky. The weapons turrets had been neutralized in rapid succession, and the remaining complex pounded for hours with everything from antimatter to tunneler rounds to knock out any deeply buried bunkers. Much of what was left had melted in the nano-D clouds.

Close by the Fortress was an area that had been a residential zone, stone and cast 'crete housing set in orderly rows among parkland and market squares. At least that was how the downloaded maps described the area. Though the region had not been deliberately targeted, it was now an almost homogenous landscape of rubble and partially melted stone.

As they picked their way through the wreckage, Ramsey and Chu came upon a scene of nightmare horror.

Several Marines in armor were clearing rubble, revealing what had been a basement. On the basement floor, dimly visible in smoky light . . .

"Jesus," Chu said . . . and then Ramsey heard retching sounds as the Marine turned away suddenly. Ramsey continued staring into the pit, unable to stop looking even as he realized that he would never be able to purge his brain of the sight. There must have been thirty or forty people huddled in the basement, though the nano-D cloud had made sorting one body from another difficult. The tangled, tortured positions of the bodies suggested they'd known what was happening to them, and that death had not been quick.

They were civilians, obviously. The Islamic Theocracy did not permit female soldiers, and there'd been children down there as well. Clearly, they'd been trying to find shelter inside the basement.

Equally clearly, the deaths had been inflicted by Theocrat weapons; the assault force had not employed nano-D.

It was said that the life expectancy of an unarmored person on a modern battlefield was measured in scant seconds. These people had never had a chance. Ramsey felt a sullen rage growing within—rage at the Muzzies for their blind use of indiscriminate weaponry and their placement of military targets close beside civilian enclaves, rage at the op planners who'd targeted a heavily inhabited planet, rage at the very idea of war, of doing *this* to innocent bystanders.

Turning away, finally, he grasped Chu's elbow and steered him clear of the scene.

He didn't think he was going to be able to get rid of the memory.

He wasn't sure he wanted to.

And at the same time, he wasn't certain he could live with the nightmare.

4

0507.1102

USMC Skybase
Paraspace
0946 hrs GMT

Lieutenant General Martin Alexander completed the final
download encompassing the Alighan operation. Casualties
had been God-awful high—almost twenty percent—and a
disproportionate percentage of those were irretrievables,
men and women so badly charred by heat or radiation or
so melted by nano-D that they could not be brought back to
life. *Those* were the tough ones, the ones requiring a virtual
visit to parents or spouses.

With a mental click, he shifted his awareness to the Map
Center, a noumenal chamber with a three-D navigable representation of the entire Galaxy. For a moment, his mind's eye
hovered above the broad, softly radiant spiral, taking in the
nebulae-clotted spiral arms, pale blue and white, unwinding
from the ruddier, warmer core, a vast and teeming beehive
of suns surrounded by gas-cloud ramparts, like luminous
thunderheads at the Core's periphery. Four hundred billion
stars across a spiral a hundred thousand light-years across.

How many of those pinpoint stars making up those
banked, luminous clouds and streaming arms were suns,
with worlds and life and civilizations?

An unanswerable question.

A majority of stars had planets, of course. That fact
had been certain as far back as the twenty-first century or

before, when extrasolar planets had first been discovered. Worlds with life were common as well; wherever there was liquid water or, more infrequently, liquid ammonia or liquid sulfur, life, of one kind or another, seemed to arise almost spontaneously.

How many of those worlds with life developed intelligence, however, and communicative civilizations, was a much more difficult, and darker question. Once, the answer would have been "millions" or even "tens of millions," a guess based partly upon statistical analyses and partly upon xenoarcheological discoveries within the Solar System and elsewhere that showed technic civilization, starfaring civilization, exploding across the Galaxy in wave upon wave.

But that was before the discovery of the true nature of the Xul.

"General Alexander?"

"Yes, Herschel."

Herschel was the artificial intelligence controlling the Galaxy display.

"Your aide wishes to link with you.

Damn. Never a moment's peace. "Very well."

Cara, his electronic assistant, entered his noumenal space, her EA icon materializing out of the void. "Excuse the interruption, General."

"Whatcha got?"

"Sir, we have a final plot on the *Argo*. And a partial synch with the ship's AI."

"Only partial?"

"Whatever happened out there happened very quickly."

"I see." He sighed. "Okay. Feed it through. And let's see the plot."

A white pinpoint winked brightly within the depths of one of the spiral arms. At the same time, he felt the surge of incoming data, an e-brief, only, representing the synch with the *Argo*'s AI.

Perseus. The name of the AI had been Perseus.

"A group of delegates from the Defense Advisory Council wants to link with you to discuss the Xul threat," his aide continued as he skimmed the brief.

"I'll just bet they do. Okay. When?"

"Fourteen minutes. Ten-hundred hours."

"Huh. The *Argo* incident has them worried."

"Terrified, more like it. And can you blame them, sir? There hasn't been another peep out of the Xul for five hundred years."

Alexander completed the brief, then stared into the sea of teeming suns hanging before him. "I wouldn't call the bombardment of Earth by high-velocity asteroids a 'peep,' Cara. Earth was nearly destroyed."

"Yes, sir. But they didn't finish us. In fact, they seem to have lost track of us entirely."

"Garroway's attack at Night's Edge—" He stopped himself. He had a tendency, he knew, to slip into lecture mode, and his aide knew the history of Night's Edge as well as he did. Better, perhaps.

"Exactly, sir," she said. "Garroway gambled that information about our whereabouts in the Galaxy had not been disseminated yet beyond the Xul base that launched the attack on us. And apparently his gamble paid off. Only now . . ."

"Now the Xul appear to have picked up the trail again."

"We have to assume that if they captured the *Argo*, they know where we are. And they'll be better prepared next time. Stronger, more careful, and in greater numbers."

"We damned near didn't survive their last attack," Alexander pointed out. "And that was just one Xul huntership!"

In the year 539 of the Marine Era, or in 2314 c.e. as the Commonwealth measured the passing years, a single kilometer-long Xul vessel had appeared out of the emptiness between the stars, destroyed several human ships, then proceeded to fling small chunks of asteroidal debris at the Earth. The fragments were small, but somehow the Intruder had boosted them to very high velocities—on the order of half the speed of light—giving them the kinetic energy of much larger bodies when they struck.

Deep space facilities designed as part of the High Guard asteroid defense network had succeeded in destroying many of the infalling rocks, but enough pieces had struck Earth to do terrible damage, obliterating much of Europe and eastern

North America in firestorms and tidal waves and plunging the rest of the planet into an ice age—what the histories persisted in calling a "nuclear winter," even though the impacts were purely kinetic, and not nuclear at all.

The only thing that had saved civilization from complete collapse had been the fact that Humankind possessed a considerable off-world presence—numerous space stations, factories, colonies, and military bases in Earth orbit, on Luna and Mars, in the Asteroid Belt, and farther out, among the satellites of Jupiter. Billions died on the Motherworld, first in the holocaust of falling debris, then of starvation and exposure as the snows deepened and the oceans began icing over. But technological help had begun pouring in from the space-based colonies, especially from the orbital nanufactories, untouched by the devastation wrought on Earth. Nanufactured food, power plants, and constructors had been loaded into immense one-trip gliders by the megaton and deorbited for recovery in the ice-free equatorial zones of Earth's oceans. Within another century, one, then dozens of space elevators had been lowered into place, connecting points along the equator with matching points in geostationary orbit, after which the supplies had really begun flowing down the pipelines from space. Ground-based agricultural nanufactories had begun producing food locally, then, along with nano designed to break down ice, lower the skyrocketing planetary albedo, and clean up the detritus of a wrecked technic civilization.

Slowly, then, the recovery had begun.

And five centuries later, that recovery was continuing. New cities were growing now along the shockingly altered Atlantic coastlines. Most of the gangs and local warlords had long since been suppressed, or incorporated into the new government. North America and most of Europe were no longer dependent on supplies from space.

Of course, the former United States was now a special protectorate of the Commonwealth, a necessary adjustment in the face of the aggressive expansion of the Chinese Hegemony. And the Islamic Theocracy continued to be a perennial problem, ruled from the Principiate of Allah, at Mecca.

Sharp wars had been fought with both states to protect both the Americas and Europe.

Alexander allowed himself an inner, unvocalized sigh. The real enemy, as always, remained the Xul, and for half a millennium Humankind had continued its divided, petty squabblings among its various fragmented religious, political and economic factions. This current unpleasantness with the Theocracy was only the latest in eight hundred years of bloodshed that stretched all the way back to WWIII, and which some historians insisted went back even further, to the Crusades of the Middle Ages.

Still adrift just above the galactic plane, Alexander gave a mental command and allowed his mind's eye to descend into the sea of stars, moving out toward the spiral arms, toward one spur of a spiral arm in particular, about 23,000 light-years from the center. The vast majority of the stars in this simulation were approximations only, with no hard information about the stars or the worlds that might be circling them. Some day, perhaps . . . but for now Humankind's knowledge of its celestial neighborhood was sharply restricted to an unevenly shaped blot perhaps 800 light-years across in its longest dimension, less than one percent of the vast and pinwheeling whole.

Ahead, the stars embraced by the Commonwealth and the other governments of Humankind glowed within a soft, green haze of light. Individual star systems were labeled with alphanumerics giving names and provenance—with Sol imbedded roughly at the center. Another mental click, and the green light fragmented into various shades of yellow, blue, and green, identifying the Islamic Arm, the Chinese Arm, the Pan-European Arm, the Latino Arm, the Commonwealth, and the rest.

He brought up a red icon marking the position of the lost *Argo* . . . 500 light-years from Sol, and on a direct line with the Andromedan Galaxy. She'd been well outside of human space when the Xul had discovered her; the outer fringes of Islamic space lay a light-century or so in her wake.

Orange pinpoints marked those outposts and garrisons of the Xul that had been identified over the past few hundred years, a fuzzy and diffuse cloud outside of human space; none lay close to *Argo*'s outbound route, but that was scarcely surprising. The Xul empire spanned the Galaxy and stretched well beyond it; Humankind thus far had identified only a few hundred Xul outposts and bases, and the best guess suggested that the Xul held a million star systems, or more.

"We now have a candidate star for another Xul base," Herschel whispered in Alexander's ear. "Here . . ."

A star was highlighted in blue, and Alexander zoomed in on it. Nu Andromedae, a type B5 V blue-white sun some 440 light-years from Earth. From Earth's perspective, the star by chance appeared just to the east of M-31.

"The *Argo* must have passed quite close to Nu Andromedae," Herschel added. The AI painted a red contrail streaming from the *Argo*, like a thin, taut thread stretching all the way back to Sol, and the line skimmed past Nu Andromedae, almost touching it. "Less than three light-years, in fact."

"Maybe. But that was still over a hundred years ago. Why should the Xul wait that long before pouncing?"

"For the same reason the Xul have not found Earth, General. The term once in use was 'a needle in a haystack.'"

Alexander had never seen either a sewing needle or a haystack, but the phrase was descriptive enough in its own right. Even the Xul, powerful and technologically advanced as they were, couldn't be everywhere, couldn't watch every star system or world where life might have evolved. The Galaxy was far too large for that level of omnipotence, even for beings with powers indistinguishable from those of gods.

"Herschel's right, General," his aide pointed out. "The *Argo* was a hollowed-out asteroid. Its passengers were in deep cybe-hibe. Even at close to the speed of light, it wouldn't have been giving off much in the way of anomalous radiation."

"I don't buy it, Cara. We know now it would have been giving off a kind of wake as it plowed through the dust and hydrogen atoms floating around in its path—the interstellar medium. We can detect that sort of thing ourselves. If *we* can do it, the Xul can as well." He studied the display a moment longer, rotating the display and studying the contrail. "Herschel . . . check distances from the contrail to nearby stars, and correlate with the one-way time lags. Assume radio noise expands from the *Argo* at the speed of light, and a more or less immediate response from the target star once the RF wave front reaches it."

"Yes, General." Angles and geometric designs flickered from star to star, touching the contrail at various points as the artificial intelligence searched for a better fit.

"Actually . . . *that* star is a better candidate," Alexander said after a moment, indicating a particular geometry.

"Epsilon Trianguli," Cara said, calling up the data window on the indicated star. "Type A2 V. Four hundred fifty light-years from Earth—"

"And 110 lights from the contrail at its closest passage," Alexander said. "The *Argo* streaks by, disturbing the interstellar medium. The radio noise spreads out, like the wake of a boat on a calm lake, and reaches Epsilon Trianguli 110 years later. A Xul ship or base takes note and dispatches a force to investigate."

"There are twenty-five other stars with corresponding distances, angles, and lag times," Herschel told them, "albeit with lesser probabilities."

"Store the data, Hersch," Alexander said. "We may want to do a careful analysis, maybe even send a sneak-and-peek team out there for a look around."

"Aye, aye, sir."

For centuries, the Marines and Navy had dispatched scouting forces out from human space—sneak-and-peek teams, as they were popularly known—in order to try to identify specific stars where the Xul maintained a presence. The idea was that if Xul bases or colonies could be found, they could be watched, with an eye to noting any sudden activity that might presage a new assault against human space.

The sheer vastness of space, the grains-of-sand numbers of stars, worked both ways, however. For centuries, they'd hidden Sol from the Xul, protecting the existence of Humankind, but those same numbers allowed the vast majority of the Xul outposts to remain hidden as well.

But the further into interstellar space Humankind probed, the greater the chance, the more certain the *inevitability*, that it would once again trip the Xul sentries, as it had on several occasions already. And it seemed all but certain that, when the Xul returned to the Motherworld of Humankind, they would come with sufficient force to finish the job they'd begun several times before.

Humans had been lucky so far . . . lucky despite the fact that half a millennium ago Earth had so nearly been rendered uninhabitable. Only during the past few centuries had they begun piecing together the full history of human-Xul interactions, a relationship that extended back, it was believed, as far as half a million years.

As Cara and Herschel began preparing the virtual space for the electronic arrival of the Advisory Council, Alexander allowed his implant processors to cull through the data, reviewing past, present, and several darkly disturbing possible futures. As the data fell into place, he allowed himself a moment's reverie, induced by the electronic flow from the local AI through the mingling of organic and inorganic regions of his brain.

Some five hundred thousand years ago, an advanced nonhuman intelligence—robotic intelligences unimaginatively dubbed variously the "Builders" or "the Ancients" by popular histories and the entertainment and news sims—had created an empire spanning all of today's human space, and presumably extending far beyond. The Builders had terraformed Mars, and, for a brief time, at least, employed reasonably bright bipedal creatures imported from the third planet as workers—genetically altering them to boost their intelligence, and in doing so creating the species that later would call itself *Homo sapiens.*

But the Xul had attacked the Builders, however, the Xul or their militant predecessors. Ruins on Mars and on Earth's Moon, on Chiron in the Alpha Centauri system, and on numerous other worlds attested to the violence and the completeness of the genocidal Xul campaign. One of their enormous ships, part machine and part downloaded intelligence, had been badly damaged in the conflict and crashed into the ice-locked world-ocean of Europa. The Builders, who called the invaders "The Hunters of the Dawn," were destroyed, their empire reduced to broken ruins and rubble on a thousand far-strewn worlds. Of the Builders themselves, apparently, nothing had survived. Their genetically altered creations, however, had escaped the notice of the Xul, and survived, even flourished, on Earth.

Half a million years later, and some ten to fifteen thousand years ago, another spacefaring civilization had entered Earth's Solar System. The An were in the process of establishing a much smaller, more modest interstellar empire, one embracing a few score star systems scattered across perhaps fifty light-years. They'd planted colonies on Earth and on Earth's Moon, mined precious metals, and enslaved human nomads to raise food and work the mines. In making slaves, farms, and stone cities, they'd managed to become the prototypes of the gods and goddesses of ancient Mesopotamia. But then the An had attracted the notice of the Xul—the name itself had survived in the Sumerian language as one meaning "demon"—and the An, too, were annihilated.

The Xul had missed one Earthlike world populated by the An, however. The satellite of a gas giant well outside its sun's habitable zone, perhaps it had been overlooked. On Ishtar, in the Lalande 21185 system eight and a half light-years from Sol, a few An and their human slaves had survived, remaining unnoticed in the holocaust when their technological infrastructure collapsed. On Earth, again, the An all were killed, but humans had survived to wonder about the cyclopean and monolithic ruins at places like Baalbek, submerged Yonaguni, and Tiahuanaco, and to tell stories of a universal deluge and the wrath of the gods.

Thousands of years passed, and humans on Earth again developed high technologies, this time on their own, and again they walked on other worlds. They found mysterious ruins on Mars and on Luna, and a few devices miraculously intact. They found the lost Xul ship, poetically dubbed "The Singer" for its eerie and insane radio transmissions, submerged deep beneath the Europan ice, and on Ishtar they found descendents of both An and humans.

From that time on, late in the twenty-second century, Humankind had existed in a kind of secretive balance with the Xul, who, it turned out, were still very much in existence after all those millennia. Like mice or cockroaches living in the walls of a very large dwelling, human starfarers sought to improve their own lot while avoiding the notice of the heavy-footed giants living nearby. Archeological teams spread out among the nearer star systems, seeking remnants of lost technologies left by the Builders, by the An, and by other civilizations. Eventually, another alien species had been discovered, the amphibian N'mah, living within an enigmatic Ancient-built stargate in the Sirius system.

In 2170, Marine and Navy forces at the Sirius Stargate had destroyed a Xul ship as it came through the Gate. In 2314, another Xul ship had appeared, this time within Earth's solar system . . . and Earth had very nearly died. In 2323, a Navy-Marine task force had proceeded through the Sirius Gate to another, unknown and distant star system, Night's Edge, using a freighter-load of sand scooped from the surface of Mars and accelerated to close to the speed of light to eliminate a Xul fleet and planetary base. As Cara had pointed out, the obliteration of that Xul outpost appeared to have wiped out any data the Xul had acquired pertaining to Humankind or Sol . . . and bought Earth a precious few more centuries to prepare for her next encounter with the Xul threat.

That there would be another encounter, Alexander had no doubt whatsoever. Since the early twentieth century, Earth had been broadcasting her presence; Sol now rested at the center of a sphere over 1,700 light-years across, a pulsing, restless bubble of electromagnetic radiation at radio wave-lengths expanding outward at the speed of light—a certain indicator of intelligent, technic life at its center.

Alexander allowed himself a mental grin at the memory of an old joke. Perhaps it wasn't an indicator of *intelligent* life, given the nature of much of the entertainment content of that bubble. Still, anyone with the appropriate technological know-how could hear that babble of noise, and know that technic civilization was responsible.

And The Singer had broadcast *something* to the stars back in 2067 when it was freed from its icy tomb. No, there was no way Humanity could keep its existence secret much longer.

And how was Humankind to survive in a contest against a technology half a million years more advanced?

It was a problem the Marine Corps had been struggling to resolve since the twenty-first century. So far, for the most part, they'd been able to fight isolated and tightly controlled battles, applying tactics that emphasized Marine strengths while sidestepping Xul technology. As commanding officer of the 1st Marine Interstellar Expeditionary Force, Alexander was responsible for keeping on top of the Xul threat, and keeping the Commonwealth government informed of any changes in the situation.

And the situation certainly had changed now, with the taking of the *Argo*.

"General?" Cara said, interrupting increasingly grim thoughts. "Will you want your full filters for the meeting?"

"Eh? What was that?"

"Your e-comm filters, sir. The delegates will begin linking in before too long. How do you want to be dressed?"

He grimaced. Personal filters were an important part of modern electronic communications. Within a noumenal setting—literally inside the participants' heads—your personal icon could take on any appearance desired, anything within the programming range of the AIs giving the encounter substance. Filters allowed the image projected into the group mind's virtual space to be of your own choosing, with apparent dress, body language, even inflection of voice under your control.

He didn't like it, though. He never had. Though e-filters had been around for centuries, a necessary outgrowth of noumenal projection, they still seemed . . . dishonest, somehow, a kind of social white lie.

"You can't," Cara told him, a disapproving tone to her words, "receive the Defense Advisory Council like *that*."

Mentally, he looked down at himself. As usual, he was projecting his real-world appearance into the galactic imagery . . . which, at the moment, was of a lean, middle-aged man with graying hair and a dour expression. He was also naked.

Causal nudity was perfectly acceptable within most modern social situations, but Cara was right. This was not the proper appearance to put before twenty-four of the more powerful and important of the arbiters of Commonwealth government policy.

"What do you suggest?" he asked her.

"Something," she said, "more like this." She gave his sim an electronic tweak, and his body morphed into something leaner, tauter, and with more presence, and wearing Marine full dress, his upper left chest ablaze in luminous decorations and campaign holos. The brilliant gold Terran Sun-burst, awarded for his role at the Battle of Grellsinore as a very raw lieutenant, was emblazoned on his right breast. His head and shoulders were encased within a lambent *corona flammae*, another social convention granted to officially designated Heroes of the Commonwealth.

"I think we can lose the decorations," he said. He gave a commanding thought, and the medals vanished. His uniform dwindled a bit into plain dress blacks. "*And* the damned light show." The corona faded away.

"With respect, sir," Cara told him, "you *need* the bric-a-brac. The council's chairperson is Marie Devereaux. She is impressed by proper formal presentation, and you will need to enlist her support for your plan."

He sighed. "Okay. Medals, yes. But not that damned glow. Makes me look like an ancient religious icon, complete with halo."

"The *corona flammae* is part of your sanctioned uniform, sir. For your service at and after the twenty-third Chinese War. And the delegation members will have their own."

"Fucking trappings of power. I hate this."

"Indeed, sir," Cara said as the light came back on . . . but a trifle subdued, this time. "But how many times have you lectured me on the need to blend in with the local social environment? To do otherwise will elicit disapproval, and might well send conflicting signals or, worse, could alienate your audience."

Alexander looked sharply at Cara's icon—which was presenting itself, as usual, as an attractive, dark-haired woman of indeterminate years wearing a Marine undress uniform. It was tough at times to remember that "Cara" was, in fact, an electronic artifice, an AI serving as his personal military aide and electronic office manager. A resident of the noumenon and virtual workplaces, she had no physical reality at all.

"Okay, boss," he said at last. "Light me. But no parade or fireworks, okay? Even heroes of the Commonwealth should be granted a little dignity."

"I'll see what I can do, sir," she told him. "But no promises!"

And then, with Cara serving as gatekeeper and announcer, the first of the council delegates began linking in.

5

USMC Skybase
Paraspace
1005 hrs GMT

It was, Alexander decided, a bit like being in an enormous fish tank. The delegates of the Defense Advisory Council appeared in the simulation as small and relatively unobtrusive icons, until one or another spoke. At that point, the icon unfolded into what appeared to be a life-sized image, standing on emptiness and aglow with its own corona. With a swarm of golden icons surrounding him, together with a larger swarm of smaller, dimmer icons representing the group's cloud of digital secretaries and personal electronic assistants, he felt as though he were a large and somewhat clumsy whale immersed within a school of fish.

There was also the feeling that the entire school was studying him intently, and not a little critically. They included, Cara had reminded him, eight delegates from the Commonwealth Senate, ten senior military officers from the Bureaus of Defense, five members of the President's Intelligence Advisory Group, and Marie Devereaux, the President's personal advisor and representative.

Alexander shrugged off the feeling, and continued with his presentation. They were adrift in an absolute blackness relieved only by a fuzzy circle of light surrounding them all, a ring dividing the darkness into two unequal parts. Within the smaller part, the ring shaded into blue, the leading edge. The trailing edge shaded into red.

This was how space had looked from the point of view of Perseus, the AI commanding the colony asteroid ship *Argo* during her flight across the Galaxy. The luminous ring was the bizarre and beautiful relativistic compression of space as seen at near-*c* velocities, a three-dimensional panorama overlaid here and there by the flickering alphanumerics of Perseus's functional displays.

"We don't have a lot to go on," Alexander was telling the watching delegates. "From the time the Xul ship materialized alongside the *Argo*, to the moment of *Argo*'s destruction, less than five seconds elapsed. The AI in command of the vessel was in time-extended mode. He did not have time to fully react."

Artificial sentients like Perseus were designed to control their own subjective passage of time. For machine intelligences that could note the passage of millionths of a second, the passage of a truly long period of relative inactivity—such as the subjective decades necessary for interstellar flight—could literally drive the AI insane. That, it was believed, was what had happened to The Singer, the Xul huntership trapped for half a million years beneath the ice of the Europan ocean.

Perseus had been experiencing time at roughly a thousand to one—meaning that a year was the same as roughly nine hours for a human. At that setting, though, those four and a half seconds after the appearance of the Xul ship had been the human equivalent of 4.5 thousandths of a second; it was amazing that Perseus had managed to do as much as he had.

In Alexander's mind, and in the minds of the watching delegates, those last seconds played out in slow motion.

"As you see," Alexander continued, indicating one of the numeric readouts, "the time scale has been altered so that we can experience the encounter at a ratio of about ten to one . . . four seconds becomes forty. Perseus would have been perceiving this about one hundred times more slowly."

Abruptly, a shadow appeared against the eldritch starlight. One moment there was nothing; the next, it was there, immense against the luminous ring. With its velocity matched perfectly to that of *Argo*, the Xul huntership appeared undistorted, a convolute and complex mountain of curves, swellings, angles, spires, and sheer mass, the whole only slightly less black than the empty space ahead and behind, forbidding and sinister.

In fact, Alexander reminded himself, the Intruder was somewhat smaller than the *Argo*—perhaps 2 kilometers long and one wide, according to the data now appearing on the display, where the *Argo* was a potato-shaped rock over 8 kilometers thick along its long axis. But most of *Argo* was dead rock. The totality of her living and engineering areas, command and defense centers, storage tanks, and drive systems occupied something like three percent of the asteroid's total bulk. The asteroid-shell of the *Argo* itself was invisible in the data simulation. Without the asteroid as a reference, the Intruder, slowly drifting closer, felt enormous.

"That looks nothing like the Intruder," Senator Dav Gannel said. "The ship that attacked Earth . . . and the hunterships we encountered at the Sirius Stargate, they were shaped like huge needles. That thing is . . . I don't know what the hell it is, but it's a lot fatter, more egg-shaped. How do we know it's Xul?"

Alexander didn't answer. The slow-motion seconds dragged by as the monster drew closer, until it blotted out a quarter of the light ring. The flickering alphanumerics indicated that Perseus was aware of the threat, and attempting to open a communications channel.

"They're not responding," another Council delegate said. "Of course they might not understand Anglic."

"English, Senator," Alexander said. "When *Argo* was launched, the principal language of trade and government was English. Perseus is signaling on several million channels, using microwave, infrared, and optical laser wavelengths. Remember, we've at least partially interfaced with a number of Xul vessels, and we were able to study The Singer, the one we recovered on Europa eight centuries ago. We know the frequencies they use, and some of their linguistic conventions. You can be sure the Intruder hears, and it understands enough to know *Argo* is *trying* to communicate. It's just not listening."

"Shouldn't the *Argo* be trying to get away?" Devereaux asked.

"Madam Devereaux, the *Argo* is traveling at within a tenth of a percent of the speed of light. At that velocity, it would take a *staggering* amount of additional power to increase speed by even one kilometer per hour. She could decelerate or try moving laterally, adding a new vector to her current course and speed, but that means rotating the entire asteroid, and that would take time. And . . . the Intruder clearly possesses some type of faster-than-light drive, to have been able to overtake *Argo* so easily. No, Madam Chairman, there's not a whole lot Perseus *can* do right now but try to talk."

"Does she have any weapons at all?"

"A few. Beam weapons, for the most part, designed to reduce stray rocks and bits of debris in her path to charged plasmas that can be swept aside by the vessel's protective mag fields. But if any of you have seen the recordings of the defense of Earth in 2314, you know that huntership shrugged off that kind of weaponry without giving it a thought. It took whole batteries of deep-space anti-asteroid laser cannons just to damage the Intruder, plus a Marine combat boarding party to go in and destroy it from the inside."

"At the Battle of Sirius Gate," General Regin Samuels pointed out, "the Earth forces used the thrusters from their capital ships as huge plasma cannons. What if—"

"No," Alexander said. "*Argo* is employing a magnetic field drive we picked up from the N'mah, not plasma thrusters." He didn't add the obvious—that this wasn't a problem-solving exercise, damn it, and it wasn't happening in real time. What was revealed by this data sim had already happened.

The government delegates, he reflected, were a little too used to, and perhaps a little too reliant on, instantaneous communications.

There was no indication that the alien vessel even heard Perseus' communications attempts. One point seven three seconds after the Intruder appeared, large portions of the AI's circuitry began to fail—or, rather, it appeared to begin working for another system, as though it had been massively compromised by a computer virus.

"At this point," Alexander explained, "the *Argo* is being penetrated by the alien's computer network. It is very fast, and apparently evolving microsecond to microsecond, adapting in order to mesh with Perseus's operating system. The pattern is identical to that employed by Xul huntships in other engagements."

It was as though the alien virus could trace the layout of Perseus' myriad circuits, memory fields, and get a feel for the programs running there, to sense the overall pattern of the operating system before beginning to change it.

Beams and missiles stabbed out from the *Argo*, focusing on a relatively small region within the huge Intruder's midship area. So far as those watching could tell, the result was exactly zero. Beams and missiles alike seemed to vanish into that monster structure without visible effect.

More alphanumerics appeared, detailing massive failures in the *Argo*'s cybe-hibe capsules. The Intruder was now infecting the colony ship's sleeping passengers by way of their cybernetic interfaces.

"We're not sure yet how the Xul manage this trick," Alexander went on, "but we've seen them do it before. The first time was with an explorer vessel, *Wings of Isis*, at the Sirius Stargate in 2148. It apparently patterns or replicates human minds and memories, storing them as computer data. We believe the Xul are able to utilize this data to create patterned humans as virtual sentients or sims."

Three point one seconds after the attack had begun, Perseus realized that all of its electronic barriers and defenses were failing, that electronic agents spawned by the Intruder's operating system were spilling in over, around, and through every firewall and defensive program Perseus could bring into play. Perseus immediately released a highly compressed burst of data—a complete record of everything stored thus far—through *Argo*'s QCC, the FTL Quantum-Coupled Comm system that kept *Argo* in real-time contact with Earth.

Abruptly, the record froze, the alphanumeric columns and data blocks halted in mid-flicker.

"Four point zero one seconds," Alexander said. "At this point, Perseus flashed the recording of *Argo*'s log back to Earth."

"But . . . but everyone has been assuming that the *Argo* was destroyed," Senator Kalin said, a mental sputter. "We don't know that. They could still all be alive. . . ."

"Unlikely, Senator," Alexander replied dryly. "First of all, of course, there's been no further contact with the *Argo* during the past three days. There is also this. . . ."

Mentally, he highlighted one data block set off by itself—an indication of *Argo*'s physical status. Two lines in particular stood out—velocity and temperature. The asteroid starship's velocity had abruptly plummeted by nearly point one c, and its temperature had risen inexplicably by some 1,500 degrees.

"When Perseus sent off the burst transmission, these two indicators had begun changing during the previous one one-thousandth of a second. We're not sure, but what the physicists who've studied this believe is happening is that *Argo*'s forward velocity was somehow being directly transformed into kinetic energy. A very great deal of kinetic energy. And liberated as heat. A very great deal of heat."

"These data show *Argo* is still completely intact," Marie Devereaux noted. She sounded puzzled. "Senator Kalin is right. That doesn't prove that the *Argo* was destroyed."

"Look here, and here," Alexander said, indicating two other inset data blocks. "The temperature increase is still confined to a relatively small area—a few hundred meters across, it looks like . . . but the temperature there in that one spot has risen 1,500 degrees Kelvin in less than a thousandth of a second. The physics people think the Xul simply stopped the *Argo* in mid-flight—and released all of that kinetic energy, the energy of a multi-billion-ton asteroid moving at near-c, as heat in one brief, intense blast. Believe

me, Senator. That much energy all liberated at once would
have turned the Argo into something resembling a pocket-
sized supernova."

"But *why*?" Kalin wanted to know.

"Evidently because the Xul had copied all of the data
they felt they needed. They're not known, remember, for
taking *physical* prisoners."

There was evidence enough, though, of their having uploaded human personalities and memories, however, and
using those as subjects for extended interrogation. He'd seen
some of the records taken from a Xul huntership, of what
had happened to the crew of the *Wings of Isis* in 2148. He
suppressed a cold shudder.

"*If* it's the Xul," Devereaux added.

He hesitated, wondering how forceful to make his response. It was vital, *vital* that these people understand.
"Madam Chairperson, Senator Gannel asked a while ago
how we could know that *Argo* was destroyed by a Xul huntership. The answer is we don't." He indicated the vast, convoluted ovoid hovering close by *Argo* in the frozen noumenal
projection. "It's not as though they've hung banners out an-
nouncing their identity. But I'll tell you this. If that vessel is
not Xul, then it's being operated by someone just as smart,
just as powerful, just as technologically advanced, and just
as xenophobic as the Xul. If they're not Xul, they'll do until
the real thing comes along, wouldn't you say?"

"If it's Xul," Devereaux continued, "how much does this
. . . incident hurt us?"

He sighed. "That's the question, isn't it? Fifty thousand
twenty-fourth century politicians, plutocrats, bureaucrats,
specialists, and technicians. How much damage could they
do?"

That asteroid colony ship presented an interesting window
into the politics of Humankind's past. Shortly after the Xul
attack on Earth, many of the survivors—especially those
wealthy enough or politically powerful enough to buy the
privilege—had elected to flee the Motherworld rather than
remain behind to face a second attack that all knew to be
inevitable. At that time, Humankind had not yet unraveled

the secrets of faster-than-light travel. With N'mah help and technology, however, they'd constructed four asteroid starships each capable of carrying tens of thousands of refugees and which could accelerate to nearly the speed of light using the reactionless N'mah space drive.

From Alexander's point of view, the decision to flee the Galaxy entirely, to travel over two million light-years to reach another galaxy, seemed to be a bit of overkill. Still, he had to admit that, judging by the interstellar vistas recorded at Night's Edge and elsewhere, the Xul did appear to have a presence embracing much of the Galaxy. Two of their known bases—Night's Edge and a Stargate nexus known only as Cluster Space—were actually located well outside of the Galactic plane, where the Galaxy's spiral arms curved across the sky much as they did in Alexander's noumenal simulation. Their empire, if that's what it could be called, might well extend across the entire Milky Way—four hundred billion suns, and an unknown hundreds of billions of worlds.

The refugees of the twenty-fourth century had desperately hoped to find a new home well beyond even the Xul's immensely long reach through space and time. It would take over two million years to make the trip, but relativistic time dilation would reduce that to something like thirty years; with the prospective colonists in cybe-hibe stasis, even that brief subjective time would vanish as they fled into the remote future.

The only question had been whether or not the refugee ships could slip out of the Galaxy without being spotted by the Xul. That hope, unfortunately, had failed.

"Our problem, of course," Alexander went on, "is that we *must* assume that the Xul now know exactly where we are, and who we are. Most of the people on board probably didn't have useful information that would lead the Xul back to Earth. A few would have, however, though I'm actually more concerned about the data Perseus might have been carrying. He probably had a complete record of the 2314 attack, for instance, and would have had the galactic coordinate system we use for navigation.

"The Xul are smart. They'll put that data together with the elimination of their base at Night's Edge, and know we were responsible. They might also be able to see enough of the stellar background in any visual records to positively locate Sol. And . . . there's also *Argo*'s path. The refugee ships were supposed to make a course correction or two on the way out, so they didn't draw a line straight back to Earth, but doing that sort of thing at relativistic speeds is time consuming and wastes energy. I doubt the changes were enough to throw the Xul off by very much. At the very least, they'll figure the *Argo* set out from someplace close to the Sirius Stargate. That bit of data alone might be enough. It's only eight and a half light-years from Earth."

In fact there was so much Humankind didn't know about the Xul or how they might reason things through. No one could explain why, for instance, they didn't share data more freely among themselves. The only reason the Xul hadn't identified Humankind as a serious threat centuries ago was the fact that the Night's Edge raid did appear to have obliterated any record of the Xul operation against Earth nine years earlier.

"What about the other three refugee ships?" Navin Bergenhal, one of the Intelligence Advisory Group members, asked. "They're all in danger now."

"We'll need to send out QCC flashes to them, of course," Alexander said. "I doubt there's anything they can do, though, since it'll take a year of deceleration for them to slow down, and another year to build back up to near-*c* for the return trip. If they wanted to return." He shrugged. "Their escapist philosophy may prove to be the best after all. If the Xul find Earth and the rest of our worlds, the only hope for Man's survival might well rest in one or more of those surviving colony ships making it to M-31."

"The destruction of the *Argo* is tragic, yes," Devereaux said. "But I still don't see an immediate threat. This all took place five hundred light-years away, after all. And the Xul have always been glacially slow in their military responses."

Alexander nodded. "Agreed. If they behave as they have in the past, it might be some time before that information disseminates across all of Xul-controlled space. But, Madam Devereaux, we would be foolish to assume they won't disseminate it, or that they won't act upon it eventually. Our best xenopsych profiles so far suggest that the Xul are extreme xenophobes, that they destroy other technic races as a kind of instinctive defense mechanism. We've bloodied them a couple of times now, at Sirius, at Night's Edge, and at Sol, so you can bet that they're going to sit up and take notice."

"We're going to need to . . . consider this," Devereaux said. "In light of the current difficulties with the Islamic Theocracy, we must proceed . . . circumspectly. Perhaps Intelligence can run some simulations plots, and come up with some realistic probabilities."

Damn. He was going to have to turn up the heat. "With all due respect, Madam Devereaux," he said, "that is fucking irresponsible. It's also *stupid*, playing politics with the whole of Humankind at stake!"

There was a long pause. Devereaux's head cocked to one side. "With all due respect *what*, General Alexander?"

"Eh?"

"Your filter blocked you," Cara whispered in his mind.

"Oh, for the love of . . ." Angrily, he cleared part of the filter program, dropping it to a lower level. The software had decided that his choice of language left a lot to be desired, and had edited it.

"Excuse me, Ms. Devereaux," he said as the program shifted to a lower level. He glanced down at himself. At least he was still in uniform. "Social convention required that I have my e-filters in place, lest I . . . give offense. But we don't have time for that nonsense now. What I said, ma'am, was that delay, any delay—giving the matter further study, running numbers, whatever you wish to call it—is irresponsible and stupid. I believe the term my e-filter didn't like was 'fucking irresponsible.'"

"I see." Her own e-filters were in place of course, but they didn't stop a certain amount of disapproval from slipping through in those two short words. "And just what do you expect us to do about this, General Alexander?"

"A raid, Madam Devereaux." At a thought, the frozen view from the *Argo* at the moment of the ship's destruction vanished, and was replaced by the galactic map he'd been studying before the delegates had arrived. The viewpoint zoomed in on the irregular green glow of human space, on the path of the *Argo*, and on a tight scattering of red pinpoints marking the nearby systems from which the huntership might have emerged—Nu Andromeda, Epsilon Trianguli, and a few others. "What the Marines call a sneak-and-peek."

The display continued to animate as he spoke, the viewpoint zooming in until Epsilon Trianguli showed as a hot, white sphere rather than as another star. An A2 type star, Epsilon Trianguli appeared imbedded in a far-flung corona of luminous gas, and even in simulation was almost too brilliant to look at directly.

A hypothetical planet swung into view, a sharp-edged crescent bowed away from the star, attended by a clutter of sickle-shaped moons. A swarm of dark gray and metallic slivers materialized out of emptiness and scattered across the system. Other planets appeared in the distance, along with the gleaming, wedding-band hoop of a stargate.

"First in are AI scouts, to show us the terrain. We also need to know if there's a stargate in the target system. The scouts will find out if there is a Xul presence in the system, and map it out so we're not going in blind."

Obedient to his lecture, a Xul station revealed itself, menacing and black, positioned to guard the stargate. A swarm of new objects entered the scene, dull-black ovoids, descending toward the Xul structure in waves. Pinpoints of white light flickered and strobed against the surface in a silent representation of space combat.

"The Marines go in hot, wearing marauder armor and accompanied by highly specialized penetrator AIs," Alexander went on. "Details depend on what the scouts turn up, of course, but the idea will be to insert a Marine raiding party into the Xul, grab as much information as we can, and blow the thing to hell."

On cue, the camera point of view pulled back sharply, just as the Xul base in the scene, in complete silence, detonated—a searing, fast-expanding ball of white light that briefly outshone the brilliant local sun.

"Very pretty," Devereaux said as the display faded into darkness once more. The noumenal scene flowed and shifted once more, becoming a more conventional virtual encounter space. "But just what would be the point?"

They now appeared to be seated around the perimeter of a sunken conversation pit three meters across, the representation of the Galaxy as seen from above spiraled about itself at their feet. Here, the individual icons all expanded into images of people, though their electronic secretaries and EAs remained visible only as tiny, darting icons of yellow light orbiting their human masters. The walls and ceiling of the room appeared lost in darkness.

"The point, Madam Devereaux, is to avoid being put on the defensive again. We were on the defensive in 2314. You know what happened."

'Yes," General Samuels said. "We beat them."

"At a terrible cost, sir. Earth's population in 2314 was . . . what?" Alexander pulled the data down from the Net. "Fifteen point seven billion people. Four billion died within the space of a few hours during the Xul bombardment. *Four billion.* Exact numbers were never available, given the chaos of the next few decades, but an estimated one to two billion more froze during the Endless Winter, or starved to death, or died of disease or internal electronics failure or just plain despair."

"We *know* our history, General," Devereaux said.

"Then you should know that the human race came within a hair's breadth of becoming extinct. Over a third of the human race died, murdered by one Xul huntership. *One!* We were lucky to be able to destroy it. And if General Garroway hadn't backtracked the Intruder through the Sirius Stargate to Night's Edge and found a way to take out the base there, we wouldn't be sitting here now discussing it!"

"And you know, General," Devereaux said, "that the current political situation may preclude a major operation such as you seem to be suggesting. The Monists and the Starborn both are threatening to side with the Islamic Theocracy. If they do, the Commonwealth will fall." She spread her hands. "If that happens, how are we supposed to defend ourselves if the Xul *do* come?"

"I submit, Madam Devereaux, that the Human species right now has more to worry about than the exact nature of God. If we do not take a stand, an active stand, against the Xul threat, if we don't deal with it now, while we have a chance of doing so, then none of the rest matters. We'll be settling the question of God's nature by meeting Him face to face!"

"He does have a point, Marie," another delegate in the circle said. He wore the uniform and the corona of a Fleet admiral, and the alphanumerics that popped up when Alexander looked at him identified him as Admiral Joseph Mason. As he spoke, the light brightened around him, drawing the eye. "We can't ignore what's happened out there."

"Five hundred light-years, Admiral. It's *so* far away."

"It's a very short step for the Xul, Marie. We've survived so far only because we've been lost within . . . what? Ten million stars, or so. Even the Xul can't pay close attention to every one. But we know the Xul. We know what they did to the Builders. And to the An. And probably to some ungodly number of other civilizations and species scattered across the Galaxy over the past half million years or so. If they locate Sol and the other worlds of human space, they *will* do the same to us."

The light brightened around another delegate. "And I concur, Madam Devereaux." The speaker was a civilian, his noumenal presentation wearing the plain white robes of a Starborn Neognostic.

"You do, Ari?" Devereaux said, surprised. "I'd have thought you would be solidly opposed to this kind of . . . of interstellar adventurism."

"I may be a Starborn," Arimalen Daley said, inclining his head, "but I'm not *stupid*. Lieutenant General Alexander is right. We need to be careful in setting our priorities. I believe even our Theocrat friends would agree that there are times when religious or philosophical differences must be set aside for the sake of simple survival."

Alexander was startled by Daley's statement, but pleased. He had little patience with religion, and tended to see it as a means of denying or avoiding responsibility. Daley's response was . . . refreshing.

He opened a private window in his mind, accessed an e-pedia link, and downloaded a brief background on the Starborn, just to make sure he hadn't missed anything. No . . . he'd remembered correctly. The Starborn had been around for two or three centuries, but had arisen out of several earlier belief systems centered on The Revelation. For them, all intelligence was One . . . and that included even the Xul. They opposed all war in general, and most especially war based on a clash between opposing faiths. Within the Commonwealth Senate, they'd been the most vocal of the opponents of the military action against the Islamist Theocracy, for just that reason.

Alexander wondered why Daley had sided with him.

For himself, Alexander had no patience whatsoever with religion of any type. Beginning in the twentieth century, Humankind had been wracked by religious mania of the most divisive and destructive sort. World War III had been brought on by Islamic fundamentalism, but other sects and religions demanding rigid boundaries and unquestioning obedience to what was imagined to be God's will had added their share of terror, insanity, and blood to the chaos of the late twentieth and early twenty-first centuries. And then had come the discoveries on Mars, of buried cities and the Builders, of the mummified bodies of anatomically modern humans beneath the desiccated sands of Cydonia and Chryse.

Science fiction and the more sensationalist writers of pop-science had long speculated that extraterrestrials had created humans, but now there was *proof*. The Builders had tinkered with the genetics of *Homo erectus* in order to create a new species—*Homo sapiens*. It had always been assumed that if such proof was ever uncovered, it would once and for all end the tyranny and the comfort of religion. If God was a spaceman, there scarcely was need for His church. Religion would die.

Surprisingly, the opposite had happened. Though the older, traditional faiths had been badly shaken, the discoveries on Mars and elsewhere, far from destroying religion, had before long fostered new sects, religions, cults, and philosophies by the dozens, by the hundreds, some of them bizarre in the extreme. Throughout the first half of the new millennium, new faiths had spawned and vied and warred with one another, some accepting the vanished Builders or even the still-extant An or N'mah as gods, creators of Humankind, if not the cosmos. Others—in particular the stricter, more fundamentalist branches of Christianity and Islam—had adhered even more closely to the original texts, and condemned the nonhumans as demons.

Things had stabilized somewhat over the past few centuries. The attack on Earth had killed so many, had so terribly wounded civilization as a whole, that few religions, old or new, could deal with it, save in apocalyptic terms. And when Earth had, after all, survived, when Humankind began to rebuild and the expected second Xul attack had not materialized, many of the more extreme and strident of the sects had at last faded away.

There remained, however, some thousands of religions . . . but for the most part they fell into one of two major branches of organized spirituality, defined by their attitude toward the Xul. The Transcendents, who represented most of the older faiths plus a number of newer religions emphasizing the nature of the Divine as separate and distinct from Humankind, either ignored the Xul entirely, or associated them with the Devil, enemies of both Man and God.

The Emanists embraced religions and philosophies emphasizing that god arose from within Man, as a metasentient emanation arising from the minds of all humans, or even of all intelligence everywhere in the universe. For them, the Xul were a part of the Divine . . . or, at the least, His instrument for bringing about the evolution of Humankind. For most Emanists, the key to surviving the Xul was to follow the lead of the An on Ishtar—keep a low profile, roll with the punches, abjure pride and any technological activity that might attract Xul notice. The hope was that, like the Biblical

Angel of Death, the Xul would "pass over" humanity once more, as it had before in both recent and ancient history.

While not as widespread as the Transcendents, Emanist religions were popular with large segments of the population on Earth, especially with the Antitechnics and the various Neoprimitive and Back-to-Earth parties. Neognostics like Daley even advocated a complete renunciation of all activities off the surface of the Earth, especially now that the ice was retreating once more.

That was why Alexander—and Devereaux too, evidently—were surprised at his position.

As Alexander closed the e-pedia window, he realized Daley was still speaking, and that he was looking at him as he did so. "Whatever the tenets of my faith might be," the Neognostic was saying, "Humankind cannot evolve, cannot grow to meet its potential, and can never contribute to the idea we know as God if we as a species become extinct. So long as we remained beneath Xul notice, survival and growth both were possible. But now?" He spread his hands. "I dislike the idea. My whole being rebels against the very idea of war. But . . . if there is to be war, better it be out *there*, five hundred light-years away, than here among the worlds of Man."

"Good God," General Samuels said in the silence that followed this speech. "I thought it was nuts including a Paxist on the Advisory Council, Ari." The Paxists included those who believed in peace-at-any-price. "But you're okay!"

"The Paxists," Devereaux said sternly, "were invited because they represent the views of a large minority of the Commonwealth population. Very well. General Alexander, thank you for your presentation. The Council will retire now to its private noumenon and vote the question."

And the Council was gone, leaving Alexander alone in the imaginal room.

If the reaction to Daley's speech was any indication, though, he would need to begin preparations.

The Marines would be going to war.

6

USMC Recruit Training Center
Noctis Labyrinthus, Mars
1512/24:20 local time, 0156 hrs GMT

Garroway opened his eyes, blinked, and flexed his hands. This was . . . *wonderful*. The crisp reality of the sensations coursing through his imaginal body was almost overwhelming.

The hellish *empty time* was over.

"Pay attention, recruit! This is important!"

Warhurst's order snapped his attention back to the exercise. He tried to let the feelings flow through his mind, but to keep his focus on the scene around him.

The landscape was barren and unforgivingly rugged, a volcanic mountain of black rock and sand cratered and torn by a devastating firestorm and draped in drifting patches of smoke. He was standing in the middle of a battle . . . an ancient battle, one with unarmored men carrying primitive firearms as they struggled up the mountain's flank. Gunfire thundered—not the hiss and crack of lasers and plasma weapons, but the deeper-throated boom and rattle of slugthrowers, punctuated moment to moment by the heavy thud of high explosives.

Something—a fragment of high-velocity metal—whined past his ear, the illusion so realistic he flinched. He reminded himself that he had nothing to fear, however. This panorama of blood, confusion, and noise was being downloaded into his consciousness from the RTC historical network, the sights and sounds real enough to convince him he really was standing on that tortured mountainside. But the Marines around him were noumenal simulations—literally all in Garroway's head. Two days earlier he'd received the nano injections which had swiftly grown into his new Corps-issue headware, and this was his first test of its capabilities.

"Move on up the slope," Warhurst whispered in his ear. He obeyed, feeling the gritty crunch of black gravel beneath his feet. A Marine lay on his back a few meters away, eyes staring into the sky, a gaping, bloody hole in his chest. Garroway could see bare ribs protruding from the wound.

It's not real, he told himself. *It's a sim.*

"Yeah, it's a simulation, recruit," Warhurst told him. Garroway started. He hadn't realized that the DI could hear him. "But it *is* real, or it was. These Marines are members of the 28th Marine Regiment, 5th Marine Division. They really lived—and died—to take this island."

From the crest of the volcanic mountain, Garroway could see the whole island, a roughly triangular sprawl of black sand, rock, and jungle extending toward what his inner compass told him was the north to northeastern horizon. Offshore, hundreds of ships—old-style seagoing ships, rather than military spacecraft—lay along the eastern horizon. A few moved closer in, periodically spewing orange flame and clouds of smoke from turret-mounted batteries, and the beaches near the foot of the mountain were littered with hundreds of small, dark-colored craft like oblong boxes that had the look of so many ugly beetles slogging through the surf.

"The date," Warhurst told him, "is 2302, in the year 170 of the Marine Era. That's 23 February 1945, for you people who still think in civilian. The mountain is Suribachi, a dormant volcanic cone 166 meters high at the southern end of a place called Sulfur Island—Iwo Jima in Japanese. For the past four days the 4th and 5th Marine Divisions, plus two regiments of the 3rd, have been assaulting this unappealing bit of real estate in order to take it away from the Japanese Empire. For two years, now, the United States has been island-hopping across the Pacific Ocean, closing toward Japan. Iwo Jima is the first territory they've reached that is actually a prefecture of Japan; the mayor of Tokyo is also the mayor of Iwo. That means that for the Japanese defending this island, this is the first actual landing on the sacred soil of their homeland. They are defending every meter in one of the fiercest battles in the war to date.

"Yesterday, the 28th Marines started up the slope of Suribachi which, as you can see, has a commanding view of the entire island, and looks straight down on the landing beaches. In an entire day of fighting, they advanced perhaps 200 meters, then fended off a Japanese charge during the night. They've suffered heavy casualties. Lieutenant General Tadamichi Kuribayashi, the Japanese commander, has honeycombed the entire island, which measures just 21 square kilometers, with tunnels, bunkers, and spider holes. The defenders, 22,000 of them, have been ordered to fight to the death . . . and most of them will.

"This battle will go down as one of the most famous actions in the history of the Corps. In all of World War II, it was the only action in which the Americans actually suffered more casualties than the enemy—26,000, with 6,825 of those KIA. The Japanese have 22,000 men on the island. Out of those, 1081 will survive.

"The battle will last until 2503, a total of thirty-seven days, before the island is declared secure. Almost one quarter of all of the Medals of Honor awarded to Marines during World War II—twenty-seven in all—were awarded to men who participated in this battle.

"Ah. There's what we came up here to see. . . ."

Warhurst led the recruits farther up the shell-blasted slope. At the landward side of the summit, a small number of Marines were working at something, huddled along a length of pipe.

"The mountain now, after a fierce naval and air bombardment, appears cleared of enemy soldiers, and several patrols have reached the top. Half an hour ago, a small flag was raised on the summit of the mountain to demonstrate that the mountain has been secured, but now a larger flag has been sent to the top. The men you see over there are part of a forty-man patrol from E Company, Second Battalion, 28th Marines, of the 5th Marine Division, under the command of Lieutenant Harold Schrier.

"Those men over there are Sergeant Michael Strank, Corporal Harlon Block, PFC Rene Gagnon, PFC Ira Hayes, and PFC Franklin Sousley, all United States Marines. The sixth man is Navy, a Pharmacy Mate—what they later called Navy Hospital Corpsmen, P.M./2 John Bradley.

"Of those six men, three—Strank, Block, and Sousley— will be killed a few days from now, in heavy fighting at the north end of the island. P.M./2 Bradley will be wounded by shrapnel from a mortar round."

The men completed doing whatever it was they were doing to the pipe. Grasping it, moving together, they dug one end into a hole in the gravel and lifted the other end high. A flag unfurled with the breeze; nearby, one man turned suddenly and snapped an image with a bulky, old-style 2-D camera, while another man stood filming the scene.

The whole flag raising took only seconds. As the flag fluttered from the now upright pipe, however, Garroway could hear the cheering—from other Marines on the crest of Suribachi and, distantly, from men on the lower reaches of the island to the north. The rattle of gunfire seemed to subside momentarily, replaced by a new thunder . . . the low, drawn-out roar from thousands of voices, so faint it nearly was lost on the wind.

"Have a peek down there on that beach," Warhurst told them. As Garroway turned and looked, it seemed as though his vision became sharply telescopic, zooming in precipitously, centering on a party of men wading ashore from one of the boxlike landing craft. Two of the figures appeared to be important; they were unarmed, though they wore helmets and life preservers like the others around them. One took the elbow of the other, pointing up the slope toward Garroway's position. He appeared jubilant.

"That," Warhurst continued, "is the secretary of the Navy, James Forrestal, just now coming ashore with Marine General Holland 'Howlin' Mad' Smith. When they see the flag up here, Forrestal turns to the general and says 'Holland, the raising of that flag on Suribachi means a Marine Corps for the next five hundred years.'"

There was a surreal aspect to this history lesson—especially in the way Warhurst was describing events in the present and in the future tense, as though these scenes Garroway was experiencing weren't AI recreations of something that had happened 937 years ago, but were happening *now*.

"As it happens, the future of the Marine Corps was far from secure," Warhurst told them. "Only a couple of years after this battle, the President of the United States attempted to enact legislation that would have closed the Corps down. He referred to the Marines as 'the Navy's police force,' and sought to merge them with the Army. The public outcry over this plan blocked it . . . but from time to time, cost-cutting politicians looked for ways to slash the military budget by eliminating the Marines."

The simulation had continued as Warhurst spoke, the primitively armed and equipped Marines on that volcanic slope continuing to move about as the flag, an archaic scrap of cloth with red and white stripes and ranks of stars on a blue field, continued to flutter overhead.

Gradually, though, the scene began to fade in Garroway's mind. He was sitting once again in a simcast amphitheater back at the training center on Mars, his recliner moving upright along with all of the others arrayed in circles about a central stage. The image of six men raising a flag continued to hover overhead, a holographic projection faintly luminous in the theater's dim light.

Warhurst paced the stage, lecturing, but with an animated passion. This, Garroway thought, was not just information to be transmitted to another class of recruits, but something burning in Warhurst's brain and heart.

"As Forrestal predicted, however," Warhurst went on, "the Corps *did* endure for the next five hundred years—and then for over three hundred years after that. For most of that time, the politicians tended to dislike us . . . or at least they never seemed to know what to do with us. We've been on the budgetary chopping block more times than we can count.

Civilians tend to like us, however. They see us as the holders of an important legacy—one embracing duty, honor, faithfulness. *Semper fi*. Always faithful.

"In fact, though, the raising of the flag on Suribachi probably had less to do with the Corps' survival than did certain other factors. A century after the Battle of Iwo Jima, we left the shores of our home planet, and discovered the Ancient ruins on Mars and on Earth's moon, and later at places like Chiron and Ishtar. Both the Builders and the An left a lot of high-tech junk lying around on worlds they visited in the past . . . the Xul, too, for that matter, if you count what we found out on Europa. Started something like a twenty-first-century gold rush, as every country on Earth with a space capability tried to get people out there to see what they could find. Xenoarcheology became the hot science, since it was thought that reverse-engineering some of that stuff could give us things like faster-than-light travel or FTL radio. The Navy, logically enough, became the service branch that ran the ships to get out here . . . and where the Navy went, the Marines came along. The Battle of Cydonia. The Battle of Tsiolkovsky. The Battle of Ishtar. The Battles of the Sirius Gate, and of Night's Edge. 'From the Halls of Montezuma, to the ocher sands of Mars.' We've written our legacy in blood across a thousand years and on battlefields across two hundred worlds.

"And in all that time, and on all those worlds, the Marine Corps has done one thing . . . what we've always done. *We win battles!*

"And you, recruits, have come here to Mars in order to learn how to do just that."

Garroway felt a stirring of pride at that—not at the promise that they would win battles, but at the way Warhurst was addressing them now. This was now the twelfth week of training, with just four more weeks to go. At some point during the last couple of months—and Garroway honestly could not remember when—Warhurst had stopped calling the men and women of Recruit Company 4102 *children*, and started calling them *recruits*.

Step by step, their civilian individuality had been broken

down; step by step Warhurst and the other DIs had been building them back up, forging them into . . . something new. Garroway wasn't sure what the difference was yet, but he felt the difference, a sense of confidence, of *belonging* that he'd never before known.

The feeling that he belonged had just taken a major boost skyward, of course. The nano injected into his system on 0710 had grown into standard-Corps issue cereblink hardware, and now, for the first time in three months, he was again connected.

It had been a rough time without connections—no downloads, no direct comm. Or, rather, downloads and incoming comm messages had entered his brain via his ears and his eyes, without mediation or enhancement by AI software. It had been like starting all over again, learning how to *learn*, rather than allowing headware and resident AIs to sort and file his memories for him.

He had a new personal electronic assistant, too . . . or, rather, a Corps platoon EA guide he shared with everyone else in the company. The EA's name was Achilles; Warhurst had told them to think of him as a kind of narrowly focused platoon sergeant. Achilles was a bit short in the personality department, but the system was *very* fast, very efficient, and was working hard at its first task, helping him learn how to get the most out of the new headware.

Later, at evening chow, he discovered one down side to Achilles.

"So, whatcha think of the new headware?" he asked Sandre Kenyon, a recruit who'd been born and raised in one of the new arcologies off the coast of Pennsylvania. She'd been a vir-simmer, a programmer of simulation AIs, before she'd joined the Corps. He followed her out of the chow line and toward a couple of empty seats at one of the tables. Noise clattered and echoed around them; meals were among the very few times when recruits were free to socialize with other recruits, at least after the first month of training.

"It's okay, I guess," she said. "It's gonna take some getting used to, though."

"I know. It's so damned fast. . . ."

"It's also damned creepy," she told him.

"What do you mean?"

"Having your platoon sergeant perched on your shoulder every minute of every day? Watching everything you do? Even everything you think? And reporting it all back to HQ-RTC, complete with images in glorious color and infrared? I don't know about you, Aiden, but there are a few things I do or think about doing that I don't care to share with half the base, y'know?"

"Oh . . ."

He'd not thought about *that* aspect of things, at least not before now.

In fact, privacy was an alien concept in boot camp. Male and female recruits trained together, shared the same barracks, and used the same head. Toilets had stalls but no doors, and no recruit was *ever* really alone for more than a few moments at a time. In fact, come to think of it, standing barracks fire watch in the middle of the night was probably the closest any recruit came to having some private time—but then you never knew when the sergeant of the guard was going to show up on one of his rounds.

Mostly, it wasn't a hardship. The recruits were too damned busy, moving at a flat run from reveille to taps every day, for it to be a problem . . . and most human cultures accepted casual social nudity as the norm.

"Is Achilles listening to you gripe about it now?"

She shrugged. "I asked it. It told me it monitored everyone in the company for breaches of regulations and compliance to orders . . . but that it didn't record or transmit anything else. It . . . it's a machine. A program, rather, so I guess it shouldn't bother me. Still . . . how do we *know*?"

Garroway began digging into his meal—a nanassembled steak indistinguishable in taste and texture from live steaks culture-grown in the Ring agros. One thing you had to say about the Marines: they fed well.

He assumed Sandre was talking about sex. Technically, fraternization between recruits was forbidden, though in fact the authorities didn't seem to pay much attention to oc- casional and harmless breaches of the rules. If a recruit on fire watch was caught in the rack with a fuck buddy, they both would probably be bounced out of the Corps and back to Earth or wherever they'd come from so fast their eyes would be spinning in their heads, but Garroway knew that several recruits in Company 4102 were enjoying one another's physical companionship—at least if their break-time war stories could be believed.

His only question was how they found the time—or the energy—with the daily schedule that ruled their lives—up at zero-dark thirty, followed by eighteen hours of marching, drilling, classroom work, lectures, testing, and downloading, with lights out at 2200 hours.

Having a personal daemon was nothing new. Most humans had them, the only hold-outs being the various neo-luddite or neoprimitive cultures which had abandoned high-tech for religious, esthetic, or artistic reasons. Achilles was a daemon, nothing more. In fact, he seemed just like Aide, except that he was more powerful, faster, and he linked all of the recruits in Company 4102 into a close-knit electronic network.

But he had to admit that Sandre had a point. Having Achilles watching him was just like having Warhurst watching him, except that the watching was taking place every second of every day. His stomach tightened at the thought.

"Recruit Kenyon is correct," a voice whispered in his mind.

Garroway looked up, startled. "Achilles?"

"What?" Sandre asked. Garroway hadn't realized he'd spoken the name aloud. He waved his hand back and forth, requesting her silence.

"Affirmative," the voice continued. *"Think of me as a part of yourself, not as a spy for your superiors."*

But you do report to the DI shack, don't you? This time, Garroway thought the question silently, employing the mindspeak he'd always used with Aide.

"Technically, yes, but only in matters involving gross negligence of duty. In any case, Marines are supposed to be of superior moral character. By this point in your training,

those with serious moral flaws have already been weeded out."

"Oh . . ."

Company 4102 had dwindled a lot in the past few weeks, it was true. Only forty-five recruits remained out of the over one hundred who'd originally mustered at Noctis Labyrinthus. But he'd assumed the DORs—the Drop Out Requests—had quit because they couldn't get along without their headware.

"*That is a large part of it,*" Achilles agreed. "*One aspect of moral character is the ability to rely on yourself rather than on technology.*"

Carefully, Garroway took another bite of faux steak and chewed, thoughtful. Achilles seemed to be a bit more dominant than Aide had been. And the damned thing was reading his thoughts, rather than waiting for him to encode them as mindspeak.

"*You will simply have to learn to trust me, Garroway,*" Achilles told him. "*Trust that I am not sharing your thoughts with others.*"

"Unless I deserve it."

"Do you always talk to yourself?" Sandre asked him.

Achilles, tell her I'm holding a conversation with you.

A moment later, Sandre's eyes grew very large. "Did you send that?"

He nodded. "Pretty slick, huh?"

"Damn it, Garroway!" she snapped. "Get out of my head!" Abruptly, she stood, picked up her tray, and walked away. Garroway considered calling to her, but decided that using telepathy would just make matters worse.

They were all going to have to work with the new technology for a bit, in order to get used to it.

Exactly, Achilles told him. He could have sworn the AI sounded smug.

* * *

Married Enlisted Housing
USMC Recruit Training Center
Noctis Labyrinthus, Mars
1924/24:20 local time, 0620 hrs GMT

Gunnery Sergeant Warhurst stepped out of the flyer and onto the landing deck outside his home. It was a small place, but with lots of exterior spaces and enclosed garden patios surrounding a double plasdome growing from a canyon wall. Other base housing modules were visible up and down the canyon, extruded from the ancient sandstone walls.

A billion years ago, this part of Mars had been under a sea a kilometer deep; the relentless rise of the Tharsis Bulge, however, had lifted the Noctis Labyrinthus high and dry; as the water drained away, it had carved the maze of channels from the soft stone. The northern ocean had rolled again, briefly, under the touch of the Builders half a million years ago, but by that time the Noctis Labyrinthus was far above mean sea level.

Apparently, the Builders had not colonized this part of Mars, restricting their activities to Cydonia, far to the north, to Chryse Planitia, and to Utopia on the far side of the planet. Some of the base personnel spent off hours pacing up and down the canyon with metal detectors, however. A handful of people out here had made fortunes with the chance find of a fragment of cast-off xenotech.

Warhurst never bothered with that sort of thing, however. His career—the Corps—was everything.

A fact that was making things difficult at home.

"Honey?" He stepped in off the deck, dropping his cover on a table. "I'm home."

The place seemed empty, and he queried the house AI. "Where is everybody?"

Julie and Eric are home, the house's voice whispered in his mind. *Donal and Callie are still at the base.*

Warhurst was part of a group marriage and, as was increasingly the case nowadays, all of the other partners in the relationship were also Marines. It was simpler that way

. . . and the partners tended to be more understanding than civilians. *Usually.*

A door hissed open and Julie emerged from the bedroom. She was naked, and she looked angry. "Well, well. The prodigal is home. Decided to come visit the family for a change?"

"Don't start, Julie."

"Don't start what?"

"Look, I know I haven't been home much lately—"

"I know that too." She ran a hand through her short hair. "Look, Marine, I'm having sex with Eric, so give us some privacy. Fix yourself dinner. When Don and Cal get home, we need to talk, the five of us."

"What do you—"

But she'd already turned away and padded back into the bedroom.

Damn.

It had been a few days since he'd come home. How long? He pulled a quick check of his personal calendar, and saw the answer. Eight days.

Damn it, Julie knew the score. When a new recruit company started up, he spent all of his time with the company, at least for the first few weeks. After that, he shared the duty with the other DIs, sleeping in the DI shack, or in one of the senior NCO quads across the grinder one night out of four. But even late in the training regime, there were particular times when it was important that he be there. This past week had been the last week for the recruits of 4102 in naked time, without their civilian headware, a time when lots of them came close to cracking. He needed to be there, to see them through. He'd almost stayed over tonight as well, but Corrolly had insisted that he and Amanate could handle things.

He wished he'd stayed.

Julie's flat statement about a family meeting probably meant an ultimatum, and that probably meant a formal request that he move back into the BOQ, the Bachelor Officers' Quarters.

In other words, a divorce.

It had been coming for a long time. He knew she'd been

wanting to talk to him about the marriage, and his part in it, for a long time, but he'd been hoping to postpone it, at least until after 4102 had graduated. Damn it, he didn't have time for this nonsense, for all this *sturm und drang*, and Julie ought to know that. He didn't have the emotional stamina to deal with it now, either. There was just too much on his plate. Angry, he walked into the kitchen unit and punched up a meal.

Warhurst was the most recent addition to the Tamalyn-Danner line marriage, having been invited in by Julie just fifteen months ago. Like many Corps weddings taking place on Mars, the vows had been declared, posted, and celebrated at Garroway Hall, at Cydonia, and half of RTC command had attended.

Marriages outside the Corps were discouraged. Not forbidden . . . but discouraged. A Marine might be at any given duty station for a year or two, but then he or she might be deployed across a hundred light-years, or end up on board a Navy ship plying a slow run between stargates. The routine played merry hell with traditional relationships.

At that, it was better than in the bad old days, before FTL and stargates, when a 4.3 light-year hop to Chiron took five and a half years objective, which meant a couple of years subjective spent in cybe-hibe stasis. Back then, Marines were assigned on the basis of their famsits, their family situations—whether or not they were married, had parents or other close relatives, and how closely tied they were psychologically to the Motherworld.

Long ago, the Corps had adopted the habit of assigning command staff as discrete groups, called command constellations, to avoid breaking up good working teams through transfers and redeployments. A similar set of regulations now governed marital relationships. While the Corps couldn't promise to keep everyone in the family together—especially in group marriages that might number ten or more people—the AIs overseeing deployments did their best, even shuffling personnel from one MarDiv to another, when necessary, to make the numbers come out even. The tough part was when kids were involved. Each major base had its own crèche, nurseries, and schools, but Navy ships on deep survey or remote listening outposts at the fringes of known Xul systems didn't have the resources for that kind of luxury. Those assignments still required Marines with Famsits of two or better.

What none of this took into account was the workload at established bases like Noctis-L. Training a company of raw recruits, breaking them out of their smug little civilian molds and building Marines out of what was left—that was a full-time job, and then some. Warhurst and five assistant DIs supervised Company 4102, now down to just forty-three recruits, and still it was never enough.

He closed his eyes. That one kid, Collins. After six weeks without her implants, she'd just . . . snapped. The messy and very public suicide had hit everyone hard, and the DI staff especially had been badly stressed. Damn it, he should have *been* there. . . .

Warhurst leaned back in his chair, his meal half finished but unwanted. He summoned a cup of coffee, though, and waited while a servo extended it to him from a nearby wall-mar. He knew there was nothing he could have done, and the board of inquiry had almost routinely absolved him and his staff of blame. But . . . he should have been there. Collins had stolen that thermite grenade one evening from a malfunctioning training arms locker when he'd been *here*, at home.

Angrily, he pushed the thought aside, then mentally clocked on the wallscreen, looking for the evening news. He wanted an external distraction, rather than an internal feed, telling himself he needed to keep his internal channels clear, in case there was a call from the base.

Which was pure theriashit, and he knew it. An emergency call would override any feed he had going. And either Achilles, the company AI, or Hector, who was reserved for the training staff, could talk to him at any time. He was avoiding the real issue, which was the strain within his marriage.

Damned right I'm avoiding it, he thought. *And a good job I'm doing of it, too.*

The news was dominated by the war, of course. The capture of Alighan was being hailed in the Senate as the defining victory of the war, the victory that would bring the Theocrats to their senses and bring them to the conference table.

"In other military news," the announcer said, her three-meter-tall face filling the wall, "the Interstellar News Web have received an as yet unconfirmed report of hostile contact with what may be a Xul huntership outside of the Humankind Frontier. If true, this will be the first contact with the Xul in over 550 years.

"For this report, we go livefeed to Ian Castriani at Marine Corps Skybase headquarters in paraspace. Ian?"

The announcer's face faded away, replaced by a young man standing in the Public Arena of the headquarters station. He looked intense, determined, and excited.

And what he had to say brought a cold, churning lump to the pit of Warhurst's gut.

7

Marine Listening Post
Puller 659 Stargate
1554 hrs GMT

Lieutenant Tera Lee unlinked from the feed and blinked in the dim light of the comdome. "Shit," she said, and made a face. "*Shit*!"

"What's the problem, sweetheart?" Lieutenant Gerard Fitzpatrick, her partner on the watch, asked.

She ignored the familiarity. Fitzie was a jerk, but a reasonably well meaning one. She hadn't had to deck him yet. *Yet....*

"That's four transgate drones we've lost contact with in the past ten minutes," she said, checking the main board, then rechecking the communications web for a fault. Everything on *this* side of the Gate was working perfectly. "Something's going down over there. I don't like it."

"You link through to the old man?"

"Chesty's doing that now," she told him. She wrinkled her nose. "I smell another sneakover."

"Yeah, well, it's your turn," he said, shrugging. Then he brightened. "Unless you wanna—"

"Fuck you, Fitzie," she said, keeping her voice light.

"Exactly."

"Forget it, Marine. I have standards."

He sighed theatrically. "You wound me, sweetheart."

"Call me 'sweetheart' again and you'll know what being wounded is like, jerkface. *If* you survive."

She dropped back into the linknet before he could make another rejoinder.

The star system known to Marine Intelligence as Puller 659 was about as nondescript as star systems could get—a cool, red dwarf sun orbited by half a dozen rock-and-ice worlds scarcely worthy of the name, and a single Neptune-sized gas giant. The French astronomers who'd catalogued the system had named the world *Anneau*, meaning Ring, and the red dwarf *Étoile d'Anneau*, Ringstar. None of Ringstar's planets possessed native life or showed signs of ever having been life-bearing. And despite frequent sweeps, no one had ever found any xenoarcheological tidbits, none whatsoever, save one.

And that one was why the Marine listening post was here. As Lee linked through to another teleoperated probe, she could see it in the background—a vast, gold-silver ring resembling a wedding band out of ancient tradition, but twenty kilometers across.

Just who or what had created the Stargates remained one of the great unanswered riddles of xenoarcheological research. Most academics, striving for the simplest possible view of things, assumed that the Builders—that long-vanished federation of starfaring civilizations half a million years ago—had created them, but there was no proof of that. It was equally likely that the things were millions of years old, that they'd been old already when the Builders had first come on the scene . . . back about the same time that the brightest creature on Earth was a clever tool-user that someday would receive the name *Homo erectus*.

Whoever or whatever had built the things evidently had scattered them across the entire Galaxy. Gates were known to exist in systems outside the Galactic plane; Night's Edge was such a place, where the sweep of the Galaxy's spiral arms filled half the sky. Gate connected Gate in a network still neither understood nor mapped. Each Gate possessed a pair of Jupiter-massed black holes rotating in opposite directions at close to the speed of light; shifting tidal stresses set up by the counter-rotating masses opened navigable pathways from one Gate to another, allowing passage across tens of thousands of light-years in an eye's blink. More, the vibrational frequencies of those planetary masses could be tuned, allowing one Gate to connect with any of several thousand alternate Gates.

The alien N'mah, first contacted in 2170, had been living inside the Gate discovered in the Sirius system, 8.6 light-years from Earth. Though they'd lost the technology required for faster-than-light drives, they'd learned a little about Gate technology, and they'd taught Humankind how to use the Gates—at least after a fashion. Thanks to them, Marines had scored important victories over the Xul, in Cluster Space, and at Night's Edge.

If it had simply been a matter of destroying Stargates to keep the Xul out of human space, things would have been far simpler. Unfortunately, it turned out that there was more than one way to outpace light. The Xul used the Gates extensively—indeed, a large minority of those academics felt that the *Xul* were the original builders of the Stargates—but their hunterships could also slip from star to star in days or weeks without benefit of the Gates.

In the past five centuries, Humans had learned at last how to harness quantum-state vacuum energies and liberate inconceivable free energy, and how to apply that energy to the Quantum Sea in order to achieve trans-c pseudovelocities—high multiples of the speed of light. They'd located some dozens of separate Stargates, and sent both robotic and manned probes through to chart the accessible spaces on the far side.

Most probes found only another Stargate, usually circling a distant star, like Puller 659, with lifeless worlds or no worlds at all. A few led to planetary systems possessing earthlike worlds, though, so far, no other sentient species had been found this way, and, in accord with the Treaty of Chiron, none had been opened to human colonization.

A very few, mercifully few, opened into star systems occupied by the Xul.

The Ringstar Gate at Puller 659 was one such. One of the

regions accessed through the Puller Gate was in a system dominated by a hot, type A star, seething with deadly radiation burning off the galactic core, and host to a major Xul base.

As was the case every time a Xul base was discovered, a Marine listening post had been constructed close by the Puller 659 Gate, and a careful watch kept. Periodically, AI-controlled probes were sent through the Gate to record signals and images from the Xul base. The probes were tiny—the size of volleyballs—and virtually undetectable. The probes would slip through, make their recordings, then double back through the Gate to make their reports.

The usual routine was to send one probe through at a time, to minimize the chances of the reconnaissance being detected. Faults and failures happened, however, and losing contact with one or even two was not unusual, especially through the turbulent gravitic storms and tides swirling about the mouth of a Gate. But Lee had just sent the third probe in a row through to check on number one, and its lasercom trace—kept tight and low-power to avoid detection—had been cut off within twenty seconds of passing the Gate interface.

Not good. Not good at all . . . especially since the lasercom threads carried no data about what was going on down range, save that the probe was functional.

And standing orders described in considerable detail what happened in such cases.

It was time for a sneak-and-peek.

"Package up the log," she told Chesty over the telencephalic link. "Beam it out NL. And recommend to Major Tomanaga that we go on full alert."

"Major Tomanaga is already doing so," the base AI told her, "and he has just authorized a level-2 reconnaissance through to Starwall."

"Excellent." *Starwall* was the name of the system on the other side of the Gate, the location of the Xul base.

"Will you be taking an FR-100 through the interface?"

"Yeah. Prep one for me, please."

"Number Three is coming on-line now."

In a larger base, there would have been a standby pool of Marine fighter pilots ready to fly recon, but the listening post was manned by six Marines at a time, standing watch-in-three. The main base complex was a space station orbiting the system's gas giant, camouflaged from detection by the planet's far-flung radiation belts and now almost two light-hours away. Non-local com webs bridged that gulf instantly, but it would be hours before fighters could get here.

Marine listening posts like Puller 659 were deliberately kept tiny and unobtrusive; Fitzie was right, damn him. It was her turn.

She dropped out of the link and rose from her couch. Leaving Fitzpatrick in his commlink couch at the monitor station, she caught an intrastation pod and dropped to the fighter bay, two decks down. The uniform of the day was Class-One VS, a black skinsuit that served as her vacsuit in a depressurization emergency, so she needed only to pick up a helmet, gloves, and LS pack on the way.

Her FR-100 Night Owl was warmed and ready for her when she arrived.

The Night Owl was dead black, pulling at the eye, a flat, smooth ovoid with teardrop sponsons and swellings for drives and sensor equipment, its sleek hull designed to absorb or safely redirect everything on the EM spectrum from long-wave radar to short-wave x-rays. It was sophisticated enough to fly itself without a human at the controls, but Corps doctrine still emphasized the need for a human at the controls in any situation where things might go suddenly and catastrophically wrong. The craft was tiny—three fluidly streamlined meters, with a cockpit barely large enough to receive her vacsuited body as it folded itself closely about her and automatically made the necessary neural links.

"Link me in, Chesty," she thought, and felt the connections open in her mind. The Night Owl's AI was technically a Chesty$_2$, a smaller, much more compact version of the software running on the station proper. She felt a slight thump as the Owl slid down on magnetic rails through a deck hatch and into its launch lock.

"You are linked and ready for boost, Lieutenant,"

Chesty told her. "Lock evacuated. Station clearance for exit granted."

She ran through a final check on her instrument feeds, and let the hull embracing her fade away into invisibility. This was always the scary part, the feeling that she was being dumped naked into hard vacuum. No amount of training, no thousands of hours of flight time could ever entirely override that deep-seated, thoroughly human terror of the ultimate night outside.

All systems cleared green. "Let's do it, then."

The drop hatch yawned and the sleek, tiny fragment of night fell into darkness.

In her mind, Lee was flying through space unencumbered by such incidentals as a ship or vacsuit. Above and behind her—though such notions as up and down were suddenly meaningless as she fell clear of the LP's grav field—the listening post hung against the stars, a small asteroid, dust-shrouded and almost lost in the wan light from the distant, red pinpoint of the local sun. Ahead, the Stargate appeared as a vast, red-gold hoop, canted at a sharp angle to the listening post, which stayed well clear of the entrance. In the 112 years that Puller 659 had been in operation, nothing had ever emerged from that gateway other than returning Marine probes.

But there was always that inevitable first time. . . .

Under Chesty's guidance, the Owl's N'mah reactionless drive switched on, propelling it toward the Gate, which filled Lee's view forward now, an immense, flattened band that, from this distance, appeared perfectly smooth and seamless. As moments passed, however, that illusion faded, as lines and geometric shapes became visible by the shadows cast by the distant, bloody sun.

At ninety gravities, the Owl shot forward, and the Gate swiftly grew larger, larger, then larger still. Shielded from the brutal acceleration inside the tiny craft, Lee told Chesty to maneuver closer to the ring wall as the FR-100 crossed into the tidal field, then turned sharply, falling into the ring's turbulent lumen.

At the last possible moment, Chesty cut the drive, and the

Owl dropped through the Gate, the red-gold-gray wall flashing past Lee's awareness, the sudden gut-twisting wrench of gravitational tides clutching at her. . . .

And then she was through, an explosion of light bathing her wide-open mental windows. *Starwall . . .*

An apt enough name. Ringstar, Puller 659, was located in a relatively sparsely populated area of space, out in the Orion Spur of the Cygnus Galactic Arm, just a few hundred light-years from Sol. The Starwall system, however, was an estimated eighteen thousand light-years closer in toward the Galaxy's central hub. From here, inside the dense banks of interstellar dust and gas that enclosed the Hub and shrouded its glow from the suburbs of the spiral arms, the galactic core literally appeared to be a near-solid wall of stars, presenting a vista like the heart of a globular cluster, but on an impossibly vaster scale, a teeming beehive of billions of closely packed suns, their clotted masses wreathed through with twisted and tattered ribbons of both dark and incandescent nebulae. That mass of stars had an overall reddish tinge to it; most of the stars of the Hub were ancient Population II suns, poor in metals, cooler than the predominantly hot, metal-rich and spendthrift blue stars of the spiral arms.

Lee's warning systems began their steady and expected drumbeat. Radiation levels on this side of the Gate were high—high enough to fry an unprotected human in seconds, high enough to overwhelm even the Night Owl's protective shielding within an hour or two at most. For safety's sake, the clock was running; Lee had a stay-time of forty minutes on this side of the Gate, a quite literal deadline by which she had to return to the listening post, or die.

She scarcely noticed those warnings, however, for her attention had been grabbed by a danger far more immediate. Movement and proximity snatched at her awareness, and she looked *up*, relative to her own alignment. . . .

It was a Xul huntership. Of that, there could be no doubt. It appeared small, thanks to its distance, but her sensor inputs were giving her a mental download giving the thing's range, size, mass . . . gods, it was *huge*.

The Xul warsips encountered by Humankind so far had

come in a variety of sizes and configurations, but all were enormous, well over a kilometer in length, and more often two. The Xul, for whatever reason, liked to build *big*.

This model had been named the Type III by Marine Intelligence, and was designated as the *Nightmare* class. Unlike the slender needles of Types I and II, the Nightmare was an immense flattened and elongated spheroid two kilometers across, its surface pocked and marked by countless structures and surface irregularities laid out in geometric arrays of almost fractal complexity. The Singer, discovered eight centuries before beneath the ice of Europa's world-ocean, had been of this type. The monster was larger than the asteroid shrouding the Puller listening post . . . but was entirely artificial, apparently grown through the Xul equivalent of nanotechnology.

Just why they built their ships and bases on such a large scale remained one of the deeper mysteries of Xul technology. Encounters with the Xul over the past eight centuries had demonstrated that they almost certainly did not possess an organic component; as near as the various human intelligence services could determine, the Xul was a gestalt of myriad machine intelligences, some of them artificial like AIs, but some possibly originally recorded and uploaded into machine bodies from the organic originals millions of years ago.

These UIs, as they were now known, Uploaded Intelligences, were virtually immortal. Imbedded within the tightly meshed and folded circuitry that filled most of the huge Xul ships, they couldn't be said to be truly alive, not in the human sense, and they certainly didn't require the life-support systems found on any human-manned spacecraft.

Lee watched the complicated surface of the Xul monster glide slowly past—nearly ten kilometers away, near the center of the Gate opening, but large enough even at that range to occult the massed stars beyond like an ink-black shadow, sharp enough and detailed enough that she felt like she could reach up and touch it. It took her a moment to realize that she was on a parallel course; like her, it had only recently emerged from the Stargate behind her and was also moving into the Starwall system, but at a slightly slower speed so that she was catching up with and slowly passing it. From her perspective, it seemed to her that the Xul vessel was standing still, or even moving past her in the other direction, *toward* the Gate.

The Nightmare's presence suggested answers to several questions. This side of the Gate must have been retuned by the Xul to another Gate, one other than the one at Puller 659. As a result, the four missing probes had been lost either because they'd passed through the returned Gate to that other system . . . or just possibly because they'd been in the process of returning and been brushed aside by this giant just as it emerged into the Starwall system.

To a monster like the Xul Nightmare, those probes must have been insignificant, dismissed as drifting fragments of meteoric debris. On that scale, Lee's FR-100 was little larger; so long as she didn't change her vector, she should be ignored.

Should be. So much about the Xul—both the limits of their technology and the leadings of their psychology—still were utter unknowns.

But it's so far, so good, she thought, watching the monster slide past in the distance. She was glad she'd told Chesty to steer her closer to the ringwall, though. Had she emerged from the Gate near the center of its opening, she might well have slammed headlong into the ass end of that thing.

That didn't let her out of the woods, though. If she applied power to decelerate in order to reverse course and return to the Gate, the Xul monster might easily pick up her energy signature; scraps of interstellar debris did *not* reverse course on their own, nor did they radiate the clouds of neutrinos that were the waste product of tapping the virtual energy of the Quantum Sea.

Lee felt a small shiver at the base of her neck, a prickling warning of danger. If she couldn't reverse course, she would die of radiation poisoning in short order. And, even if she did reverse course . . . the Xul Nightmare's presence suggested that the Stargate on this side was now attuned to a different star system. If she went through, she would not emerge at Puller 659, but in some other unguessable but absolutely guaranteed remote location. Chesty could retune the Gate for a return, of course; the Puller 659 Gate's coordinates were programmed into him.

But that would be a rather nasty give-away to the Xul here at Starwall, who would certainly be monitoring the Gate's settings. Regulation One-alpha, drilled into every Marine standing duty at a Gate listening post, was to lay low and keep a low profile, to not attract Xul attention to human activities. Humankind had survived for the past eight centuries *only* because they'd managed, on the whole, to stay off the metaphorical Xul radar.

"Chesty?" she asked. "Are you picking anything up from over there? Can you piggyback it?"

"We are intercepting the usual RF leakage," the AI replied. "I am attempting to locate a viable frequency with which to establish a tap."

Xul ships leaked, at least at radio frequencies. The millions of kilometers of nanoelectronic circuitry and processors packed into each of those immense hulls gave off a constant hiss and murmur of radio noise as a kind of metabolic by-product, and the Xul never seemed to bother with shielding. Some theorists suggested that the radio noise served an almost organic function, helping to reassure individual Xul ship-entities that others of their kind were near.

Ever since the first studies carried out on the Singer eight centuries before, humans had looked for ways to turn this fact to their advantage. It was possible, for instance, to use some Xul frequencies as carrier waves, allowing human-developed AI programs to upload into a Xul computer network and have a look around. The technique was called piggybacking, and Marine listening posts often used it in attempts to gather yet more intelligence on the poorly understood and still mysterious Xul.

There was an ancient aphorism, something all Marines learned in boot camp, something from the writings of Sun Tzu in *The Art of War*. It stated that if the warrior knew himself, but not the enemy, he would be victorious only half the time. If he knew the enemy, but not himself, he would, again, be victorious only one battle out of two. Only if the warrior knew the enemy and himself could he hope to win every battle. . . .

The Marine philosophy, begun in the crucible of recruit training, was designed to create a sure knowledge of self. Unfortunately, even after eight centuries, the Xul were still largely an utterly alien quantity. Xenocultural theorists were still divided as to whether the Xul could properly be called living beings . . . or even whether they were self-aware, both sentient and conscious in the same way that humans understood the terms. In most ways, they appeared to be machine intelligences, like human-designed AIs, but on a far vaster and more powerful scale.

There were hints, however, that each Xul ship contained hundreds, perhaps thousands of organic minds patterned and downloaded into the vessel's circuitry, separate identities arrayed in a gestalt, a group mind, in an interconnected collection referred to—ever since the discovery of The Singer—as a chorus.

There were hints, too, that a Xul chorus included the downloaded minds both of the original, biological Xul, beings whose organic bodies had died and decayed countless millennia ago, and the minds of other intelligent beings captured and incorporated into the Xul matrix for purposes of interrogation . . . the Xul version of knowing both self and adversary. So far, the Xul definitely had the advantage in the arena of knowing, but progress had been made in that direction during the past eight centuries.

As Chesty$_2$ was about to demonstrate. . . .

Chesty$_2$
Starwall System
1608 hrs GMT

Unlike humans, the artificial intelligence, dubbed "Chesty" after the nickname of a legendary Marine of long ago, did not rely exclusively on vision to model his surroundings. Merging with the data streams flowing like myriad streams and rivers through the tightly packed and tangled electronic pathways of the alien vessel, the closest sensory analogue he possessed was that of sound.

Human understanding of Xul mentalities had actually taken an enormous leap forward in the twenty-fourth century, when communications breakthroughs with dolphins in Earth's oceans had helped forge a new understanding of how they perceived their watery surroundings as magical, somehow crystalline panoramas of sound rendered palpable.

From Chesty's point of view, he was slipping deeper into a vast and hauntingly resonant meshing of rhythms and harmonies, a blending of tones and pulses and throbbings and even voices in a shifting, ever changing whole that felt both self-directing and self-contained, but which also felt like a fragment, a discrete but dependent shard of something far larger, tantalizingly beyond the reach and scope of Chesty's awareness.

The trick was twofold—remaining invisible within that harmonic chorus while retaining the ability to probe and peer and penetrate, winkling out useable data from the incoherent ocean of information pulsing around him and recording it for later analyses. As he slipped into the Xul data stream, Chesty manifested a data shell around the essential core of his operating software, taking on the virtual appearance of a minor counterpoint to the thronging choral harmony about him. So long as he played the part and kept it low-key, he should be able to remain undetected. His distant ancestors would have recognized the technique at once. Chesty$_3$ was, for all intents and purposes, a computer virus slipping in through an unguarded back door.

Key to the strategy, of course, was compatibility. The Xul was the ultimate in an alien operating system. Fortunately, there were only so many ways to encode and manipulate data, and both modern human computer technology and that of the ancient predecessors of the Xul shared essential basics. Both had begun, in their infancy, with the yes/no, on/off simplicity of binary, but Xul systems had later evolved the more adaptable yes/no/yes-and-no flexibility of trinary, similar in many ways to the fuzzy logic of the most powerful human systems.

As a result, and beginning with the extensive code-breaking and reverse engineering projects carried out on the recovered corpse of The Singer centuries ago, human computer technicians had learned enough of the Xul operating system, communications protocol, and essential language to understand perhaps twenty percent of a rich-content Xul data stream.

Twenty percent . . . one word in five. In some ways it wasn't much.

But it was all Humankind had if it was ever to understand the nature of its Enemy.

Moving through vast caverns of sound, then Chesty$_2$ sampled the currents, seeking matches for certain known concepts. In effect, he was listening for key words and phrases . . . most importantly among them the identifier phrases "Species 2824," "System 2420–544," or "Gateway 2420–001."

Thanks to the painstaking analyses of data brought back by other AI probes of Xul hunterships, Intelligence now understood that System 2420–544 referred to none other than Earth's solar system, evidently the 544th star system within a galactic sector designated 2420. Gateway 2420–001 was a particular Stargate—the gate at Sirius through which Xul hunterships had first entered human space, and through which humans had attacked Xul bases at Night's Edge and, earlier, in Cluster Space.

Species 2824, it was now known, was none other than Humanity.

If Humankind had survived this long, it was because the Xul had lost track of those identifiers within the incalculable, unfathomable immensities of a Galaxy of four hundred billion stars. Xul memories appeared to have noted Earth and Humankind a long time ago indeed, in records that quite possibly went back to the time of the Builders and their genetic tinkerings creating *Homo sapiens* out of *Homo erectus* half a million years before, but more recent information had, thankfully, been destroyed at Night's Edge.

If there was new information on Species 2824, however . . .

And there was. With an inward shock, Chesty$_2$ felt the match-up of duplicated chunks of code.

Briefly, he heard the interweaving voices of the Xul choral harmonies. . . .

" . . . *Species 2824 has been noted in the past* . . . ."

" . . . *Species 2824 has been of interest in the past.* . . ."

" . . . *Species 2824 has been of significant danger in the past.* . . ."

" . . . *Survival remains the first and only law.* . . ."

" . . . *Species 2824 may well pose a threat to We Who Are.* . . ."

" . . . *Survival remains the first and only law.* . . ."

" . . . *Species 2824 shall not be allowed to circumvent the first and only law.* . . ."

" . . . *Species 2824.* . . ."

Each line of code was linked by threads of coded logic to other lines, and as verse followed verse, Chesty$_2$ probed and listened and recorded, gathering a treasure trove of raw data, cascades of data, most of it too intricately complex to permit analyses or even translation here and now.

But everything he heard, he recorded and transmitted, sending it back over the initial carrier wave as a weak, low-frequency, and highly directional modulation just strong enough to reach the FR-100 Night Owl, some ten kilometers distant.

Chesty$_2$, as an artificially sentient software package, was both powerful and sophisticated in terms of creative scope, but there was no room in his coding matrix for such data-extravagant luxuries as emotion. He could not feel fear or excitement as the chorus sounded and resounded about him, speaking of the patterning of a host of alien soul-minds from an artifact identified as *Argo*. He couldn't even feel the thrill of recognition when he touched a familiar pattern of code indeed . . . another artificial intelligence that called itself Perseus.

But Chesty could and did recognize the seriousness of the encounter, and its importance to Humankind.

Earth had to be warned, and swiftly . . .

. . . or "Species 2824" might very soon become extinct.

8

2410.1102

Lieutenant Tera Lee
Starwall System
1609 hrs GMT

Lieutenant Lee watched the stream of returning data from Chesty$_3$, her alarm growing with each fresh revelation. She could only hear what Chesty was able to translate, but he'd picked several "voices" out of the background chorus and singled them out for special attention.

And now Lee and Chesty$_2$ listened to the ebb and flow of harmonies from the huntership now drifting a few kilometers away, an eerie symphony of voices crying out, echoing one another, merging, branching, merging once more. The Xul knew of Humankind's modest pocket of habitation in the Orion Arm, knew that it had destroyed several of their hunterships in the past, knew it represented a threat, at least in principle, to Xul long-term survival.

This last made absolutely no sense to Lee. How could beings as powerful and as technologically advanced as the Xul feel threatened by the insignificant likes of *Homo sapiens*? Still, the fact that *they* believed it was significant.

It was vital that she get this data back to the listening post.

But actually pulling that off was going to be a bit more difficult than thinking it. The Night Owl was falling directly away from the Stargate at a relative velocity of 217 meters per second—a bit over 700 kph. To return to the other side of the local Gate, she needed to kill that speed, then accelerate back the way she'd come. But as soon as $Chesty_2$ powered up the Owl's drive, they risked immediate detection.

Normally, this wouldn't have been a problem. The main Xul base in the Starwall system was some twelve light-seconds distant, ten times the distance between Earth and Earth's moon. Lee could have reversed course and slipped back through the gate before the Xul ever realized she'd been there.

That was not a good option, though, with a Xul huntership ten kilometers off her beam. For long seconds, she watched that other ship as it slowly drifted farther and farther astern, willing it to switch on its own drive and vanish into the blaze of starlight ahead. Damn it, what were they playing at over there? They'd come through the Gate from the gods alone knew where; why didn't they now move in-system, to dock with the Xul base here?

The longer she waited, though, the more she wondered if the Xul huntership had been deliberately parked there, squarely above the center of the Gate's opening, as a sentinel, as a guard on perimeter watch. It made sense; if the Xul were now suddenly concerned about Species 2824, they might be taking extra security precautions at all of their gateway bases. Or, worse, they might already know that humans possessed a listening post accessible through this gate—659—and be guarding against exactly such reconnaissance missions as Lee was now carrying out.

"$Chesty_3$ reports that he cannot access more deeply without risking discovery," $Chesty_2$ told her, a whisper in her mind. "He suggests that he remain in place as a rear guard while we attempt the vector change. He will wait to dissociate until after we pass through the Gate."

Lee thought about this, but didn't like it. Like most Marines, she thought of the Chesty iterations as sentient and autonomous life forms—artificial, perhaps, but as much alive and aware in terms of their thought processes as any organic life form. There were cybernetic tech specialists and theoreticians who would have disagreed with her, of course; the debate over whether a string of software commands and associated data clusters was alive or merely mimicking life through clever responses had been raging unabated in those circles for the entirety of the current millennium. The Turing Test, that ancient assessment of machine intelligence, said far more about human programming skills than it did about the presence or the nature of sentience itself.

Leaving Chesty$_3$ behind was tantamount, in her mind, to leaving behind a fellow Marine.

"It's not the same, Lieutenant Lee," Chesty$_2$ whispered in her thoughts, apparently reading them. "We would have left him in any case. Beaming a data package requires duplication. What remains behind must dissociate in order to avoid detection."

"I know, I know," she snapped, angry. "I understand all that. But it's not as though I have to *like* it."

"I do not understand the distinction."

"No." She sighed. "No, you wouldn't. Damned soulless machine. . . ."

Chesty$_3$ had been an exact copy of Chesty$_2$, beamed into the Xul huntership as a subtle modulation of an existing RF carrier wave. That identity had ended, of course, the instant Chesty$_3$ began to experience—and to record—events different from those experienced by Chesty$_2$ back on board the Night Owl, but Chesty$_2$ was being brought up to speed as the data from Chesty$_3$ continued to stream back across the ten-kilometer gap between them.

From the points of view of the two AIs, there was no point to "rescuing" Chesty$_3$ from the Xul ship. Neither Chesty$_2$ nor his duplicate possessed significant information about Sol or humanity, but it was good technique to leave behind no traces of the recon. Intelligence work was all about assembling small bits of discrete data from many discrete sources, like a jigsaw puzzle, to build a coherent picture of enemy plans or activities, and no one knew just how good the Xul were at that ancient game.

"Chesty$_3$ suggests we move quickly," Chesty$_2$ told her. "I concur. We are already beginning to push the safety factor for organic systems in respect to the local radiation fields."

She checked the time readout. The AI was right, damn

him. She'd been on this side of the Gate for nearly twelve minutes now. Depending on how hard she decelerated, then boosted for the Stargate, she might well be up against the forty-minute stay time allowed for this mission.

"There's some wiggle room in the safety factor," she said. "And we can't do this suddenly, or our Xul friends over there will have us nailed to the wall. Here's what I want to try. . . ."

In swift, concise thoughts, Lee explained what she wanted to do. The AI sounded dubious. "Shutting down life support could expose you to a fatal dose of radiation. I cannot comply."

"Nonsense. The hull will shield me long enough. As long as we get back through the Gate in, oh, half an hour or so."

"I trust you are aware of the old military aphorism, Lieutenant, the one declaring that no plan survives contact with the enemy."

"And Murphy's Law applies too. I know, Chesty. But if we just cut and run, that huntership over there will be on top of us before we move three meters."

"I am required to protect you from—"

"You are required, Chesty, to see to it that the mission succeeds. Right now, that is your only directive. Is that understood?"

"Understood." The inflection of Chesty's mental voice was neutral, but she could still hear a certain reluctance. Or was that her projection of emotions into an AI interface?

It didn't matter. She didn't like the possible ramifications of her idea, either, but right now it was all they had to work with.

"Systems are ready for implementation, Lieutenant. At your word."

"Very well. Implement. *Now*. . . ."

An instant later, the surface of the Night Owl began to shift, blur, and change.

Nanoflage had been a standard technology within the human military inventory for centuries. Beginning with pho-toreactive paints late in the twentieth century, objects like body armor or vehicles could be set to reflect ambient light and color in such a way that the article in question blended in nearly seamlessly with its surroundings, no matter what the current lighting conditions. At night, it was black; by daylight, it reflected the surrounding colors of desert, jungle, or ocean.

Eventually, camouflage paint became a thin layer of smart molecules that rearranged themselves to change the object's color, reflectivity, and even texture in response to the surroundings. With sufficient processing power, provided by long-chain molecules designed to process data like submicroscopic computers, light could actually be absorbed by the paint on one side of the object and re-emitted at the correct angle on the other, providing effective invisibility.

There were still serious limitations inherent in that bit of technological trickery, however. It worked well for small objects at long range and for long wavelengths only; the old dream of rendering a man invisible was still pure fantasy. The outer surface of the Night Owl was indeed invisible at microwave and radar wavelengths, but the technique still couldn't be applied to larger craft. Phase-shifting was another high-tech bit of protective camouflage, but that took a hell of a lot of power, and was not one hundred percent effective, either as camouflage or as shielding.

But what the Night Owl *could* do was rearrange the outer layers of its hull, transforming that sleek and light-drinking surface into something rough, rugged, and dusty-looking, giving it an appearance radically different from the sleek, black set of curves it exhibited now.

At the same time, Lee applied a full one hundred gravities of thrust for a fraction of a second, killing the Owl's forward momentum and putting it on a new vector, moving back toward the Stargate at a bit over 500 kilometers per hour. As an added bit of camouflage, she put the FR-100 into a gentle tumble, setting the blazing panorama of stars and nebulae into a slow spin about her head. Then she shut down all power, including shielding and even her life support.

She had enough air inside the cockpit to last for several hours. More serious was the lack of magnetic shielding. The adaptable nanosurface of the ship would handle some of the radiation sleeting across the hull, but not all of it, and not for long. She was already being burned, though she felt nothing . . . yet.

To any observer on the outside, however, the tiny spacecraft now looked precisely like a three-meter-long planetoid—a dusty, cracked, and rugged lump of nickel iron adrift in space. That sudden burst of energy would have been detected by the Xul, of course; the question was how closely they'd been monitoring their immediate surroundings. In its earlier configuration, the FR-100 would have been invisible at a range of 10 kilometers, but by changing vector she'd just done the equivalent of sending up a flare.

The question now was just how paranoid the Xul actually were—and how observant. Would they dismiss that brief burst of neutrinos as an anomaly, the random product of that brilliant background of massed stars? Or would they associate it with what appeared on the surface to be a lifeless and tumbling bit of rock?

She waited. The Owl's computer network used only a trickle of energy, as easily shielded as the electrical field of her own body, so she was able to continue watching through Chesty$_2$'s electronic senses, monitoring the Xul huntership. So far, there'd been no response . . . not yet . . .

The tumble threatened to make her dizzy. "Can you adjust the visual input for the spin?"

"Affirmative." And the tumble seemed to cease from her vantage point, though the Night Owl continued to fall end over end. She was facing the Stargate, now fifteen kilometers ahead and slowly growing larger. The Xul huntership was a flattened oval in the distance, slowly passing her on her left. There'd been no reaction whatsoever that she could detect.

"A message from Chesty$_3$," Chesty$_2$ told her. "The Xul—"

She never heard the message, because suddenly the alien machine was *there*, twenty meters away, a flattened ovoid sprouting unevenly planted tentacles like black whips. Three of those tentacles snapped out and grasped the Night Owl, and with the inertial damping fields down, she felt the gut-wrenching jolt as the ship's tumble was arrested, and as the alien machine decelerated.

On several occasions, Marines had fought Xul combat machines—in the bowels of hunterships at Sirius and at Sol, and within the depths of a Xul space station at Night's Edge—and always they seemed to be variations on this same theme, egg-shaped, with bumps and swellings and convolutions, with sensory lenses and implanted tentacles in patterns that appeared to differ from one individual to another. This model possessed a single, very large sensor, a glittering crystal as big across as a dinner plate, and the thing appeared to be narrowly watching her with a cold and unblinking gaze.

Lee stifled a raw instinct to scream, to thrash, to struggle, to *fight*; from her perspective, the monster was holding her in the implacable grasp of its manipulators. The thing could easily drag her back to the Xul ship for a more lingering inspection . . . or it could blast her into randomly drifting atoms right here. She could see the snouts of several plasma weapons protruding from that black, slick shell.

The Xul inspection lasted only a second or two . . . and then it released her. Stunned, she watched it recede once more, rapidly dwindling toward the huntership in the distance.

"Looks like we passed inspection," she managed to say after a few shaky moments.

"There is a problem, however," Chesty$_2$ told her. "That machine has reduced your velocity. Unless you accelerate, you will not reach the Stargate for another two hours, forty-seven minutes."

"Great."

"I do not understand your use of that word. The ambient radiation levels are already harming you physiologically."

She sighed. "It's called sarcasm. Can you get this thing back through to the listening post?"

"Of course."

"Then do it. Deliver everything from Chesty$_3$ you can extract." She could feel something already, that faint, scratchy tingle that presaged a sunburn at the beach. This was going to be *bad*. . . .

* * *

Marine Listening Post
Puller 659 Stargate
1904 hrs GMT

The alarm went off and Gerard Fitzpatrick nearly fell out
of his commlink couch. He'd been discussing the situation
with Chesty, preparing to send out a follow-up probe, when
an FR-100 transponder had lit up half a kilometer this side
of the Gate. He started to check the ID, but Chesty confirmed it before he could link through.

"It's Lieutenant Lee's Night Owl," Chesty told him in
maddeningly even tones. "I am linking with my uploaded
counterpart now . . ."

"Well? What does he say, damn it?"

"Lieutenant Lee's mission was successful. They electronically penetrated a Xul huntership and have confirmed
that news of *Argo*'s capture had extended to the Xul base at
Starwall, at the very least. They have also made contact with
the AI from the *Argo*, which should prove to be informative.
Lieutenant Lee is a casualty."

"Oh, Christ. How bad?"

"Not good. The radiation flux within the Starwall system
is—"

"I *know*, damn it! How is she?"

"Alive. Barely. My counterpart informs me she may be
near death. . . ."

"Well, scramble a work pod, damn it! Drag her in here!"

"Lieutenant Fitzpatrick, I must advise against that. The
Night Owl is itself highly radioactive. We could contami-
nate the entire—"

"Chesty, I've got the watch, okay? That puts me in command of this listening post. Patch a Class-One emergency
NL call through to Major Tomanaga. Upload the data Tera
brought back, and tell him I've gone out to retrieve the lieutenant's ship."

"But—"

"That's a goddamn fucking order!"

"Aye, aye, sir," the AI replied, with rigidly correct service
protocol.

Fitzpatrick knew he *could* buck the decision up to the Old Man—Major George Tomanaga at the LP's main station two light-hours away. Either Tomanaga would immediately order him to send out robotic tugs to bring the lieutenant in—in which case, why the hell wait? Or he would delay while he conferred with his superiors at paraside HQ, which could mean hours of delay, hours that Lieutenant Lee did not have. Or he would say no, order Fitzpatrick to sit tight until properly equipped tugs could arrive from the main base, and that would take God-knew how long. Work tugs with rad screening were not exactly interplanetary greyhounds.

And Fitzpatrick was going out after her *now*, no matter what. This way, if the Old Man flashed back an order to him to sit tight, he wouldn't have to disobey it.

A small but very guilt-feeling part of him was telling him that *he* should have gone on the sneak-and-peek, not her. Damn it, if she died. . . .

In a way, things had been easier in the old days, before the widespread introduction of nonlocal communications. A few centuries ago, he would have flashed off his intent to go pick up Tera, gone, and been back at the LP long before his message had even reached HQ. Having faster-than-light communications was a royal pain in the ass, since it invited micromanagement by the jerk-off remfies in their comfortable habitats far from the point of action.

Well, the hell with orders, and the hell with the remfs. Marines did *not* leave their own behind. . . .

USMC Skybase
Paraspace
2355 hrs GMT

"General Alexander. Please wake up."

Cara's voice brought Alexander upright in bed. "This had better be goddamned important," he mumbled aloud.

Tabatha rolled over at his side. "Mmph. Martin? What is it?"

"Call from the office, Tabbie," he said, caressing her thigh. "Don't worry about it. Go back to sleep."

"I'll get us caff." Nude, she slid out of bed and made her way in the near darkness to the bedchamber door.

He sighed. "Thanks, kitten." Though they'd not formally married, Tabatha Sahir had been his domestic partner for a good many years, now, and she knew what a call from his assistant at this hour almost certainly meant.

"We have an upload coming in NL from one of our Xul listening posts, General," Cara told him. "It sounds serious."

"Tell me."

Briefly, Cara filled him in on the bare bones of what had happened. Listening Post Puller 659 had noted the loss of some automated probes at a targeted Stargate. A Marine lieutenant and an AI had gone through to check things out up close and personal, and encountered a Xul huntership. The AI had successfully linked with the Xul, and they'd brought some hot data out.

As Alexander listened to a précis of that data, he felt his gut constrict, a hard, cold knot. *Damn! The bastards found us. . . .*

"Put that Marine down for a medal," he told Cara. "We owe him a lot."

"Her," Cara corrected him. "And the LP reports she is seriously injured. She may not survive."

"Shit. Keep me informed of her condition," he said. "Okay. Pass the data up the line, Intel and the Joint Chiefs."

"Very well."

"And give me a map. Where the hell is this place, anyway?"

Currently, the bedchamber's walls and domed ceiling were set to display the dark and murky blue fog of paraspace. Other Marines, he knew, tended to display scenes from Earth or Earth's Rings, or generic starfields, or even keeping the displays blank and neutral, but he'd always found the shifting blue murk to be relaxing, a definite inducement to sleep.

As well as to *wonder.* Paraspace, more poetically known as the Quantum Sea, lay at the very foundation of what modern physics was pleased to call reality, whatever the hell *that* was. It was here that, in accord with the laws of quantum physics, particles and antiparticles popped into existence for too brief a space of time to measure, then winked out again, where standing waves of virtual particles formed the basis of matter and energy at higher reality levels. The two-million-ton bulk of Skybase had been constructed in Mars orbit, then phase-shifted into the Quantum Sea, so the station could not be said to have a location in normal space/time at all. The idea had been to put the main operational headquarters for the U.S. Marine Corps outside the reach of any possible sneak attack, either by human foes or by the Xul.

He checked the hour, and groaned. Since there was no day or night here—indeed, no means of measuring time at all save by instruments brought through from normal space—by old, old tradition, the station operated on Greenwich Mean Time. As commanding general of the station, he could set any personal schedule he wished, and so several hours ago had turned in with Tabbie for the "night," whatever *that* might mean here in this eldritch space-that-was-not-space. By Greenwich Mean, it was just before midnight.

But the CO of any ship, base, or station was always on call. *Always.*

At his thought-click, the blue murk faded to dark, and a three-dimensional representation of human space hung high in the dome over the bedchamber. Sol glowed bright yellow at the center, surrounded by a thin haze of other stars in a many-lobed blob stretching across eight hundred light-years at its greatest extent, perhaps three hundred light-years at its smallest.

The amoebic shape of human space had been dictated by the uneven expansion of colonizing expeditions outbound from Sol over the course of the past six or eight centuries. Colony ships searched for worlds as close to Earth in terms of climate and habitability as possible, bypassing hundreds of frozen or poisonous rock balls in favor if those rare worlds that could be made livable with a minimum of terraforming. The statistics appeared in a window to one side of the display. All told, human space embraced roughly 120 million cubic light-years containing some 10 to 12 million stars.

Of those millions, however, about five hundred systems, all told, contained a human presence, ranging from tiny mining or military outposts to a scant handful of systems like Sol or Chiron, with populations numbering in the tens of billions. Of those 500, roughly a quarter—128, to be precise—were members of the Terran Commonwealth. All of the rest belonged to the nonaligned governments—the Islamics, the PanEuropeans, the Chinese, the Hispanics, the Russians.

"Drop in the known Gates, please," he told Cara. Instantly, seventeen of the fainter stars on the display turned bright and purple. Four were in space claimed by the Commonwealth. The other thirteen belonged to other stellar governments.

The closest Gate to Sol, of course, was Sirius C, the Gateway orbiting in the planetless Sirius star system 8.6 light-years from Sol. Over the centuries, though, as human colonies reached farther and farther out, other Gates had been discovered; the second closest Gate was at Gamma Piscium, a Type K0 giant 91 light-years from Sol. The Gates were unevenly sprinkled across human space with a randomness that suggested that the network, if it had ever possessed an order to begin with, had been distorted over the eons by the natural drift of the stars in their individual orbits about the galactic center.

Probes and research conducted at each of the seventeen gates located within human space had demonstrated that none of those seventeen linked with one another, that all available destinations were other Gates scattered across the Galaxy at extremely long ranges indeed—usually on the order of several thousand to several *tens* of thousands of light-years. Many, in fact, like the Gate nexus in Cluster Space, were well outside of the Galaxy proper, out in the thin halo of dim and distant stars thinning out endlessly into intergalactic space.

If there was anything like a large-scale order to the galactic network of Stargates, human research had not yet

been able to determine what it was. Neither was it known
yet whether the Gate network had been built by the Xul in
the first place, by the Builders, or by someone else entirely.
That the Xul *used* the network was definite. Of nearly five
thousand gateway possibilities so far investigated among
those seventeen Gates, almost two hundred opened into star
systems occupied by Xul bases. Marine Listening Posts had
been established at each of those systems, in order to attempt
to monitor Xul activities on the far side.

That strategy had just paid off, thank God.

But at a damned high cost.

"Which one is Puller 659?" he asked.

One of the purple points of light flared brighter on the display. Puller 659, he saw, officially Ringstar in the PanEuropean ephemera according to the windowed description, was
a red dwarf star near the fringes of human-explored space,
283 light-years from Sol and located within the misshapen
lobe of habitation known as the PanEuropean Arm. The
star system was nondescript and otherwise unimportant—
possessing a single gas giant, Ring, and its coterie of moons,
a few dwarf-planet rock-and-ice balls, and a large population
of asteroids and comets.

And the base there was illegal as hell. "*Shit!*" he said
aloud, with some feeling.

Human politics had just shoved its ugly nose under the
tent flap.

This was *not* going to be easy.

9

0511.1102

Senate of the Terran Commonwealth
Earth Ring
1445 GMT

It was, Alexander thought, a less than auspicious start to his
mission to Earth. He'd expected the Commonwealth Senate
to debate his plan for combating the Xul threat. That much
went without saying. He'd not expected that the Marine
Corps itself would be within the Senate's sights, that they
would actually be debating whether or not to bring the
Corps' eleven-hundred-year history to a close.

After reviewing the data transmitted back from Puller
659, he'd routed the full text back to Earth, to USMC-HQ,
to the Military Intelligence Agency, and, as required by
regulations, to the Senate Military Oversight Committee.
The reaction of that last was uncharacteristically swift; he'd
been ordered to return to Earth Ring in person, to face a full
Senate meeting and to present his recommendations.

To that end, he'd taken the somewhat unusual step of pulling Skybase out of its paraspace anchorage and returning it
to the Sol System. The Quantum Sea, existing outside of the
normal boundaries of four-dimensional space/time, did not
relate to space/time with a point-to-point correspondence.
If you had a well-plotted set of special coordinates, it was
possible to use paraspace as a means to bypass enormous
distances in 4D space.

Dropping into Sol space had enabled him to get back

to Earth Ring much more quickly than an FTL shuttle. He was wondering, however, if the trip had been worth it. He'd delivered his recommendation—a carefully parsed blueprint for action by the 1st Marine Interstellar Expeditionary Force—1MIEF—minutes ago.

And already the vultures were descending like harpies, scenting blood and eager for a meal.

Madam Marie Devereaux drew herself up to her full 150 centimeters, chin held high, defiant. She was standing at her seat in the Commonwealth Senate, an enclosed box high up within one of the ascending ranks of Senatorial platforms, but her repeater holo image stood at the chamber's center, towering over the Senate Chamber pit, matching each move, each dramatic pose, each gesture and expression. Alexander wondered if the holo was projecting the woman's personal e-filters to achieve that seeming perfection of face and form, or if what he was seeing reflected reality.

Not that reality had that much to do with this charade. He grimaced. Devereaux was putting on the show of her life. She appeared to be relishing this moment.

"Ladies and gentlemen of the Senate," she declaimed. "We've heard the arguments in favor of striking at the Xul, heard them *endlessly* in round upon round of discussion within these sacred halls, both in open debate and in closed committee. Is anyone else here as tired as I am, as sick to death as I am, I wonder, of hearing yet more excuses for this collection of odd bits and pieces of military technology and tradition and self-serving alarmist brinksmanship that calls itself the U.S. Marine Corps?"

A chorus of boos and shouted catcalls sounded from the surrounding rings of seats . . . but Alexander heard cheers and applause as well. It was impossible at this point in the proceedings to calculate whether the Senate was going to go along with his recommendation . . . or side with the newly constituted Peace Party.

What he'd not anticipated, though, was that this session was going to become a referendum on the very survival of the Corps.

"The Marines," Devereaux continued, "may once have

had a place in history, a role to play within the disparate collection of military services that once served the United States of America." The huge, holographically projected face smiled down beatifically at the watching senators. "They were very good, I understand, at scrambling up into the rigging of ancient warships, back in the Age of Sail, and shooting enemy officers on other ships. Some centuries later, they served as a kind of police force on American wet-navy vessels, and as ceremonial guards at American embassies in other countries. I suspect they were chosen because of how pretty their red, white, and blue dress uniforms were. . . ."

Chuckles and isolated bits of laughter rose from several quarters, and Alexander scowled. Damn the woman. Playing politics with the Corps at a deadly time like this. . . .

"Many of us love and admire the Marines, admire them for their sense of duty, their sense of tradition going back over eleven hundred years, now. But even as we admire them, we must admit to ourselves that these Marines have never really fitted in with their brothers-at-arms in the other services . . . the Army, the Air Force, even with the Navy, though historically they draw their strongest support from them. The Marines, admittedly, have served us well in the past, but we see from this incident just brought to our attention that the U.S. Marines are . . . extremist in their views. And this is *not* a time, Senators, for extremists.

"You see, the Marines, as we have seen repeatedly in the past, are not . . . not *team players*, as the old expression puts it. They take a disproportionate share of scarce resources and financing for their own service needs—for training, for supply, for transport, for administration—and give nothing back.

"They do *nothing* that the Army could not do just as well. Once, perhaps, the argument could be made that the Marines served a vital role as a ready amphibious landing force. In the days of wet navies, they could land on any beach, anywhere in the world, creating a beachhead through which regular Army forces could arrive and deploy.

"But the day of amphibious landings is long, *long* past, Senators. Marines have for centuries deployed through suborbital transports or orbit-to-surface landing craft, not wet-navy *boats*. Their very name—*Marines*—reflects a bygone age when 'marine soldiers' could be deployed on Navy ships to carry out missions on Earth's seas. Why, I wonder, deploy them into space? Because the Navy builds and operates the majority of our military spacecraft? Is that reason enough to keep them . . . like aging pets? Marines, I submit, are anachronisms, a piece of our past as anachronistic as armored knights on horseback.

"But more than being military anachronisms, I submit, Senators, that Marines are *political* anachronisms. Ask any Marine. Ask General Alexander, up there in the visitor's gallery, who brought this affair to our attention. Their first loyalties are not to Humankind, nor to our Commonwealth, but to an outmoded political concept called *America*, and to the Marine Corps itself.

"And that, Senators, that makes them, to my way of thinking, just a little *dangerous*."

Again, that smattering of applause. Alexander closed his eyes, trying to feel the emotion in the room. How many supported Devereaux? How many supported the lame duck administration?

How many simply hadn't yet made up their minds?

"Senators," Devereaux went on, "the Marines like to present themselves as being the guardians of our liberty. But when their heavily armed mobile base appears off our Ring docking ports, when Marines in their pretty uniforms and with their steely expressions suddenly walk the corridors of our orbital habitats . . . how safe, how *free* can we actually feel?"

Alexander's fist closed. He nearly stood, nearly shouted protest, but forced himself to remain in his seat. Damn it,

He'd ordered Skybase to transit out of paraspace and dock at Earth Ring. It was unusual, but it was the fastest means of getting here. Strictly speaking, Skybase was not a space craft, but a deep space habitat, similar to the colony facilities in use in the Asteroid Belt and the mining settlements out in the Oort Cloud. It had no motive power of its own, other than station-keeping thrusters, and it required a small fleet of tractor tugs to move it around in normal space. The bulky structure was designed to dock periodically at major port facilities—those large enough to receive it—for resupply and maintenance.

As for Marines entering the Ring, well, hell, of *course* he'd permitted liberty for the base personnel. The men and women under his command were people, not robots. Skybase had been deployed in paraspace for fifteen months—five longer than usual, and it was about time the crew had a chance to go shoreside for a little downtime.

But Devereaux's tirade was continuing, unfolding like a thunderstorm. "I submit that the Marines, far from being guardians of our liberty, represent a clear and present danger to our cherished way of life. For centuries now, the Marines have not even been a part of our world culture, not in the way that Army soldiers or Air Force High Guardsmen are. They don't, they *can't* fit in. They live for their precious Corps, maintain their own self-contained culture, their own laws, their own religion, even . . . and rarely mingle with civilians. Indeed, I suspect many of our Marine friends consider mere civilians to be somehow inferior to them.

"The Army is much more connected to our culture, our society, than are the Marines. Marines are extremists in all of their views, and anytime you have extremists, you run the risk of a total disconnection with society.

"And that, my friends, is *dangerous.* A danger greater than Theocratic fundamentalism, a danger more sinister than this so-called Xul threat! How are we to maintain our freedom with these trained killers in our midst?"

Gods above and gods below. Did the creature just like the sound of her own voice, or did she really mean even half of the crap spewing from that ugly hole in her face?

Furious now, Alexander opened an inner window, calling up a bio on Marie Devereaux. She'd been born, he saw, in Saint-Jean-sur-Richelieu, which was located in the province of Quebec. The old sovereign nation of Quebec had finally joined the old North American Federation in the twenty-fifth century, but never had been wholly comfortable with that union. Quebec had never accepted statehood, as

had several of her Canadian sister-provinces. After a plebi-
scite, however, the 2740 Act of Common Union had granted
all of North America full and equal representation in the
Commonwealth Senate, which was how she'd ended up as
a senator. She'd also been an officer in the last war with
the Chinese Hegemony, rising to the rank of general in the
Commonwealth Army, which explained how she'd wangled
a slot as a representative on the Military Advisory Council.

There was nothing, though, to suggest why she had such
a hair up her ass about the Marine Corps.

Or possibly . . .

Okay, *that* might explain it. Saint-Jean-sur-Richelieu was
located south of the St. Lawrence—in a part of Quebec once
and briefly known as *occupied* Quebec.

That reflected a bit of history dating all the way back to
the First UN War, back in the twenty-first century. Quebec
had invaded the then-United States as part of a much larger
UN offensive involving Mexico, France, and Japan; the U.S.
Army had handily knocked back the invaders, then swept
in and occupied everything north to the St. Lawrence, from
Lake St. Francis to New Brunswick.

That had been the *army*. But, he noted, elements of the
U.S. Marine Corps had assisted with the occupation in the
late 2050s.

Damn it! That was ancient history! He knew the PanEu-
ros and the Islamics tended to hold grudges that lasted for
thousands of years, but he hadn't thought that that kind of
narrow-minded Dark Ages thinking extended to the Québecois! Besides, the Marines had been a small, almost inci-
dental part of a much larger and complicated history. Why
single them out for this . . . this persecution?

He read further.

Clearly, Marie Devereaux was ambitious. She'd been
President Rodriguez's principal political rival for five years,
now, and in the general elections three days ago, the whole-
sale defection of her Peace Party from its sixty-year alliance
with the Liberty Party to the more conservative Constitutionals had won the election for the Constitutionals. Rodriguez,
a staunch conservative, would be out in two months; Sher-

rilyn Simmons, the new president elect, was a liberal but a hard-line fiscal conservative . . . *and* an anti-militarist.

That must be it. Devereaux supported Simmons. More, she was positioning herself to be noticed by the new administration. If she were seen as a champion of cutting back the military—principally by eliminating or severely restricting the Marine Corps—she was all but assured of a strong position within the new government. Hell, she might even be angling for a shot at the presidency herself, eight years down the road.

The hell of it was, the election results of the other day were being widely interpreted by the news media as a rejection of the hardliner conservative stance against the Islamic Theocracy. That was scarcely a surprise; lots of people, Alexander included, had some doubts about the nature and the necessity of the current war.

But the media loved the word "mandate," and the election was being presented as a mandate to end the ill-starred war with the Theocracy . . . and, what was more, to draw down on the military in order to banish any future risk of interstellar war—whether it be with the Theocrats, or with the Xul.

Disarming in the face of a clear and imminent danger. From Alexander's perspective, that was sheer lunacy . . . but he'd seen it before, and knew enough history to know that the same thing had happened time after time after time throughout history, going back long before there'd been a Marine Corps.

The problem was that sooner or later, Humankind would face an enemy that didn't give a damn if humans were unarmed or not, and which would be strong enough and technologically advanced enough to send humanity the way of the dinosaurs.

An enemy, for instance, like the Xul.

Devereaux, he realized, was still speaking, but it sounded like she was on the point of wrapping things up. "Senators, this proposal placed before us this morning by Lieutenant General Alexander and his staff should be, *must* be rejected. We cannot act preemptively against the Xul. When they come, if they come, we must trust to the gentle art of diplomacy to convince them that we are no threat to them, that we and they can share this vast Galaxy without threat or dominance of one over the other.

"Furthermore, I submit that the Marines themselves should be allowed to retire, to fade away into the mists of history . . . and to cease once and for all in their meddling and in their interference in the *modern* affairs and political ministrations of a united Humankind! It is, in my humble opinion, Marine belligerence, their martial spirit and outlook, their tendency to look at anything strange or unknown as a military foe that threatens the peace more than any presumed threat by an ancient and distant alien empire!"

Devereaux sat down, and a moment later the high-vaulted Senate chamber filled with a roar of applause. There were jeers and boos as well, but it sounded to Alexander's ear as though the senator from Quebec had successfully swung the majority to her way of thinking.

He thought-clicked a request to speak.

It took several moments for the noise to die away. A number of the senators in the boxes nearer to the visitor's gallery, he could see, were looking up at him expectantly. Maybe they were just waiting to see if he would react to Devereaux's tirade with a tirade of his own. Politics could be boring, and maybe this sort of infighting was the only entertainment they could expect this day.

He considered a tirade, a broadside in return, but dismissed the idea. That would be fighting on ground of her choosing.

But he *had* to respond. . . .

"General Alexander," Ronald Chien, the Senate president said. "You have a reply or a rebuttal?"

Slowly, he stood up, and now an immense image of *him* towered over the assembly. He tried not to look at it. The scowl, the craggy eyebrows, the jut of the chin all conspired to make him look angry, even darkly sinister, and that made him self-conscious.

"Ladies and gentlemen of the Senate," he began, keeping his voice low, "I am not, of course, a member of this body. I am a guest and, I suppose, a kind of expert witness, whom you have kindly invited to come here and share my views on the *Argo* incident, and on the necessity of adopting War Plan 102–08." A babble of voices, protests, and catcalls rose, and he shouted through the noise. "Yes, *necessity*! Because if we duck back into our shells and ignore the crisis before us, I *promise* you that we will cease to exist as a species, that you, me, and every man, woman, and child in this system, on the world beneath us, and among the stars around us, will be hunted down and exterminated!

"But before I get to that, I feel that I must comment, briefly, on some of the things Madam Devereaux has said. You see . . . as it happens, I *agree* with her, in two important ways, at least."

At that moment, the Senate chamber became deathly silent. Currently, there were within the Commonwealth government 494 senators, two representing each state, district, major orbital colony, and world within the Commonwealth, and even some major corporate entities as well. Each of those senators had his or her own oval seating box, and each was accompanied by his or her own entourage of secretaries and personal assistants. Several thousand people were watching Alexander at that moment in complete and utter silence.

And a far vaster audience, he knew, was present virtually, watching through their personal links from home.

"Madam Devereaux has said that she believes Marines to be 'a little dangerous.' I really must take exception to that. Marines are not a little dangerous. We are *very* dangerous. We are trained to kill, and we are very, very good at what we do.

"She has also called us extremists, pointed out that we are not a part of the overall culture of Humankind, and suggested that our extremism is more of a threat than are the Xul.

"Extremists? Maybe so. We are extreme in our pride. We are extreme—I would say we are *insufferable*—in our devotion to our Brotherhood, to one another, and to what we stand for. We are extremists in that way, in the *depth* of our devotion, to our Corps, to our traditions, and to the memory of those Marines who've gone before, to the blood shed by all of the Marines who have served in the past eleven hundred years.

"And we are extremists when it comes to our devotion to duty, to service, to country, to you senators, and to the people and the government you represent.

"Marines *are* different from the men and women of the other branches of service. I admit that. I am *proud* of that. And that distinction is an important one.

"In the Army, you have riflemen . . . and you have supply clerks, and you have cooks, and you have electronics specialists and sims technicians and cartographers and comm personnel and pilots and drivers and military police and all the rest. What is it, now . . . four, maybe five hundred distinct military specialties?

"In the Marines, though, it's different. We have specialization skills, yes . . . but in the Marines *every* man and woman is a rifleman first. I don't care if a Marine is unloading cargo pallets at a spaceport, or flying an A-410 Kestrel, or programming combat sims at Skybase, or sneaking drones through a Stargate into a Xul base at the Galactic Core. I don't care if that Marine is a general officer, or fresh out of boot camp. He or she is a Marine combat rifleman *first*.

"I daresay General Lisa Devi, the General of the Army, would not call herself a soldier. The General of the Aerospace Force would not call himself an aerospaceman. The Chief of Naval operations does not call himself a sailor. General McCulloch, the Commandant of the U.S. Marine Corps, however, is damned proud to call himself a Marine. As *I* am proud to call myself a Marine.

"Does that make us extremists? Maybe . . . but if it does, I submit, ladies and gentlemen of the Senate, that the Commonwealth *needs* that kind of extremism. That kind of dedication. That sense of purpose and that devotion to duty!

"In five more days, ladies and gentlemen, the Marine Corps will have its birthday, celebrating eleven hundred and three years of service, first to the United States of America, then to the Commonwealth of Terra. Eleven hundred years.

"It's true, you know, that the Marines have their own culture. I admit that. In fact, I'm damned proud of that. We call a floor a deck, a door a hatch, a hat a cover, our living spaces quarters, a bed a rack. We have our own brand of humor, jokes *only* Marines can appreciate or even understand. Marines have had their own culture ever since they lived crowded together on the stinking lower decks of wind-driven wet-navy sailing ships, ever since seven of them led an army of revolutionaries across the Sahara Desert to Derna, ever since they charged time after time after bloody time the German machine-gun nests in Belleau Wood. It's a part of being a member of this fraternity, this brotherhood of heroes.

"Is that such a bad thing? We still have God knows how many distinct cultures on Earth, and we call it diversity and say it's an important part of being human. And the people living in Earth Ring have their own distinct way of looking at things . . . as do people in Mars Ring, or in Luna, or out in the Belts or the Jovians or Chiron or Ishtar or anywhere else where humans have gone and made homes for themselves. We Marines are no different. We've made a home for ourselves within the family we call the Corps. If we're proud of that, it's no worse than being proud of being American, or Japanese, or Lunan.

"How does having a unique culture make us a threat?

"Yes, we have our 'pretty uniforms,' as Madam Devereaux said, where each part carries its own tradition, each color its own meaning. Black for space, blue for the ancient oceans of Earth. And red. Let's not forget the red in that thin red stripe down the trouser legs of our full-dress uniforms. Red for the blood of Marines shed at places like Chapultepec and Belleau Wood, Suribachi and the Chosin Reservoir, Cydonia and Ishtar.

"Blood, I might add, shed for *your* ancestors, so that they, and you, might be free to hold these deliberations in this chamber today!"

Alexander was startled by a sudden burst of applause from the chamber. He hesitated, looking across the pit, wondering what it was that had inspired this display. He didn't think of himself as a demagogue, and certainly not as a politician or a speechmaker. He'd been speaking from the heart, from a very *angry* heart, not so much trying to sway the audience as to simply get them to hear, to understand.

He took a deep breath, calming himself. He did have their attention now, so if he was going to make his point, now was the time to do it.

"You have a choice before you, Senators. You can do nothing, and wait for the Xul to arrive . . . and they *will* arrive, I promise you that. Sooner or later, they will be here, just as they were here in 2314, but this time it will be an *armada* flinging rocks or worse at Mars, not a solitary, arrogant, and cocksure huntership.

"And if that happens, I promise you that the Marines will stand and fight. We will fight, as we have always fought in desperate actions, and we will die protecting you, and your children, and our children, and our worlds. We will stand and we will fight and we will die . . . because there will be no place else to which we can withdraw if the enemy comes to us with his full, vast, and overwhelmingly advanced technological might.

"Do you understand that? We will die. Earth will die. And on every one of 512 planets scattered across eight hundred light-years, *Humanity* will die! We know something similar happened half a million years ago, with the destruction of the Builders. It happened to the An. It will happen to us.

"Or . . . you can adopt the proposal I have placed before you, a plan drawn up by my staff on Skybase and incorporating the best intelligence on Xul basing and deployments that we have. We can go on the offensive, take the war to them in a dozen different star systems. We can hit them and keep hitting them and never be there when they muster a retaliatory force, and we can hurt them enough that they will send their full strength after *us*, rather than to Sol and Earth. We will lead them deeper and deeper into the sea of stars that is our Galaxy, far away from Earth, and we will continue to fight them while you, here, decide how best to preserve that 'precious way of life' invoked by Madam Devereaux.

"That, Senators, is the choice I give you. Stand and fight and die here . . . within Earth's own solar system. Or send the Marines, dangerous and extremist as we are, to fight this war out there, in *their* backyard, not ours.

"And because we are loyal to the Commonwealth and to the rule of civilian law, we will wait and do what you command.

"I only ask that you make up your minds swiftly . . . because we, all of Humankind, do not have much time left."

Again, thunderous applause filled the chamber. As Alexander took his seat, he turned his gaze on Devereaux, in her box on the far side of the pit. His link with the local Net allowed him to zoom in on her face from almost 80 meters away. She was watching him, he saw, with a cold look of absolute contempt.

"I don't think she likes you, General," Cara whispered in his thoughts.

"No, I don't think she does." He shrugged. "Does make me wonder, though."

"Wonder what, General?"

"Why it always seems that our most vicious enemies aren't the aliens who want to wipe us off the face of the universe . . . but our own friends and neighbors."

"Truthfully, General, I've never understood that about humans. If you don't have enemies, you seem peculiarly adept at creating them. If you don't mind my saying so."

"Mind? No. Why would I mind the truth?" He checked his internal time sense. "Looks like they're going to be debating for a long time to come, Cara. I need food."

He electronically logged out, then stepped through the doorway at the back of his visitor's box. He could already tell that it was going to be a long afternoon, one that would probably extend well into the evening.

And the die was cast, as another general had commented three thousand years earlier.

There was nothing else he could do to influence events, however much he might wish it.

10

USMC Recruit Training Center Command
Ares Ring, Mars
1020 hrs GMT

Like Earth, Mars possessed a ring.

Like its counterpart encircling the Motherworld of Humankind, the Ares Ring was not solid, but was composed of some tens of thousands of separate orbital facilities, colony habs, nanufactories and power stations, dockyards and spaceports, research stations and living quarters. Each structure pursued its own orbit about the planet, though many were magnetically locked with the neighbors, creating the illusion of a solid structure. They were positioned at about 20,000 kilometers above the planet's surface, locking them in to an arestationary orbit—the equivalent of geostationary for Earth. From this height, Mars appeared some eleven times larger than did the full moon from Earth, and four times brighter.

Unlike Earth, Mars possessed only a single ground to synchronous-orbit elevator, the Pavonis Mons Tower. Pavonis Mons, the middle of the striking set of three volcanoes in a row southeast of the vast swelling of Mons Olympus, reached seven miles into the sky and by chance exactly straddled the Martian equator—the perfect ground-end anchor for a space elevator. The habitat housing the Marine Recruit Training Center Command was positioned close by the nexus with the P.M. Tower, which looked like a taut, white thread vanishing down into the mottled ocher and green face of Mars.

PFC Aiden Garroway stood at attention on the Grand Arean Promenade, together with the thirty-nine other Marines of Recruit Company 4102 who'd completed boot training, and tried not to look down. The deck they were standing on was either transparent or a projection of an exterior view from a camera angled down toward Mars—the resolution was good enough that it was impossible to tell which—and it was easy to imagine that the company was standing on empty space, with a twenty-thousand-kilometer fall to the rusty surface of the planet far beneath his feet.

The effect of standing on empty space, the gibbous disk of Mars far beneath his feet, could be unnerving. He could just glimpse the planet when he turned his eyes down, while keeping his head rigidly immobile.

Garroway and his fellow newly hatched Marines had spent a lot of time looking at that sight since they'd made the ascent from Noctis three days before. The world was achingly beautiful—red-ocher and green, the pristine sparkle and optical snap of icecaps, the softer white swirls and daubs and speckles of clouds, the purple-blue of the Borealis Sea.

For many of them, those from Earth's Rings, Garroway included, it brought with it a pang of homesickness. Not that Mars resembled Earth all that closely, even with its reborn seas and banks of clouds . . . but the oceanic blues and stormy swirls of white echoed the world they'd watched from Terrestrial synchorbit; for the handful of recruits from Earth herself, it was the colors—the blues and greens, especially—that reminded them of home.

All things considered, perhaps it was best that he was standing at attention and looking straight ahead, not gawking at the deck. Somewhere behind him were the ranks of seats filled with friends and families of graduating Marines. No less a luminary than General McCulloch, Commandant of the U.S. Marine Corps, was delivering a speech, his head and shoulders huge on the wallscreen ahead and slightly to Garroway's right.

"The Marines," McCulloch was saying, "have been criticized for being different, for being out of step with the society that they are sworn to protect. And it's true. Marines look at the world around them differently than most people. Marines are dedicated to the ideal of service.

"I don't mean to say that joining the Marines constitutes the *only* valid form of service. Certainly not. Nor do I mean that military service is the only way to serve one's country.

"But military service is one of the very few, unambiguous ways by which a young man or woman can declare themselves in support of the common good. It's one of the few means remaining today by which young people *can* make a deep and lasting difference, both in their own lives, and in support of their homeland, even their home world.

"And Marines—these Marines—have selflessly chosen service to country at considerable personal risk, have chosen service to others above comfort, above profit, above every other mundane consideration popular with young civilians these days. . . ."

Garroway listened to the words, but somehow they didn't connect for him. The seats above and behind him, he knew, were filled almost to capacity, but not one of the Giangreco line had come out to watch his graduation. Not one.

Estelle, he knew, had wanted to come, but an e-transmit from her last week had told him the money for a flight out to Mars just wasn't there. He wondered if that was the reason . . . or if Delano Giangreco had put his pacifist foot down. Delano, he knew, held the purse strings for the entire Giangreco line family.

He wished that, at least, his birth mother could have been there.

McCulloch was still talking.

". . . and it is within the Corps that these young people learn the heart and soul of altruism. They learn to value the person standing next to them more than they value themselves, learn to regard sacrifice as the sacred gift they give to their comrades, and to their home.

"There was a time, a thousand years or more ago, when service in the military was a prerequisite for public service as a leader of the community or of the larger state. It was the military that taught a young person character, and half or more of the people attending the institutions of higher learning first served in the military.

"Eventually, however, and unfortunately, such service, such altruism, became unfashionable. Today, I might point out, only a tiny fraction of our leaders actually have military service in their records.

"Does that mean that our Commonwealth leaders are of poor character? No . . . and I wouldn't be allowed to say so if they were." That brought a small chuckle from the audience. The commandant, Garroway thought, was skating kind of close to the edge, here. Service personnel were required to be completely apolitical so long as they were in uniform.

"But I do wonder," McCulloch continued, "just where in this day and age a future leader can better develop that altruistic ethic, that willingness to sacrifice for others, that comes from military service in general, from service as a Marine in particular. . . ."

Garroway stifled a yawn. His feet were hurting, and his back, and he thought-clicked the appropriate anodynes into his system, mixed with a mild stimulant. He was operating now less on a willingness to sacrifice than terror of what Gunnery Sergeant Warhurst would do to him if he screwed up.

"*Duty*," McCulloch said, the word reverberating through the Arean Promenade. "Honor. Loyalty . . . to comrades, to country, to the Corps. . . ."

There was more, lots more, but the rhetoric ended at last. Warhurst, at the head of the graduating class, crisply attired in Marine full dress, rasped out the command. "*Comp*'ney, forrard . . . *harch*!" As one, forty new Marines stepped out, left foot first, the sharp clash of sound shivering the air as they began the first leg of their march around the Arean Promenade.

"*Right* turn . . . *harch*!" and they swung in-column, four abreast to the right. As they passed the reviewing stand, Warhurst snapped, "*Comp*'ney, eyes . . . *right*!" He then raised a sharp salute toward the stand. A live band waiting

in the wings burst into the surging strains of the Marine
Corps Hymn.

Garroway snapped his head to the right, and so was able
to see the assembled brass in the reviewing stand rise to
their feet and return the salute. . . .

Afterward, they attended one hell of a party.

Sloan Residence
Ares Ring, Mars
1720 hrs GMT

Warhurst stepped off the elevator and onto a broad, open
deck of artificial wood overlooking a lake. A forest crowded
close around the house—he couldn't tell if the trees were
real or artificial, but they *smelled* real in the gentle breeze.
Whichever they were, the illusion was that of a forested
mountain on Earth; the illusion broke down only when the
visitor looked up, toward the hub, and, beyond the hub's
artificial sun, saw the green and sculpted landscape—woods,
streams, and other buildings—etched into the other side of
the colony arching overhead.

And, of course, when he turned around, he found himself
looking through the hab's transparent end cap, to see the
green and ocher half-disk of Mars turning gently with the
rest of the sky. Stars and an endless night rotated beyond
the opposite end cap, the two transparencies sandwiching
between them this strip of green and blue.

"Welcome, Gunnery Sergeant Warhurst!" a young servant
in scarlet livery announced.

Warhurst had never met the man, and he assumed that the
guy had just pulled his ID off the local Net. "Thank you. It
was kind of you to invite me."

"It was the senator's pleasure. Would you care for a drink?"

A serving robot hovered at the man's side, a selection of
drinks of various sizes, shapes, and colors on its tray.

"Not just now, thank you," Warhurst replied. He looked
about, puzzled. "I'm not the first one here, am I?"

The servant laughed. "Certainly not, sir! People have
been coming in since early this morning!"

"Oh. Good." He felt terribly awkward. He wanted to ask if Julie, Callie, Donal, or Eric were here . . . or if they were expected. He didn't want to see them right now, or relive any of *those* memories, not the pain, not the injustice, not the anger.

God it still hurt. . . .

But the servant was still speaking, gesturing toward the sliding glass doors leading into the main house. "You'll find refreshments inside, sir. Or you can follow the guidelight on the deck around the corner, there, and go straight back to the pools. Make yourself at home, have a good time . . . and happy birthday!"

"Thank you," Warhurst replied, terse. He didn't like being here alone. And quite apart from his . . . *personal* problems, social galas like this one always gave him a pain.

As did the pretensions of the rich. But he appreciated the greeting.

Wherever there was a Corps presence, the date of 1011—the tenth day of November, old-style—was celebrated, the birthday of the U.S. Marines.

On that date, in 1775, the Second Continental Congress had enacted legislation, resolving that "two battalions of Marines be 'inlisted' to serve for and during the present war between Great Britain and the colonies." Two weeks later, a Quaker innkeeper named Samuel Nicholas had been commissioned as the first officer of the Marines, and recruiting had begun at the Tun Tavern in Philadelphia. Less than four months after that, on 3 March 1776, four full months before the signing of the Declaration of Independence, Captain Nicholas led 268 Marines ashore on New Providence Island in the Bahamas, capturing two forts, cannons, and a supply of gun powder in the Corps' very first amphibious operation.

Eleven hundred two years later, the Corps continued to celebrate that birthday, in this case with an elaborate party. The graduation of class 4102 had been arranged to coincide with the festivities.

Normally, Marines took care of their own celebrations. The festivities within the Arean Ring, though, had been hijacked this year. Warhurst made a face as he looked around the expansive, rotating hab module. Senator Sloan was not a Marine. According to his Net bio, he hadn't even served in the military.

But he *was* one of four Commonwealth senators representing Mars, and the two chief pillars of the Martian economy were xenoarcheological research and the Marines. Both the 1st Marine Division and the 1st Marine Interstellar Expeditionary Force had moved their headquarters to Mars centuries ago, and any political representative of that world knew that his hopes of staying in office resided with the Marine constituents.

Danis Sloan was also ostentatiously rich, as the lavishness of his personal quarters suggested. The hab was enormous, a squat, rotating cylinder similar in design to some of the larger O'Neil-type space colonies, but only about 1 kilometer long, and twice that in diameter. The ends were capped in transplas, giving constantly turning views of the stars, the sun, Mars, and the other nearby habs making up this portion of the Area Ring as the structure rotated, producing its out-is-down spin gravity. Visitors docked at the hub airlock, then traveled out and down one of the elevators to reach the landscaped terrain. The main house, where the party was being held, occupied nearly ten percent of the hab's internal terrain, tucked in between one of the transparent end caps, and a broad, sparkling lake.

And the whole damned thing belonged to Danis Sloan.

Half a million years ago, the Builders had left a vast array of faster-than-light communicators in a subsurface complex called the Cave of Wonders, beneath a weathered plateau in Cydonia. Those communicators still possessed real-time visual and audio links with similar devices on Chiron, Ishtar, and elsewhere, but it had taken centuries to reverse-engineer the process and learn how to use quantum entanglement to instantly bridge distances measured in light-years.

A quantum dynamicist named Victor Sloan, among others, had been instrumental in making modern FTL communication possible, and that, in turn, made both interstellar business and government possible.

The Sloan fortune now was rumored to exceed the economies of several small nations. Hell, the guy could probably *buy* small countries if he had a use for them. Warhurst had heard that Sloan's Arean Ring hab was only one of his dwellings, that a larger one existed in Earth's First Ring, and that others existed in at least three other star systems. The guy, through his company, Sloan Stellartronics, had his own FTL starship, for God's sake, and that was certainly no cheap date.

Fair enough. FTL communication was vital in tying together the far-flung worlds of Humankind. The Commonwealth wouldn't have been possible without it. More than that, humanity's survival might depend upon it; late in the twenty-sixth century, shortly after they'd become commercially feasible, faster-than-light starships had caught up with the *Argo* and the other fleeing asteroid starships, offering to share the new technology, and offering them evacuation, a chance to come home. The offers in every case had been rejected, but *Argo* and her sisters all had accepted Sloan units in order to maintain real-time communications with Earth.

Likely, Warhurst thought, they wanted to know if and when the Xul found and destroyed Earth, thereby justifying their flight.

But if that hadn't happened, if *Argo* had not possessed an FTL transmitter quantum-entangled with a Sloan unit back in the Solar System, Perseus would not have been able to flash news of the Xul appearance instantly back to Earth, and word of *Argo*'s destruction would not have been received on Earth for more than another four hundred years.

By then it almost certainly would have been too late.

So Sloan was welcome to his fortune. His family had come by it honestly, at least. Warhurst just wished the man wasn't so damned ostentatious about it. Importing and growing those gene-tailored trees alone must have cost tens of millions of newdollars . . . enough to fully equip a modern Marine rifle company at least.

Possibly, he thought as he followed the guidelight moving before him across the decking, the problem lay in the implication that the Marines—or at least 1MarDiv—somehow belonged to Sloan personally. That wasn't the case, to be sure, but the press and often parts of the Commonwealth government seemed to think it was. Sloan had been chairperson of the Defense Advisory Council three times running, losing out in the elections four years ago only because Marie Devereaux and the Peace Party had insisted on the change as part of the price of their support.

He wondered if the Peace Party's swing to support the Constitutionalists would bring Sloan back to chairpersonship of the council. He doubted it. Current politics were way too volatile to permit long-term government fiefdoms.

And there were all those rumors that Danis Sloan hoped to launch his own bid for the presidency four years from now.

Warhurst stepped around the corner of the house and onto the raised deck above the pool area behind the house. Sonic suppressor fields had kept the noise levels low, but as he stepped through the field interface, the babble of conversation, laughter, music, and noise assaulted his ears. Sloan had been planning a lavish ball in honor of the Marines for a long time, and the party promised to be a long one—several days at least.

Several hundred people were gathered on the tiers of decks behind the residence already. Perhaps a quarter, he saw, wore Marine dress uniforms, complete with gloves, glowribbons, and red-striped trousers. The rest wore a dazzling array of costumes, from formal ball gowns and dressuits to holographic light displays and sim projections to complete and fashionable nudity. Sloan's invitation, obviously, had gone out to his own social set as well as Marine personnel . . . and that griped Warhurst as well. This . . . this ritual honoring this date in history belonged to the Corps. Civilians shouldn't have any part of it, no matter how rich or well connected they might be.

"Sergeant Warhurst, is it?" a woman's voice said at his back. "Michel?"

He turned. The speaker was a tall and beautifully sculpted blond woman, technically nude, but with a fan of what looked like gorgeously colored peacock feathers arranged in a full, 2-meter circle behind her body, reaching from her knees to well above her head, and with nanorganic emitters within her skin giving off a constant, golden radiance that perfectly matched her hair. Her nipples alone, he estimated, were giving off enough light to read by, had it been dark.

"*Gunnery* Sergeant Warhurst, ma'am," he said, correcting her.

"Larissa Sloan," she told him, extending a hand. "Danis's first wife, don't you know. Welcome to our little gathering!"

He took her hand and gave a slight, perfunctory bow above it. "Pleased to meet you, ma'am."

"Now, Sergeant! Don't 'ma'am' me! I'm Rissa to my friends!"

He made a noncommittal sound, more of a grunt than an assent, but softening it with a smile. Warhurst wasn't entirely sure yet if the woman was actually offering that level of friendship . . . or if he should accept it if she did. Her exuberance was just a little disturbing, as was her misunderstanding of the Marine rank structure.

For a moment, she had a faraway look in her eyes as she accessed data. "And are your wives and husbands here yet?" she asked brightly. "I haven't seen them so far. . . ."

"Actually, I'm here alone tonight, Ms. Sloan."

"Oh, but you *must* know this affair is for Marines and their spouses and other partners! Feel free to call them and have them come right over!"

Briefly, he considered replying with a blunt, "I'm divorced. They kicked me out a month ago." If the woman had bothered to look more deeply into his public data stats, past the front page, at least, she would have seen that.

But it didn't matter. And he certainly didn't want to have to explain the circumstances to this . . . naked butterfly. He let the comment pass. She was already taking him by the arm and leading him deeper into the crowd. "There are *so* many people for you to meet! Please, help yourself to food, drink, drugs, whatever suits your fancy! And inside there's so much going on. If you want a companion, we have a number of *lovely* girls here as personal entertainers . . . boys too, if you prefer." She patted his arm. "I might look you up myself after a while, if your partners don't mind!"

"Ah, excuse me, ma'am," he said, stopping abruptly. "I see a couple of Marines over there I know. If you'll forgive me?"

He disentangled his arm and strode across the deck, not waiting to find out if he was forgiven or not. He came up between two young PFCs in full dress blacks at a buffet and put his arms over their shoulders. "*Semper fi*, Marines," he said.

The two Marines started, whirled, and came to attention. "Sir, yes, sir!"

Warhurst grinned and shook his head. "You can always tell the ones straight out of boot camp. Danvers? Garroway? What are you two fucking dipshits doing in a galahole like this?"

Garroway stammered, swallowed, and tried again. "Sir! We were invited, sir!"

Warhurst raised an admonishing white-gloved finger. "Negative on the 'sir,' son. You both are *Marines*, now, and that means that I am no longer a 'sir.' I may still be God, so far as you sorry-assed PFCs are concerned, but I do work for a living. 'Gunnery Sergeant' will do perfectly well."

"Thank you, s-, uh, Gunnery Sergeant."

"That's better." He looked around. "So this is how the other half lives."

Garroway turned, his eyes following a small group of attractive and naked young women as they made their way through the crowd toward the pool. "Must be nice," he said. "I wouldn't mind having a couple of mil, if it meant living like *this*."

"Dream on," Ami Danvers told him. "You'd need a couple of *bil* for a spread like this!" Eyeing a couple of equally nude men who'd just joined the women, "Of course, I must admit that the scenery *is* very nice."

Garroway sighed dramatically. "Such a tough job, living like this, but someone has to do it." He popped a purple-iced something into his mouth and chewed reflectively. "At least they feed well."

"So, Gunnery Sergeant," Danvers said conversationally. "Now that 4102 has flown the nest, will you be taking on a new boot company?"

"Negative, Danvers. I've had it with diaper duty and babysitting. I've put in for 1MIEF."

"Maybe we'll be serving together, then," Garroway said. "Our orders are for 1MIEF, too!"

"I know," Warhurst said, nodding. "The whole company. God help me. I thought I was free of you clowns." He shrugged. "But, hey, who knows? Maybe I'll get lucky and they'll stick me on a listening post on some God-forsaken asteroid at the other end of the galaxy instead. Then at least I wouldn't have to look at the likes of you two!"

"We love you, too, Gunnery Sergeant," Danvers said. "Where do we go around here to get a drink?"

Garroway pointed to a bar at the other side of the nearest swimming pool. "They've got booze there. Or there's a bigger bar inside."

"Marines, I'm going to attach myself to you two—just temporarily—because I am using you for protective cover. Shall we perform a reconnaissance in force?"

Garroway grinned. "Yes, *sir*, Gunnery Sergeant, sir!"

Together they entered the house.

The mansion's interior was, if anything, more decadently luxurious than outside. The rooms were large and sprawling, most with soft-carpeted floors that rearranged with a thought into any size or shape or design of furniture imaginable. Most walls and ceilings were taken up by projection screens, some showing outdoor or undersea views, other showing erotic scenes with such high resolution it was possible to bump into a wall that looked like an archway into yet another bed- or playroom. Food was everywhere, available at small buffets, or straight out of niches in the walls. Many of the guests wore sensory helmets, which picked up and enhanced sights, sounds, tastes, touches, and smells according to preset programming. He noticed that most of those folks had bypassed the food, and gone straight to the caressing and sex.

One large, circular room, in fact, proved to be the source

of several of the erotica projections they'd seen on various walls. A dozen people of various sexes were grappling with one another in an impromptu orgy. The three Marines had to carefully pick their way over and past a number of thrashing bare limbs to reach the doorway on the other side.

The house wasn't entirely devoted to orgies, however. One room they passed through had been set up with sim projectors, so that people walking in saw and heard and smelled the claustrophobic bustle of the Tun Tavern late in the year 1775, with Samuel Nichols seated behind a large wooden barrel, puffing at a long-stemmed pipe as a recruiter regaled the listeners with the benefits of service with the Marines. The lines about bounty payments and a ration of grog brought amused chuckles from the twenty-ninth-century spectators . . . especially the handful of men and women in uniform.

That raised a question, though. Warhurst wondered why most of the people he was encountering were in civilian clothing, or no clothing at all. This was supposed to be a Marine function, after all.

Or were the Marines all shucking their uniforms to join in the orgies? A disquieting thought.

"So . . . Gunnery Sergeant Warhurst?" Garroway asked.

"Yeah?"

"This is the Commonwealth way of life we're supposed to be fighting for?"

"Well, you won't find it in the Theocracy or the Hegemony."

"Sure, you would," Danvers said. "They're just not as blatant about it."

"Bullshit," Garroway said.

"No, it's true. The prudes of every age in history had orgies. They just didn't admit to them."

Warhurst bent over and dragged one white-gloved finger up the curve of a naked, heaving female butt cheek. The owner didn't seem to notice the touch. He looked at the fingertip critically. "Dust. They need to field-day this barracks."

Warhurst was feeling a little giddy, and he wasn't sure why. He always felt a bit up-tight around civilians, especially in this sort of social milieu. Damn it, they just weren't *Marines.*

And that, he thought, explained the giddiness. He'd seen and recognized two of his erstwhile recruits, and the relief he'd felt had been palpable.

"Good evening, gentlemen."

They'd found the inside bar and been making their way toward it when a silver-haired man wearing a golden glow and little else greeted them. Warhurst did a fast ID check, and almost came to attention. "Senator Sloan?"

"Correct. And you are . . . Gunnery Sergeant Warhurst, and Privates Danvers and Garroway. Welcome to my home."

"It was good of you to host this party, sir."

"Not at all, not all. Least I could do. I, ah, see by your public data, you're on your way to the MIEF."

"I've requested the transfer, sir, yes. Don't know yet that they'll give it to me."

"Mm. Yes. A Marine goes where he's sent. Still, I should think that a man with your record will get that billet, especially since the MIEF is going to be rather dramatically expanded over the next few months."

"Sir?" He'd heard scuttlebutt, but nothing certain.

"General Alexander's proposal *did* pass, Gunnery Sergeant. A reinforced Marine Expeditionary Force is going to be sent into Xul space." Sloan gave Warhurst an appraising look. "What do you think about that, anyway?"

"As you say, sir. A Marine goes where he's sent."

"Yes, but . . . against the Xul? That's a tall order if I ever heard one."

"The Xul are not invincible, Senator. We've proven that several times over."

"What do you think about General Alexander?"

"I don't know the man, sir."

"Yes, but you must have an opinion."

Warhurst shrugged. "From everything I've heard, he's an excellent officer. And a good Marine."

"Good enough to take on the Xul?"

"Why are you asking me this, sir?"

"Oh, just taking advantage of an opportunity. I have several hundred Marines in my home for the day. Seemed like a good opportunity to get a feel for their morale, their caliber. Their *esprit*. How about you, Ms. Danvers? What do you think about fighting the Xul?"

"Sir! The Marines are gonna kick Xul ass. *Sir*!"

Sloan laughed. "And you, Private Garroway?"

"Doesn't much matter what *I* think, sir. It's all up to you people in the government."

"How's that?"

"Sir, the Marines will do their job, no matter what. Their job is whatever the government tells them to do."

"Yes?"

"So, the way it seems to me . . . the government just needs to make up its collective mind, if it has one, about just who the enemy is, what it wants done to him, and give the appropriate order. And we'll do the rest."

"In other words," Warhurst added, "you start it. The Marines will finish it. Sir."

Sloan looked serious for a moment, then nodded. "That, Gunnery Sergeant, is not as easy as that. But we'll do the best we can." He studied his drink. "My question for you is, though . . . the Xul are so far ahead of us in technology. Ahead of us in numbers, too, if they're really spread across the entire Galaxy, the way it appears they are. The MIEF is going to be horrifically outnumbered, outgunned, outclassed, right from the start. Do you really think you have a chance in hell of pulling this off?"

Warhurst pulled himself up straighter. "Sir. Like the private here said . . . we will kick Xul ass. Assuming, of course, that they have one."

"I sincerely hope you're right, Gunnery Sergeant," Sloan said. "I sincerely hope you're right."

11

1811.1102

UCS Samar
In transit, Alighan to Sol
1430 hrs GMT

The passage from Alighan to Sol took six weeks. For most of that time, the Marines on board the Marine assault transport *Samar* would be in cybe-hibe; four companies of Marines required a lot of consumables—air, food, water—and took up a lot of space. It was far more economical to ship them in electronic stasis, sealed inside narrow tubes and stacked ten-high in the cavernous vessel's cargo holds, the meat lockers as they were known to the men and women who traveled in them.

Escorted by the destroyer *Hecate*, the Marine transport *Samar* had departed Alighan three weeks earlier, engaging her Alcubierre Drive as soon as she was clear of the bent spacetime in the vicinity of the local star. Almost three hundred men and women were in meat-locker storage, passing the voyage in blessed unconsciousness.

For Gunnery Sergeant Charel Ramsey, however, sleep—or at least the dreamless emptiness of cybernetic hibernation that mimicked real sleep—had been deferred. He was one of seventeen Marines in the 55th Marine Regimental Aerospace Strikeforce designated as psych casualties.

And they weren't going to let him sleep until he was cured.

"We can edit the memories, you know," Karla told him gently. "That would be the easiest course for you, I think."

"Fuck that," Ramsey said. "I don't *want* to forget. . . ."

"I understand. But it's going to mean a lot of work on your part. Very difficult, even painful work."

"So what are we waiting for?" He took a deep breath. "Tell me what I'm supposed to do."

In Ramsey's mind he was in a forest in eastern North America, back on Earth—oaks, tulip trees, and maples; rhododendrons, ferns, and mountain laurel, and a fast-moving stream splashing down across tumbled piles of limestone boulders, many thickly blanketed with moss. The sky glimpsed through the leaf canopy was bright blue, with sunlight slanting through the branches at a low angle, as if in the late afternoon.

It didn't matter that the woods scene was an illusion.

Within his external reality, he knew, he was in *Samar*'s sick bay, in one of the compartments reserved for this type of treatment. Karla was the ship's psychiatric specialist AI; "Karla" was derived from Karl Jung, the name given the feminine ending because Ramsey found it easier to talk with women than with men. The AI appeared to be a handsome, middle-aged woman in a blue jumpsuit, seated on a boulder next to him. With her dark and lively eyes, black hair, and square jaw, she actually looked a bit like his mother, going back to perhaps twenty years before she'd died; he wondered if that detail was deliberate.

Probably. The Corps' psych AIs didn't miss very much.

"You can start," Karla told him, "by telling me about your relationship with Thea Howell."

"We met about a year and a half ago. She was in the 55th MARS already, Alpha Company, First Platoon . . . though she hadn't gotten promoted to staff sergeant yet, and been moved up to the platoon sergeant's billet. I was transferred in from 2/1. . . ."

He went on to tell the AI about how they'd met, how the relationship had developed. He was a bit nervous about that. Talking to a medical AI was exactly like talking to a human medical officer, and a serious breach of regulations *would* be reported.

And there *were* regulations about having sex with some-

one in your own platoon, and even stronger ones about sleeping with your leading NCO—with anyone higher or lower
on the chain of command, in fact. The fact was, though, that
everyone did it, and for the most part the powers-that-were
turned a blind eye to casual sex between fellow enlisted
Marines.

The emphasis was on the word *casual* and on the word
enlisted. If two Marines became so close that they wanted
to establish a formal contract, one was generally transferred
to a different platoon, because no Marine could be permitted to show favoritism to a sex partner over another fellow
Marine in combat. If jealousy became an issue, the Marine
with the problem would have to enter therapy, possibly to
have the possessive aspects of his or her libido adjusted.

And officers *never* slept with enlisted personnel. *That*
particular sin could lead to a general court and dismissal
from the Corps for both parties, as it had since women had
first entered the Corps in 1918. The same went for pregnancy
or sexually transmitted disease, though neither issue was the
problem it had been before the advent of medinano late in
the twenty-first century.

The fact that Ramsey had been sleeping with his platoon
sergeant for ten months might well be reported, and it could
come back to bite him. Hell, he thought, as another wave of
depression surged up from the blacker corners of his mind,
it had already bitten him. He'd damned near been incapacitated when Thea had been hit on Alighan. They never had
let him see her; her wounds were serious enough that she'd
been popped straight into cybe-hibe and loaded into a medical support capsule for medevac back to Mars.

Two months afterward, word had finally trickled back
down the chain of command to the 55th MARS, still deployed in mopping up Muzzie resistance on the planet. At
the Naval Hospital in the Arean Ring, on 3007, Staff Sergeant Thea Howell had been declared an irretrievable.

She was dead, and he hadn't even been able to tell her
goodbye.

"What was that?" Karla asked him.

"What was what?"

"You just registered an extremely strong surge of emotion while you were speaking—extremely depressive emotion. Was it thinking about Staff Sergeant Howell that triggered it?"

He sighed, leaning back on the boulder and closing his eyes. "Of course. What did you think it was? Fucking indigestion?"

"Emotion does not map linguistically . . . at least, not with one-to-one correspondence. I can easily sense the emotion within you, but the source, the triggering thought or thoughts, can be numerous and they can be subtle."

"Look, it's not complicated," he told the AI. "I was in love with Thea—with Staff Sergeant Howell, okay? She was my platoon leader, but we had a . . . a thing. We were sex partners, yeah, but we also cared for each other. A lot. We'd been—" He stopped himself. He'd felt as though once the words started flowing, he wouldn't be able to hold them back, wouldn't be able to hold back the emotion, or the memories that caused them.

"You'd been what?"

"We'd started talking about a long-term contract. Marriage." He said the words with an almost defiant edge to them.

"I see." The program paused for a moment, as though considering the best way to reply. That, Ramsey knew, was sheer nonsense. Even expert software as complex as a psych AI ran so much faster than human thought that any pause in the conversation at all would be for the program the equivalent of waiting hours before responding.

No, the hesitation, he knew, was a tool the AI was using to let him better respond to it as if it were a human.

"Charel, I know you must be concerned about telling me this. Regulations prohibit relationships of this sort, particularly when they result in harm to the Marines involved, to general productivity, good order, and discipline, and especially to the mission."

"Yeah." He thought about it. "You know, I had a buddy once, a PFC, who fell asleep while sunbathing, back on Earth. Second-degree burns over half his body. When he got out of the hospital, he got a court-martial. The charge was 'damaging government property,' meaning him."

"What happened to him?"

Ramsey shrugged. "A slap on the wrist. I think they fined him part of his pay for three months. And he got himself a new asshole drilled by his platoon sergeant."

She nodded. "Legally, Charel, Marines are not 'government property,' as you put it. But regulations do allow military personnel to be charged and punished if their actions, inattention, or irresponsibility causes them bodily or psychological harm, or causes others to be harmed.

"However, I do not foresee that to be the case in this instance. Others in your company have suffered psychological injury simply from the fact that many of you had close friends and comrades irretrievably killed on Alighan." Again, a human-sounding pause. "Five hundred eighty Marines of the 55th MARS made the combat assault on Alighan. During the assault, they suffered two hundred five casualties—and one hundred twelve of those were irretrievables. That's over nineteen point three percent killed, Charel."

He shrugged. "We knew it would be rough going in."

"For most military units throughout history, losses of anything above ten or twelve percent were considered crippling. The unit in question effectively ceased to operate as a fighting group, especially when it was a company-sized unit or smaller, where most of the personnel actually knew one another, where the losses represented friends or, at the least, acquaintances.

"In your assault on the Theocrat position on top of the building, two of the ten involved were killed. Twenty percent. And the ten of you knew one another, were close to one another, on a personal level."

"So? Allison said we'd be lucky if it was twenty-five. What's your point?"

"That everyone in your unit suffered considerable loss. You would not be human if all of you weren't grieving."

"None of the others in my squad are here, I notice," he said. "Maybe they're grieving, but they're handling it, right?"

"Each person handles grief differently. How are you handling it, Charel?"

He shrugged again. "I don't know. Mostly, I guess I'm not. I was thought-clicking stim releases off my implants for a while, to kind of keep me going, get me moving in the morning, y'know? But after a couple of weeks my software reported me."

"Yes. And for a good reason. Nanostims are not addictive physically, but it is very easy to become psychologically reliant on them. And that would reduce your usefulness to the Corps."

"Yes. Always the Corps. First, last, and always."

"You sound bitter."

"About being one tiny circuit in a very large board? A number, one among hundreds of thousands? Now, why would that make me bitter?"

"I will assume that you mean that sarcastically. You knew when you enlisted that the needs of the Corps came first, that you would surrender certain rights and privileges in order to become a Marine."

"Yes. . . ."

"That the good of the mission comes first, then the good of the Marine Corps, then that of your own unit . . . and only then can your personal good be considered."

"I know all that."

"Good." Another hesitation. "Were you aware that Lieutenant Johnson, your platoon CO, has recommended you for platoon sergeant?"

That startled him. "Shit. No. . . ."

"It's true. The decision has been deferred, pending my recommendation."

"Don't defer on my account. I don't want it."

"Why not?"

He had to think about that one for a moment. He'd wanted the slot once. He and Thea had joked frequently about him gunning for her billet, and how he would have to transfer to a different platoon to get it.

"I'm not sure," he said after a moment. Where the hell was Karla going with all of this? "I think . . ." He stopped. He didn't want to go there.

"What do you think, Charel?"

"I think I don't deserve the slot."

"Why not?"

"I screwed up. It was my idea, mounting up on Specter guns and going up the outside of the building like that. If we'd gone in another way . . . or called down sniper fire from orbit . . ."

"According to the after-action reports," Karla told him, "orbital bombardment was restricted in that sector due to the presence of civilian noncombatants. And assaulting that tower from the ground up would have resulted in unacceptably high Marine casualties. You made the correct choice, and your platoon sergeant agreed with your assessment. In what way did you 'screw up?'"

"I didn't get all the APerMs."

"There were other Marines in the area. In any case, APerMs are generally deployed in numbers sufficient to overwhelm individual suit countermeasures. In combat, remember, chaos effects tend to outweigh both planning and advance preparation. You did what you could, what you'd been trained to do, and you did it to the best of your ability. Unfortunately, two APerMs got through and killed Howell and Beck. What could you have done differently that would have resulted in a different outcome?"

"I don't know. I don't know! If I knew, I would be platoon sergeant material, okay? But I don't know, and the Corps isn't going to risk a platoon with someone who doesn't know the answers."

"I believe, Charel, that you are setting standards for yourself that are too high, and too rigid."

"They're mine to set."

"Not if in the setting you do harm to yourself. 'Government property,' remember?"

The session continued, but Ramsey listened with only half an ear, making polite noises where necessary to convince Karla that he was paying attention.

Or could the AI tell by monitoring his brain waves? Ramsey didn't know, nor did he care. The depression was settling in closer, deeper, until it threatened to smother him.

He wanted the damned AI out of his head.

USMC Skybase
Dock 27, Earth Ring 7
1015 hrs GMT

Lieutenant General Martin Alexander's concept, as so-far approved by the Commonwealth Senate, had been designated Operation Gorgon. The strategic option of a strike into Xul space to delay or block a likely Xul attack against human space by drawing them off in pursuit of a large Navy-Marine task force was a go.

Now all that remained was to come up with a viable ops plan. To that end, he'd called a general staff meeting.

"Map Center open," Lieutenant General Martin Alexander said. In his mind, the dome of the virtual briefing room shimmered, then deepened into the gently curved clottings of stars that made up one small section of the Orion Arm of the Galaxy. With a thought, he began rising into the mass of stars, focusing now on the amoebic blot of various-colored translucence marking the various regions of space claimed by Humankind. One star, just inside the outer periphery of one of the colored areas, was highlighted a bright green—Puller 659.

"Our problem," Alexander told his audience, "is primarily a political one. Puller 659 is the location of a Stargate leading to a region of Xul-controlled space designated Starwall. Intelligence says that Starwall is an important Xul nexus—and we know they have information about Earth at the base in that system. Take out Starwall, and we *might* arrange to have that information become lost again. Even if we don't, Starwall is a big enough target that we know we'll hurt the bastards if we hit them there.

"Unfortunately, the Gate leading to Starwall, as you can see here, is located inside space claimed by the PanEuropean Republic. The Commonwealth Senate is not enthusiastic about starting a war with the Republic and opening a third front, not at a time when we're already engaged with the Theocracy . . . and may be about to face a new Xul incursion as well."

His virtual audience was represented in the briefing area

by the icons of over two hundred men, women, and artificial intelligences making up 1MIEF's ops planning staff, which included intelligence, communications, and administrative staff constellations from all organizational levels.

"Our best hope against the Xul, obviously," he continued, "would be to get *all* of the human governments pulling together . . . ending the war with the Theocracy, and getting them, the PanEuropeans, the Chinese, the Hispanics, the Russians, *all* of them pulling together and pooling their space-military resources to fight the Xul.

"In my estimation, our survival as a species almost certainly will depend on the human species working together."

"Yeah, well, good luck with that," the rough voice of Vice Admiral Liam Taggart put in, and several in the audience chuckled. Taggart was Alexander's opposite number in Gorgon, the commander of 1MIEF's naval contingent.

No one else in the virtual space would have dared to interrupt Alexander's exposition.

"Thank you, Liam," Alexander replied. "Fortunately, uniting Humankind is a job for the politicians, not the military. While they're working on that, we need to consider our strategic alternatives for Gorgon, and—just as with the original gorgons of Greek myth—so far we have three.

"The first, and least desirable in my opinion, is that we wait . . . hold back and wait for the political situation to resolve itself. The advantage is that we don't have to commit ourselves at once. The downside is that we can't assume that the Xul are going to give us the luxury of waiting. Our intel from Puller 659 is solid; we know the Xul know where we are and how to get at us. We can assume they're gathering their forces for a strike as we speak. Absolutely the only unknown factor in the equation is how long we actually have.

"Second, we trespass into PanEurope space, take the whole MIEF right through the Republic, and the hell with the consequences. We *might* win Aurore's approval and support . . . but no one's betting money on that." Aurore was Theta Bootes IV, the capital of the PanEuropean Republic.

"Now, the Senate won't approve a head-on invasion . . . but they *might* allow us to pull an end run. Puller 659 is close

to the outer periphery of Republican space. We might swing
out this way . . ." As he spoke, a yellow course line moved out
through Commonwealth space from Sol, leaping from star
system to star system to enter an as-yet unexplored region
beyond the frontier, then looping back and around to come
in to the Puller system from *outside* human space. "Technically, this would still constitute an invasion of Republican
space . . . but we might be able to slip the whole MIEF into
the Puller system and out through the gate to Starwall before
the Republicans know what's going down. The downside:
if Aurore finds out and gets ticked off, the Commonwealth
might find itself at war with the Theocracy, the Xul, *and* the
Republic.

"Third." Four white pinpoints lit up within Commonwealth space. "We forget about Puller 659 and Starwall
entirely. There are a total of seventeen known Stargates,
offering a total of about two hundred known routes into
Xul systems, all of them now being actively monitored by
Marine or Navy listening posts. Four of those Gates lie
inside Commonwealth space—Sirius, of course, Mu Cygni,
Gamma Piscium, and Lambda Capricorni." Each pinpoint
on the map display brightened as he named it.

"These four gates offer us a total of twenty-nine routes
into star systems we know to be occupied by the Xul. We
select one of those twenty-nine potential paths and send the
MIEF there.

"The disadvantage of this choice is that we know the
space controlled by the Xul is unimaginably vast . . . so vast
that what happens in one part might simply not matter to the
rest of it."

At Alexander's command, the viewpoint of the watchers'
assembled minds seemed to pull back sharply. The gleaming starscape of near-Sol space dwindled into the distance,
revealing the entire sweep of the Galaxy, three milky-haze
arms wrapped tightly about a bulging, ruddy-hued central
core. In an instant, the patch of space occupied by Humankind vanished, a dust speck lost against that teeming backdrop of stars.

"For instance," Alexander continued, "if we go through

the Sirius Gate, we could strike *here* . . ." A white nova flared near a globular star cluster above the galactic plane.

"Those of you who've studied your Corps history remember the Marine incursion at a system designated Cluster Space, about five hundred years ago—a single star system in the galactic halo that possessed very large collection of multiple star gates, a kind of switching station for tens of thousands of different gate routes. That route was slammed shut when the Marines destroyed the Cluster Space end of that gatepath . . . but we've found similar systems elsewhere. This is one—designated CS-Epsilon. According to our listening post at Sirius, it possesses five separate gates in the same star system. Obviously a high-value target.

"Unfortunately, we're really in the dark as to just how important any one stargate nexus is to the Xul. Remember, they didn't build these things, so far as we've been able to determine. They just use them . . . and guard as many as they can. Like us, really, but on a *much* larger scale.

"So . . . if we hit CS-Epsilon, we don't know that the news would reach any other Xul base, or that it would make the slightest difference to them or their plans." Two hundred more stars lit up, scattered from one end of the Galaxy to the other. "Remember that we only know of about two hundred systems with a Xul presence. There may be thousands, even *hundreds* of thousands of other Xul bases. The MIEF might rampage across the Galaxy and take out every single known Xul strongpoint . . . then return to Sol in a few years and find all of the worlds of Humankind reduced to blackened cinders because nothing we did really hurt the Xul badly enough to attract their attention. If Operation Gorgon is to succeed, we *must* hit the Xul in a vital spot, hurt them so badly they send everything they have after us, and leave our worlds alone, at least for the time being.

"I'm ready to entertain any ideas any of you might have. . . ."

"Sir," Colonel Holst, of 3rd Brigade Intelligence, ventured after a long moment's silence . . .

"Go ahead."

"Sir . . . with respect, this is just flat-out impossible! How do we know if any of the systems we can reach are important enough to get the Xuls' attention if we hit it? Like you said, we could blow their bases from now until Doomsday, and they might not take any more notice of it than we would of a fleabite. How do we *know*? . . ."

"We don't, Colonel. Hell, even with a human enemy, ninety percent of intelligence work is WAG—wild-assed guesses. You probably know that better than I do. And with . . . entities like the Xul, it's a lot worse."

"We do know the Xul are xenophobic in the extreme," Major General Austin pointed out quietly. He was the CO of the MIEF's ground combat division, but he'd put in a bunch of years in Intelligence on his way up. "In fact, that appears to be their defining characteristic. Anything, any species, that poses a threat to them, even a potential threat, they take notice. The Fermi Answer, remember."

Eight hundred years before, according to legends rooted in Earth's pre-spaceflight era, a physicist named Enrico Fermi had wondered why, in a galaxy where advanced technical life *ought* to be common, and the radio emissions and other evidence of their existence *ought* to be easily detected . . . there was nothing. Humankind had appeared to be alone in the cosmos. That contradiction had become known as the Fermi Paradox.

Only gradually had the answer to that paradox revealed itself. When humans first ventured out to other worlds within their own Solar System, they'd found ample evidence of extrasolar intelligence—evidence even of the large-scale colonization of Earth, the Moon, and Mars in the remote past. Later, when they began exploring beyond the Solar System, they found the blasted, wind-blown ruins of planet-embracing cities on Chiron and elsewhere. The Fermi Answer, evidently, was that intelligence *did* evolve, and frequently, but that someone was already out there, waiting and watching for any sign of technological evolution.

In all the history of the Milky Way Galaxy, among all those hundreds of billions of stars, if even *one* species evolved with the in-born Darwinian imperative to survive by eliminating all possible competitors, and if that species

survived long enough to achieve an advanced enough technology, they would be in the perfect position to wipe out any
nascent species long before it became a serious threat.

The Fermi Answer. Humankind was alone because the
Xul had killed everyone else.

There were exceptions, of course. The An Empire had
been destroyed thousands of years before, but a few had survived on Ishtar, overlooked when they lost any technology
that might attract Xul notice—like radio. The N'mah had
survived by giving up star travel and living quietly inside
the Sirius Stargate—the strategy now known as "rats-in-
the-walls." And there might be other exceptions out there
among the stars as well.

Humankind had so far avoided destruction thanks to a
combination of luck and the fact that the Xul appeared to respond to threats in a cumbersome and unwieldy manner; the
sheer size and scope of their Galaxy-wide presence worked
against them.

But that unwieldiness now would be working against the
Marine MIEF.

"General Austin is correct," Alexander said. "Basic strategy 101: use the enemy's weaknesses against him. Xul weaknesses, at least in so far as we've been able to determine over
the past few centuries, include their xenophobia and their
glacial slowness in responding or adapting to threats. The
xenophobia makes them predictable, after a fashion. Their
slow response time gives us a chance to hit them multiple
times before they land on us with their full weight.

"But we *do* need to identify those systems that will make
them sit up and take notice if we hit them. Ideas?"

"Starwall," a major in the 55th MARS intelligence group
said after a moment. "We know it's a major Xul transport
nexus, and we know the intel they took from the *Argo* is
there. Option B, going into Republic Space and through the
Puller gate to Starwall is our best option."

And with that, the discussion was off and running, with
various members of the planning staff contributing thoughts
and suggestions, others offering objections and criticisms.
Alexander stepped back mentally, listening to the debate.

After a few moments, he assigned Cara the job of monitoring the discussion, while he focused on the far more boring topic of Expeditionary Force logistics.

Gorgon represented a God-awful mess when it came to supply. An MIEF was an enormous and sprawling organization, so intricate and complex that dozens of specialist AIs were required simply to maintain internal communications, logistics, and routine administration. It was a joint-service unit, comprised of some 52,000 Marine and Navy personnel and eighty ships. The Marine component included a full Marine division—16,000 men and women—plus a Marine Aerospace Wing and a force service support group.

Currently, 1MIEF drew on 1MarDiv for personnel and support, but ever since the Commonwealth Senate's vote to accept Alexander's operational proposal, both units had been heavily reinforced, both by drawing personnel and assets from other Marine divisions, and from newly graduating classes out of the recruit training centers, both on Mars and at Earth/Luna. When 1MIEF departed for the stars—the date of embarkation was now tentatively scheduled for mid-January, eight weeks hence—it would be fully staffed independently of 1MarDiv, which would remain in the Sol System as part of the standing defense against a possible Xul strike.

The sheer logistical complexity of Operation Gorgon meant that a small army of planners were needed to work out each detail before embarkation. Vast quantities of expendables were already being routed to the Deimos Yards over Mars—most of them in the form of water ice, methane, and ammonia, with lesser amounts of trace elements. The ice would serve both as shielding and as a water supply; nanoassemblers would pull carbon, hydrogen, oxygen, and nitrogen from the raw materials and rearrange them as needed to create air and food. Resupply during the mission would be accomplished by mining outer-system worlds and asteroids each time they entered another star system. The supply lines back to Sol would be too long and tenuous to permit cargo ships to keep the fleet supplied.

But even if the MIEF was able to "live off the land,"

as some wag had put it already—meaning picking up all necessary elements in other star systems for reassembly as needed—the Expeditionary Fleet needed to have robot miners and transports enough to collect the raw materials, storage tankers to hold them, and mobile processing plants to convert and distribute the finished consumables. Besides that, there were critical decisions to be made concerning mechanical spares and replacement parts, especially for complex electronic components that couldn't be batch grown in the fleet's repair ships.

And there were the weapons, the Mark 660 battlesuits, the ammunition, the power cores and converters . . . the list seemed endless, the storage space for it all sharply limited. Alexander and his planning staff were still hard at work determining if the thing was even possible. It wasn't enough simply to add an extra few AKs, ANs, and AEs to the fleet roster, because each of those vessels—cargo ships, nanufactory transports, and ammunition ships—in turn needed their own small mountains of spare parts and extra equipment.

Where 1MIEF was going was a long, long way out into the dark, and resupply was going to be a bitch. The situation was made even tougher by the fact that Alexander couldn't even begin to guess how long 1MIEF would be deployed starside.

"No!" a voice in his mind called, rising above the others. "You young rock! We do that and we leave our lines of retreat wide open and vulnerable! Doing that would be tantamount to suicide!"

Judging from the acrimony of the debate going on within the staff planning group, it might be a while before the MIEF could depart in the first place. *Rock* was an old, old Corps epithet for a particularly dumb Marine—as in "dumb as a rock."

"With respect . . . *sir*," another voice came back, biting. "How the hell are we going to maintain our lines of retreat across twenty thousand light-years? The EF will be cut off as soon as it goes through the first Gate!"

"People!" Alexander cut in. "Let's keep it civil." A webwork of varicolored lines and brightly lit stars now stretched across the Galaxy map, showing alternate routes and objectives, known Stargate links, and known Xul bases. Cara had been tagging and color-coding each idea as it was presented, attaching to each lists of pros and cons.

As Alexander looked at the tangle, a new surety began to make itself felt. Leadership styles differed, of course, from officer to officer, and since the beginning of his career Alexander had tried to be democratic in his approach, soliciting the ideas and opinions of his subordinates and giving each due consideration.

But in the final analyses, the Marine Corps was not a democracy, any more than was the chain of command on board a Navy warship. One voice was needed to give the orders; one mind was required to make the necessary decisions.

He wanted their input, but ultimately, this decision was his, and his alone.

"Okay, people," he said, speaking into the hard, new silence. "It's clear that what we lack more than anything else is decent intel. We need to identify, and quickly, the best way to hit the Xul, and to hit them *hard*, hard enough to draw their interest away from human space.

"To that end, I'm authorizing increased surveillance on known Xul bases, with an emphasis on astrogational mapping. We need to know where these bases are relative to one another, and how they interconnect."

"Sir," General Austin asked. "Does that include Stargates outside the Commonwealth?"

"You're damned straight it does. Keep the ops black. We don't need any more political problems, here. I'll get the authorization we need. Okay?"

"Yes, sir."

"Good. I am also authorizing an AI search of all known astronomical databases. I want to compile every bit of data possible that might reveal unexpected or unknown links between known Stargates and known areas of deep space." He thought a moment, then added, "Include in that search any deep space anomalies or unexplained phenomena that might indicate a Xul presence or interest." A number of agencies kept track of such data, he knew, though he wasn't sure if anyone ever actually *used* it.

But the data were there, and AI agents could find it, compile it, and present it to the ops planning team. Reports of gamma or x-ray ray bursts, for example, from a particular star system might indicate a normal and natural process—stellar material from a companion star falling onto the surface of a neutron star, for example—or it could indicate the presence of a Xul fleet.

"So far as ops planning goes, we need to pick *one* mode of approach and focus on that. So here's what we're going to do. . . ."

12

UCS Samar
In transit, Alighan to Sol
0730 hrs GMT

The transport was two weeks out from Sol. For the past four weeks, Ramsey's sessions with Karla had continued, with hours out of each ship's day passing in virtual conversations with the AI in a variety of imagined "safe" environs.

Slowly, he was coming to grips with his ghosts.

It hadn't been easy.

"I don't know how the Navy pukes stand it, man," Staff Sergeant Shari Colver told him. "The boredom would drive me straight out the nearest airlock ricky-tick."

"Hey, that's why they spend most of their time in cybe-hybe," Ramsey said with a shrug.

They were sitting in the ship's lounge, a small and Spartan compartment that combined rec hall with mess deck and was normally reserved for the use of the shipboard in-transit watch. The domed overhead showed a backdrop of stars; if one studied the star patterns closely enough, individual stars appeared to move from hour to hour—the nearest ones, at any rate . . . but the effect was a lie, an illusion generated by the *Samar*'s navigational AI.

The fact of the matter was that it was impossible to see outside of a starship traveling within an Alcubierre spacetime bubble.

In 1994, a physicist named Miguel Alcubierre had first laid the groundwork for the space drive that later bore his name, when his equations demonstrated that—in theory, at least—a wave of distorted spacetime, expanding behind and contracting ahead, could carry a spacecraft along at faster-than-light speeds. No basic physics were violated in the movement; Einstein's prohibitions against FTL had been directed at mass and energy, *not* at the fabric of space itself, and, in fact, it was eventually determined that the entire universe had naturally expanded faster than the speed of light in the opening moments of its own birth. A ship in the warp of the Alcubierre Metric might slip quietly across flat spacetime at the rate of nine light-years per day, but since it was motionless relative to the encapsulated spacetime immediately around it, it avoided completely such inconvenient effects as acceleration, relativistic mass increase, or time dilation.

But by the nature of the space-bending field around it, a vessel under Alcubierre Drive, also was effectively cut off from the universe outside. There were no navigational vid views outside the hull for the simple reason that there was nothing to see out there save the enveloping black. Encased within a bubble of severely distorted space and time, *Samar* and her passengers remained completely deaf and blind to their surroundings, and the slow-drifting stars electronically painted on the lounge overhead represented the navigational AI's best guess as to what *should* be visible outside. It was, in fact, little more than an elaborate planetarium display.

But even the display of an educated guess was essentially boring, the patterns of stars changing so slowly the novelty wore off after a very few hours.

Still, Ramsey and the other waking psych-wounded on board tended to spend a lot of their off-hours here. The cool, K0 star circled by Alighan was located in the constellation Ophiuchus, as seen from Sol, and after the first three weeks or so, star patterns in the sky opposite Ophiuchus, ahead of the *Samar*, had begun to drift into recognizable constellations, albeit shrunken and distorted. Day by day, those constellations opposite Ophiuchus in Earth's sky, including the easily recognizable sprawl of Orion with the prominent three-in-a-row suns of his belt, became more and more evident.

Ramsey and Colver were sitting in one of the double lounge recliners, a side-by-side seat that let them watch the stars. They'd been watching Orion, and wondering if Sol was visible yet somewhere within that dusting of stars ahead.

No wonder, Ramsey thought, passengers and crew alike in A.D. ships spent the passage in cybe-hibe, save for a small, rotating watch. The planetarium display did little but emphasize just how tiny *Samar* was within a very large galaxy. That sort of thing could wear unpleasantly on the healthiest of minds.

"Did you ever wonder," Colver asked him after a long while, "why we're doing our therapy time shipboard? Why didn't they just pack us away with everyone else, and start unscrambling our brains once we get home?"

Ramsey looked around. Three Navy enlisted ratings were playing cards at a table on the other side of the compartment. They didn't appear to be listening to the two Marines, though the space was small enough that they could have, had they wanted.

"I never thought about it, no," Ramsey replied. "I mean, they have the psych AI resident in the ship's Net, so it's there and available. They'd need it for ship's crew, just because the isolation *could* drive people off the deep end. So, as long as the software's there anyway . . ." He shrugged. "Why, is it important?"

"I dunno. I've just been in the Corps long enough to know they do everything for a reason, even if that reason doesn't make a whole lot of sense up front. I was just wondering if they do it in-transit because we *are* so isolated out here. No distractions. Nothing to do but count the days until we get home."

Ramsey managed a chuckle. "Well, hell. I can just imagine Karla trying to talk to me back at the Ring, and all I want to do is put on my civvies and hit the airlock. The Arean Ring is pretty good for liberty."

"You call it Karla?" she asked. "Mine is Karl. For Karl Jung."

"Yeah. Depends on whether the patient relates better to men or women. You know, another possible reason for shrinking us out here . . . they can control what they put in our heads."

"How do you mean?"

"Think about it. Out here, it's just us and our . . . our memories, right?"

She nodded. Ramsey didn't know exactly what had happened to Colver on Alighan, but it was probably one of a relatively few but common problems. Stress shock—what once had been called post-traumatic stress syndrome—or survivor guilt or anxiety attacks or, like Ramsey, she'd lost someone important to her and was dealing now with the depression. Whatever it was, he could see echoes of grief, fear, and sadness in her eyes.

He wondered if his own eyes betrayed his inner demons that clearly.

"Well," he went on, "if we were back on the Ring—unless they quarantine us all—we'd be going out on liberty and visiting family, getting drunk, getting simmed—"

"Getting laid," she put in.

"Sure, that, too. We'd probably get ten kinds of advice from family and friends back there, all about how to put all the bad memories away, get over it, forget about it, and move on, y'know?"

"And what they're telling us here, Karl and Karla, I mean, is that we have to look at the memories. Deal with them."

"Yeah. Something like that. Unless we let them mem-wipe us, we've got to deal with our shit. We can delay it, we can play all kinds of games, we can pretend it never happened, but, sooner or later, we've got to face it."

"You sound like Karl." She smiled.

"I wonder why?"

"So you think they don't want us contaminating our minds with input from our families?"

"Yeah."

"Okay, but they let *us* talk together. They don't have us isolated from all human contact. They even have the group sessions, where all of us get together and talk."

"True. But then . . . we're all in the same boat, literally, right? Same general experiences. Same problems. And Karla, Karl, I mean, is there to facilitate." He thought about it a moment. "It's kind of like being in the Corps. We're *all* Marines. Family, y'know?"

"The Green Family."

"Yeah. Semper fi. . . ."

Green Family was a term out of the days before FTL, when Marines deployed starside might be gone for decades, objective. Over the course of the past eight centuries, the Marine Corps had been strongly shaped in certain key ways by the physics of interstellar travel.

Back at the dawn of Humankind's migration into space, all that had been known for sure about faster-than-light travel was that it was impossible. Einstein and relativity had convincingly demonstrated that converting all of the mass in the universe into energy would not be enough to accelerate a single atom to the speed of light, much less pass it. If humans wanted to travel to the stars, they would have to settle for decades-long voyages in cybernetic hibernation, on board ships that approached, but could never actually reach, the magic velocity of c. Relativistic time dilation slowed the passage of subjective time, but the fundamental way in which the universe was put together forbade the FTL warp drives of the popular fiction of the time.

As a result, Marines deployed to the worlds of other stars would return to a culture that had changed dramatically during the intervening decades. Time dilation meant that the Marines might have aged five or six years, subjective, while twenty or thirty years objective had passed on Earth. The resultant temporal isolation had guaranteed that large numbers of Marines simply couldn't fit in with the civilians they were sworn to protect; while they were out-system, most of the cultural markers they'd known and grown up with had changed. Music, language, fashion, art, politics, technology, everything that connected them with others had transformed, while the people they'd left behind were dead or changed by age.

More and more, Marines had relied on the Corps as family. A Marine might return from the stars and find that Marines back on Earth possessed a different cultural background, true, but they were still Marines. Somehow, the similarities always outweighed the differences.

Eventually, of course, Einstein was proved to be a special case within the broader scope of quantum physics, just as Newton had been a special case within the mathematics of relativity. The Stargates had demonstrated that it was possible to bypass enormous gulfs of interstellar space. Encounters with the Xul proved that FTL travel was possible without the Gates, though for centuries no one could figure out how they did it.

What no one had ever imagined was that, when the problem was finally cracked, there would be not one solution, but *many*. It was still not known how the Xul hunterships bypassed light, but humans now possessed not one but *two* non-Gate modes of FTL travel of their own—the Alcubierre Drive and the much more recent paraspace phase-shift transitions, or PPST, used by large structures such as the Corps' Skybase. And there were suggestions within the wilderness of theoretical physics that promised other modes of FTL travel as well.

Neither the Alcubierre Drive nor PPST involved acceleration, and, therefore, time dilation didn't enter into the equation. Voyages between the stars now required weeks or months rather than decades. It was with some surprise, then, that Marine psychologists noted that Marines, enlisted Marines, especially, still failed to connect with the cultures from which they'd emerged.

There were some who joked that Marines weren't human to begin with, but the problem was becoming worse and needed to be addressed. The Marines possessed their own culture, their own societal structure, language, calendar and timekeeping system, heroes, economy, history, goals, and concerns.

Most Marines would have pointed out that this had *always* been the case, going at *least* as far back as the global wars of the twentieth and twenty-first centuries. The psychs didn't need to invoke star travel to suggest that Marines were different . . . or that most of them gloried in the difference.

As an ancient Corps aphorism had it, there are only two kinds of people: Marines, and everyone else.

Ramsey leaned back in his chair, watching the almost imperceptible drift of the nearest stars on the overhead. Thea's death still burned in his gut, hot, sullen, and he still tended to flinch when he let his mind slip back to the final moments of the firefight on the skyscraper roof, to the sight of her battlesuit torn open and bloody as he cradled her, as he watched her consciousness slip away. He didn't know if he could ever *heal.* . . .

Awkwardly, he lifted his arm and placed it along the back of the reclining seat, behind Colver's head. She moved a little closer to him, her leg touching his, and he let his arm drape over her shoulders. They continued to watch the illusion of stars.

Whatever happened, he knew he had family—the Green Family—and, for the moment, at least, that was enough.

PanEuropean Military Hospital Facility
1530/31:05 hours, local time

"Lieutenant?" a woman's voice said in her head. "Lieutenant Lee? Can you hear me?"

Lieutenant Tera Lee opened her eyes—then squeezed them tight once more as the blast of light speared its way into her skull. "Where the hell am I?"

"You're in the medical facility at Port-de-Paix."

"Where . . . where is that? . . ."

"You're at Aurore. Perhaps you know it as Theta Bootes IV? Actually, we're on Aurore's inner moon. We brought you here from the star system you call Puller."

The words were spoken within Lee's mind, coming through her cranial implants, and that fact alone was . . . disturbing.

Aurore, Lieutenant Lee knew, was deep in the heart of the PanEuropean Republic, the fourth planet circling a hot, F7 V star some 48 light-years from Sol, a world of broad oceans, rugged mountains, stunning auroral displays from which it took its name, and a trio of large moons. At least, that's how it was described on the *Worlds of Humankind* database she'd studied back in the Naval Academy.

It was also the capital of the Republic . . . and what the hell was she doing here when her last memories were of being adrift at Starwall, umpteen thousands of light-years from the listening post at Puller 659?

"How . . . long? . . ." Her lips were cracked and dry, and her throat was sore. She was aware of terrible pain, but at a distance, held at bay, she imagined, by whatever anodynano-meds they'd given her.

"Please don't try to talk," the woman's voice said. "I'm using your implant channels to communicate with you directly. If you focus your words in your mind, I will hear you."

The security implications of that were ominous. How had the PEs gotten hold of her personal comchannels?

For that matter, what the hell was she doing at the PE capital in the first place?

"How long have you been here?" the voice in her head continued. "You were brought on board the *Sagitta*, one of our light cruisers, on the third of November. That was about three weeks ago. You arrived at the Theta Bootes system yesterday. You've been in deep cybernetic hibernation since your . . . exposure to radiation somewhere beyond the Puller Stargate.

"You were very, very badly burned. I'm told your condition was beyond the scope of the small base where you were stationed. If our task force had not arrived when it did, if your commanding officer had not chosen to communicate with us, your condition would have deteriorated to the point where you would have been an irretrievable."

Major Tomanaga had called in the Europeans? That didn't sound right.

"Who are you?" Lee asked. "And why the hell should I want to talk to you?"

"I am Monique Sainte-Jean. You may think of me as your . . . your therapist. You have been unconscious for a very long time, and we want to be sure you awake with your mind, memories, and personality intact, *non*?"

Alarm bells were figuratively ringing in Lee's mind, now. As a rule, she'd paid scant attention to interstellar politics, but she *had* been thoroughly briefed before her deployment to the Puller star system. The Puller system, she knew, was uninhabited and of zero importance to anyone, with the single exception of the Puller Gate.

The Gate's connections had been explored in the half-dozen years following its discovery, some three decades earlier. A total of twelve established gatepaths had been uncovered there, one of them the route to the large Xul base at Starwall.

The problem with the stargates was that the multiple paths to other stars they provided never seemed to go to anyplace known or useful. All appeared to open at gates circling other stars scattered across the Galaxy, from the outer halo to the Galactic Core itself, but until more was known about those possible destinations—and whether or not entering them would alert the Xul to Humankind's presence—it had been decided to avoid using them entirely.

Ever since the discovery of the very first gate at Sirius, astronomers, cosmologists, and physicists from every human starfaring government had been clamoring for the chance to use the Gates as research tools—opportunities to explore close-up such cosmic wonders and enigmas as black holes, neutron stars, the large-scale structure of the entire Galaxy, and the weird zoo of mysterious phenomena ticking away at the Galaxy's heart. Since a significant number of those paths—two-hundred or so—led to Xul-occupied systems, and since the Xul appeared to use the far-flung network of Gate connections for their own long-range movement through the Galaxy, the various interstellar governments had agreed at the Treaty of Chiron in 2490 not to permit any human movement through the gates for any reason, without the fully informed consent of *all* starfaring governments.

And that was why the Puller Listening Post, and all of the others like it, were illegal, at least within the often murky arena of international treaty law. Under the auspices of the

DCI², the Department of Commonwealth Interstellar Intelligence, the Marines had been tapped to build and operate the system of listening posts . . . and as part of that operation, they routinely sent robotic probes and even—upon occasion and when necessary—manned surveillance spacecraft to keep an eye on the various identified Xul bases.

"My therapist, huh?" Lee replied. "Since when is the *Direction Général* interested in the emotional health of junior Marine officers?"

The DGSE—*Direction Général de la Sécurité Extraterrestrial*—was the Franco-PanEuropean counterpart to the DCI². It was a guess on Lee's part, but Ste.-Jean had to be either military or Federal-Republic civilian intelligence, and the DGSE was the largest and best funded of all of the Republic's intelligence organizations.

The long silence that followed her jab suggested that she'd been on-target, or close to it. She might be consulting with her superiors on a different channel, or with a military intelligence AI.

"Very well," Ste.-Jean said after a moment. "Perhaps we should play this in a more, ah, straightforward fashion. As it happens, I am DST, not DGSE, but it was a good guess on your part."

The DST was the *Direction de la Surveillance du Territoire*, a kind of civil police intelligence unit tasked with keeping tabs on people, organizations, and traffic within French territory that could pose a threat to the government. Other Terran nationalities within the PanEuropean Republic had their own intelligence organizations, the Germans and British especially, but the French held the lion's share of planetary colonies within the Republic, and they claimed the Puller system as their own, even if the place wasn't populated.

"Yeah, well," Lee said in her mind. "I don't think I have anything to say to you."

"Not even in exchange for our medical assistance?" Ste.-Jean said. "Look. I will be honest with you. We know all about your observation post at the Puller gas giant. And we know that you went through the stargate in that system to investigate a Xul base. Your government, it seems, has much to answer for . . . beginning with the arrogant breaking of solemn interstellar treaty, and with placing the security, even the very survival of *all* human worlds at grave risk. *You* needn't worry, Lieutenant. We have brought no charges against you . . . at least, not yet. We recognize that you were simply doing what your superiors told you to do . . . and were caught in the middle, yes?"

"If you say so."

"However, we do require your cooperation. We want to know exactly what you saw and experienced on the other side of the gate. And we want your cooperation in identifying Marine installations that we suspect are imbedded within other Stargate systems in sovereign *PanRépublique* space."

"Go fuck yourself."

That response elicited another long silence.

Lee managed to open her eyes, and this time she could keep them open. She was lying in what obviously was a hospital bed, her body completely enclosed in a plastic sheath that left only her face exposed. Unable to move, she couldn't see much of the room, but it appeared to be sterile, white, and lacking in any amenities whatsoever. She couldn't even see a door.

Presumably, they had her body hooked up with tubes for feeding, for medication, and for waste removal, though she couldn't feel much of anything from her neck down save for that general, far-off-in-the-background sense of pain. Presumably, too, her bloodstream was now crawling with nano-agents—microscopic devices programmed to busily swarm through her circulatory system and repair the damage caused by her exposure to the Galactic Core's radiation fields, but they might be programmed for other things as well.

The big question of the moment was how they'd managed to tap into her private internal communications channel. If they could manage that, then theoretically they should be able to download her entire on-board memory. They wouldn't need to ask her questions or elicit her cooperation; all they'd need to do was pull a full memory dump.

Okay, girl, she thought. *Think it through. But keep it low-channel, in case they're listening in . . .*

If they hadn't pulled a memory dump, then they *didn't* have access to her cerebral link hardware. Tentatively, she tried to connect with Terry, her personal software EA, but the AI resident in her hardware remained silent. She tried again, searching for Chesty or any of his iterations. Again, nothing.

Okay, that suggested they'd deliberately disabled Terry . . . or that he'd been fried by the Core radiation. Chesty was too large a program to reside within her personal hardware, so he might be off-line because of range. Had her cereblink been damaged on the other side of the Gate?

She ran a fast diagnostic, ignoring the fact that her captors—she thought of them in those terms, now—would be able to monitor what she was doing. There was damage, but her hardware appeared to be more or less complete. The software was running at about forty percent efficiency.

Her personal software might have been taken off-line in order to facilitate her treatment. More likely, her captors had tried to access the software directly while she was unconscious, and either botched it, or caused some physical damage in the retrieval process. If the former, questioning her would be the only alternative they had in order to get the information they wanted. If the latter, they might have a partial memory dump already in-hand, and simply wanted to confirm what they had, or to fill in some missing blanks.

Either way, Lee was in no mood to be helpful.

"That is . . . unfortunate," the woman's voice said, and Lee cursed to herself. Apparently, the PEs had managed to establish quite a deep communications link through her implants, enabling them to read most of her surface thoughts. If Terry or Chesty had been operational, they would have been able to block the intruding channel; hell, Terry would have not only been able to block the intrusion, he'd have been able to impersonate Lee so closely over an electronic net that her interrogators would never have been able to tell the difference. That, after all, was what personal AI secretaries did, among other things.

"We have quite a few different means of getting the information we want," the woman's voice went on, relentless. "And we will have it. If you choose to voluntarily cooperate, you will be permitted to return to your people within a few weeks, at most.

"If you refuse, the alternatives could be . . . distressful. Just think about it. We could vivisect you very slowly, peeling away your skin, your muscles, your tissue bit by bit, and with enough control of your nervous system that you would not be able to lose consciousness at any point in the procedure. And throughout it all, you would never know if what was happening was a virtual simulation being played into your brain . . . or a horrible and very bloody reality. That is the nature of direct mental feeds, you know. *You have no way of knowing what is simulated, and what is real.*

"The trouble is, such techniques also violate interstellar treaty, as you know well. Sooner or later you would break and beg us to let you tell us what we wanted to know . . . but either way, whether we'd tortured you only in your mind or actually cut your body to pieces, we could never allow you to return to your own people. Even a total mindwipe would not remove all of the emotional scarring from such torture.

"Or . . . consider this. We could fashion for you an elaborate simulated fantasy . . . one involving you being rescued by your comrades. You would be freed, be taken back to Earth, and there you would undergo a perfectly natural debriefing by your superiors. Again, how could you tell if what you experienced was real, or a simulation downloaded into your brain?

"And there are other alternatives as well. We have medinano that could suppress your own will and hijack your implants. We could rape your mind and your memory, take from you what we want by force. Unfortunately, I very much doubt that Lieutenant Tera Lee would have much of a personality left when we were done. And, again, that entity, that living shell, could not be permitted to return to Earth, ever. I imagine that shooting it would be a mercy.

"So, think about it, my dear. Imagine the possibilities. Cooperate voluntarily and you will see your home and family again. We might even see our way clear to recompense you generously. The alternatives, you must agree, are far more . . . unpleasant."

And then Lee was alone in the hospital room, alone with her thoughts, and her fears.

Where were Major Tomanaga and the rest of the Marines stationed at Puller? Where was Fitzie?

And there was something else, something her interrogator had omitted . . . and it was suddenly vitally important that Lieutenant Lee *not* think about it, given that they might well be monitoring her thoughts. . . .

13

USMC Skybase
Dock 27, Earth Ring 7
0950 hrs GMT

"General?" Cara said within his mind. "I think the AI search has found something."

Lieutenant General Martin Alexander had been seated at his office desk, going over an unsettling report from Intelligence. A Marine—specifically, the Marine who'd gone through the Puller Stargate and discovered that the Xul at Starwall knew of Humankind's recent activities—was missing.

Worse, it seemed likely that the PanEuropeans were behind the disappearance.

But Cara would not have interrupted his work if this hadn't been something important. The MIEF staff constellations had been hard at it for almost a week, now. Six days ago, at the ops planning session, he'd given them the outlines of what he wanted, but they still had to churn out the hard data. Actually, he'd not expected any real progress for another week or two yet, so complex was this strategic problem.

"Okay," he said, leaning back in his chair. "Whatcha got?"

"You requested an AI search of astronomical databases, specifically seeking information that might reveal unexpected or unknown links between known Stargates and known areas of deep space."

"Yes."

The worst problem the planning team faced at the moment was the lack of hard data on stargates and exactly how they interconnected across the Galaxy. Several ongoing database studies were being carried out by astronomical institutes on dozens of worlds, both in the Commonwealth and elsewhere. Alexander had hoped that the staff planning constellations might be able to mine data from those studies, acquiring a better understanding of just how the various stargates were linked together.

"You also requested," Cara went on, "a list of anomalies associated with areas we researched . . . anomalies that might indicate Xul presence or interest."

"Yes. What did you come up with?"

"The Aquila Anomaly. The information is very old . . . pre-spaceflight, in fact."

"I've never heard of it."

"The name is relatively recent. The information, however, was first gleaned from an astronomical compilation known as the Norton Star Atlas before such information was even available on electronic media. While we can't be certain at this point in the research, the anomaly is significant enough that we felt it necessary to bring it to human attention."

"Show me."

A window opened in his mind, opening on to a view of deep space, scattered with stars—one bright star, five or six somewhat dimmer stars, and a background scattering of stardust.

"This is the constellation of Aquila, as seen from Earth," Cara told him.

"The Eagle," Alexander said, nodding. He hadn't recognized the pattern of stars when it first appeared, but he knew the name.

Lines appeared in the window connecting the brighter stars—a parallelogram above, a triangle below, both slanting off to the right. With *great* imagination, an observer might imagine a bird of prey, wings raised in flight.

"As with all constellation groupings," Cara told him, "the identification with a person, animal, or object is problematical, at least from the AI perspective. But an eagle is the historical designation, yes."

"Beauty, and eagles, are in the eye of the beholder," Alexander quipped. "That bright star is Altair—Alpha Aquilae." It was, he knew, a shade over sixteen and a half light-years from Earth, and was one of the nearest outposts of the PanEuropean Republic. Commonwealth military planners had been working on contingency plans focused on how to fight a war with the Republic if things came to that unpleasant juncture. If the Commonwealth went to war with the PanEuropeans, getting past Altair would be their first big strategic requirement.

Cara ignored his sally—AIs had trouble understanding certain concepts, like "beauty"—and continued. "You are aware of the astronomical phenomenon of novae," the AI said.

"Of course. Stars that explode—become much, much brighter in a short period of time. They're not as violent as supernovae, of course, but they're violent enough to cook any planets they might have. A handful are reported every year. Most aren't naked-eye visible, but there have been a few bright ones."

"Correct. Most novae appear to occur in close-double star systems, where material from one star is falling into the other. At least, that is the conventional theory, which seems to hold for a majority of the novae studied so far. And, as you say, novae are observed and recorded every year. My AI colleagues went through all such lists, among many others, in pursuance of your authorization for a data search on 1811, six days ago."

"What did you find?"

"An intriguing fact. During a single thirty-seven-year period in the early twentieth century, a total of twenty bright novae—exploding stars—were observed from Earth."

"Go on."

"Five of those twenty novae occurred within the arbitrary boundaries of the constellation Aquila."

It took a few seconds for the import to sink in. "My God—"

"Twenty-five percent of all observed and recorded novae, in other words, occurred within *point* two-five percent of the entire sky. This, we feel, is statistically important.

"One of these novae," Cara went on, as a bright, new star appeared on the skymap just to the west of Altair, "was Nova Aquila. It appeared in the year 1918, and was the brightest nova ever recorded until Nova Carina, almost six centuries later. Two of the other novae appeared in the same year—1936—here, and here." Two more bright stars appeared as Cara spoke, followed a moment later by two more. "And the last two, here in 1899, and here in 1937."

"Five novae, though," Alexander said slowly. He didn't want to jump to unreasonable conclusions. "That's still too small a number to be statistically significant."

"It *could* be a random statistical clustering, true," Cara told him. "Statistical anomalies do occur. But the extremely small area of sky involved—one quarter of one percent—seems to argue strongly against coincidence as a factor. And there is this, as well, a datum not available to twentieth-century cosmologists."

The group of stars showing in Alexander's mind rotated. The geometric figures of parallelogram and triangle shifted and distorted, some lines becoming much longer, others growing shorter.

A constellation was purely a convenience for Earth-based observers, a means of grouping and identifying stars in the night sky that had nothing to do with their actual locations in space. With a very few exceptions, stars that appeared to be close by one another in Earth's sky—all members of the same constellation, in other words—*appeared* to be neighbors only because they happened to lie along the same line of sight. That was the fatal flaw in the ancient pseudoscience of astrology; one might as well say that a building on a distant hill, or the sun rising behind it, were physically connected to a house three meters away—or to one's own hand—simply because they all appeared from a certain viewpoint to overlap.

Rotating the volume of space that included Aquila demonstrated this fact clearly. On a 2D map, the stars of Aquila

appeared close together—the three brightest, Altair, Alshain, and Tarazed, for example, lay almost directly side by
side in a short, straight line. Viewed from the side, however,
Altair—Alpha Aquilae—was only 16.6 light-years from
Earth, while Alshain, Beta Aquilae, was 46.6 light-years
distant. Both, in fact, were quite close to Sol as galactic distances went. Gamma Aquilae, however, the third brightest
star in the constellation and better known as Tarazed, was
330 light-years from Earth. Epsilon was 220 light-years distant; a few others were *extremely* distant; Eta Aquilae, for
instance, was 1,600 light-years away, while dim Nu Aquilae,
so distant it vanished off the window to the left when the
display rotated, was actually a type F2 Ib supergiant 2,300
light-years distant.

The novae could be expected to show a similar range of
distances, but this, Alexander saw, was not the case. They
were clustered; Nova Aquila was about 1,200 light-years
from Earth. The other four were all positioned at roughly
the same distance, though they were spread across the constellation like a sheet, defining a flat region of space roughly
fifty light-years deep and perhaps 200 to 300 light-years
wide, some 800 light-years beyond the borders of human-
colonized space.

Alexander felt a stirring of awe as he examined the 3D
rotation. "Just when did these novae actually light off?" he
asked.

"That represents a second anomaly," Cara told him. "The
light from all five novae arrived at Earth within that single
thirty-eight-year period between 1899 and 1937. Again, that
might have been coincidence, but, as you see, they actually
are located in relatively close proximity to one another. All
of them, we estimate, exploded within a few years of one
another, right around the year 700 c.e."

In the year 700, Alexander knew, Byzantines and Franks
had been battling it out with the Arabs for control of the
Mediterranean world on Earth, and the most startling advance in military technology was the stirrup. Twelve hundred light-years away, meanwhile, *someone* had been
blowing up suns.

Random statistical anomalies happened, yes . . . but as Alexander studied the 3D constellation map, rotating it back and forth for a better feel of the thing's volume and the relationship of the stars within it, he was dead certain that something more than chance was at work here.

"If this is . . . artificial," he told Cara, "if this is *deliberate* . . ."

"We estimate a probability in excess of sixty percent that this clustering of novae is the direct result of intelligent action."

"Intelligent action." Alexander snorted. "Funny term for something on this scale."

"We know of several sapient species with technologies sufficiently high to effect engineering on such a scale," Cara told him. "The Builders, the Xul . . . and possibly the N'mah of several thousand years ago, though they would not be capable of such activities now. The artificial detonation of a star is certainly feasible, given what we know of the three species."

"I wasn't questioning that," Alexander said. "It's just, well, I see three possibilities here, assuming that those novae were artificially generated. One, of course, is that the star-destroyers were the Xul."

"Possibly. We have no evidence that they have blown up stars in the past."

"No. I agree, it's just not their style." The Xul's usual *modus operandi* was to pound a target planet with high-velocity asteroids, quite literally bombing the inhabitants back into the Stone Age . . . or into extinction. "But the Xul have been around for at least half a million years, now, and if anyone has the technology to blow up a star, they should."

"Agreed. What are your other two possibilities?"

"One, and the most intriguing one, I think, is the possibility that *another* technic species was detonating stars out there in Aquila over two thousand years ago."

"That is the possibility that we noted when we uncovered this data," Cara said. "Another high-technic species fighting a war to the death with the Xul. If we could make contact with such a species, ally with them, it might mean the difference between survival and extinction for Humankind. I do not see a third alternative, however."

"It's possible that what happened in Aquila had nothing to do with the Xul," Alexander told the AI. "It was a civilization busy destroying itself. It might even have been an accident."

"What kind of *accident* could—"

"An industrial accident on a colossal scale. Or an engineering accident . . . an attempt to manipulate whole stars gone terribly wrong?"

"I have no data that will permit me to evaluate these ideas."

"Of course you don't. We're not used to thinking about engineering on an interstellar . . . on a *galactic* scale. But it is a possibility."

"Perhaps the data was not as useful as we first believed," Cara told him. The AI sounded almost crestfallen, and Alexander smiled. Artificial intelligences were superhumanly fast and possessed a range and scope and depth of knowledge that far surpassed anything humans were capable of, even with the most sophisticated cybernetic implant technology. Where they had trouble matching their human counterparts was in creativity and in imagination. Being able to imagine a cosmic engineering project on a scale that could annihilate stars was for the most part still beyond their operational parameters.

"No, Cara," he told the AI. "The data are *tremendously* useful. This is exactly what we're looking for . . . a focus, a direction in which we can work." He thought for a moment. "The question is how to get out there. It's a long way."

"Which brings up the second bit of information our research has uncovered. Look at this." The image changed, showing what appeared to be a photograph of open space. A number of stars were visible, but one in particular stood out—a dazzling, white beacon. "That is the star Eta Aquilae," Cara told him. "A star's spectrum is unique, as unique as human fingerprints. There is no doubt as to the star's identity."

"Right. You just pointed that one out on the constellation image."

"Actually, this image is in our files from one of our early Gate explorations. Our probes moved through a particular Gate pathway, took a series of photographs for later analyses, and returned."

"Ah! And which Gate? . . ."

"As it happens . . . Puller 659."

"God. . . ."

"This pathway appears to open into a star system four hundred light-years from Eta Aquilae."

"Four hundred . . . Then, the other end might be close to the area of novae?"

"A distinct possibility. Further, there did not appear to be a Xul presence there. For that reason, we have not been monitoring that path, but the original photographs were still on file."

"Out*stand*ing," Alexander said with feeling. He was seeing all kinds of possibilities here.

"You concur that an expedition to this region of space might allow us to contact another technic species, one sufficiently powerful enough to help us withstand the Xul?"

"Yes, although we seem to be back to needing to enter Republic space. Again . . . we have several possibilities in front of us."

"Perhaps you should list them," Cara said. "I don't seem to be seeing as many options and outcomes as are you."

"Well . . . the big possibility is that there's someone out there who beat the Xul two thousand years ago. If we can make contact with them, ally with them, like you said, we might have a chance to beat the Xul on their own terms."

"Yes. This was the possibility we had noted when the data first turned up in our research. But . . . you also said the novae could have been caused by the Xul. If so, the species we'd hoped to ally with might have been wiped out two thousand years ago. A mission to the Nova Aquila region would be futile if that was the case."

"Not at all. If the Xul resorted to blowing up stars—incinerating whole star systems—then they must have been up against someone or something that scared the liver out of them . . . assuming they have livers to begin with. Even if this hypothetical technic species is now extinct, we might find remnants . . . like the ruins on Chiron and elsewhere. We might learn why the Xul feared them that much." He shrugged. "At least it's a damned good place to start."

"That possibility had not occurred to me."

"Here's another one. Imagine you're the Xul, hard-wired to be paranoid about anyone different or advanced enough to be a threat. Two thousand years ago, someone in that one region of space gives you such a damned bad scare that you detonate stars to get rid of them. You think they're all dead, wiped out when their worlds were incinerated . . . but two thousand years later, someone with a large battle fleet shows up in that same region and starts nosing around the wreckage of those stars. What do you think?"

"Either that the old enemy has reappeared, and is still a threat," Cara said, "or, somewhat more likely, that another technic species is examining the wreckage of that former civilization—"

"And might learn something from the ruins. Exactly."

"At the briefing, you emphasized that we needed to find a means of getting the Xul's full attention," Cara said. "A means of getting them to follow the MIEF off into the Galaxy instead of striking into Humankind space. The perceived threat posed by the MIEF at Nova Aquila might be sufficient for this." The AI paused. "But suppose the Xul are not involved at all? You mentioned the possibility of a cosmic engineering or industrial accident involving some other species."

"If all we find are the leftovers of a colossal cosmic engineering experiment gone bad," Alexander said, "it still might help us. Even a mistake on that scale, something capable of detonating multiple suns, would represent an extremely advanced, extremely powerful technology. I would be willing to bet my pension that the Xul keep a watch on any such system, just in case."

"Unless the system in question was so completely obliterated that, literally, nothing remains."

Alexander shook his head. "Not possible. A supernova might vaporize any inner planets the star once had, and even then, I wonder if there wouldn't be rubble of some sort left over, moving outward with the outer shell of explosion debris."

"According to current astrophysical theory, supernovae are generated only by extremely massive stars," Cara told him. "Stars that massive do not have planetary families, and in any case would be too young and short-lived to support the evolution of life, much less advanced technology."

"Yeah, yeah." He waved the remark aside. "That wasn't my point. In Aquila we're dealing with ordinary novae, not supernovae. The explosion blows off the outer layers of the star's surface, and what's left collapses down to a white dwarf. Any planets in the system would be cooked, maybe have their outer crusts stripped away, but the planetary cores would remain."

"I fail to see how that helps us. Surely, the wreckage of any advanced technology would be obliterated by any wave front energetic enough to strip away a planet's crust. Buildings, power generators, spacecraft, they all would be vaporized."

"But the Xul watching the system, wouldn't *know* that every trace had been vaporized," Alexander replied. "Not with one-hundred-percent certainty. And with a spacefaring technic culture, there might be asteroids or outer-system moons with high-tech bases on them or inside them, or starships or large space habitats that rode out the nova's expanding wave front relatively undamaged, or bases hidden inside some sort of long-lived stasis field." He shrugged. "Endless possibilities. The chances of our going in and actually finding anything like that are remote in the extreme, granted, *but the Xul won't know for sure why we're there, or what we might find*. If they're as paranoid as our xenosapientologists think they are, they'll by God *have* to respond."

"I take your point." The AI hesitated. "It must be comforting to know—or at least to have a good idea—how the enemy will react in a given situation."

He grunted. "There are still too damned many variables,

and we still just don't know the Xul well enough to predict
how they'll respond, not with any degree of certainty. The
idea of them being xenophobes certainly fits with what
we've seen of them up until now, as does the idea that they
are extremely conservative, and don't change much, if at
all, over large periods of time. But, damn it, we don't *know*.
They're still aliens . . . which means they don't think the
same way we do, don't see the universe the same way we
do, and we'd be arrogance personified if we thought we
understood their motives or their worldview at this point in
time."

"But this gives us a starting point," Cara observed.

"That it does," Alexander agreed. "I'm actually more
concerned—"

"Just a moment," Cara said, interrupting. "Just a moment. . . ."

Alexander waited. He knew the AI well enough to recognize that she was momentarily distracted by something
entering her electronic purview. Whatever it was, it had to
be a very large something to so completely monopolize her
awareness, even for just a few seconds.

"General McCulloch's EA is requesting connect time,"
Cara told him. "Will you accept?"

"Damn it, Cara, when the Commandant of the Marine
Corps requests an electronic conversation with a mere lieutenant general . . ." Alexander replied, letting the statement
trail off.

"Will you accept?"

He sighed. AIs could be narrowly literal to the point of
obsession. "Of course I will."

"General McCulloch's EA states that the general will be
on-line momentarily, and to please hold."

"Then I guess we'll hold.

"Give me a quick update," he told the AI. "I'm actually
a lot more concerned about the PanEuropeans and how
they're reacting to the political situation than I am about
the Xul right now. Is there anything new this morning on
NetNews?"

"I've prepared your regular daily digest, which you can
download at your convenience," Cara told him. "Two hun-

dred ninety-five articles and postings concerning the PanEuropean crisis. Most of those are classified as opinion pieces or commentary, and most tend to be alarmist or sensationalist in nature."

"Nothing I need to be briefed on before I talk to the commandant?"

"In my estimation, no."

"The usual crap, then." He sighed. "Why do we have more trouble understanding ourselves and those like us than we do entities as alien as the Xul?"

"Human history suggests that this has always been a factor in human politics."

"Mm. Yes. Agreed."

"I am opening a virtual room for your conference with General McCulloch."

"Thank you." Alexander felt the familiar, lightly tingling surge across his scalp as the external reality of his office on board Skybase was swept away, replaced by a star-strewn void. The poly-lobed sprawl of human space filled his visual field; Puller 659, near the outer fringes of PE space, was highlighted as an unnaturally brilliant white beacon, outshining the strew of other stars.

"It appears General McCulloch is concerned about PanEuropean reaction if 1MIEF enters Republic space," Cara told him.

Alexander snorted. "I'm concerned that we're, both of us, Republic and Commonwealth, acting like apes around the water hole, thumping our chests, shrieking and grimacing at each other, and all the while the leopard is watching from the underbrush, getting ready to pounce. We should be working *together*, damn it, working toward the common cause, not clawing at each other's throats."

"Again, this appears to be a common pattern in human history. I submit that it represents a hard-wired feature of human psychology, and no doubt derives from the pre-tribal evolutionary period you refer to. Humans *are* apes, remember, and still possess the ape's instincts regarding territory, protectiveness, threat, and strangers."

"Tell me about it." He realized Cara would take his words

literally, and hastily added, "Belay that. *Don't* tell me. The question is whether or not we're going to have to go to war with the PanEuropean Republic in order to force them to help us against the Xul."

"Would their cooperation be worth the effort?" Cara asked.

"Good question. They have a large fleet, and we're going to need warships, both to protect the home front, and to carry out 1MIEF's long-range mission. Their ground forces aren't as good as ours, though." He didn't add that PE planetary assault units in particular didn't measure up to U.S. Marine standards. "But the stargates they control could be the key to hurting the Xul. Especially the Puller Gate . . . and Starwall. There's also the alert flashed from Tomanaga's LP. That, I imagine, is what General McCulloch is going to want to discuss."

"I have an incoming data feed from his EA, which I've been processing as we speak," Cara told him. "It includes intelligence reports concerning PanEuropean fleet elements and activities within the Puller 659 system, which supports your supposition." There was a brief hesitation. "Channel opening from General McCulloch."

And General Vinton McCulloch appeared, his icon bright with his official *corona flammae*, his full-dress uniform bright with luminous decorations and awards. "Good morning, General," McCulloch said, voice gravel-rough. "Sorry to keep you waiting."

"Not at all, sir." In fact, Alexander suspected that the higher the rank, the more you needed to keep subordinates waiting, just to keep them aware of who they were dealing with.

"We have a final go from the Senate," McCulloch said. "It was damned close, but Operation Lafayette has been approved."

"Lafayette?"

"Obscure historical reference, I'm told—'*Lafayette, we are here.*' Don't ask me. I just work here."

"But we're going in to get our people."

"Ay-firmative."

"When?"

"Riki-damned-tick. As soon as you can get an assault team together."

"I've tapped the 55th MARS," Alexander told him. "They're only just back from Alighan, but that means they haven't scattered to the four corners yet. The platoon COs are authorizing liberty, but no leave."

"Tough break for them."

Alexander shrugged. "They're Marines. They're squared away and set to boost. We just need to load their AT with fresh supplies and expendables. We have some more data, though, that you should see. I'm uploading to you now."

He waited as General McCulloch assimilated the data. "It seems Puller 659 has become doubly important," the older man said after a moment.

"Yes, sir. A bit of serendipity, actually. It gives us a choice from the same Stargate . . . Starwall, which appears to be a major Xul base, or the Nova Aquila region." He briefly outlined his ideas about the Aquilae novae, and why they might be important. "I was recommending Starwall," he concluded. "I need to study this data from the AI research team, but right now my inclination is to try that route instead."

"Have you considered both options?"

"Not yet. I will. Of course, we're so badly outnumbered and outgunned as it is. Splitting my force in the face of the enemy might not be the brightest of ideas."

"Well, it's going to be your call," McCulloch told him, "pending Senate approval, of course. Just keep me in the loop."

"Aye, aye, sir."

"I actually came down here to see what you could tell me about the Puller situation. What's the latest on that front?"

Alexander lifted his eyebrows. "I'd think you would know more about the situation out there than me."

"Hell, son, no one tells me anything. By the time the EAs finish filtering out the news they think I shouldn't be burdened with, there's not enough left to let me ask intelligent questions. I just know the PEs have some of our people at Puller in custody, but that some of them are still loose and lying low."

"That's right, sir." Alexander thought-clicked an animation into view, showing the tiny, red Puller sun, the orbit of the system's lone gas giant, and the wider orbit of the stargate. "Our covert base in that system consisted of two facilities. The larger, main base is dug into the surface of an ice-covered moon of this gas giant, here. The giant's radiation belts mask any electronic leakage. The smaller facility is out here, dug into the interior of a 10-kilometer asteroid that's in orbit around the stargate itself.

"Lieutenant Lee reemerged from the Gate on 2410. One month later, on 1911, a PanEuropean battlefleet arrived in-system—we think from the base at Aurore. Assault troops landed on the gas giant moon and took over our facility there. The LP commander, Major Tomanaga, reported PE troops inside the base, and then all communication with the unit was lost.

"Our best guess is that the PEs had a small, probably robotic probe in the Puller system, and that it detected and tracked the ships Tomanaga sent out to pick up Lieutenant Lee when her Night Owl reemerged from the Gate. It would take about a month for Republic ships to get out there.

"Apparently, however, the Republican forces did not detect the asteroid LP near the Gate. There are still five Marines there, under the command of a Lieutenant Fitzpatrick. Fitzpatrick has been sending us regular updates via QCC."

QCC, Quantum-Coupled Communications, possessed two singular advantages over any other form of long-range communication. It was instantaneous, and there was no way an enemy could tap into the transmission because there was no beam or wave to tap. A message spoken or typed at one console simply appeared at the designated receiver without passing through the intervening space, a satisfyingly practical application of what the long-dead Einstein had called "spooky action at a distance."

"So Fitzpatrick and his people are still undetected?" McCulloch asked.

"As of their last report, yes, sir. He was able to tell us that the PE squadron consisted of twelve ships, including the fast cruiser *Aurore*, a heavy monitor identified as *Rommel*, and a fleet carrier, *Le Guerrier*."

"I saw the list," McCulloch said. "They came loaded for bear, didn't they?"

"I'm not sure what 'bear' is, but, yeah. They came in with their heavies. Our best guess is that Tomanaga, Lee, and thirty-five other Marines and naval personnel are now being held on board the *Aurore*. She will be our chief target."

McCulloch nodded. "I just had some intel passed down from I-squared. You're going to have help when you get there."

Alexander felt an internal twist of hard suspicion. "What kind of help?"

"You're aware of the religious problems in the French sectors?"

Alexander nodded. "Somewhat. I don't *understand* them. . . ."

"The Republic's French sectors are officially Reformed Catholic. But there's a strong Traditionalist Catholic element in their fleet. DCI² tells us that the T.C. is set to mutiny if and when our forces appear. If they can take over the French warships before we can deploy, they will . . . and they've promised to try to protect our people."

Alexander groaned. "Gods. . . ."

"What's the matter?"

"That complicates things, General. You realize that, don't you?"

"I know."

"We're going to need to go in hot and hard. We do not need a bunch of friendlies running around, getting in our way and maybe taking friendly fire. That could get real nasty, real fast."

"Affirmative. But we work with what we've got."

"Ooh-rah." Alexander looked at the animation of the Puller star system for a moment. "Maybe we'll get lucky and the PE fleet will pull out before we get our act together."

"Don't count on that, General. So far, they haven't admitted that they have our people . . . and we haven't admitted that we know they have our people. Their safest bet is to sit tight at the Puller system, especially since they're probably questioning our people on exactly what Lee saw on the other side of the Gate."

"Starwall. Right. Okay, General. We'll take them down and we'll get our people out. But . . ."

" 'But?' "

"Nothing. But when we go in, those so-called friendlies in the PE fleet had better stay the hell out of our way. Our Marines are going to be moving fast and kicking ass, and they will *not* have the time to find out what church their targets attend."

"Understood. Just do your best."

Damn, Alexander thought. *It's going to be a cluster-fuck.*

And there wasn't a damned thing he could do about it.

14

Suit Locker
UCS Samar
Dock 27, Earth Ring 7
1315 hrs GMT

"So? How does it feel?" PFC Sandre Kenyon asked him.

Garroway blinked, testing the mental currents. "It feels . . . empty. Kind of like back in boot camp. When we didn't have our implants activated, y'know?"

She nodded. "That's exactly what it's like. Because that's what it is, at least up to a point. You still have Net access, comm access—"

"But we can get Achilles back?"

"Oh, sure! He's still there," she reassured him. She laughed and nudged Garroway in the ribs with an elbow. "He just doesn't know what he's missing!"

They were sitting side by side on one of the benches in the locker, surrounded by the silent, hanging shapes of emergency pressure suits. All of his attention, however, was focused inward as he took a self-inventory of his electronic systems. His implant software was still running. Achilles, however, the platoon AI, did not appear to be on-line.

He shook his head, partly in confusion, partly in admiration. "How the hell did you learn this, Sandre?"

She shrugged. "I'm a vir-simmer, remember? Back in my misspent civilian youth, I programmed the micro-AIs in sensory helms. I knew there had to be a back door. I just needed to find it."

"It's still amazing."

Garroway continued testing the feel of his internal hardware. In a way, it *was* like that horrible stretch of time in boot camp, the empty time, when he'd been deprived of any cereblink hardware at all. He still had most of his connections for communication, for linking into other computers, or for downloading data off the Net. What was missing was Achilles, the AI Electronic Assistant that served both as guide through the military cyberworld and as an unofficial tattletale and voice of authority.

"Yeah, well, I had some expert help, too," Sandre told him. "Did a favor for Vince, down in the 660 maintenance shack back at RTC Mars. He uploaded some secure code for me, gave me a head start."

"Vince? Staff Sergeant Gamble?"

"That's right."

"I didn't think that old son-of-a-bitch ever had a helpful thing to say to anyone!" He made a face, and imitated Gamble's acid tones. "*Especially* puke-recruits."

She laughed. "You never tried, um, feminine wiles on the poor dear. Besides, we're not recruits any more. We're *Marines*."

"Ooh-rah." He said it automatically, almost sarcastically, but he still felt a small, sharp chill of excitement as he spoke. Boot camp was over, the initiation complete, the metamorphosis from civilian to Marine accomplished.

Even so, he'd been feeling a bit of anticlimax. For almost two weeks after their graduation ceremony on the tenth of November, Garroway and the rest of the newly minted Marines had sat around in a temporary barracks at Noctis Labyrinthus. The forty survivors of Recruit Company 4102 had expected to be shipped out to different units almost immediately, but when their orders didn't come, speculation and rumor—"scuttlebutt" in ancient Marine and naval parlance—had fast become their primary, if highly unreliable, source of intel. Day after day, they'd stood watch, held practice drills, and carried out field days in various buildings across the compound, scrubbing, mopping, waxing, and polishing, "doing the bright work" until, as Ami Danvers had put it, the rising albedo of the base threatened them all with blindness. Robots and nanocleaning aerosol fumigants, Garroway had observed, could have done the job with far greater, microscopic precision; all of the hard manual labor, it was patently obvious, was make-work, designed to keep them busy and out of trouble.

They'd still had plenty of free time, though, and a lot of the conversation in the squad bay had turned naturally enough to their new life as Marines, in addition to the more traditional topics like sex, liberty ports, and more sex. The fact that they all now housed an artificial intelligence—Achilles—griped a lot of them. Achilles was, in effect, the eyes and ears of their superiors, always watching, always listening. When they were busy, Achilles' presence didn't bother them much; when they were practicing a combat evolution, he was treated as a part of the company, linking them, all together and guiding their movements, warning them of danger, and linking them into the larger combat net.

But when they were just sitting around the squad bay talking, Achilles' presence became a constant stressor, invisible, not discussed, but always *there*.

And morale had plummeted.

But Sandre, evidently, had decided to do something about it. She'd struck up a friendly acquaintance with one of the base personnel, and learned how to switch Achilles off.

A few days later, Company 4102 had been loaded on board a tiny military intersystem transport and shuttled to Earth Ring, where they'd been hustled across to their new duty station, a titanic assault transport named *Samar*. The word around the squad bay was that *Samar* had just returned from Alighan with the 55th Marine Aerospace Regimental Strikeforce on board, or what was left of it, and that the forty new Marines were destined to fill out the 55th's combat-depleted ranks.

But their orders still hadn't arrived.

A short time before, Sandre had approached Garroway on the mess deck, with the suggestion that he accompany

her down to the emergency suit locker after chow. He'd readily agreed; the two of them had snuck some playtime several times during the long stretch in the holding barracks at
Noctis, and he'd been hoping to pursue the relationship.

With Achilles blocked, he would be able to continue his
trysts with Sandre. Not that the AI had caused them any
trouble at Noctis. Their platoon commander had probably
been informed of all of their meetings up until he'd received
the software that let him disconnect from the AI, but had
chosen not to intervene—quite probably because morale
had been so bad, and disciplining a couple of Marines because they'd been having sex after hours would have made
things a whole lot worse.

Still, so far as Garroway was concerned, it would be a
lot better if Achilles was out of the picture entirely, at least
once in a while. After sixteen weeks of boot camp, he valued
his privacy more than ever, and grated under the knowledge
that anything he did, from scratching his balls in the head
to just *thinking* about how he hated Gunny Warhurst could
be recorded and fed up the chain of command. And almost
everyone else in Company 4102 he'd talked to felt the same
way.

"You're sure Achilles doesn't know he's being cut out?"
Garroway asked. He was trying to imagine the AI's point
of view. Wouldn't he know that he wasn't getting data from
certain members of the company, and become suspicious?

"The way it was explained to me," Sandre told him, "is
that he's only programmed to respond to certain situations,
thoughts, or words. We don't know what those triggers are,
of course, but as long as he doesn't receive them he's content. Artificial intelligences aren't curious unless they're
programmed to be curious."

"Or suspicious, I guess."

"Exactly."

"So," Garroway said, with just a trace of hesitation in his
voice, "this means you and I could? . . ."

"Of course. Why do you think I did it?"

"Just checking." He slipped his arm over her shoulders,
drawing her closer.

And the next hour or so was the most pleasant and unfettered hour Garroway had yet enjoyed in the Marine Corps.

The Comet Fall
Terraview Plaza, Earth Ring 7
2226 hrs GMT

"So, did y'hear the latest scuttlebutt?" Staff Sergeant Shari Colver asked.

"About what?" Ramsey asked.

"Yeah," Sergeant Vesco Aquinas said. "The rumor mill's been grinding overtime lately. Everything from peace with the Xul to war with the PEzzles."

"It'd damned well be better than your *last* butt-load of scuttlebutt," Sergeant Richard Chu said. "I didn't like that one at all."

"Roger that," Ramsey said. "They fucking gave it away. . . ."

The entire platoon had been grumbling since their arrival back in the Sol system, with morale at absolute rock-bottom. The word was—still unconfirmed but apparently solid—that the Commonwealth was giving back Alighan. *Two hundred five Marines hit,* Ramsey thought with dark emotion, *over half of them irries . . . and they fucking go and give that shit hole back to the Muzzies. . . .*

Colver leaned forward at the table in approved conspiratorial fashion. "It's war with the PanEuropeans," she said in a throaty half-whisper. "They're shipping us out next week."

"And how do you happen to be privy to *that* little tidbit?" Ramsey asked.

"Yeah," Sergeant Ela Vallida added. "You been talking with the commandant lately?"

"No, but I *have* been talking with Bill Walsh." Walsh was a staff sergeant over in Ops Planning. "He says it's already decided. They're pulling together the battlefleet now. And the 55th is on the ship-out list."

"Aw, shit!" Corporal Franklo Gonzales said.

Chu shook his head. "Well, our luck's true to form, isn't it?"

"Shit," Ramsey said. "*Can't* be. We just freakin' got back from Alighan!" Even as he spoke the words, though, he knew how hollow they were. The Corps could do anything it damned well wanted.

"Fuckin'-A, Gunnery Sergeant," Corporal Marin Delazlo put in. "We're *due* some freakin' down time!"

"Maybe," Ramsey said, taking in the noise and bustle of their surroundings with a grin, "just maybe this is it!"

The six of them were in the Comet Fall, a popular bar and nightlife center on the Seventh Ring Grand Concourse. It was large, murkily red-lit, and crowded; perhaps half of the other tables had privacy fields up, making them look like hazy, translucent ruby domes. The house dancers on-stage and the wait staff navigating among the tables all were stylishly nude, with eye-tugging displays of light and color washing across every square centimeter of exposed skin. The club patrons, both those at non-shielded tables and up on the stage with the professional dancers, wore everything from nothing at all to elaborate formal costumes. Music throbbed and pounded, though you needed a sensory helm for the full effect. Ramsey and the other Marines had elected not to wear helms, preferring unfiltered conversation instead.

His mind drifting, Ramsey found himself following the gyrations of one young woman on-stage wearing what looked like a swirling, deck-sweeping cloak of peacock feathers, a glittering gold sensory helm, and a dazzling *corona flammae*; she'd been enhanced either genetically or through prosthetics with an extra pair of arms, and her dance movements were eerily and compellingly graceful.

He was feeling wretchedly out of place. Aquinas and Gonzales both were wearing fairly conservative civvie skinsuits, but the rest of them were in undress blacks. Both sets of attire, by regulations, were acceptable wear for liberty, but it tended to make them stand out somewhat against the gaudy and sometimes extravagant background of evening wear sported by the other patrons in the establishment.

"Like hell," Gonzales said after a long moment. "I don't know about you clowns, but me, I'm just getting started! I'm not ready to redeploy!"

"That's right," Chu said. "I have a *lot* of catching up to do in the drinking and socializing departments before my next deployment!"

"Ooh-rah!" the others chorused, and Colver raised her glass in salute. "To downtime!"

"Downtime and down the hatch!" Ramsey added, lifting his own glass, then tossing it off. "*Semper fi!*"

The drink was called a solar flare, and the name was apt. He felt the burn going down, then the kick, and finally the rolling swell of expanding consciousness as the drink's nano activators kicked in.

If his platoon implant AI had been activated, he thought, it would be screaming at him by now. Marines were *not* supposed to imbibe implant-activators, for fear it would scramble their hardware and invalidate their government warranties or whatever. He didn't care. After Alighan, he *needed* this. Hell, they all did.

How the hell could they just give it away, after what we went through out there?

"Well, the brass is ramping up for something big," Ramsey told the others, perhaps three or four flares later. He had to focus on each word as he brought it to mind, then tried to say it. He was pleased. No slurring of speech at all, at least that he could detect. "I just heard this morning that we're getting a shuttle load of fungies in from RTC Mars."

"Yeah," Delazlo said, nodding. His speech *was* slurred, but it didn't matter. "'Sh'right. I heard that, too."

"Shit. Check your daily downloads, guys, why don't ya?" Vallida put in. "The fungies arrived yesterday. Forty of them, straight out of Noctis Labyrinthus."

"No shit?" Ramsey asked. He hadn't heard about that. Still, *Samar* was such a huge vessel, and she was swarming right now with technicians, computer personnel, cargo handlers, mechs, and shipwrights. A freaking regiment could have come on board and he wouldn't have noticed.

"No shit," Vallida said. "Seems they want all units up to full strength, even if we have to raid a nursery to do it."

"Shee-it," Gonzales said with considerable feeling. He was looking a bit the worse for the wear as multiple solar flares continued to burn their way through his circulatory system. "Just what we need. Babies to baby-sit."

"Hey," Colver said with a shrug. "Fresh meat. Don't knock it."

"We all had to start somewhere," Chu said, the words slurring slightly.

"The Corps is home, the Corps is family," Ramsey recited. It was an old mantra focused on the *belonging* of Marines. "And to hell with the politicians."

A waitress walked up to their table, her face a brilliant, sapphire blue, with rainbow luminescence rippling across the rest of her body. "You folks with the 55th MARS?" she asked.

"Yeah," Ramsey said. He felt a cold chill prickling at the back of his neck, and some of the drunken haze began evaporating from his mind. The Comet Fall was one of hundreds of nightspots along this stretch of Ring Seven. How the hell could they have tracked the six of them?

"You heard about us, eh, babe?" Gonzalez said, leering as he reached for her.

"Nope," the waitress said, slapping his hand away. "Can't say that I have. But your CO sure has. You're wanted back at your ship, immediately. *All* of you. What'd you do, switch off your AIs?"

"How about another round for the table?" Aquinas asked.

"To hell with that," the waitress said, as she began collecting empty and half-empty glasses. "I could get fired and the boss could lose his license! You people just move on now, before the SPs show up."

"So, what have we here?" a young man seated at the next table over exclaimed. "Pretty-boy Muh-*rines*?"

The atmosphere turned suddenly cold. That next table was a big one, with fifteen tough-looking men seated around it, all of them with similar patterns of blue-white luminous tattoos on the left sides of their faces—which meant either a punk gang or a fraternity. The privacy screen had been up until a few moments ago, but now it looked like they'd just taken an unhealthy interest in the party next to them.

"You'd better go," the waitress told the Marines, dropping her voice.

"The lady's right," Ramsey told his friends, pressing his palm to the credit reader on the table to pay the outstanding bill, then standing. "Let's move on. We don't want trouble."

"Yeah!" a civilian called from the next table. He sniggered. "Run home to mommy and daddy!"

"Back off, mister," Ramsey growled. "This isn't your business."

"Not my business, *Muh*-rine?" the kid said, standing and turning to face Ramsey. "I'll fucking make it my business if I want. You freaks aren't wanted here."

"That's right," another of the punks said. "You pretty-boy gyrines're nothin' but trouble. Who let you out without your keepers, huh?"

"You lousy little civilian shit—" Aquinas said, starting forward.

Ramsey put a hand on his arm. "Belay that, Marine. Outside. *Now*."

A moment later, they stepped onto the plaza beneath the Comet Fall's strobing sign. The concourse was a wide, sweeping mall lined with multi-tiered shops, bars and eateries, with a vast arch of transparency stretched overhead. Earth, half-full, hung directly overhead.

Chu looked up at the blue and white-mottled orb, frowning through his alcoholic haze. "Why aren't we falling?"

The question, though garbled, wasn't as drunken-wrong as it sounded. Each structure within the Rings circled Earth once in twenty-four hours, maintaining geostationary position. They should all have been in free fall, but the gravity here was roughly equivalent to the surface gravity on Mars, about three-tenths of a G.

Vallida laughed at him. "Jesus! You just now noticing, Chu-chu?"

"Gravity . . ." Ramsey started to say, then tripped over a hiccup. "Gravity engineering," he finally said. "Quantum-state phase change in the . . . in the . . ." He stamped his foot. "Down there. Subdeck infrastructure. Haven't you ever been to th' Rings?"

"Nope. Born'n raised on Mars. Never left until I joined up, and they fuckin' send me to Alighan. . . ."

"There they are!"

Harsh voices sounded behind them. Ramsey turned, and saw the gang from the Comet Fall spilling out into the street. They were looking for trouble, looking for a fight.

"Heads up, Marines," Ramsey said. He was fumbling through the mental commands that would revive his personal AI. If he could connect with the watch on board *Samar* . . . or even with the nearest Shore Patrol base. . . .

"You pretty-boys need to be taught a lesson!" one of the gangers growled. He was big, heavily muscled, and evidently having some trouble focusing. "You pretty-boys shouldn't be coming into *our* part of th'Ring. . . ."

"They ain't *all* pretty-boys," another civilian said. He pointed at Colver and Vallida. "Them two are kinda cute, for Muh-rines."

"Then we'll be gentle with them," the first said, with a nasty laugh.

"Yeah," another said. "We'll give them *special* treatment. But the *rest* of 'em—"

Ramsey slammed the heel of his palm into the kid's nose before he completed the statement, snapping his head sharply back. The other Marines flowed into action in the same instant; Ramsey heard the crack of one punk's arm as Vallida broke it, heard another ganger choke and gurgle as Gonzales drove stiffened fingers into his larynx, but he was already stepping across the body of the one he'd downed to block a punch thrown by a screaming punk, guiding the fist harmlessly past his head, locking the wrist, and breaking it. The kid shrieked in pain, then went silent and limp as Ramsey hammered the back of his head with an elbow.

The whole encounter was over within five seconds. The six Marines stood above fourteen bodies, some of them unconscious, some writhing and groaning as they cradled injured limbs or heads or groins. A fifteenth punk was disappearing down the street, running as fast as his legs could carry him.

"Not bad, Marines," Colver said. "Considering our, uh, slowed reaction times."

"Slowed, nothin'," Ramsey said. He reached down and extracted a tingler from the unconscious grip of one of the civilians. He checked it, switched it off, then snapped the projector in half, flinging the pieces across the street. Several of the punks were armed, and the other Marines proceeded to similarly disable the weapons. "We just gave them the first shot . . . to be . . . to be *fair.* Right?"

"Whatever you say, Gunnery Sergeant," Gonzalez said. "But maybe we should hightail it before the SPs show up."

"Yeah," Vallida said. "Someone's bound to've reported this."

"Roger that." He looked around. She was right. Habitats, even extraordinarily large ones like the Ring habs orbiting Earth, tended to have lots of cameras and other unobtrusive sensor devices, both to monitor the environment and to watch for trouble of a variety of types—including crime. He didn't see any cameras, but that meant nothing; most covert surveillance cameras, such as the ones the Marines themselves used to monitor battlespace, tended to be smaller than BBs, floating along on silent repulsor fields.

As he completed a full three-sixty of the concourse terrain, he became aware of another problem, one more immediate than having the local police watching the Marines mop up with some local thugs. "Uh . . . which way?"

His hardware included navigational systems, but he'd not bothered to engage them when they left the *Samar* earlier that evening. He suddenly realized that, in his current somewhat befogged state, he had no idea as to which way Dock 27 and the *Samar* might be.

"I think, boys," Colver said, "we'd better switch on our AIs. Otherwise we're going to be going in circles."

That was easier said than done.

Most enlisted Marines learned how to disable their company AIs temporarily within days of leaving boot camp, and some probably figured out how to do it while they were still boots. Hell, for that matter, Garroway was pretty sure that officers did it, too, right out of OCS or the Naval Academy.

No one ever talked openly about it, of course, because it was against regs. Getting caught was at the very least worth "office hours," as commanding officer's nonjudicial punishment had long been known in the Corps, and in some situations, like combat or while embarked on board ship, it could get you a general court and a world of hurt.

The process was simple enough, and involved visualizing a certain set of code numbers and phrases, which you brought to mind one by one and held for a second or so. It provided a kind of back door to the AI's programming. It saw and recorded the code, then promptly forgot about having seen it, or anything at all about the person doing the coding, until another set of codes was visualized to reset the software.

The problem was that you needed to have a clear and highly disciplined mind to be able to pull the visualization trick off. At the moment, all six of the MARS Marines were somewhat less than clear in the mental department. Not only were their minds sluggish with alcohol, but under the influence of the nano activators in their drinks they were having trouble focusing on *anything* with much clarity or discipline, much less memorized strings of alphanumeric characters.

"Wait a sec," Chu said. He was standing still, eyes closed, arms outstretched. "I almost have it. . . ."

They waited, expectant.

"No. I guess I don't."

"Someone write the code down. We can focus on that."

"No . . . no . . ." Colver said. "I've got it. Yeah! *There*. . . ."

She was silent for a moment, as the other Marines waited. "C'mon, c'mon," Gonzales said. "We gotta *move*! . . ."

"Okay," Colver said. "Dock 27 is *that* way."

"I coulda told you that," Chu said miserably.

"And I have the recall coming through. Shit. I think we're all gonna be AWOL. They passed the word at 1830 hours. We were supposed to check in at 2000."

Absent without leave meant NJP for sure. The six of them had checked out at *Samar*'s quarterdeck at 1800 hours, and switched off the company AI minutes after that. It was now just past 2300 hours, three hours after they were supposed to be back on board.

"Well, let's get the hell back there, then," Ramsey said. "We'll just have to face the music."

"Sure," Colver said. "What can they do to us . . . ship us back to Alighan?"

"Don't even *joke* about that, Staff Sergeant!" Delazlo scolded.

Unsteadily, the Marines began making their way back toward Dock 27 and the *Samar*.

Unfortunately, as soon as Colver's AI was switched back on, the Shore Patrol had a fix on her, and her name was flagged as being AWOL.

And so the six Marines of 55th MARS ended up spending the rest of the local night in the brig at Shore Patrol headquarters.

15

Platoon Commander's Office
UCS Samar
Dock 27, Earth Ring 7
0910 hrs GMT

"What the *hell* were you thinking, Marines?" Either Lieutenant Kaia Jones was furious, or she was one hell of an actress. The muscles were standing out like steel rods up the sides of her neck, and the anger behind her words could have melted through Type VII hull composite. "Switching off your AI contacts like that?" She paused, sweeping the six Marines standing in front of her desk with a gaze like a gigawatt combat laser. "Well?"

"Sir, we were *not* thinking, sir!" Ramsey snapped back, his reply militarily crisp.

"No, I should think the hell you weren't."

The six of them stood at attention in Jones' office on board the *Samar*. After an uncomfortable night in the SP brig ashore, they'd been escorted back to the ship by a pair of square-jawed Navy petty officers with no-nonsense attitudes and little to say. Master Sergeant Adellen had met them at the quarterdeck, signed off on them, and ordered them to stay in the squad bay, except for meals, until they could see the Old Man.

"Old Man," in this case, was a woman; long usage in the Corps retained certain elements of an ancient, long-past era when most Marines were male. The commanding officer

was the Old Man no matter what his or her sex. Just as a
superior officer was always *sir*, never ma'am.

Of course, the joke in Alpha Company was that in
Jones' case, you couldn't really tell. She'd been a Marine
for twenty-three years—fifteen of them as enlisted. She'd
been a gunnery sergeant, like Ramsey, before applying
for OCS and going maverick, and her face was hard and
sharp-edged enough that she looked like she'd been a
Marine forever.

Rumor had it that she'd been a DI at RTC Mars, and
Ramsey was prepared to believe it.

"What about the rest of you?" Jones demanded. "Any of
you have anything to say?"

"Sir . . ."

"Spit it out, Chu."

"I mean, sir, *everyone* does it. If we didn't have some
privacy once in a while, we'd all go nuts!"

Jones leaned back in her chair and watched them for a
moment, her gaze flicking from one to the next.

"Privacy to jack yourself on nanostims," Jones said at
last.

"Sir!" Gonzales looked shocked. "We would never—"

"Spare me, Gonzo," Jones said, raising her hand. "You
were all medscanned at the Shore Patrol HQ, and I've downloaded the reports. You were all buzzed. The wonder of it
was that you were still able to stand up . . . much less inca-
pacitate that group of . . . young civilians."

"Sir, you . . . know about that, too?" Ramsey asked.

"Of course. Your little escapade was captured on three
different mobile habcams, as well as through the EAs of two
of your . . . targets the other night. As it happens, you single-
handedly took out half of the hab's local militia."

"What?" Colver exclaimed. "Those punks? Sir! There's
no way!"

"Don't give me that, Colver. You've been in the Corps
long enough to know about gangcops."

Ramsey digested this. He'd run into the practice at several
liberty ports, but he'd not been expecting it at a high-tech,
high-profile facility like Earth Ring 7. Gangcops and police

militias were widely tolerated and accepted as a means of ensuring the safety of the larger cities and orbital habs.

It was the modern outgrowth of an old problem. Police enforcement could not be left entirely to AIs, neither practically nor, in most places, by the law. When local governments had problems recruiting a police force, they sometimes resorted to enlisting one or another of the youth gangs that continued to infest the more shadowy corners of most major population centers. The idea was to clean them up and give them a modicum of training—"rehabilitate them," as the polite fiction had it—and send them out with limited-purview electronic assistants tagging along in their implants. Whatever they observed was transmitted to a central authority, usually an AI with limited judgment, keyword response protocols, and a link to city recorders that stored the data for use in later investigations or as evidence in criminal trials.

Defenders of the policy pointed out that crime in targeted areas did indeed tend to drop; its critics suggested that the drop was due less to crime than to less *reporting* of crime; paying criminals to act as police militias was, they said, nothing less than sanctioned and legalized corruption.

In any case, a certain amount of graft, of intimidation, even of violence was unofficially tolerated, so long as the peace was kept. Wherever humans congregated in large and closely packed numbers, there was the danger of panic and widespread violence. Political fragmentation, religious fanaticism, rumors about the Xul or about government conspiracies all spread too quickly and with too poisonous an effect when every citizen was jacked in to the electronic network designed to allow a near instantaneous transmission of information and ideas, especially within tightly knit and semi-isolated e-communities.

Most citizens accepted the minor threat of being hassled by street-punk militias if it meant the authorities could identify and squash a major threat to community peace quickly. The Earthring Riots of 2855—in Corps reckoning the year had been 1080, just twenty-two years before—were still far too fresh in the memories of too many, especially within the orbital habitats where a cracked seal or punctured pressure hull could wipe out an entire population in moments. The Riots had begun less than twenty hours after the appearance of a rumor to the effect that the Third and Fourth Ring food supplies had been contaminated by a Muzzie nanovirus. That rumor, as it turned out, had been false—a hoax perpetrated by an anti-Muzzie fundamentalist religious group—but over eight hundred had died when the main lock seals had been overridden and breached in the panic.

And so the authorities had begun cultivating various street gangs and civil militias, with the idea that the more people there were on the streets with reporting software in their heads, the sooner rumors like the one about a terror-nanovirus one could be defused.

"Sir," Ramsey said, "we didn't know those . . . people were militia."

"That's right," Delazlo added. "They came after *us*, not the other way around! Started hassling us. They started it!"

"I don't give a shit who started it," Jones said. "As it happens, I agree that hiring young thugs off the streets as peacekeepers is about as stupid an idea as I've seen yet. Politicians in action. However, the Ring Seven Authority *has* requested that you be turned over to the civil sector for trial. The charges are aggravated assault and battery."

Shit. Ramsey swallowed, hard. In most cases, civil law took precedence over military law, at least within Commonwealth territory. They could be looking at bad conduct discharges, followed by their being turned over to the civilian authority.

No . . . wait a moment. That wasn't right. ABCD was a punishment that a court-martial board could hand out, not a commanding officer.

"Before we go any further with this . . . do any of you want to ask for a full court?"

That was their right under regulations. They could accept whatever judgment—and punishment—Jones chose to give them under nonjudicial punishment, or they could demand a court-martial.

But there was absolutely no point in that. They'd all been caught absolutely dead to rights—AWOL and fighting with the civilian authorities. Better by far to take whatever Jones chose to throw at them; whatever it was, it wouldn't be as bad as a general court, which could hand out BCDs or hard time.

"How about it? Ramsey?"

"Sir," Ramsey said, "I accept nonjudicial punishment."

"That go for the rest of you yahoos?"

There was a subdued chorus of agreement.

"Very well. You all are confined to the ship for . . . three days. Dismissed!"

Outside the lieutenant's office, the six Marines looked at one another. "That," Colver said, "was a close one!"

"She could have come down on us like an orbital barrage," Chu added. "Three days?"

"I don't get it," Delalzlo said, shaking his head. "A slap on the wrists. What's it mean, anyway?"

"What it means," Ramsey told them, "is she's keeping us out of worse trouble. Two days from now we're shipping out."

They'd learned that fact yesterday, shortly after coming back on board the *Samar*, but with other things on their minds, they'd not made the connection. The civil authorities might request that the six miscreants be turned over to them for trial, but unless and until they were handed over, they were part of *Samar*'s company. The needs of the ship and of the mission always came first; by restricting them to quarters, Lieutenant Jones was making sure that the civilian authorities didn't get them.

Marines always took care of their own.

USMC Skybase
Dock 27, Earth Ring 7
1030 hrs GMT

General Alexander floated against the backdrop of the Galaxy, surrounded by the icons of the Defense Advisory Council. Despite the naggingly unpleasant presence of Marie Devereaux, it was actually a bit of a relief to be here. "Operation Lafayette," he told them, "is on sched, with T-for-Translation Day now set for three days from now."

For days, now, Alexander had been submerged in the minutiae of ops preparation. The actual strategic planning he tended to enjoy, with a sense of roll-up-the-sleeves and get things moving accomplishment. Going over the endless downloaded lists of logistical preparations and supply manifests, however, was sheer torture, and he found he was willing to endure even Devereaux's acidly uninformed tongue to escape it, even if only for a little while.

"I don't understand your use of the word 'translation,'" Devereaux put in. "What does language have to do with it?"

"It has to do with a mathematical concept, Madam Devereaux, not with language," he replied. "You can download the details here." He paused, ordering his thoughts. How to explain the inconceivable? "Any point in space can be precisely defined in terms of its local gravitational matrix. If it can be so defined, it can be given a set of detailed spatial coordinates.

"Now, the paraspace plenum we call the Quantum Sea is co-existent with . . . or, rather, think of it as *adjacent* to every portion of four-dimensional space-time. Practically speaking, that's where we draw vacuum energy from . . . the realm of quantum fluctuations and zero-point energy. If we know the precise special and gravitational coordinates of where we are, and the precise coordinates of where we want to go, we can translate one set of coordinates to another by rotating through paraspace."

"General, that makes no sense whatsoever."

He sighed. "In simple terms, Madam Devereaux, the Quantum Sea allows us direct, point to point access through paraspace to any place in the entire universe."

"This is something naval vessels can do?"

"Not naval *vessels*, Madam, no. I don't know the engineering specifics, but in essence the translation requires enormous amounts of energy. Skybase is large enough to accommodate the zero-point energy taps necessary to effect a translation . . . but nothing smaller could pull down that much power.

"So what we've worked out is a kind of shuttle plan. We take on board as many of the 1MIEF heavies as we can . . . the first load will consist of a Marine fleet strike carrier, a Marine assault transport, and either three destroyers or a destroyer and a light missile cruiser for fire support. We make the first translation from Sol to the Puller system, drop those four or five ships off, then translate immediately back to Sol to take on board the next load of ships, which will be queued up and waiting. It will take, we're now estimating, a total of sixteen such transitions to get all eighty vessels of 1MIEF shifted out to Puller. Obviously, we can take on more light ships in one load, or fewer heavies. We're only limited by the docking storage space on Skybase's main hangar deck."

"Essentially," Admiral Orlan Morgan added, explaining, "they intend to use Skybase as an enormous fleet carrier." His icon grinned. "In the case of a fleet strike carrier like the *Chosin*, Skybase becomes a *carrier*-carrier!"

"If you'll recall," Alexander continued, "Skybase was designed to reside in paraspace. It's a fairly simple operation to move out of paraspace and into 4D space at any point of our choosing, *if* we have the proper field metrics and coordinates to make the transfer."

"Why weren't we told this before?" Senator Gannel put in. He sounded irritated. "It seems to me that this represents a significant strategic advantage, not only in war against other human stellar nations, but against the Xul."

"That's right," Senator Kalin put in. "It also means we could send your battlefleet straight to Starwall or to Nova Aquila or wherever we want to go without having to pass through the Puller gate, without trespassing in PanEuropean territory!"

It was an effort not to lose patience with them. "To translate from one point to another," he told them, "we need extremely exact coordinates for both points. We know the metric throughout Sol-space quite well, of course. We know the Puller system because we've had Marines out there for several years, now, and one of the things they've been doing, besides watching the Xul on the other side of the Stargate there, is taking gravitometric readings on local space . . .

just in case. The stargates all put a considerable dimple into space-time, thanks to the pair of high-speed black holes each one has racing around inside its structural torus, and we take those measurements as a matter of course so that we can better understand the local matrix.

"We do not, however, have gravitational readings on places like Starwall. We've had Marine recon probes out there, but they had other things to keep them busy than flit around taking gravity readings. As for Nova Aquila, we have not yet had *any* probes out there, either manned or AI. We have absolutely no data on the local matrix out there.

"Does that answer your objections, Senator?"

"Adequately."

"And have I answered your questions, Madam Devereaux?"

"Yes. You're saying you can get the fleet to Puller, but not to any place on the other side of the Puller Gate?"

"Exactly. We are fairly confident we can make the translation to Puller, and each successful translation would give us additional data on the metric. We would not even be able to attempt a translation to Nova Aquila, however. We simply don't have the requisite information."

"We will be able to use Skybase translations out to both Nova Aquila and to Starwall once we have secured them," Admiral Morgan added. "We simply need to have the time and equipment out there to make the necessary readings."

"We think," Alexander said. "The gravimetric situation at Starwall is pretty complicated. When I say we need exact readings, that's not a matter of measuring the gravity from the local star and a couple of the closest planets. Starwall is close to the outer fringes of the Galactic Core, and literally millions of nearby stars are affecting the local picture. As for Nova Aquila . . . well, we'll know more when we actually get some instrumentation out there. For now, though, it's first things first. We need to secure the Puller system, and that we can do using Skybase as our transparaspace shuttle. We have the queue orders drawn up and transmitted. According to our current schedule, we will begin loading the first ships on board Skybase later today, using L-3 as our rendezvous point. The first translation to Puller space is now set for 1800 hours GMT, on 0112, three days from now. Operation Lafayette will commence as soon as the first ships are released at the Puller Gate. Any questions?"

"Yes, sir," General Regin Samuels said. "I note in your plans that this operation will be depending heavily on a Traditionalist Catholic mutiny in the Puller system. Just how reliable is this element, anyway?"

"I believe I can answer that, Regie," Navin Bergenhal, of the Intelligence Advisory Group, said. "We have good, solid intelligence assets throughout PanEuropean space, including inside both the DST and the DGSE. Those assets, in fact, are how we determined that the French are indeed holding some of our people for questioning."

Not entirely true, Alexander thought. The initial data had come from Lieutenant Fitzpatrick, still watching and listening quietly from the hidden asteroid base orbiting the Puller stargate. But the Commonwealth's DCI[2] had developed that intelligence further, and brought home a lot of data concerning both the political and the military situations inside Republic space.

"From the Marines' point of view, General Samuels," Alexander said, "we will welcome help from local forces if it is available. We will *not* count on it."

And that was the final decision made after a very long series of discussions and ops planning sessions, including many hours of virtual-reality simulations playing out each aspect of the mission. Most Marine officers, from the MIEF's platoon commanders up to Alexander himself, felt the possibility of Traditionalist assistance at Puller was going to be more trouble than it was worth. The situation presented endless possibilities for targeting the wrong PE units, for friendly fire incidents, and for outright deception by the Republic's defensive forces.

"So, are you saying you don't trust the Catholics, General?" Devereaux asked.

"I'm saying, Madam Devereaux, that the MIEF will have the greatest chance for success if we welcome any help that's offered, but go in prepared for no help at all. As a matter of fact, our defensive stature will assume that the T.C. mutiny is actually a PanEuropean deception, a trick. We would be foolish to act in any other way, or to lower our guard without *very* solid reasons to do so."

"Quite right, General," Samuels said, and other military officers in the assembled council murmured agreement.

It was impossible to get a feel for what Devereaux actually thought. Her Net persona was well filtered, her icon image emotionlessly bland in affect. When she'd asked if he didn't trust Catholics, however, it had been impossible not to get the idea that she was fishing for something—a weakness, perhaps, or an opening for an attack. She was, he knew from her public records, from a Traditionalist Catholic family, but he also knew she wasn't herself a believer . . . at least not to the extent of going to Mass or accepting the word of the Papess in Rome as law.

What the hell was her game?

He didn't trust the woman, not after her attempt to shut down the Marine Corps. He still wished he knew what her personal stake was in the Corps—why she seemed to hate it so. Further searches of available public data had turned up nothing more on her background. So far as he could tell, she was simply a political opportunist who saw in the current situation a possible way of making political capital at the Corps' expense.

That made her no less of a viper, however. She would need to be watched, and carefully, by the few friends the Marines still had within the Senate. He did not think it impossible that she might even be working for the PanEuropeans; the Québecois link, certainly, suggested that possibility. Quebec and France had been in each other's pockets for centuries, since the First UN War at least, and possibly even well before that.

At least the chances were good that the woman wasn't working for the Xul. The Xul, Alexander thought with a wry and inward grin, didn't work with *anyone* unless they were Xul, and even Madam Devereaux wasn't capable of bridging a gap like that.

"My ops planning staff has put together an assault plan,"

Alexander continued, addressing the group at large. As he spoke, an animated diagram unfolded in the assembled minds of the audience. "The first ships in will act to set up a local defended space into which we can continue to drop ships and men. As you see here, there are two primary centers of interest within the Puller 659 system . . . here at the stargate, where our covert listening post is still in operation . . . and far in-system, here, at one of the moons of this lone gas giant. As of our last set of reports from the LP, the French fleet is in orbit around the gas giant. So far they've made no move at all to investigate the stargate.

"We will materialize *here*. . . ." He indicated an area some 10 light-seconds away from the stargate, and nearly 30 light-minutes from the gas giant's current orbital position. "With luck, we'll be able to bring the entire MIEF into position before the PEs even know we're in-system."

"Won't they be aware of your ships when they arrive?" General Samuels asked. "Neutrino emissions from your ships' reactors."

Samuels had a valid point. The QPTs or Quantum Power Taps utilized by Commonwealth naval vessels required massive input from conventional antimatter power plants to open the zero-point channels. Once those channels were open and functioning, energy from the zero-point field itself was more than sufficient to keep those channels open and working, but the power-up procedure required a lot of initial seed energy . . . and they wouldn't be able to go through the paraspace translation with their power taps on. That, any good QPT engineer knew all too well, was an excellent way to release a *very* great deal of energy into a small volume of space in an accident—a "casualty," in naval parlance—that would almost certainly result in the complete vaporization of Skybase.

With a thought, Alexander switched on a doughnut-shaped swath of red light surrounding the glowing point of light that marked the Jovian gas giant. "We hope that the answer to that, General, is 'no.' At the moment the PE fleet is deep inside the radiation fields of the Puller Jovian. If their sensors are finely tuned enough, they might pick up our reactor leakage, but they would have to know exactly where to look to have much of a chance of picking us up. We're hoping that the radiation belts in this area—and their own shields against that radiation—are going to keep them pretty well blind to our approach."

"Isn't that a rather slender hope, General?" Devereaux demanded.

"Not at all. According to our LP, the Republic forces have been paying no attention at all to the Gate. Even if they do pick up on what's happening before our fleet is fully in place and ready to deploy, we anticipate being able to achieve local battlespace superiority in relatively short order. Their current fleet in the system consists of twelve ships. Of those, only two could properly be considered heavies—a monitor and a fleet carrier. The flagship appears to be a fast cruiser, and the rest of the ships are destroyers, escorts, frigates, and three supply-cargo vessels.

"Because we're trying to rescue our own personnel and because we wish to limit the scale of destruction, we intend to use Marine boarding tactics rather than ship-to-ship combat. That will give us our best chance to capturing the ships, freeing our people, and resolving the situation with relatively low casualties."

He kept to himself the corollary . . . that saving the lives of naval personnel on the ships of both sides meant spending the lives of a number of Marines, possibly a large number. The tactical situation, however, demanded it.

"This is one instance where we absolutely need the Marines and their special capability in naval engagements," he continued. He looked at Devereaux's icon as he spoke, looking for a reaction, wishing again that he could read the emotion behind that bland, corona-haloed projection. "Modern space warfare is a notoriously all-or-nothing affair. Most missiles mount thermonuclear warheads. Beam weapons are designed to overpower shields and pick off point-defense batteries, so the nukes can get through. *When* a nuke gets through, usually, only a single one is necessary to obliterate the target vessel and everyone on board. That sort of thing would be very hard on the POWs we hope to rescue, and on the T.C. mutineers if they happen to be in the way. The Marines give us an alternative—the ability to burn our way onboard, capture or knock out the command centers, hijack their AI nets, and force each ship's surrender.

"We *could* launch a Marine strike solely with the personnel on board the strike carrier and on the assault transport, the assets that we will be sending through in the first translation. Tactical prudence, however, suggests that we wait until we have sufficient ships in place to provide us with decent fire support.

"With that in mind, we will begin deploying our Marine strike forces immediately upon entry into the Puller system. We will not commit ourselves to the assault, however, until we have a naval force in-system that at least matches the PanEuropean fleet already present . . . say, a total of two to three translation runs. Are there any questions?"

There were questions . . . most of them small and nagging and micromanaging bits of annoyance. The council appeared for the most part to have accepted at least the broad outlines of the plan. Technically, they couldn't dictate strategy or tactics, but technically, also, the President could, in his guise as commander in chief of the Commonwealth's armed forces. The council sought to understand the plan well enough to give the President decent feedback. And, slowly, thanks in part to the military and ex-military personnel within their number, and to their EA links to the Net, that understanding was forthcoming.

But Alexander had tangled with politicians often enough to know that it was never that simple.

Especially, he thought, when one of those politicians was Marie Devereaux.

16

0112.1102

USMC Skybase
LaGrange-3/Puller 695
1750 hrs GMT

Skybase drifted in empty space, alone and unattended, now, as the last of the supply and shuttle vessels pulled back to a safe distance. Most ships, and most especially the cis-Lunar tugs and more massive cargo vessels that had been servicing Skybase, used gravitic engineering both for their drives and to maintain artificial gravity on board. Such units warped and wrinkled the fabric of space, rendering useless the Skybase's mathematical understanding of the local metric. From a distance of 10 kilometers, though, with drives switched off, the minor warping from the argrav generators was trivial enough to ignore.

General Alexander was in his office on board Skybase, awaiting the translation to Puller 659, but he was linked in to the scene transmitted from the transport *Aldebaran*, the image electronically unfolded in his mind. From this vantage point, some 10 kilometers off, Skybase looked like a huge pair of dark gray dishes fastened face to face, rim to rim, with one side flattened, the other deeper and capped by a truncated dome. The structure's surface looked smooth from this distance, but Alexander knew that up close its skin was a maze of towers, weapons mounts, sponsons, surface buildings, and trenches laid out in geometric patterns that gave it a rough and heavily textured look.

The perimeter of the double saucer was broken in one place as though a squared-off bite had been taken from its rim, at the broad opening leading into Skybase's hangar deck, a deep and gantry-lined entryway nearly 100 meters wide jokingly referred to as the garage door. Harsh light spilled from that opening, illuminating the gantry cranes and the massive shapes of the starships nestled inside.

"Ten minutes," an AI's voice announced in his head. It wasn't Cara, this time, but one of the battalion of artificial intelligences resident within the MIEF net, tasked with co-ordinating the entire operation.

Was there anything else that needed to be done, anything forgotten? God help them all if there was. Alexander expected no serious trouble with the PanEuropeans at Puller, but after that, when they jumped through to Nova Aquila. . . .

Three days earlier, a fleet of gravitic tugs had gentled the behemoth clear of Dock 27 and into open space well beyond the outer ramparts of the outermost Earthring. Hours later, Skybase had translated to the fleet rendezvous area to begin the final loading. The gravimetric picture was complicated close to Earth and to the artificial gravity-twisting engineering of the Rings themselves, but the translation was a tiny one, only about a quarter of a million miles, from geosynch out to the Moon's orbit. There'd been the faintest of shudders, and Skybase had quietly vanished from Earth synchorbit, to reappear a heartbeat later at L-3.

L-3, the third of the five Earth-system LaGrange points, was located at the Moon's orbit, but on the far side of Earth from the Moon's current position, so that Luna was perpetually masked from view by the larger disk of Terra. The point was gravitationally metastable; the gravitational metric was relatively flat, here, with Earth and Moon always positioned in a straight and unchanging line, but ships or structures parked at L-3 still tended to drift away after a few-score days due to perturbations by the Sun and by other planets, especially Jupiter.

However, that metastability would not affect Skybase, which wouldn't be there long enough to be perturbed by much. The important thing was that local space was flat enough in terms of gravitational balances, providing a good starting point for the coordinate calculations that would allow Skybase to transit through a much, much longer jump, not through but *past* the Void.

A jump of some 283 light-years, all the way out to Puller 659.

For *that* transition, local space had to be as flat as could be managed, with a metric far less complex than the scramble of interpenetrating gravity fields found in geosynch. There could be no drift of Moon relative to the Earth, no hum of nearby artificial agrav fields, no space-bending pulse of a passing ship under Alcubierre Drive. L-3 was ideal as a jump-off point, as ideal as could be found, at any rate, this deep inside the Solar System.

"There is something I do not understand," Cara said as he watched the view of Skybase from the transport.

"What's that?"

"The QST appears to be a highly efficient means of crossing interstellar distances," the AI said. "I'm curious why more mobile habitats like Skybase have not been built."

Alexander let the comment about being *curious* pass. From his first introduction to the EA years ago, Cara had continued to surprise him with what seemed to be a genuinely human range of behaviors. AIs weren't supposed to exhibit curiosity, but the more powerful ones did, indisputably.

"Well, there *are* plans on the drawing boards," Alexander said, "for true starships using Quantum Space Translation . . . but I don't think any of them are funded for development yet. At least, not beyond the wouldn't-it-be-nice stage."

"I have seen some of those plans on the Net," Cara told him. "But you're right. None has been funded past the initial research stage."

"The Arean Advanced Physics Institute has been using Skybase as a testbed to study paraspace," Alexander said, "both to improve energy tap technology and to investigate the possibility of very long-range transport. But ships built around translation technology . . . they'd be damned expensive. They'd also have to be huge, to accommodate the necessary power taps and the translation drive itself. A lot of military decision-makers don't think it's feasible."

"Skybase is still considerably smaller than a typical Xul huntership," the AI pointed out. "And it would be simple enough to mount gravitic drives to provide the necessary maneuverability for combat and in-system travel. A fleet of such vessels equipped as warships would be most formidable."

"And you want to know why we're not developing such ships more . . . aggressively?"

"Exactly. It is as though human governments, the people who make such decisions, do not realize the gravity of the Xul threat."

Alexander sighed. It was almost embarrassing admitting to the non-human artificial intelligence in his head what most senior military officers had lived with for their entire careers, worse, what humankind had lived with for centuries.

"That's a complicated question, Cara. I guess the short answer is . . . they know the Xul are a threat, sure, but after five centuries, they don't seem to be an *urgent* threat. There are always more important things to attend to closer at hand."

"Even after the Xul incursion of 2314, when humankind was nearly annihilated?"

Alexander shrugged. "But we weren't, were we? Humans have a lot of trouble connecting with something that happened centuries ago . . . or that might not happen until centuries in the future. Download the history. Remember global warming? The fossil fuel crisis? The e-trans crisis? The genetic prosthesis crisis? The chaos of the nanotechnic revolution? If it doesn't threaten us, immediately and personally, it's someone else's problem—especially if it's government that has to take action to fix it. Hell, politicians have trouble keeping their focus on problems just from one election to the next. The Roman Senate probably had the same problem with the barbarian crisis three thousand years ago."

"But it is the politicians—specifically the Senate Mili-

tary Appropriations Committee—that would be responsible
for funding a fleet capable of fighting the Xul, is it not?"

Cara sounded genuinely confused, and Alexander wondered how much of that was personality software miming
human patterns, how much was genuine perplexity. There
was no way to tell.

"That's right," he said. "And they're not eager to increase
taxes just so the military can have some expensive new toys."
He hesitated. While Cara was his electronic assistant alone,
she did share data with many other people, both civilian and
military, and with innumerable other AIs. How well could
he trust her not to share with the wrong people?

The hell with it. They would be gone, soon, gone and
far beyond the reach of anyone—officious bureaucrat, ass-
covering general, or self-serving politician—who might
object to him giving voice to his opinions. "The truth is,
Cara, it's not just the civilians who are a little slow on the
uptake, sometimes. In fact, if the military really pushed for
it, we would probably get those fancy new ships. The al-
locations for the designing, for the building . . . hell, the
shipyards at Earthring, at the Arean Rings, at Luna, at L-5,
they'd all be falling all over themselves to win *those* contracts. And the civilian sector would profit with a whole new
means of traveling between star systems."

"You're saying the work would stimulate the economy."

"Definitely. Military contracts have always been a big
factor in keeping the economy going. That's one reason war
was so hard to get rid of over the centuries."

"Why, then, would the military sector not wish to see
these ships developed?"

"Because the military sector has always been *extremely*
conservative. They don't trust new technology."

"But advanced technology has always won wars. The
development of nuclear weapons to end World War II, for
instance, would be a case in point."

"Which actually began as a *civilian* initiative, instigated
by the U.S. President at the time when he learned that the
enemy had a chance of developing those weapons first. But
check your historical files. Naval vessels continued to have

masts for *decades* after the steam engine made sails obsolete. When General Custer's command was wiped out at the Little Bighorn, the native forces attacking him were armed with repeating rifles; most of Custer's men were not, because the military bureaucracy of the time was convinced that repeaters wasted ammunition. Custer also left behind a couple of Gatling guns—primitive machine guns—because they slowed up his column. In other words . . . he refused to change his tactics to take advantage of new technological developments.

"Later, navies continued to cling to the battleship even after repeated demonstrations that they didn't stand a chance against carrier-based aircraft. Then they clung to carriers after orbital railguns and microcruise missiles made those monsters into fat, wallowing targets. Two centuries after that, Marines were *still* being issued slug-throwers as standard weapons because of concerns about the reliability of lasers and man-portable batteries under combat conditions. As a rule, military leaders don't like *anything* new or different."

"But why would that be, given that change is the essence of history?"

"Major changes in how we do things usually means waiting around until the last generation dies off. It's a basic truism of military history: we're always ready to fight the *last* war, and the methods and tactics of the *next* war always catch us by surprise."

"That would seem to be a depressing philosophy for someone in your line of work, General," Cara told him. "Or do you embrace such conservative viewpoints as well?"

He thought about that one for a moment. "There are never any absolutes in this business," he told the AI. "No blacks or whites. In point of fact, space-combat doctrine right now favors lights over heavies."

"You refer to the tactical doctrine of using many small, cheap, and expendable spacecraft, rather than a few large and expensive ones."

"Exactly. A Skydragon masses less than a hundred tons, and can still carry a dozen long-range missiles with thermonuclear warheads. One such warhead can cripple or even destroy a hundred-thousand-ton battlecruiser, if it gets through the point defense field. The powers-that-be are perfectly happy to sacrifice a few Skydragon squadrons in exchange for a high-value heavy, no problem." He felt his own bitterness rising as he said that. "It remains to be seen if being able to translate ships as big as Skybase makes it worthwhile changing tactical doctrines."

"It seems that there is a certain inertia resident within any given approach to warfare," Cara observed. "Once a government is committed to a given way of doing things, it is difficult to change."

"You could say that." He sighed. "In fact, the conservative factions are usually right in holding on to the tried and true . . . *up to a point.* We know what works, so we stick to that. If it's not broken, don't fix it, don't risk creating a real mess.

"But . . . and this may be the single most important 'but' in any military leader's lexicon, we must be aware that change—technological change, social and cultural change, demographic change, religious change, political change—*all* of them are going on around us all the time, even when we don't actually see it happening. If we get so mired in the past that we don't see the next new wave coming, if we can't recognize it in time to adapt, then we're doomed to go the way of the dodo, the elephant, and the blue whale, a dead-end trap and ultimate extinction."

"It still seems short-sighted to ignore the potential for this type of interstellar transport," Cara observed.

"Cara, I couldn't agree more. Maybe, if Operation Lafayette and Operation Gorgon are both successful, if Skybase really shows her stuff out there, that by itself will nudge things along in a positive direction. At least we can hope."

"Hope is one aspect of humanity I've never been able to fully understand," Cara told him.

"Three minutes," another AI's voice announced. Pure imagination, really, but to Alexander it seemed that he could sense the gathering of energy within the bulk of Skybase. Windows open to one side in his mind showed that all of the base systems were standing ready, all personnel at battle stations, the antimatter reactors at the station's core already pouring terawatts of energy into the slender channel now opening into the Quantum Sea.

"Cara," he said in his mind, "has there been any word from the Puller listening post?"

"Not for eight days, five hours, twenty-seven minutes," the AI told him. "Lieutenant Fitzpatrick's last report indicated a possibility of failing power systems, however. He may not be able to communicate."

"QCC units don't need much power," Alexander said. "And they can't be tapped or intercepted. If he's not able to communicate, it's because the PEs found him . . . or his life-support systems failed." He watched the inner panorama, of Skybase adrift against a star-scattered emptiness, for another moment. "I don't like jumping into an unknown tacsit," he said at last.

"We've known there would be considerable risk, General. The connection with Lieutenant Fitzpatrick has been tenuous and intermittent ever since the PanEuropean fleet entered the Puller system."

"I know." He was thinking about the ancient military maxim: *no plan of battle survives contact with the enemy.*

During ops planning, they'd considered putting a hold on the actual translation to Puller 659 until they actually received an all-clear from Fitzpatrick and the listening post. That idea had been dropped, however. There were reasons, psychological as well as engineering, that Skybase could not be kept on perpetual alert waiting for the next contact from the distant Marine listening post.

So they would make the jump, and simply try to be ready for *whatever* they found at the other end.

"Two minutes."

He opened another window, sending out a connect call. "Tabbie?"

There was a brief pause.

"Hi, hon," was her reply. "Almost up to the big jump-off?"

The link was via conventional lasercom relays, so

there was a speed-of-light time lag of about three seconds between the moment he spoke, and the moment he heard her reply.

"Yeah. But I do hate leaving you behind."

"I hate it, too. But . . . you'll be back. And I'll be here waiting for you."

They'd talked about that aspect of things a lot during the weeks before this. Normally, Skybase was home not only to nearly eight hundred Marines and naval personnel, but also to some five hundred civilians. Most of them were ex-military, or the children of military families, or the spouses of military personnel serving on Skybase. Most worked a variety of jobs on the base, ranging from administration and clerical duties to specialized technical services to drivers and equipment operators in the docking bay.

In fact, they represented the way the Marine Corps, in particular, had over the centuries evolved its own microculture. The retired Marine staff sergeant or colonel, the spouse of a Marine pilot, the child of Marine parents both stationed at Skybase, all shared the same cultural background, language, and worldview that made them a single, very large and extended family.

But Skybase was about to take part in an operation utterly unlike anything tried in the past. This time, the MIEF's headquarters would be traveling with the expeditionary force. It would be the target of enemy assaults, and it would likely be gone for many years.

Active duty Marines at Skybase had been given their orders. The civilians, however, had been given a choice—a choice to be worked out by both civilian and military members of each family. Many civilians had preferred to stay behind at Earthring, though the decisions of many had been swayed by the military members of those families, who'd wanted loved ones to be safe.

According to the final muster roster, two hundred five civilians were accompanying the Marines and naval personnel to the stars on board Skybase. Among them were the research team from the Arean Advanced Physics Institute, crucial members of the technician cadre, and a number of civilian family members who'd refused to be separated from loved ones.

Tabbie, though, was staying at Earthring. She had family there . . . and though she'd not wanted to stay at first, Alexander had finally convinced her that she would be better off making a home for herself there, rather than enduring the hardships—and the danger—of life aboard the base during this new deployment.

"I still don't entirely agree with your reasoning," she told him after a moment.

"You mean about Earth not being safe?"

"You've said it often enough yourself," she replied after the three-second delay. "If the Xul come to Earth again, *when* they come, there won't be any behind-the-lines. Everybody will be taking the same risks."

In fact, the original rationale behind giving Skybase its paraspace capability was to ensure that the MIEF headquarters would survive if the Xul *did* manage to find and slag the Earth. It would be a terrible irony, Alexander thought, if Skybase survived the coming campaign . . . and Tabbie and the other civilians left at Earthring were killed.

"Yeah, well, there's a big difference between the Xul coming to Earth again, and us going out hunting for the bastards," he told her. "We'll be out there looking for trouble, and we're going to find it. And if we're successful, we'll shake the Xulies up enough that they won't come to Earth."

"I know, I know. But I don't have to like it."

"One minute," a voice said in his head.

"Okay, Kitten," he told her. "I just got the one-minute alert. If everything goes as planned, I'll be back in a few hours for the next set of ships."

"I love you, Marty."

"I love you." He hesitated, then added, "I'll be back before you know it."

He could feel the hard and familiar knot of anticipation tightening in his gut. He wished this next translation was the one taking them to the Xul. He wanted to get it over with . . . but unfortunately Operation Lafayette had to come first. Secure the jump-off system—and get those captured Marines back—

and then it would be time to deal with the much vaster threat of the Xul.

"Thirty seconds."

What perverse insanity emanating from the gods of battle demanded that humans first tear and kill one another, when the Xul were the real threat, the most terrible and terrifying threat the human species had ever encountered?

"Ten seconds."

"Five . . . four . . . three . . . two . . . one . . . systems engaged. . . ."

The mental window through which Alexander was watching the scene suddenly turned to white snow and crashing static. *Damn*! He hadn't even considered the self-evident fact that once Skybase translated, the camera on board the *Aldebaran* would suddenly be left far behind, and the abrupt loss of signal had jarred him. He switched to a different input channel, one connected to a camera feed from Skybase's outer hull.

For just an instant, Skybase would have dropped through the blue-lit haze of paraspace, but Alexander had missed it. What he saw now was a view of deep space, star-strewn and empty, the constellations unrecognizable. Two hundred eighty-three light-years was far enough to distort the familiar patterns of stars in the sky into strangeness.

In fact, there was nothing much to see. Other downloads from Skybase's command center, however, began providing a more complete picture of their surroundings as the base's sensitive scanners began sampling the background of ambient electromagnetic and neutrino radiation. The star gate, as expected, was about 10 light-seconds in one direction, the tiny red spark of the local sun in another, the star marking Puller 659's solitary gas giant just to one side of the star, and thirty light-minutes away.

Seconds after translation, Skybase began releasing her first riders—sixteen F/A-4140 Stardragons of VMA-980, the Sharpshooters, one of three fighter squadrons in 1MIEF's aerospace wing. Sleek, black-hulled, and deadly, the fighters dispersed around Skybase in a globular formation, the base protectively at its center. They continued to move outward at a steady drift of nearly 4 kilometers per second relative to the Skybase, flight and combat systems shut down, drawing energy solely from their on-board batteries, watching for a sign, *any* sign, that the enemy knew they were there.

Skybase, too, continued sampling ambient space, building up a detailed picture of its new surroundings. One by one, PanEuropean ships were picked up by their electromagnetic signatures despite their being submerged within the hash of charged particles enveloping the Puller gas giant. In all, seven enemy vessels were picked up and identified, just over half of the expected twelve. Those five missing PE ships were a minor worry; most likely, they were simply too well masked by the gas giant's radiation belts, or they might be hidden by the bulk of the planet itself, on the far sides of their orbits. They might even have departed the system . . . but it was also possible that they were closer at hand, well-shielded and effectively invisible.

If so, the fighter screen would sniff them out soon enough. Skybase's sensors, meanwhile, scoured the surrounding sky, searching.

There were no ships close by the stargate. The tiny planetoid housing the Marine listening post, however, was spotted and identified after a few moments. A small shuttle slid from a secondary docking bay in Skybase's hull, accelerating toward the stargate.

The first flight of starships was already being off-loaded as the shuttle departed. First to emerge from Skybase's maw was the destroyer *Morrigan*, 24,800 tons and 220 meters in length overall, and with a crew of 112. Her antimatter reactors were already powering up; she would be ready to engage her primary drive within another fifteen minutes.

Alexander, meanwhile, switched to the downloaded view being recorded from the *Morrigan*, and was able to watch the second starship slip her magnetic moorings and exit Skybase's hangar bay, edging gently into hard vacuum, guided by a quartet of AI-directed tugs.

She was the *Thor*, and she was sister to *Morrigan*, her masculine name notwithstanding. Both *Cybele*-class destroyers were fast and maneuverable, designed originally to serve with the Solar High Guard fleet, protecting worlds and habitats from incoming asteroids or cometary debris. Each possessed a powerful spinal-mount plasma gun as primary weapon, but their hull superstructures bristled with secondary laser turrets, missile batteries, and railgun accelerators, as well as automated point-defense mounts.

With the two destroyers launched and positioned a few thousand kilometers to either side of Skybase, Alexander let himself begin to breath more easily. The most dangerous part of Operation Lafayette was the possibility that PanEuropean warships would be close enough to pick up Skybase's transition into normal space. While Skybase did possess defensive weapons, the structure was still not primarily intended for combat. The two destroyers would provide the fledgling in-system beachhead with some decent fire-support.

Third out of Skybase's cargo deck was the Marine assault transport *Samar*, huge, blunt-prowed, and massive. Measuring 310 meters long, and with a beam of 85 meters, *Samar* massed nearly 35,000 tons. She carried a crew of 79, as well as her cargo—four companies of the 55th Marine Aerospace Regimental Strikeforce, a total of nearly 600 Marines. Half of those Marines would already be loaded into their ship assault pods, or SAPs, ready to engage in ship-to-ship boarding actions.

The final ship nestled within Skybase's hold was the largest, the Fleet Marine Carrier *John A. Lejeune*, massing 87,400 tons, and measuring 324 meters, stem to stern. Cocooned within *Lejeune*'s hangar deck were two more squadrons of F/A-4140s, as well as a squadron of A-90 ground-support strike craft and a number of support and auxiliary vessels—ninety-eight aerospace craft in all.

The *Lejeune* was a tight fit inside Skybase's hangar bay; in fact, several outriggers and deep-space communications and tracking masts had been removed in order to let her slip through Skybase's garage door at all. Getting her out was a tediously exacting exercise in geometry and tug-facilitated maneuvering that would take nearly an hour *if* all went well. It was for that reason that the *Lejeune* had been the first ship loaded on board the Skybase, and the last out; Alexander had wanted the fleet carrier to be with the first translated load, however. Her three Stardragon squadrons—forty-eight aerospace fighters in all—would be invaluable in achieving and maintaining battlespace superiority, and greatly expanded the fleet's reach and sensitivity.

An eighth PanEuropean ship was picked out of the radiation fields around the gas giant. By now, neutrino and electromagnetic energy emitted by the newly emergent Commonwealth vessels would have reached the vicinity of the PE fleet. The question now was how good the enemy was at picking those radiations out of the storm of particulate radiation surrounding them at the moment. The Commonwealth squadron might be detected at any moment; Alexander was gambling on the enemy—even his AIs—being less than perfectly vigilant.

Even so, every passing minute increased the chances of discovery.

And so *Thor* and *Morrigan* stood guard as Skybase slowly, even grudgingly gave birth to the *John A. Lejeune*, while the *Samar* drifted nearby, her waiting Marines encased in their SAP pods, unable to do anything but watch, fret, pray, or sleep, according to individual habit and preference.

And once *Lejeune* drifted free in open space, the tugs dragged her clear and, after a brief gathering of inner power, the Skybase winked out of existence once again, returned to distant Earth.

The four capital ships, a small cloud of fighters and auxiliaries, and some twelve hundred men and women remained behind, alone, outnumbered, and expendable almost three hundred light-years from home.

And everything was riding on a single unknown: was the enemy aware of their arrival?

The question would be settled, one way or the other, within the next few hours.

17

0112.1102

SAP 12/UCS Samar
Assembly Point Yankee
Puller 695 System
1935 hrs GMT

PFC Aiden Garroway could scarcely move. He had a little bit of wiggle room inside his 660-battlesuit, but the embrace of his Ship Assault Pod made any real shift in his position impossible. His confinement was beginning to gnaw at him. He'd been sealed in here since 1700 hours, long before the Skybase had even made its translation. Two and a half hours, now.

Worst of all he couldn't scratch. There was a point midway up his back, below his shoulder blades and on the left, that had been tingling and prickling for the past hour, and there wasn't a thing he could do about it. Theoretically, he could have used his system nano to anesthetize the spot—a process that happened automatically if he was wounded—but so far his thought-clicks hadn't done a damned thing. In fact, when he tried to isolate the itch in his mind, it moved, shifting one way or another until it was impossible to really pin it down.

The failure of the anesthetic release probably meant the sensation was purely psychosomatic, but that made it no easier to bear. In any case, he'd experienced worse. In boot camp, any unauthorized movement or wiggling when the recruit platoon had been ordered to hold position, had been punished by a session in the sand pit, taken through a grueling set of exercises by a screaming Gunny Warhurst or one of the assistant DIs.

At least Warhurst wasn't going to reach him in *here*, sealed away deep in the belly of *Samar*'s launch bay. His former DI was in another SAP, possibly right next door, but as helplessly cocooned as was Garroway.

At least he had the squad data feed to keep him from going completely nuts. An open window in his mind showed an animated schematic of the tacsit, centered on *Samar*, with the *Lejeune*, *Thor*, and *Morrigan* spread across several thousand kilometers of empty space, and with the fighters farther out yet.

By pulling back on the viewpoint within his mind, the Commonwealth squadron dwindled to a bright, green dot, and he could see the icon representing the stargate falling in from the right. Pulling back still more, he could see the icons representing the enemy; zooming in on that tightly grouped pack of glowing red icons revealed seven capital ships just visible in a pale, red fog representing the radiation belts around the system's gas giant. All seven vessels were evidently in orbit about the giant, and gave no indication that they were aware, yet, of the presence of the small Commonwealth squadron.

But they would be.

Garroway kept turning inward, inspecting closely his own emotions. He wasn't sure about what he was looking for. Fear? Anticipation? Excitement? Impatience?

Maybe he was feeling something of all four. Boot camp had taken him through so many simulations of combat he couldn't begin to number them. In virtual reality simulations he'd sat inside the close, unyielding embrace of an SAP many times, until he knew exactly what to expect—the long wait, the gut-punching jolt of launch, the sweaty palmed anxiety of the approach, the strike, the penetration, the entry.

Except that, he knew very well, you could *never* know for sure what was coming. Simulations were just that, *simulations*, and the real world was certain to contain more than its fair share of the unexpected.

Marine Listening Post
Puller 659 Stargate
1935 hrs GMT

In fact, the unexpected had already happened. Seven days earlier, guided by intelligence provided by the DGSE—*Direction Général de la Sécurité Extraterrestrial*—the light cruisers *Sagitta* and *Pegasus* and the destroyer *Détroyat* had approached the Marine listening post beside the stargate under Alcubierre Drive, slowing to sublight velocities at the last possible moment. Lieutenant Fitzpatrick had noted the ships powering up, but they arrived at the stargate long before the light carrying news of their departure from their orbit around the gas giant.

Seconds after dropping back into unwarped space, *Détroyat* had released a 10-megaton thermonuclear warhead which had detonated at the asteroid's surface; the shockwave had wrecked the listening post, and incapacitated or killed the Marines inside.

Before the fireball had fully dispersed, *Pegasus* had deployed an anticommunications nanocharge, a warhead releasing a cloud of molecule-sized disassemblers that had sought out the internal wiring and optical networks interlaced through the asteroid's heart and followed it to the listening post's QCC unit, reducing it to inert plastic, ceramcomposite, and metal in seconds. QCC signals could not be intercepted—or even detected—without a second unit containing elements quantum-entangled with those of the first, but disassembler nano could be smart enough to identify an FTL unit and destroy it.

Lieutenant Fitzpatrick and the other five Marines still within the listening post never had a chance even to alert Skybase that they were under attack. Within a few more moments, FMEs—the elite French *Fusilier Marin Extraterrestrienne*—and German *Sturmjäger* had broken in and secured what was left of the facility. Lieutenant Fitzpatrick—badly injured but alive—and the other Marines had been taken prisoner.

They killed eight FMEs before they were taken, though, and wounded five more.

For the next week, then, the former Marine listening post had been occupied by a small reconnaissance unit of PanEuropean special forces. The asteroid's antennae and other surface structures had been vaporized by the nuke, but the base was now linked to the PE flagship *Aurore* by QCC, and the French troops inside had been monitoring the deployment of the Commonwealth squadron almost from the moment Skybase had translated into the Puller battlespace.

And starward, in orbit around the gas giant, *Aurore* and her sister ships were already preparing to spring the trap.

SAP 12/UCS Samar
Assembly Point Yankee
Puller 695 System
1948 hrs GMT

"Fifty newdollars," Gunnery Sergeant Charel Ramsey said over the squad com channel, "that the whole thing is called off and we get told to stand down."

"There speaks the voice of experience," Master Sergeant Paul Barrett said. "Didn't you make the same bet on the way in to Alighan?"

"Well, hey. Cut me some slack, okay? I'm bound to hit it right *some*day."

"You wish," Corporal Takamura put in.

Still packed into his SAP, Garroway listened to the banter among the waiting Marines, and wondered if the old hands in his new platoon were as confident, as relaxed as they seemed. He certainly wasn't able to hear any stress in their voices.

But then, perhaps they had more experience in masking it.

Shit. Did Marines ever admit that they were terrified? . . .

"Uh-oh," Ramsey said. "Take a look at the tacsit feed. There's something—"

A second before, the space around the squadron had been empty of all but Commonwealth ships. Now, though, something like a ripple spread across the electronic representation of the background starfield . . . and then the PanEuropean ships were *there*, in the Commonwealth squadron's midst.

There were six of them. Alphanumerics appearing alongside each red icon identified them by name, class, and tonnage. Largest was the monitor *Rommel*, an 81,000-ton weapons platform mounting multiple plasma cannon banks, high-energy lasers, three massive turret-mounted antimatter accelerators, and a seemingly inexhaustible supply of missiles with high-yield nuclear warheads. A trio of frigates and two destroyers followed, minnows to the monitor's shark.

Garroway stared into the feed for a moment, confused. The tacsit download now showed those six vessels in two places at once—here at AP Yankee, and still in orbit around the gas giant.

Then realization hit him. Of course. The gas giant was thirty light-minutes distant; the six PE warships had outpaced the radiations they'd been emitting in orbit, using their Alcubierre Drives to cross thirty light-minutes in an instant. As he watched, *Samar*'s AI updated the tacsit, erasing the obsolete data.

"Are we going to launch?" Sergeant Chu demanded. "When the hell are we going to launch?"

"Take it easy, Chu-chu," Barrett said. "I don't think any of us want to go out into *that*."

The master sergeant indicated the tacsit feed, which now showed a confused tangle of ships as the two fleets engaged. Though spread across almost 200,000 kilometers, the view compressed battlespace to a small globe filled with moving ships, the rigidly straight lancings of plasma and laser fire, the arcing trajectories of missiles. In particular, the Commonwealth Marine fighters were plunging into the heart of battlespace under high acceleration. At the instant the PE ships had materialized, the carefully drawn globe of Marine aerospace fighters had dissolved like a swarming cloud of insects, sweeping out, around, and in toward the intruding vessels.

Each F/A-4140 massed 94 tons, most of that divided between its powerful Consolidated Aerospace KV-1050 plasma drive and the Solenergia ZPE quantum power transfer unit. Two Marines, a pilot and a weapons operator, were squeezed into a tiny dual cockpit forward. The Stardragon mounted a variety of weapons, interchangeable depending on the mission profile, but its primary was its spinal mount, running forward all the way from the aft thrusters to become the distinctive needle-slim lance extending for 10 meters beyond the nose.

That lance was a plasma accelerator capable of hurling tiny masses of fusing hydrogen at near-c velocities, inertia-shielded to bleed off the incredible recoil energies that otherwise would have torn the fighter to shreds. Range was limited to about 120,000 kilometers—less than half a light-second—but the combination of fusion temperatures and high-velocity kinetic impact could be turned against almost any target with devastating effect.

In terms of both tonnage and firepower, however, the PanEuropeans held the advantage. Both *Samar* and the *Lejeune*, while sizeable vessels, possessed only relatively lightweight armament—primarily point-defense lasers to engage incoming missiles or enemy fighters. *Thor* and *Morrigan* were more heavily armed, but they were two against six, and the enemy monitor was a behemoth, slow-moving and clumsy, but possessing a devastating long-range punch in its trio of turret-mounted antimatter accelerators.

The one advantage held by the Commonwealth lay in the sixteen Stardragons of VMA-980. The fighter squadron already was beginning to live up to their nickname, the Sharpshooters, a proud name born by other Marine aviation squadrons across the centuries. As soon as each fighter was aligned with a PE target, its on-board AI, closely linked with the Weapons Officer's mind, calculated range and speed, adjusting the spacecraft's attitude to permit interception shots across a range of almost 100,000 kilometers. Like miniature suns, packets of fast-expanding fusing hydrogen snapped across the void, penetrating magnetic shielding, slicing through hull composites, liberating flashes of starcore fury with each strike. The outer hull of the immense *Rommel* seemed to sparkle with the impacts.

The *Rommel* was clearly the key to the battle, the equivalent of the proverbial high ground in a conventional surface battle. The Commonwealth destroyers and *Lejeune*'s fighter squadrons could deal with the enemy frigates and destroyers easily enough . . . *if* the PanEuropean monitor could be neutralized. And if not, the monitor's heavy weaponry would make short work of all of the Commonwealth vessels.

From the PanEuropean perspective, it was vital to knock out the two Commonwealth destroyers quickly, before they could combine their considerable firepower and cripple the monitor. Neither *Lejeune* nor *Samar* possessed heavy weapons—they were *transports*, after all, the first of Marine aerospace fighters, the second of Marines, and while they mounted considerable point-defense capabilities and some high-energy lasers for ship-to-ship actions, they lacked the more devastating firepower of antimatter accelerators or large plasma cannon.

Admiral Edan Mitchell was in command of the Commonwealth fleet, operating from his combat command center on board the *Lejeune*. He would be linked in to the battlenet now, Garroway thought, directing the Commonwealth fleet to focus its full attention on the enemy monitor. Already, fighters were issuing from the *Lejeune*'s ventral launch bays, accelerating at high-G toward the PanEuropean behemoth. Clouds of tiny, robotic probes were already scattering throughout the battlespace, each providing a steady feed of visual and electronic data for the Commonwealth C^3, allowing the battle analyses staff to build up a coherent picture of the action.

On board the *Samar*, the waiting Marines could only watch the battle unfold around them, watch . . . and wonder if they would get to take part in the battle, or if a direct hit on *Samar* was about to end their careers in a single, sun-brilliant flash. Once, a plasma bolt struck *Samar*'s hull with a savage, burning snap and an explosion of vapor into empty space, and the transport had rolled slightly, staggered by the shock. There were no casualties; armor and an AI-controlled point-defense gun turret had been all that had been hit.

But the jolt had driven home the overwhelming sense of helplessness Garroway and the other Marines were experiencing right now. And it had led him to rather forcibly remember one of the battle simulations he and the other recruits of his training platoon had experienced at Noctis Labyrinthus, after their naked time, after they'd received their Corp implants.

The historical battle had been at a place called Tarawa, in Earth's Pacific Ocean back in the late pre-spaceflight era. In that action, the U.S. 2nd Marine Division, with elements of the Army's 27th Infantry Division, had made an amphibious assault against a tiny tropical coral atoll defended by 4,500 Japanese under the command of Rear Admiral Shibasaki Keiji.

Tarawa, according to the download data, had been a royal cluster fuck, an operation that had come *that* close to being an utter and complete military disaster. The preliminary bombardment had transformed the atoll into a fire-blasted landscape reminiscent of the cratered surface of the Moon, but had utterly failed to touch the defenders, dug in to a well-protected labyrinth of trenches, log forts, and five hundred concrete bunkers. Worse, *much* worse, the first Marine waves had gone in late, and the tides had been unexpectedly low, so the incoming landing craft had gotten hung up on the coral reef 500 yards offshore. The first waves of Marines had been forced to swim and wade ashore across a fire-swept lagoon, ideal targets for the Japanese mortars and machineguns.

A few amphibious tractors—amtracks—had made it over the reef and across the lagoon, then begun shuttling back and forth between the beach and the reef, carrying stranded Marines ashore, but the Japanese fire had been accurate and heavy. Within a few hours, half of the available amtracks had been knocked out.

For the Marines huddled in those vehicles, the crossing must have been hell. All the men could do was wait . . . crowded together, helpless, wondering if the next incoming round would be the one to score a hit on their wallowing vehicle.

Garroway had been there, standing on the reef next to a blazing landing craft, then on board an amtrack churning its way across the lagoon as mortar shells sent geysers of spray skyward on all sides. He'd charged bunkers with handfuls of

Marines, had watched the battle slowly, *slowly* shift in the attackers' favor, but only after three days of savage fighting, three days collapsed into several long hours by the simulation feed at Noctis Labyrinthus.

Not until now, however, had Garroway truly felt one with those long-ago, long-dead Marine brothers.

"Listen up, Marines," Lieutenant Jones' voice called over the command channel. "We have orders. Stand by to launch!"

"Shit," Ramsey said. "This is it!"

"All you newbies," Master Sergeant Barrett said. "Your trajectories will be AI controlled. When you get on board the target, just stay close and watch your feeds. Just like your training sims."

"Yeah," Ramsey added. "And thank the Marine-green gods of battle you're not going up against the Xul first time out of the gate!"

"Let's kill the bastards!" Barrett added.

"Ooh-rah!" chorused from the ranks of waiting Marines.

Garroway watched the data feed coming through. *Samar* was rotating to bring her SAP launch tubes to bear on the *Rommel*, now 12,000 kilometers off and hammering away at both the *Morrigan* and *Thor*. Garroway watched the numbers of the countdown flicker toward zero, bracing himself . . . and then his SAP slammed into the void under nearly twenty gravities of acceleration.

With inertial dampers on and his suit cushioned within the narrow constraints of the pod by a thick, almost gelatinous liquid, he felt only a few of those twenty Gs, but they were enough to crush the breath from his lungs and blur his vision. When it cleared, when he could focus again on his link feed, he could see *Samar* receding rapidly astern, against a sky lit by intense but utterly silent flashes of light. SAPs were too small to mount the heavy generators necessary for phase-shifting, so each pod was fully visible to the enemy's fire-control radar and lidar systems. This visibility was offset somewhat by the pods' absorptive and energy-scattering outer layers, and the pods were maneuverable enough to give any fire-control AI severe headaches as it tried to predict the myriad incoming vectors . . . but the enemy was tracking the Marine assault wave almost from the instant it emerged from *Samar*'s armored belly.

Point-defense lasers snapped out, crisscrossing the gulf between the *Rommel* and *Samar*. Those beams of intense, coherent energy were invisible in hard vacuum, but the AI governing the tactical feed was painting them in, presumably to reassure the Marines on the grounds that a beam you could see had already missed you.

Somehow, Garroway didn't feel particularly reassured. It seemed as though the entire sky ahead had lit up with flashing, snapping threads of red light, that they were weaving a web of fire so thick and complex that the incoming assault pods couldn't possibly avoid them all.

Then a brilliant, eye-twisting sun erupted over *Rommel*'s aft hull as a small fusion warhead went off. *Morrigan* and *Thor* both were firing everything they had at the monitor, including nuke-tipped missiles, trying to buy precious time for the Marine assault. The superheated plasma and EMP from the blast would provide the SAPs with a bit of cover, at least for a few seconds.

But the plasma cloud dissipated all too swiftly, and *Rommel*'s own point-defenses were simply too effective to allow more missiles to reach her. Abruptly, shockingly, PFC Dulaney's pod was speared by a point-defense beam, a direct hit that vaporized half of the capsule, and sent fragments hurtling outward from within an expanding cloud of hot gas. An instant later, Sergeant Mendoza's pod was hit, a glancing, slicing strike that sheared away part of the hull, and left the remnant tumbling helplessly through the void.

One by one, the enemy fire-control systems locked onto incoming pods. One by one, the pods were being slashed from the sky. There'd been forty SAPs in the first wave. Halfway across the gulf there were thirty-four left . . . then thirty-two. Garroway felt panic rising; *none* of them were going to make it across!

All he could do was hang there in space, a naked and helpless target.

Ontos 7
Battlespace, Puller 695 System
1953 hrs GMT

"Hang on to your lunch!" Lieutenant Kesar Eden yelled over
the intercom. "We're punching it!"

Gunnery Sergeant Warhurst lay cradled in his fighting
position, linked into the Ontos' combat system. There was
a savage thump, and then the *John A. Lejeune*'s launch bay
fell away around him, the carrier dwindling rapidly astern as
the MCA-71 Ontos accelerated at fifty gravities.

Ontos was the Greek word for "thing," and this was the
second time in the long history of the Corps that a Marine
weapons system had borne that unlikely name. Eight hundred years before, during the 1950s, the Marine Corps
had developed a light tracked vehicle specifically as a fast-
moving antitank weapon. Massing just 9 tons, and squeezing
three crew members inside a hull compartment just four feet
high, that first Ontos, designated the M50A1, had mounted
six 106mm recoilless rifles on the upper deck of the vehicle.
The idea had been to allow it to engage enemy armor with
six rapid shots, guaranteeing a kill; its speed, then, would let
it withdraw to cover, allowing the exposed recoilless rifles
to be reloaded.

No one, however, had quite known what to do with the
ugly little vehicle. In fact, the Army had cancelled their
original order when the prototype testing was complete.
The Marines, however, had accepted almost 300 of the vehicles, taking them to war in a place called Vietnam—an
environment for the most part lacking enemy armor to serve
as targets.

The Marines were well known for their ability to adapt
to changing conditions and battlefield needs. The Ontos was
an awkward beast, it turned out, unable to carry much ammunition, and requiring the crew to exit the vehicle in order
to reload, making them vulnerable to enemy fire. Even so,
it proved popular with its crews, who noted that frequently
the enemy would break and run as soon as one of the ugly
little beasts arrived in the combat zone. Those six recoilless

rifles fired beehive rounds, each shell consisting of a bundle of one hundred darts that sliced through jungle foliage with devastating effect, turning the vehicle into what had been called the world's biggest shotgun. Used against bunkers and against enemy infantry, the Ontos provided Marine riflemen with effective close-fire support at the company level.

Always considered an ugly duckling, however, that first Ontos had never been accepted by decision-makers above the company level, and the weapon system was withdrawn from service after it had seen only four years of combat service. For decades after, the Ontos had been something of an embarrassment to those tasked with designing and procuring new weapons.

Eight centuries later, a new Marine weapons system had been introduced to the Corps bearing the ancient Greek name for "thing." Part vehicle, part artillery, it was designed to both provide close infantry support in combat—especially in zero- and low-gravity environments, and also to serve as transport for a Marine squad, getting them safely into combat, then providing artillery support as they made their assault. The new Ontos was undeniably ugly, as awkward-looking as its ancient predecessor, flat, stubby, and massing 383 tons, with multiply jointed legs and a ball-mounted forward blast head that gave it the appearance of a huge and ungainly insect. Twelve armored Marines and their equipment could be carried aft in the lightly armored belly. The vehicle's "wings" mounted a pair of hivel accelerator cannons that could fire antimatter rounds, tactical nukes, nano-D canisters, or conventional high explosives.

Space was sharply limited on board the transport, however. Warhurst and one other gunner were squeezed in to either side of the vehicle commander in a dorsal sponson forward, behind the blast-head mount, and cyberlinked into the Ontos' command network. The Marines aft were as tightly cocooned as their counterparts in the SAP pods now being launched from the *Samar*. Like the ancient Ontos, no one really knew what to do with the modern weapon of that name, but the Corps had adapted it especially for ship-boarding actions. Four, including Warhurst's vehicle, had been accelerated from the *Lejeune*'s launch bay, and were vectoring in on the PanEuropean monitor *Rommel* now.

Like aerospace fighters, the Ontos operated off of a Sole-nergia ZPE quantum-power transfer unit. Using the same principle as a Quantum-Coupled Communications system, the ZPE transfer unit used quantum entanglement to transmit energy from one point to another, without actually traversing the space in between. Extremely high energies were drawn from the zero-point field taps on board the *Lejeune* and the *Samar*, but routed directly to field-entangled power receivers on board individual F/A-4140s and the MCA-71 Ontos transports, without the possibility of that transmission being blocked or even detected.

The system had some important trade-offs. The advantage, of course, was that the massive quantum power taps could be left back on board the capital ships. The disadvantage, though, was that if the *Lejeune* or the *Samar* were knocked out of action, their orphaned offspring would become dead in space, with only their relatively low-powered on-board antimatter converter systems from which to draw on for life support and maneuvering.

All of that was of less importance to Warhurst now than was the simple fact that he was back in action at last.

When he left Recruit Training Command, there'd been speculation that he would end up in a rifle company with a number of his former recruits. The 1MIEF personnel department had killed that idea, however, and in fairly short order. Marine recruits were instilled with the absolute and unvarying principle of the Corps—Marines work *together*, as a unit. However, learning that basic lesson as they go through boot camp, most Marines reach graduation hating their DI. Respecting him, yes, but hating him nonetheless.

It wasn't that 1MIEF's command constellation was afraid that some former recruit of Warhurst's was going to get even some night on deployment. Platoon AIs were good watchdogs when it came to that sort of thing. They were conscious, though, of the need for a smoothly functioning structure at the squad, platoon, and company levels. Hatred—or fear—of a squad mate during a combat situation when everyone needed to work together smoothly, as a unit, might get Marines killed.

So Gunny Warhurst had been assigned to an Ontos crew, a demanding billet that required experienced combat veterans, rather than newbies. The platoon's fresh meat would do best in assault platoons where they could draw on one another—and on the old hands in each platoon—for support and strength. Serving a gun station on an Ontos required more seasoning, and the ability to link *very* closely indeed with the vehicle commander, and with the other gunner on board.

Warhurst's relief at being in action again had more, *much* more, to do with his need to get away from Mars and the still-burning pain of having been evicted from his family. The psych AIs at Ares RTC had tried to counsel him through the rough parts, but he honestly couldn't tell now if they'd done a damned thing to help.

He knew he was still spending way too much time uselessly rehearsing conversations in his head. He so wanted his family—especially Julie—to understand, to, to what? To come to their senses and *feel* how he needed the Corps, to understand that this was his family as much as the Tamalyn-Danner line marriage, because, damn it, the Corps was a part of who and what he was, that he could no more discard it than he could discard his own heart.

He was beginning to realize that a lot of his grief was centered less on losing Julie, Eric, Donal, and Callie than it was on being rejected. Dumped. As though he meant nothing to any of them, had contributed nothing, had *been* nothing. When he thought about how they'd cast him aside, it was all he could do to see through that haze of enveloping white pain . . . a searing mingling of grief and loss, of fury and hatred and broken ego and insulted honor and yearning desire.

He hated them all, now. And he still wanted them to come back, to say it had all been a mistake.

He still wanted to love them. . . .

Damn it, he was doing it again. *Focus, you idiot*! he snarled at himself, furious. *Pay attention to what you're doing or you'll get us all killed*!

The Ontos had vaulted through the emptiness between the *Lejeune* and the enemy monitor, shifting vectors wildly and rapidly in order to make things as difficult as possible for the *Rommel*'s fire-control AIs. Drawing on the ZPE energy tap on board the *Lejeune*, the Ontos could afford the added power-hungry luxury of phase-shifting, which made the enemy's job even harder in terms of target acquisition and lock, and provided some measure of defense against beams and shrapnel.

But not *complete* protection, he noted, as a small hivel slug struck the Ontos amidships. He felt the staggering shock as a few grams of depleted uranium passed through the ship. Most of the released kinetic energy, fortunately, was dissipated by the Ontos' phase-shifted state, but enough leaked through to jar his teeth.

He stayed focused on his link, however. They were still flying, so he ignored the impact, figuring that there was nothing he could do about it except to keep doing his job, which was to try to track incoming missiles or armored enemy troops or gun or sensor emplacements on the monitor's hull and knock them out with hivel cannon fire.

The ship's AI had already highlighted the turret that had loosed that slug. He dragged his mental targeting cursor over the dome and thought-clicked the number two gun starboard, sending a stream of high-velocity rounds slashing through the turret in great, pulsing gouts of white heat before it could fire another shot.

As it neared its objective, as the *Rommel* loomed huge in his downloaded mental vision, the Ontos' hull began morphing into its landing configuration, wings and weapons outstretched, clawed legs extended, blast head forward and down, seeking contact.

Then the Ontos was on the monitor's hull with a heavy, ringing thud, its ugly blast head extending and dropping to bring a torch of plasma energy, as hot as the core of a sun, into contact with the monitor's armor cladding.

Under that searing assault, the outer nanolayers rippled and flowed as they tried to distribute the heat, then burst away in clouds of vapor, exposing the tender ceramics and alloys beneath. The Ontos' claws dug in and held, as the current of vaporizing metals and composites howled past like a hurricane wind, expending itself in vacuum. A crater formed, then deepened, widening, as the Ontos *thing* continued to eat its way through the skin and into the heart of the enemy ship.

The *Rommel* carried fighters—not as many as the *Lejeune*, but enough to provide some measure of close defense against such tactics as the Ontos was now employing. His AI warned of two bogies swinging up and around over the horizon of the monitor's hull, identifying them as PanEuropean Épée fighters—robotic craft that were exceptionally fast and maneuverable because they had no flesh and blood on board to coddle.

Warhurst was screaming as he brought both starboard-side guns to bear on the stooping targets. . . .

18

0112.1102

SAP 12
PanEuropean Monitor Rommel
Puller 695 System
2004 hrs GMT

Garroway had been wondering if any of the SAPs were going to make it across the gulf between *Samar* and the *Rommel*, as pod after pod was struck down by the enemy point defenses, but then a fresh wave of blasts flashed and pulsed across the monitor's hull, targeting the point-defense turrets and fire-control sensors. *Morrigan* was now concentrating all of her fire against the PanEuropean monitor, attempting to screen the Marine assault wave, giving them a precious few seconds to complete their run, and a number of aerospace fighters had closed enough of the gap to pour concentrated devastation into the shuddering hull of the huge enemy ship. Although he hadn't seen them, the tacsit feed also showed three MCA–71 Ontos transports had touched down on the monitor's hull, and were busily tunneling into thick armor. Another nuke, one of a salvo fired from the *Thor*, got through a moment later, flaring with dazzling incandescence against the night.

But the *Rommel* was still very much in action. In seconds, three more SAPs vaporized in white-hot flashes of energy . . . and the tacsit showed enemy fighters as well, rising from the monitor to engage the incoming pods.

But by now the PanEuropean monitor was looming

huge just ahead, its surface rushing up to meet Garroway's incoming capsule. The guiding AI, Garroway noted with an almost detached interest, was directing his pod into a gaping crater blown open moments before by the plasma blast head of an MCA–71. An instant later, and despite the inertial damping, Garroway felt the savage shock as his SAP slammed into the wreckage of what had been the *Rommel*'s hull at that point.

The SAP's squared-off prow was designed to collapse against whatever it struck, releasing a ring of nanotech disassemblers programmed to ignore the pod, but to eat through hull metal or composite with which it was in contact. As the pod slipped deeper into the PE ship's armor cladding, the SAP's entire outer surface turned gelatinous with nano-D, eating away at the metal and lubricating the pod's movement. Vanishing into the ship's hull, the pod continued burrowing forward, dissolving wreckage and armor, until sensors within the drilling head detected an empty space beyond.

When that happened, nano-disassemblers halted their eating, then converted to sealant, fusing pod to hull, and the leading end of the assault craft flashed from solid to gas in a savage liberation of raw energy.

Garroway was waiting, gulping down air, heart pounding, the flamer mounted on his 660-battlesuit's left forearm already aimed and armed. As the bow of the assault pod exploded into gas, he followed up with a burst from the flamer, sending a fireball searing into the *Rommel*'s interior.

He was right behind the dissipating fireball, allowing the pod mechanism to propel him forward and through the breach into the monitor's hull as the dampening gel around him flashed into harmless vapor.

What followed next was pure training. *Rommel* possessed an artificially generated gravity field, set to about three-quarters of a gravity—roughly equivalent to the gravity of Aurore. He was entering the monitor from an unusual angle, coming down through the overhead of one of the interior decks, and the local gravity field grabbed at him as he fell through the opening.

There'd been no good way to predict where he would come out, or what the local gravity would be like. Part of his brain registered the fall, and long hours of training took over. He twisted as he fell, landing catlike, if heavily, on his boots, his left arm already sweeping up and around to engage any targets that might present themselves. His helmet sensors gave him a 360-degree view in a side mental window, but he pivoted in any case to see for himself, checking both ways.

Several bodies of the ship's crew lay on the deck both ahead and behind, within a passageway choked with an impenetrable fog of smoke and a near-total darkness relieved only by his battlesuit's shoulder-mounted lights. Whether they'd been killed by external fire, by the blast as the SAP opened up, or by his flamer, there was no way of knowing.

Nor was it important. A Marine assault was built around one simple concept—the employment of extreme and sudden *violence* to overwhelm local defenses and secure the battle initiative.

And to keep the initiative, he needed to keep moving. If he stopped, if he went on the defensive, he would in minutes be isolated, surrounded, and killed. Two of the ship's crew appeared from a side passage just ahead; he triggered his flamer and saw the two writhe and struggle and then wilt in the torchblast. Neither had been wearing armor, though both were carrying mag-pulse rifles. In another second, both were dead . . . probably irretrievables.

"Green one, one-two!" he shouted into his helmet pick-up. "On board! Request orienteering fix!"

"One moment," the voice of the platoon AI said. Then a window opened in a corner of his mind, showing an animation of the corridor he was in now, and a flashing pointer showing which way he needed to go.

That way. Strange. His instincts and his implanted hardware both had been suggesting the other way . . . but he was feeling a bit disoriented both by the shock of landing and the drop into the *Rommel*'s local gravity.

But if Achilles said go *that* way, that was the way he would go. The animation also showed the ghosted-out shadows of other passageways around him, and moving green blips representing other Marines. The sight was deeply reassuring; he was alone in that corridor, but he could see other Marines appearing one after another in other, nearby compartments and passageways, all of them moving in the same general direction.

A monitor was a huge ship, a veritable city wrapped in thick cladding, and enclosing a maze of passageways and compartments designed to house several thousand crew members. A few hundred Marines—to say nothing of however many members of the 55th MARS had actually survived the passage from *Samar*—could not hope to kill or overpower the entire crew, especially when a number of those enemy personnel would be PE armored marines trained to combat just such an assault as this.

The Commonwealth battle-command AIs had already identified the key objectives within the *Rommel*, using available schematics and ship plans from Intelligence, as well as sounding information being gathered from robotic probes already burrowing into the ship's thick hull. The combined information, transmitted back to *Samar* and the *Lejeune*, allowed Achilles and the AIs within the Combat Command Center to build up a coherent picture of the *Rommel*'s interior, and to know exactly where each Marine was at the moment in relation to a list of possible objectives. A handful of Commonwealth Marines wandering around on their own would have been lost in moments, easy targets for the enemy's counterattack. Under Achilles' guidance, however, they could be sure they were moving as a unit, with common purpose.

Garroway's primary objective was a command-and-control center buried in the *Rommel*'s core. To get there, he needed to follow this passageway for about 20 meters, then locate a maintenance shaft in the starboard bulkhead, a broad, open tunnel plunging into the monitor's core.

"Here," Achilles said in his mind, highlighting a section of the passageway's bulkhead in red. "There is an access tube just beyond that partition."

"Got it," he said, and he turned his mag-pulse rifle on his right arm on the bulkhead, slamming a rapid-fire stream of slugs into the wall. Metal and ceramplast shredded, and then he could see through the hole and into a black emptiness beyond.

He used a personal drone to check the far side, tossing the fist-sized robot sensor through the hole and watching the feedback on a helmet display. The maintenance shaft was a broad but narrow space descending relative to the local gravity field. There was no artificial gravity, but his armor thrusters ought to get him where he needed to go.

Just behind him, the overhead suddenly bulged, then exploded as another SAP broke through. Garroway decided not to wait for a possible volley of friendly fire, but he tagged the opening with a small transponder that would show the bulkhead breach to anyone following him, then plunged through himself.

The shaft interior was in complete darkness, but his armor's shoulder lights illuminated his surroundings in harsh, shifting patterns of white light and black shadow. A moment later, he became aware of other lights above him, as other Marines broke through into the shaft and began the descent into the monitor's core.

He was no longer alone . . . a very good feeling indeed.

Kicking off from the entrance breach, he drifted down several meters—"down," of course, being a relative term in the sudden falling emptiness of microgravity. He triggered his suit thrusters and moved more quickly, using his hands to guide himself along the piping and tightly tied bundles of fiber optics lining the shaft walls.

He moved through the shaft for what seemed like hours, though his implant timer insisted it was only three minutes. At last, though, Achilles highlighted an area of tunnel wall just ahead. "There," the AI told him. "That will give you direct access to your objective."

The tacsit feed continued to give him a ghosted overlay of what was behind the surrounding bulkheads. Pulling himself up short alongside the indicated section of the tunnel, he hung in emptiness for another few seconds until five more Marines reached him, snagging hold of conduits and coming to a halt at the designated level.

An armored form bumped against him, steadying itself on a conduit. The 660-armor's surface Nanoflage made the figure almost ghostly in the tunnel's gloom, but a transponder-relayed ID appeared on Garroway's helmet display—Gunnery Sergeant Ramsey. Garroway felt an almost overwhelming sense of relief, so much so he could feel his knees trembling. He'd not wanted to go through that bulkhead alone.

"Hey, Gunnery Sergeant," he said. "I guess this is it."

"Looks that way. Wait until the others get here."

Three more armored figures arrived down the shaft in short order—Sergeant Richard Chu, Corporal Marin Delazlo, and PFC Sandre Kenyon.

"Okay, people," Ramsey told them, pulling a breaching charge from an external suit pouch. "We breach and we go through, standard one-by-one assault. Everyone set?"

"Ready, Gunnery Sergeant," Garroway said. He was focusing on damping down the fear.

"Fire in the hole!" Ramsey announced, slapping the self-sticking breaching charge to the sealed hatch. The Marines rolled away, and an instant later an intense gout of white-hot metal erupted from the charge, as a nano-D thermal-decoupler turned titanium alloy to a spray of liquid and gaseous metal. The spray grew brighter, expanding into an oval patch roughly 2 meters high . . . and then the metal burned through with a brilliant flash.

Ramsey was the first Marine through the still-hot opening, but Garroway crowded through just behind him. Both Marines tumbled once more into gravity, this time within a large and circular chamber filled with control consoles, work stations, and a number of men and women in PE uniforms, reclining on link couches as they directed their side of the battle through the ship's Net.

Operating under Achilles' instructions, Ramsey turned his pulse rifle against one particular bank of instrumentation, slamming it into junk. The salvo seemed to shock the reclining enemy officers, as their link with the *Rommel*'s AI net was broken and they were dropped out of their command virtual reality.

Achilles identified one threat—an armored Marine standing near the compartment's single hatch. The guy's armor would be proof against flamer fire. Instead, Garroway triggered a burst from his mag-pulse rifle, the stream of high-velocity slugs catching the enemy marine high in the chest and slamming him backward into the hatch.

The other Marines were coming through the opening into the compartment as well. One of the enemy officers pulled an ugly handgun from a holster and fired from his couch; the round ricocheted off Ramsey's helmet. Chu took three steps and placed the black muzzle of his flamer against the man's skull. "Drop it, monsieur," he growled.

The chances were good that the language spoken by *Rommel*'s crew was Deutsch, not Français, but the message was unmistakable. The man, eyes bulging, dropped the pistol and raised his hands. Other men and women in the room were already doing the same.

Other Marines, guided by Achilles, were attaching nano-D charges to specific consoles and link stations, and Ramsey was jacking a small, heavily armored box into a particular computer access relay. Garroway and Chu, gesturing with their weapons, herded the PanEuropean personnel off of their link couches and across the compartment, lining them up on their knees, facing an empty bulkhead, their hands behind their heads.

This compartment, Garroway knew, was one of three auxiliary control rooms buried within the *Rommel*. Some of the others might be destroyed, or isolated by damage, or Marine assault squads might already be breaking into them.

All they could do now was wait. Garroway kept the POWs covered, while Ramsey worked his computer link and the other three Marines kept their weapons trained on the sealed hatch. They wouldn't fire the nano-D charges unless they absolutely had to. The idea was to capture the monitor, not junk her . . . but they *would* render the huge ship harmlessly inert if they couldn't force her to surrender.

"Okay," Ramsey said after a few moments. "Achilles has interfaced with *Rommel*'s AI suite. We're in."

"Ooh-*rah*!" Garroway cried, and several of the others

joined in. Sandre Kenyon was, by chance, standing close by. Keeping his weapon still trained on the kneeling POWs, Garroway reached out and gave Sandre an awkward one-armed hug, their black armor clashing as it came together like a pair of colliding tanks.

"It's gonna be close," Ramsey said a moment later. He was getting things on his tactical feed that weren't funneling through to the rest of the squad. "We have three more enemy ships arriving from in-system. Another destroyer . . . and it looks like a couple of light escort cruisers, *Pegasus* . . . and *Sagitta.* Our fighters are reforming to meet them."

His momentary rush of enthusiasm cooled, Garroway stood, covering the prisoners, and waited. *Rommel*, apparently, was still in the fight, though only intermittently now as more and more of her Net circuitry was shut down or compromised. Garroway tried to figure out what was going on through the platoon tacsit feed, but gave up after a few moments. The tangle of ships out there was hopelessly confused, now, with no fewer than thirteen major warships and well over a hundred fighters from both sides, plus Marine Ontos transports and shuttles, robotic sensor craft, and hundreds of circling, target-seeking missiles. Nukes were going off every few moments, and each blast tended to blank out the data transmission with momentary storms of white-noise static.

Someone was at the hatch. Garroway heard the thump, followed by a mechanical-sounding clank. Chu, Kenyon, and Delazlo hunkered down behind consoles and link couches, their weapons aimed at the hatch. Ramsey continued working with the computer feed relay. By now, a small army of artificial intelligences were being beamed across from the *Lejeune* and the *Samar*, downloading themselves into the *Rommel*'s computer net. If they could capture the electronic high ground in time. . . .

"The hatch may be a diversion," Achilles whispered in their minds. "I am detecting suspicious noises *here.*" The AI highlighted a section of bulkhead at right angles to the bulkhead containing the hatch.

"Right," Chu said. "Kenyon! Keep covering the hatch! Laz, with me!"

Chu and Delazlo shifted positions to cover the new threat. A moment later, the hatch flared with a dazzling white light, metal dissolving under a high-energy assault of nano disassemblers. Kenyon opened up with her pulse rifle as soon as the hatch started melting away and there was no longer a threat of own-goal riocochets in the compartment, sending a steady stream of high-velocity fire through the opening and into the compartment beyond.

Five seconds later, a second gout of light and hot gases exploded from the other bulkhead, burning through a communications console. A heavily armored *Sturmjäger* appeared, stepping through the gush of incandescent gasses, his dark grey combat armor outwardly similar to the Marines' 660-battlesuit, but with a flatter, more complex helmet and a different weapons loadout.

The German armor appeared to flow and distort as its surface Nanoflage blended with smoke and bulkhead, but the elite trooper's battlesuit could not render its wearer completely invisible. As he moved, a general outline of the figure could clearly be seen, and certain things like the visual pickups and external sensor gear were still plainly visible. The *Sturmjäger* stepped through the molten opening into a double stream of high-velocity kinetic-kill rounds. One round in ten contained a charge of nano-D, but the impact alone was sufficient to shred the man's plastron and helmet, opening the suit up in a shocking blossom of bright red blood. A second trooper came through behind the first, and was cut down.

After that, there was silence.

Ramsey, Garroway knew, was waiting with a coded thought-click ready. If he triggered it, the instrumentation in the compartment would dissolve. The enemy would hold off on using things like grenades, thermal charges, or nano-D because they didn't want to destroy *Rommel*'s command-center electronics any more than the Commonwealth Marines did.

Stand off.

And then, four minutes later, the incredible, the impossible happened. A white rag appeared in the opening in the bulkhead. "Marines?" a voice said over a standard com channel. "Marines? *Bitte*. We surrender. The ship surrenders. . . ."

"Stay back!" Chu demanded. "We want confirmation."

But the confirmation came through moments later. At the order of Kapitän Walther Hirsch, commanding officer of the PanEuropean monitor *Rommel*, the ship was formally surrendered. Garroway learned later that the electronic assault AIs, feeding in through the relay, had overcome the ship's electronic defenses and taken control of her computer net. *Rommel*'s captain, when he found he could no longer control his ship, had safed her weapons, then announced his capitulation.

The ship-boarding action turned the tide of the battle. Though the Marines in the assault teams wouldn't learn the details until later, *Rommel*'s capitulation triggered a full-scale disengagement by the other PE ships. One of the PE frigates and a destroyer had been knocked out of action and were now helplessly adrift, but the others had broken off the attack and begun accelerating back in-system.

Over the course of the next hour, naval personnel arrived from the *Lejeune* to try to make *Rommel* operational once more, though that was clearly going to take time. The monitor had been badly mauled in the fight, and many of her weapons systems were off-line.

The situation was still extremely serious, however. Both *Thor* and *Morrigan* had also taken heavy damage, and six aerospace fighters out of the three squadrons engaged, one fighter in eight, had been destroyed. Both *Samar* and *Lejeune* had taken light damage as well. The original operational plan for Lafayette had called for at least three loads of ship, fourteen in all, to be translated into Puller space, and for those fourteen ships to then make a concerted assault against the PE ships while they were still in orbit around the gas giant. The Marine assault was to have been directed against the cruiser *Aurore*, which Intelligence believed was the enemy command ship, and which was believed to be the vessel where the Marines captured from the Puller listening post were being held.

A hostage-rescue assault was now out of the question, since the advantage of surprise had been lost.

Still, the capture of *Rommel* had certainly changed the

tactical balance, somewhat. Admiral Mitchell elected to wait and see what happened next.

Some two hours after the end of the battle, Skybase translated in from distant Sol with five more ships crammed into her flight deck, the destroyers *Kali* and *Bellona*, and three escort gunships, *Active, Amazon,* and *Avenger*.

General Alexander entered into immediate negotiations with the PanEuropean commander and, before much longer, the Battle of Puller 659 officially was over.

USMC Skybase
Puller 695 System
2329 hrs GMT

General Alexander stared across the virtual table at the icon of his opposite number in the PanEuropean fleet, an older, diminutive, and bearded man whose personal software had introduced as Admiral Pascal D'Urville. Intelligence records indicated that D'Urville was better known in military circles by the nickname "Marlon," meaning "Little Falcon," and the man's formal *corona flammae* actually held within it the faint image of a bird of prey with outstretched wings. According to the mil-history downloads, he'd won the nickname while in command of the battlecruiser *Faucon* during a nasty little naval confrontation between the PanEuropean Republic and the Islamic Theocracy at Ubaylah twenty years before.

"We do not want to be here," Alexander was saying. "We have no wish to fight you. You are not our enemy. This is the wrong war, at the wrong time, with the wrong enemy."

"But I note," D'Urville replied with just a ghost of a smile, "that you *are* here, monsieur. Fighting us." He was speaking Anglic, rather than having his words translated by AI interpreters, with only rare lapses into Français.

"We fought you, yes. We will continue fighting you if you don't release our people."

"What people?"

"The Marines you took from our listening post."

"An *illegal* listening post, established clandestinely within PanEuropean territory."

Alexander stared at the other's virtual image for a long moment. There was no way to tell what the man was really feeling at the moment, no way to read his electronically created persona. That faint, somewhat sardonic smile might be reflecting what the man himself felt, or it could be something inserted by the AIs running the simulation.

"Admiral, I'm not going to argue with you about legalities. That's for lawyers and politicians to decide. The fact is . . . you and I are *here*, and the politicians are on Aurore and on Earth hundreds of light-years distant. I suggest that we leave the politicians out of this, just for the moment. Just possibly, we can find a means of hammering out a peace without their . . . help."

He gave a deep, Gallic shrug. "You must know, sir, that my own powers in that regard are limited. I am charged with defending PanEuropean space. I am scarcely what you could call a peacemaker."

"Admiral, I am here for two reasons, and two reasons only. I intend to free my people which you are holding as prisoners of war, and I intend to assemble the rest of my fleet here, in this system, and then depart through that stargate yonder. We offer no threat to PanEuropean sovereignty. When we move through the gate, I doubt very much that you'll see us again."

D'Urville's eyes widened slightly. "You hope to die on the other side?"

"No. Not if we can help it. What I hope is that we will find other ways home, after dealing with the Xul threat. In any case, it will take time. Quite probably years. Possibly decades."

"A long war."

"A large foe."

"Monsieur . . . have you given thought to why the Republic has refused your fleet passage here? If you should succeed . . . if you should find the Xul on the other side of the gate, if you should *awaken* him, his planet-killer ships might well come through here, in PanEuropean space. My government fears your . . . your government's impetuous nature. You don't know what you're dealing with beyond the gates. Your meddling might call down the Xul's wrath upon *la République*. Have you given thought to the possibility that it might be better, *far* better, simply to leave the Xul alone . . . and pray that they never find us?"

"It's too late for that, Admiral. You've seen the reports. About the *Argo*. If the Xul aren't already on the way, they will be soon. And when they come, no matter where they come, no human world will be safe."

He appeared to consider this. "Your Commonwealth is taking on a rather arrogant responsibility, you know, one involving the survival of all of humanity. Some of us believe that to be . . . short-sighted. And stupid."

"And which is the more short-sighted, Admiral? To face what's coming boldly? Even go out to meet it on its own ground? Or to hide our heads in the dirt until we're taken and devoured? Admiral . . . the Republic can do what it likes, but we are *not* going to sit around doing nothing while those monsters roll right over us. We've lived in the shadow of fear for too long. No more."

"Perhaps that is for the politicians to decide. We have other matters to deal with, eh?"

"The POWs. Yes."

"You must realize, General Alexander, that I have limited authority here. Even if we held the people you mention—and we do not—I cannot simply hand over prisoners of war without some . . . reciprocity? Yes. Something from you in exchange."

"Simple enough. I'm told that we hold nearly four thousand men and women, crewmembers of the *Rommel*. Including Captain Hirsch."

D'Urville gave a sour expression. "Perhaps we don't want Captain Hirsch back." He shrugged again. "In any case, our main fleet shall be here within a day or two. It might be best if you withdrew with your small fleet now, while you still can. Details of a prisoner exchange can be handled by our respective governments."

Now he *knew* the man was bluffing. "Admiral D'Urville, I'm not going to fucking play games with you. Perhaps you recognize these?" With a thought-click, he opened a data-filled window.

Hours before, when the Marines had been penetrating the *Rommel*'s electronic fastness, the uploaded AIs that had shut down the PanEuropean monitor had at the same time accessed a treasure trove of data stored in the enemy vessel's computer net. The information included updated rosters on all of the PE ships in-system, their operational orders, archived orders going back for weeks . . . and the complete communications logs recording conversations between the *Rommel* and the *Aurore*.

Lejeune's command constellation had already prepared a complete translation for Alexander, which included the text of an exchange between Admiral D'Urville and a Captain Hirsch, just before *Rommel* and the other PE ships had engaged their Alcubierre Drives for the run out to the stargate. *We are on our own, Captain,* D'Urville had told his subordinate. *They can send us nothing more. It is up to you, my friend, to hold the line here.*

We can do it if we can defeat them in detail, sir, Hirsch had replied. *If we can destroy this small squadron before more Commonwealth warships arrive. If that happens, well . . . I fear our assets are stretched too thin. We would have to withdraw.*

Do it. They are only four ships. Intelligence tells us that the two transports carry only a handful of fighters and Marines, a token force only. Kill them now, and we will be waiting for the rest when they arrive.

D'Urville was now reading those words.

Much had been written over the past few centuries regarding modern space tactical combat—especially the use of Marines in ship-to-ship actions such as the one that had taken down the *Rommel*. A tactic as old as the ancient empire of Rome, combat boarding actions seemed nonsensical on the face of it. Armchair strategists had repeatedly announced that using men to storm and board enemy ships had no more place in modern warfare than skill at swinging a sword.

But there were times when capturing an enemy warship was far, far more valuable in winning a battle than simply vaporizing it. The recovery and analyses of data from enemy computer networks constituted one entire branch of modern military intelligence. It was *information* that won battles, not mere firepower.

"We are not at war, Admiral," Alexander told the other man. "Not *yet*. But you are not now in a position to play games with me . . . to delay . . . or to fight back. You will return my people to me and you will have your squadron stand down. If you do not, my Marines will board each of your ships in turn and shut them down."

He didn't add that Commonwealth AIs had followed communications pathways in from the *Rommel* to other ships in the PanEuropean fleet. It would take time for them to compromise the entire PE data net, but, like an insidious invasion of computer viruses, they were already piggybacking into the enemy's network. At the very least, Alexander would know within another few hours exactly where any Commonwealth POWs were being held. He would target that vessel first; once the POWs were freed, he would take down the rest.

With luck, it would be simpler still. A single command from him would shut down the enemy fleet cold.

"You wouldn't dare!" D'Urville declared. "As you said, there is no war, yet! You would not . . . would not . . ."

"Admiral, I am a Commonwealth Marine . . . a direct line descendent of the original United States Marine Corps. I do *not* make threats. And I do not make a request a second time. Surrender here, now, and retain the integrity of your fleet . . . or surrender to my Marines when they board your ship."

The two men locked gazes for a long several seconds. Then, reluctantly, D'Urville broke eye contact. "You win," he said.

And the negotiations were over, the war ended before it had even been declared.

19

USMC Skybase
Anneau orbit, Puller 695 System
0950 hrs GMT

The Galaxy is a hellishly big place.

Even that minute backwater pocket of the Galaxy that held all of the worlds of Humankind was immense beyond all human reckoning. Not even faster-than-light travel or the quantum miracle of instantaneous communications could make that volume of emptiness and thinly scattered suns small enough for any mere government to truly claim to own or actually to control it.

Admiral D'Urville was the local PanEuropean military commander, and while he continued to receive orders from Aurore, he was the man who had to determine how best to implement them in the distant and out-of-the-way cosmic speck that was the Puller system—or Anneau, as the PanEuropeans called it. Aurore might suggest—even order—but D'Urville, simply by virtue of his isolation, was the one who would decide policy here.

General Alexander stood on Skybase's main observation deck, looking up at the world called Ring with something approaching religious awe. He'd assumed—like nearly everyone else within the Commonwealth who'd heard the name—that the world had been named Anneau, or Ring, and the red dwarf sun Ringstar, because of the location of the Stargate in the system's lonely outer reaches. Clearly

though, that was not the case . . . or else the presence of
the Stargate was a coincidence that permitted an amusing
double meaning.

Like many gas giants, the world of Ring was, in fact,
ringed, surrounded by broad, knife-edge-thin bands of icy
particles. And like Uranus in Earth's solar system, the planet
had an extreme axial tilt—85 degrees—so that it seemed to
be lying on its side in respect to the plane of its orbit about
Étoile d'Anneau.

As a result, twice in Anneau's brief, twenty-two-week
year, its rings were face-on to the light of its star, and by
chance that was the case now. The Commonwealth fleet had
maneuvered in-system to approach Anneau and its circling
moons, and from this vantage point, half a million kilometers out, the red-hued light of the tiny sun was diffused
through the glittering plane of the rings, transforming them
into a dazzling series of nested ruby arcs, transparently delicate, spectacularly beautiful.

The Republican fleet had gathered close by the PanEuropean base, constructed on one of the shepherd moons orbiting Anneau just outside the outermost band of sparkling red
light. The Commonwealth fleet, clustered about Skybase,
was maintaining a position farther out, on the gravitational
high ground, so to speak, well clear of the deeper reaches of
Anneau's gravity well and outside the worst of the planet's
radiation belts.

A dozen other Commonwealth ships had been dispatched
to the Stargate, where Marines were reclaiming the captured
listening post and preparing, upon the successful completion
of Operation Lafayette, to initiate Operation Gorgon.

With friendly artificial intelligences now resident
throughout the local PanEuropean computer net, the Commonwealth fleet had been monitoring a steady stream of
FTL communications between the two Aurores—the PE
flagship and the distant Republican capital. Alexander had
felt considerable compassion for Admiral D'Urville as he'd
been castigated by his superiors for his surrender . . . but
the electronic eavesdropping had proven conclusively that
there would be no help forthcoming for the PanEuropeans

in the Anneau system, and it appeared that the Auroran government would indeed be forced to accept the *fait accompli* of the Marine victory in the sharp little engagement at Puller 659. For one thing, and against all expectations, there *had* been a small but significant mutiny within the PE fleet; as promised, Traditionalist Catholic elements had tried to seize control of several PE ships, including the *Sagitta,* the *Détroyat,* and the frigate *Drogou.* As nearly as could be learned from intercepted comm messages transmitted back to Aurore, the mutinies all had been suppressed, but the momentary confusion within the PanEuropean ranks had evidently contributed to their decision to withdraw—and to not re-engage once additional Commonwealth fleet elements began making their appearance.

It left Alexander wondering just how close-run the battle actually had been. It was now clear that by putting their own special forces troops into the listening post, the PanEuropeans had known exactly when the Skybase had first translated into the Anneau system, and been able to strike when the Commonwealth forces had been at their weakest. But for the uncertainties of the promised religious uprising on the Republican ships—coupled with the valiant assault by the 55th MARS on the *Rommel*, Operation Lafayette might well have been a military disaster from the first.

And it also left him wondering what weakness might be buried within the Gorgon op plan, what overlooked aspect of the battle plan or key lack of intel on the enemy might be waiting to undo all of that planning in a single nightmare orgy of flame, death, and destruction somewhere beyond the Stargate.

Well, insofar as that went, they'd planned the best they could. Everything that could be taken into account had been. The op would succeed, or it would fail . . . but either way they'd done everything possible.

And Alexander remained convinced that Gorgon was the *only* means available to keep the Xul from finally devouring the worlds of Humankind.

And they would be making the Stargate transit with a solid victory under their belts. Yesterday, shortly after they'd

arrived in orbit around Anneau, a PE shuttle had flown up
and out of the gas giant's gravity well and approached the
Skybase. On board was Major George Tomanaga, Lieuten-
ants Fitzpatrick and Lee, and the other Marine personnel
captured when the PanEuropeans had discovered and taken
over the listening post. Lee had been in a medical stasis tube,
still undergoing treatment from her radiation exposure in
the Starwall system. She was on board the medical support
ship *Barton* now, and the doctors and med AIs all promised
a rapid recovery. Evidently, she'd already, and with some ve-
hemence, volunteered to join the MIEF's aerospace wing.

She would be welcome. The final butcher's bill, the ir-
recoverables, for the Puller system engagement had not
been bad, considering the scope of the victory—76 naval
personnel on board the *Thor* and the *Morrigan*, and 92
Marines—most of those last picked off during their approach to the *Rommel*. Fifteen Marines, though, had been
aerospace fighter pilots killed in the engagement against
Rommel and her fighters, and 1MIEF would be entering
the next phase of operations with a serious weakness in her
complement of ASF flight officers.

Damn, but that fight had been a near-run thing. If the
Marine boarding parties had not been able to take down the
Rommel, the monitor would have pounded the Commonwealth ships into scrap, and the PanEuropeans would have
been sitting there waiting when Skybase had reemerged
from paraspace. The warships she carried couldn't fight
from inside the base's hangar bay, and Skybase would have
been helpless under *Rommel*'s powerful, long-range accelerator guns.

But *Rommel* had surrendered, though her ownership still
had to be determined by negotiation. The PanEuropeans,
naturally enough, wanted the monitor back. The MIEF had
returned her crew as part of the general post-battle exchange
of POWs, but, frankly, Alexander was hoping to be able to
incorporate the *Rommel* into the expeditionary force. Certainly, there was plenty of historical precedent in naval history regarding the incorporation of captured warships into
the victor's fleet. According to his last report from Earth,

however, the politicians were going at it hot and heavy now, arguing the fine points of the battle, and trying to hammer out a peace before the situation could deteriorate any further.

Alexander didn't really care what the outcome was, so long as 1MIEF had free access through the Puller 659 system to the Stargate.

He could see much of that fleet now, from his vantage point on the Skybase observation deck. For three days after the battle, Skybase had been shuttling back and forth between the carefully measured metrics of Assembly Point Yankee and the equally precisely measured volume of space at the Earth-Moon L-3 point. In threes and in fours and in fives, depending on the masses of the vessels involved, Skybase had taken on board the ships of 1MIEF and brought them across the light-years to this system, eighty ships, ranging from sleek corvettes to massive assault carriers, attack transports, and the three centerpieces of the MIEF naval task force, the 80,000-ton planet-class battlecruisers, *Mars, Ishtar,* and *Chiron.*

The largest ship in the fleet, of course—with the word "ship" used somewhat advisedly—was Skybase itself. Four *Atlas*-class fleet tugs had been solidly anchored to the structure's hull; their gravitic drives would provide a small measure of maneuverability for the huge space-going base. Unofficially, at least, Skybase had been tagged with a new name that had tended to transform the MIEF headquarters from an "it" to a "her," from a military orbital base to an active warship.

The name was *Hermes*, and it had no doubt originally been proposed, Alexander thought, with tongue firmly in cheek. Hermes had been the swift messenger god of the ancient Greeks, to be sure. With its—no, *her*—ability to translate back into Solar space, the UCS *Hermes* would certainly fit the role of messenger in this coming campaign, but the huge structure was anything but *swift*.

Alexander was still questioning his own decision to include Skybase—*Hermes*—on the fleet roster. She was so damned slow that she would be of very little help in a major fleet action, and by providing the enemy with an easy target, she might even prove to be a serious liability. What had tipped the scales in so far as making the decision was the fact that including *Hermes* did have some important positives. *Hermes* could maintain instant communication with Earth no matter where in the Galaxy she ended up, and she was big enough to carry the gravitometric measuring gear necessary for establishing new translation points elsewhere. With that facility, *Hermes* could slip back to Earth and pick up reinforcements—personnel, ships, and supplies—no matter where among the stars the MIEF might find itself.

But there was more. Hermes had also been a trickster god, the god of thieves, the god of travelers, and the god of cunning, all traits that the MIEF was going to need when it came up against the Xul. In myth, Hermes had been the god who'd lulled Argus, Hera's hundred-eyed guardian monster, to sleep in order to free the captive maiden Io.

Alexander knew enough cultural anthropology, however, to know something else about Hermes the god. He'd been a *psychopomp*—a kind of divine escort who guided the souls of the dead down to the underworld.

And *that* association was just a little too close to the mark to bear thinking about. A lot of Marines and naval personnel were going to end up passing to whatever afterlife there might be within the next months and years, and it had been the UCS *Hermes* that had brought them here to the stargate to make that possible.

Senior commanders, Alexander thought wryly, should not be permitted such thoughts. The perils of too damned much education . . .

"General Alexander?" Cara's voice cut in.

"Yes?"

"A message incoming from Major Tomanaga on the LP—conventional lasercom. Would you care to see it?"

"Please."

A communications window opened in his mind. After a momentary burst of radiation-induced snow, the face of Major Tomanaga appeared, making his report. The major had asked that he be allowed to again take command of the LP, as soon as his debriefing on board the *Hermes* had been complete.

"Status report," Tomanaga said, "Operation Gorgon, at oh-nine-thirty hours GMT, day oh-four, month twelve. Expected time delay thirty-one minutes, twelve seconds. The xenotexpert AIs have completed retuning the Puller Stargate. We have successfully recovered three unmanned gate probes sent through earlier this morning, and verified that we now have access to the region designated as Aquila Space. So far, we have detected no indication of a Xul presence on the other side. Just maybe we've lucked out on this one.

"At your direction, we are ready to send through manned units, and then to commence movement of the fleet.

"Tomanaga, Major, commanding officer of Listening Post Puller, out.

"This message will repeat automatically. . . ."

The speed-of-light time delay for normal-space messages meant that reports like this one were monologues, transmitted without expectation of a back-and-forth discussion. Tomanaga had transmitted the message thirty minutes ago, and it had taken that long for the laser light carrying it to crawl down in-system.

"Acknowledge message receipt," Alexander told Cara. "And pass the word to the rest of the fleet, will you? They should know."

"Yes, General."

One of Alexander's chief concerns now was the issue of morale. Platoon AIs had been unanimous in their reports from the squad bays throughout the fleet. The MIEF Marines knew that the PanEuropean Republic was not their primary target now, and they begrudged the fact that ninety-two fellow Marines were dead for no good reason.

Damn it, the whole political situation with the Republic should never have come up in the first place; Operation Gorgon was, first and foremost, an action by all of Humankind against the Galaxy's ancient masters. Humans should not be killing humans. Not now. The MIEF Marines wanted to get into action, they were *eager* to get into the fight, but against the Xul threat which had held Humankind hostage now for eight centuries, not their misguided fellow humans.

They would welcome the news that the way was open for the invasion of a Xul-dominated Galaxy.

"Another call, General," Cara said. "Admiral D'Urville."

"Put it through."

Another communications window opened. Since D'Urville was on board the *Aurore* now, this could actually be a communications exchange, with a time delay of less than a second.

D'Urville's bearded face appeared in the window. "General Alexander?" Again, he spoke in perfect Anglic.

"What can I do for you, sir?"

"I've just received an FTL transmission from *Aurore*, and I thought you should know about it."

"Yes?"

"Apparently, the Commonwealth Senate has agreed to return the *Rommel* to the Republic fleet. Something about 'creating an atmosphere of cooperation and sensibility in these trying times,' I believe was how they worded it."

Alexander had, frankly, been expecting as much. There was within the Senate a strong undercurrent of appeasement—as though the good will of enemies could be purchased through concession.

In Alexander's experience, the reverse was always true.

"Very well. I will await my own orders before returning the vessel. I'm sure you understand." He made a mental note to check with Intelligence, to see if they could confirm that message from *Aurore*.

"Of course. Actually, however, General, I had something else in mind."

"Eh?"

D'Urville sighed. "I was wondering, sir, if you would accept a *foreign* contingent within your expeditionary force?"

Alexander blinked, momentarily taken aback. "Let me get this straight. You want to come along?"

"Some of us do, General." He glanced left and right, as though looking to see if anyone else was close by in the compartment he was transmitting from. "You must be aware, your intelligence service must have told you, of the schism within our fleet."

"Sir, I cannot comment on matters of fleet intelligence, either to confirm or deny. You must know that."

"Of course, of course. One must always follow the rules, *non*? But we do regard your intelligence services with considerable respect. I would be very surprised to find out that you were unaware of the split between Traditionalist Catholic and Reformed Catholic elements within our fleet."

"What does all this have to do with a . . . with the foreign contingent you mentioned?"

"A number of us happen to agree with you, General. About who, or, rather, about *what* the real enemy is. And we want to help."

"I . . . see. And just how many of you feel this way?"

"I don't have exact figures. But several thousand, at least. Enough, perhaps, to man several ships. Including the *Rommel*." He hesitated. "A number of the Traditionalist Catholics have expressed an interest in . . . serving elsewhere, for the duration of the emergency. And others of us, well, our services may no longer be required by the government at Theta Bootis IV."

Alexander considered this for a long moment. D'Urville seemed sincere . . . even eager.

But . . .

"Admiral, I'm going to have to refuse."

"But . . ."

"This is an issue for our respective governments to work out. Not a couple of old warhorses like us."

"Governments, monsieur, can rarely see past the ends of their noses." He sounded bitter. "And some of us . . . no longer have the favor of their government."

D'Urville, Alexander thought, must have been cashiered—or felt it was about to happen . . . the penalty for failure.

"Are you saying you're in trouble with your superiors?"

D'Urville shrugged. "'Trouble' is one way to say it, General."

Damn. But Alexander was in no position to accept the

man's offer. The PanEuropeans were the enemy, or, at least, *an* enemy, despite grand words and declarations to the contrary. Besides, folding a PE force into the combined Naval-Marine task force would bring its own nightmare of logistical and political problems. The 1MIEF was a team, trained, honed, and experienced. Nothing would screw that balance faster than adding outsiders to the mix.

The thought did give Alexander pause, however. The supreme hope of passing through the Puller gate to Aquila Space was the possibility that there was someone there, an alien someone—the ultimate outsiders—who might join with Humankind to fight the Xul. Any civilization 1MIEF found in Aquila Space would be infinitely more difficult to communicate with, to work with, would be far more *alien* than the PanEuropeans ever could be.

But . . . he couldn't risk it. Not for the possible gain of a few ships. Even the *Rommel*.

"There will be plenty for *all* of us to do in this war, Admiral," Alexander told the man. "It may fall upon you to defend your homeworlds, if we fail."

"I . . . understand." He shook his head. "The problem is, General, that most in my government will not be interested in helping you. They fear repercussions should you fail, and the Xul find us."

"My government has its own share of people like that. Believe me, you have my sympathy. Here." He transmitted an eddress. "That will connect you with the personal AI of Danis Sloan."

"Ah! Your Defense Advisory Council, yes?"

"He *was* chairperson of the Council, yes," Alexander said. "Four years ago he was ousted by Marie Devereaux. She holds the position now.

"Now, I don't think Devereaux will be interested in your joining in with the crusade against the Xul, either. In fact, I suspect that she's in pretty tight with some people in the PanEuropean Republic. I do know she doesn't care much for the idea of Marines poking around in Xul space. The Treaty of Chiron must stand, and all of that."

"We call them *hommes du l'apaisement*," D'Urville said. "The Appeasers."

Alexander chuckled, the sound harsh. "I think every government has them. But every government has good men as well. Sloan still has considerable power, and if he can't help you, he'll know who in the Commonwealth government can."

D'Urville recorded the eddress. "Thank you, sir. And . . . may I ask, how long before you pass through the gate?" Damn it, the man was actually trying to be friendly. But Alexander couldn't take the risk.

"I can't tell you that, sir. Security."

"I see. I wish you well, however. And I wish you all success."

"Thank you, General. We'll need it. We'll *all* need it."

Squad Bay, UCS Samar
Anneau orbit, Puller 659 System
1740 hrs GMT

"I got killed," Garroway told the circle Marines in the squad bay lounge, "three fucking times this afternoon. Frankly, I'm getting a little sick of it."

"Well, practice does make perfect," Sandre Kenyon offered, laughing.

She was sitting next to him on the lounge, and he turned and gave her a hard, playful shove. "Hey, practice getting killed I do *not* need!"

Garroway was sitting with eight other Marines of First Platoon, Charlie Company, of the 55th MARS. He was beginning to feel like he was fitting in with the unit. Oh, they still called him "newbie" and "fungie"—that last derived from "FNG," or "fucking new guy." But he was also *accepted*.

Surviving his first live combat with them had helped, of course.

"What I want to know," Corporal Marin Delazlo said, "is how they know what to program into those sims for the Xul side of things, y'know?"

"Marines have fought the Xul before," Corporal Gonzales said. "And *won*."

"Yeah, yeah, but the last time that happened was . . . when? Five hundred years ago?"

"Twenty-one August 2323, oldstyle," Sergeant Richard Chu said.

"Five hundred fifty-four years," Garroway added, running the numbers through his implant math processor.

"Okay, 554 years. Yeah . . . you'd know that, wouldn't you, fungie? You had an ancestor or something in that battle."

"Or something."

"Well, my point is that in all that time, don't you think the Xul will have evolved some new tactics? You know, they say that we're always prepared to fight the *last* war, never the next one."

"Well, if we know anything about the Xul," Corporal Ran Allison said slowly, "we know they're damned slow on the uptake. Static culture, like they're locked in to how they perceive the universe, and in how they react to it. The xenopsych guys think they haven't changed much in half a million years."

"They *think*," Delazlo said, the words almost a sneer. "And not one of them has actually met a Xul, or talked to one!"

"Well, neither have you," Kenyon pointed out. "Or any of us."

"Right! So what good are all the endless sims?" He reached across from his chair and rubbed Garroway's close-shaven scalp. "Our baby-faced fungie, here, can practice getting killed until Doomsday and it's not going to help him when the real show goes down, am I right?"

Garroway knocked the hand aside and laughed. "Fuck you very much, Corporal."

"Thank you, I'll take two."

Delazlo had a point, Garroway thought. The simulations had all been much the same . . . variations, in fact, of the assault on the *Rommel*. Time after time, in a kind of free-flowing lucid dream fed to him by the platoon AI, he'd buttoned into a SAP and been fired across a flame-shot blackness toward an immense . . . thing, a lean golden needle 2 kilometers long, or a space base like a small moon covered with towers, turrets, and domes. Each time, his SAP had tunneled through a strange hull material that seemed to grow and shift around him, and he'd emerged inside a vast maze of inner passageways and tunnels. The Xul had been represented by elongated egg-shaped machines with multiple tentacles and glittering lenses, some serving as eyes, others as weapons.

There were always a horrific lot of the things, and beating them generally meant firing fast, firing accurately, and staying in a tight group with your fellow Marines. The first two times when he'd been rudely jolted out of the simulation as a "kill" today, it had been after he'd been separated from the other Marines in his fireteam by a sudden and unexpected influx of new Xul combat machines from an unexpected direction. Sometimes, the damned things seemed to just mold themselves right out of the surrounding bulkheads.

And Delazlo had a point. The images fed into his mind had been gleaned from implants and drone recorders at the Battle of Night's Edge in 2323, and from other battles with the Xul before that. Suppose they *had* changed their tactics?

Not that their old tactics were all that bad. Victory meant holding off those swarming, glittering machine-monsters long enough to plant a satchel nuke deep enough within the bowels of the enemy ship so that the whole, huge structure was destroyed . . . or at least severely inconvenienced.

The trick was planting the charges and then getting out before they blew. The last time he'd been "killed" today, he'd planted a backpack nuke, then managed to get lost coming back out. He'd died within a tiny sun when his own charge had detonated.

A tall figure in Marine undress blacks walked into the squad bay—Gunnery Sergeant Ramsey. He stopped, looking the group over.

"Hey, Gunny!" Sergeant Chu said. "Join us as we solve the mysteries of the universe!"

"In a minute, Chu-chu." He seemed preoccupied. "Garroway! A word with you?"

"Sure, Gunny." Now what the hell? . . .

Ramsey led him to an alcove at the back of the squad bay, semi-private from the others behind an arms rack. "I've been meaning to talk to you ever since the *Rommel* engagement," he said.

"Is there a problem, Gunnery Sergeant?" He swallowed. "I mean, I was damned scared—"

"You did fine, Marine. For your first live combat? You performed splendidly. I'm proud to have you in this platoon."

"Then, what—"

"I have to ask you a question. An intensely *personal* question. What is your relationship with PFC Kenyon?"

Garroway hesitated, his mind not clicking immediately. "Uh . . . sorry?"

"When we were in that control compartment, and we found out the *Rommel* was surrendering, you two were hugging like old lovers." He smiled. "Or *trying* to. Those battle-suits make that sort of thing a bit tough."

Garroway played the moment back in his memory. "Oh, yeah. I guess we did. Well, uh, I guess we got a little excited. And we *are* good friends. . . ."

"Son, it's none of my business. None of the *Corps'* business. Fuck each other all you want, as long as you both show up for duty and don't fall asleep on watch. But . . . I lost someone recently. Someone very important to me. She got killed on Alighan, my last out-system deployment."

"Damn. I'm sorry."

He shrugged. "Life happens. And in the Corps, *death* happens. Just a friendly word of warning, and advice." He raised both hands and clasped them together. "The Marine Corps is a family. The *Green* Family. All of us together, right?"

"Sure, Gunny. I understand that."

"You think you do. You won't feel it until you've lived it a few more years, like some of the rest of us have. And maybe not until you've lost someone close, like a lot of us have already. A lover. A buddy. Someone we went through boot

camp with, or served with on some out-of-the-way hellhole
on the other side of the sky.

"I'm not telling you to break things off with Kenyon. I
just want you to be aware, okay? Fuck-buddies are one thing.
Romance—*love*—is something else. The first is fine, so long
as you do your job. The second can kill you, if it hurts you
badly enough."

"That's a damned dark way of looking at things,
Gunny."

Ramsey drew a deep breath. "Garroway, I'm only telling
you this shit because I don't want the smooth functioning of
this platoon to be affected by the emotional misjudgments of
two members of my squad. Lust is acceptable. Love is not."
He turned, then, and walked away, leaving Garroway in a
decidedly uncomfortable frame of mind.

Did he love Sandre? Well, they'd *told* each other that
often enough, during stolen moments with the platoon AI
shut out of their minds. But what did the word mean?

He decided he was going to have to think about that one.

Bemused, Garroway returned to the bull session in the
squad bay.

20

Ontos 1, Recon Sword
Stargate
Puller 695 System/Aquila Space
1220 hrs GMT

"Recon Sword, launch door is open and you are cleared for *Lejeune* departure."

"Copy that, *Lejeune* Pryfly. Ten seconds."

"Good luck, Marines."

"Thank you, Pryfly. We'll bring you back some souvenirs."

"Just bring yourselves back."

"Roger that. And three . . . and two . . . and one . . ."

"Launch!"

With a savage thump, the Ontos accelerated down the launch rails and into hard vacuum, leaving the carrier *Lejeune* dwindling astern. The sudden acceleration—better than fifty gravities—would have left the humans on board battered and broken had the inertial dampers not cushioned them, bleeding off the excess force into paraspace. Ahead and around them, a flight of twelve Skydragons adjusted their vectors to match the larger Ontos. They would accompany the larger craft, flanking and preceding it in a protective hemispherical formation.

Enough accelerative force leaked through the dampers to make all three Marines on board the Ontos grunt, hard.

"God!" Lieutenant Eden gasped over the in-ship comm. "I'm *never* going to get used to that!"

"I hear it's rougher on the guys in the ASFs," Warhurst said conversationally as the pressure eased somewhat. Within his mental window-link, he could see the green blips marking the fighters all around them. "Smaller power taps. We can goose it harder than them."

In fact, all thirteen spacecraft were now accelerating in perfect unison, their drives under the control of a single AI, named Chesty.

Chesty, he'd been told, had been the AI linking the Marine recon force hidden within the Puller 659 system—"Chesty" having orignally been the nickname for General Lewis A. Puller, a twentieth-century Marine officer, and the only Marine ever to win *five* Navy Crosses. Evidently, the Chesty AI had made several trips through the Puller Stargate—most notably into the region called Starwall, near the Galactic center. Later, Chesty downloads had piloted unmanned probes into Aquila Space, looking for signs of a Xul presence, or anything else of potential interest.

Chesty knew this Gate, and would be coordinating the activities of the entire recon formation, codenamed Recon Sword.

"*Lejeune* Pryfly, Recon Sword," Eden said. "Patrol vector established. Switching to *Hermes* flight ops."

"Roger that, Recon Sword."

Pryfly was the ancient aviator's name for Primary Flight Control, tasked with launching aircraft from the old seagoing flattops, and, in more recent centuries, with launching small spacecraft from larger ones. From now on, the mission would be directed from the Ops Center located on the *Hermes*—formerly Skybase. Warhurst imagined that every high-ranking piece of gold braid in the fleet must either be there now, or linked in, watching the tiny flotilla hurtle toward the Stargate.

They would reach the Gate in twenty minutes.

"Are we sure this thing is going to work over there?" Sergeant Aren Galena, the number two Ontos gunner, asked. "I mean, on the other side. . . ."

"Now's a hell of a time to wonder about that," Warhurst said with a chuckle.

"Yeah, well, I'm just not sure I trust the quantum-whatzis," Galena said. "How do we know we're not going to be flat out of juice when we pass through . . . *that*."

"That," of course, was the Stargate, visible now within their inner link windows as a perfect circle of dark and ruddy gold against a star-strewn night up ahead. For several days, now, the MIEF fleet had been redeploying back out from the inner-system gas giant to a staging/departure zone near the Gate, and the *Samar* had reached the jump-off point just yesterday. The gate was expanding swiftly as the recon patrol approached it at 3 kilometers per second.

"Distance doesn't make any difference, Sergeant," Eden said. "We'll still get power, even if we're on the far side of the galaxy."

"Yeah . . . but that just don't make *sense*."

Warhurst could understand the younger man's anxiety. Hell, he didn't understand the science any better than did Galena. It was hard not to picture the ZPE quantum power transfer technology as a means of *beaming* energy from the *Lejeune* to the Ontos and the fighters, when in fact the system did no such thing. Energy called into being from the Zero Point Field in the carrier's massive power taps simultaneously appeared in the Ontos' Solenergia field-entangled receivers. There was no energy beam to be tapped or intercepted by an enemy, or to be lost during violent maneuvers. And the lieutenant was right. Theoretically, they could be a hundred thousand light-years away—or even millions of light-years away, in another galaxy entirely, and still be able to tap into that power flow—exactly as though there were no intervening distance between the two at all.

That was the point of quantum-entangled technologies: power *here* was instantly and simultaneously *there*, just as with quantum FTL communications, through the application of the immortal Einstein's "spooky action at a distance." Theoretically, the only thing that could cut the energy flow on board an Ontos or an aerospace fighter was the destruction of the *Lejeune* . . . and there were back-up entanglement receivers keyed to other carriers and transports in the fleet, and to Skybase itself.

No problem.

But while he'd downloaded the explanation and knew the words, Warhurst, like most Marines he knew, still had some trouble when it came to accepting seemingly magical technologies. After all, there was a universe of difference between the *theoretical* and the *practical*. What if passing through a stargate affected the quantum-entangled link in unpredictable ways?

He snorted to himself. Maybe Marines were just so damned used to having to go it alone and rely on their own resources that they had trouble with the concept of accepting *anything* for free or on faith . . . even high-tech magic.

"You know, Sergeant, it doesn't have to make sense," Warhurst said. "Tap into your weiji-do training. *Focus.* . . ."

"You know, Gunny, I never did buy into all that weird shit," Galena said.

"You'd damned well better. The Corps teaches that stuff for a reason."

"Yeah, well, I always had trouble understanding stuff that I couldn't wrap my brain around, y'know?" Warhurst could sense his shrug.

"Most of us don't know how an ordinary wallscreen monitor works, either," Warhurst said. "But that doesn't stop us from using our own wetware as well as the hardware, right?"

"If you say so, Gunny."

He didn't sound convinced. Galena was, in Warhurst's experience, a stereotypical "rock," a dumb-as-a-rock Marine. Sergeant Galena was a good man—there was no question about the man's credentials. The word was he'd distinguished himself on Alighan by charging a Muzzie position guarded by a dug-in battery of APerM launchers and taking them out at point-blank range with his flamer, and the guy was in line to get a Silver Star for that little action.

But he was also opinionated, mule-stubborn, and unwilling to stretch when it came to trying to understand *anything* that wasn't bloody self-obvious. Warhurst wished he'd had the guy in one of his boot companies back at Noctis Labyrinthus. Maybe a few extra after-hours rounds of being pitted would have opened up some willingness to dig in the man's stubborn shell. According to the guy's personnel records, he'd done acceptably in his T'ai Chi training in boot camp . . . but had gone into it as a means of hand-to-hand combat, and never, apparently, picked up on the system's more subtle, purely mental aspects.

And according to those records, he'd never really gotten the hang of the weiji-do exercises at all. Those, however, were not requirements for graduation since, frankly, some recruits could handle them, and some never could.

Warhurst would have felt better if Galena had been able to run through a basic T'ai chi/weiji-do kata in boot camp, though. During a recon op, as in combat, you needed to *know* you were tuned in with your buddies, a *part* of them, all acting together as one.

The Stargate continued to expand ahead, the far-flung hoop now stretched across a full third of the sky.

Probes sent through to Aquila Space had returned without detecting Xul ships or fortresses. That, at least, was a blessing. But Warhurst wished the brass had been more specific about what the probes had detected. There were rumors, but the data had not been released to the people who needed it most—the Marines going in on point.

Why were the probe reports being hushed up? The official word was that signals had been detected on the other side—RF noise which might mean technology—but that the data were still being analyzed.

Maybe so. But Warhurst was suspicious of any ops briefing that began with the words, "This one should be easy."

They *had* been shown visual downloads from Aquila Space, at least, so they had an idea of what they would be seeing. Twelve hundred light-years was not far, as galactic distances go, and the stellar backdrop—the number of background stars—seemed about the same as in circumsolar space. The local Stargate appeared to be in orbit around an A-class star imbedded in a flat disk of dust and asteroidal debris.

The big question, of course, was whether anything unpleasant might be lurking in that debris field. That was why the Ontos was going through first, in its role as scout-recon. The Ontos carried a QCC radio, allowing real-time communications with the Skybase, and—instead of a squad of Marines—its payload bay carried a very special miniature spacecraft. Warhurst, besides serving in his usual role as starboard-side gunner, had also been assigned as loadmaster for the mission. He performed a quick mental check of the craft loaded into the MCA–71's aft bay. All green.

"Ten seconds," Eden warned them. Ahead, the lead Skydragon fighter passed into the plane of curiously disturbed space at the center of the Stargate . . . and winked out of existence. Four seconds later, the three fighters spread out behind the leader reached the interface and vanished as well. The rim of the Gate cut the sky in half, now, a thread of gold light. Warhurst tried to imagine two Jupiter masses shrunken to marble-sized black holes, hurtling through the ring structure at near-c velocities, the gravitational stresses somehow focused on the space *here*, at the ring's center. Whoever—*whatever*—had constructed the Stargates had been the master of technologies still incomprehensible to Humankind.

And perhaps to the Xul as well. The Xul certainly used the Gates, as did both humans and N'mah from time to time, but most xenosapientologists were of the opinion that the Xul had not originally built the things, that they had discovered them in place whenever they began spreading across the Galaxy . . . how long ago? A million years, at least. . . .

Warhurst felt the sharp, inner twist as the Ontos passed through the gravitationally distorted interface. This was his first time through a Stargate, but he'd been through plenty of sims, and knew to expect that wrenching sensation as, just for an instant, part of his body was *here*, dropping through the Puller Gate, and the rest emerging from another Gate twelve hundred light-years distant.

"Woof!" Galena said, with feeling. "Is it always like that?"

"Damfino," Lieutenant Eden said. "First time for all of us."

"A slight feeling of discontinuity, like an inner jolt or twisting, appears characteristic of human physiological response when passing through a Gate," Chesty said, the AI voice even and measured.

"Yeah, well, it felt to me like a hard kick in the ass," Galena said.

"Heads up, people," Eden told them. "Sensors to on. Chesty is on-line. Listen for the signal, now. . . ."

Warhurst studied the downloaded imagery now feeding in from the Ontos' forward cameras and other sensors. So far, no surprises. The local sun burned in the distance, some fifty light-minutes away, as a bright, blue-white beacon imbedded in a faint and far-flung haze of zodiacal light. Despite the name for this region of space, the star, listed as HD387136 on the star catalogues, had never gone nova; Nova Aquila, or that star's white dwarf remnants, were reportedly located perhaps ten light-years distant. The star itself was invisible at that distance, but a smear of light was visible in one part of the sky—the glowing shell of ejecta blasted away when Nova Aquila had detonated, some fourteen hundred years ago.

As for HD387136, it appeared to be a normal, unremarkable A4-class star, though it did not appear to have a family of planets. The zodiacal light was, in fact, a glow off a cloud of asteroidal debris circling the star in a broad, flat plane. The material, ranging in size from minor planets a few hundred kilometers across down to sand grains and dust motes, created a thin smear of light encircling the star.

No planets . . . and no fortress bases, such as those favored by the Xul. Some, small, fear-stubborn piece of him had halfway been expecting to find a Xul monster-ship or orbital fortress base waiting for them on this side, despite earlier negative sweeps by unmanned probes.

But there was nothing. He saw the low-grade radio-frequency noise, which *might* have been leakage from a shielded, high-tech source, but which could just as easily be something natural—a hiss of radio noise from the star as its magnetic fields interacted with the orbiting ring of asteroidal debris. The lack of full-sized worlds made the system seem an unlikely place to find intelligent life, or *any* life, for that matter.

The fighter screen was spreading out, now, covering as large a volume of space as possible. Linked together through Chesty, each vessel became one component in an array of linked receivers, creating, in effect, an enormous and extremely sensitive radio telescope.

"So what do you hear, Chesty?" Warhurst asked the AI. The program was powerful enough, he knew, to hold multiple separate conversations without affecting its primary mission.

"The signal is almost certainly of intelligent origin," Chesty whispered in his thoughts. Small mental windows opened to show gain and frequency, as well as a simplified map of local space. "The origin appears to be numerous multiple points within the local star's asteroid field."

"Radios, then?"

"More likely a variety of electronic equipment," Chesty replied. "Possibly from large-scale manufacturing centers, or from the nodes of a widely distributed computer network. The signals are extremely faint—as though they have been shielded."

"Is it Xul?" Lieutenant Eden asked.

"Unknown. However, the frequencies do not match previously recorded Xul data intercepts. I believe this may be someone new."

"Right, then," Eden said. "Warhurst? Let's drop our package."

"Aye, aye, sir."

A thought-click, and the aft-ventral cargo hatch cycled open. He did a final systems check, and then, a moment later, the EWC–9 Argus/NeP Entruder dropped into vacuum and began slowly accelerating out ahead of the Ontos.

The spacecraft was designated the EWC–9 *Argus*, after the hundred-eyed guardian monster—no relative of "Argo," the mythical ship for which the lost asteroid starship had been named. One of the Marine weapons technicians who'd designed the system on board Skybase reportedly had suggested the name after hearing that Skybase was being renamed *Hermes*, and there'd already been a fair amount of good-natured ribbing back and forth about Hermes boring hundred-eyed Argus into a coma. "EWC" referred to the vehicle type—Electronic Warfare Craft.

Working closely with Chesty, Warhurst began feeding a list of potential targets into the EWC's navigational system. There were hundreds of targets to choose from; all were locked in, though the emphasis was on one particular RF source that, according to parallax measurements, was considerably closer than the rest—less than 100,000 kilometers distant.

The Aquila Space stargate orbited the local star at the ragged, outer fringe of the system's broad planetoid belt. The RF sources were widely scattered through the belt, but there were so many that a few, at least, were within easy range of the Argus' payload. Once the best targets were locked in, Warhurst gave another mental command, and the craft began accelerating under its own gravitic drive, pushing swiftly up to over two hundred Gs. Once clear of the guardian hemisphere of Skydragon fighters, the forward half of the cylindrical craft unfolded, exposing thousands of pencil-sized launch tubes, each now tracking a separate target. At a precisely calculated instant, the tubes fired, releasing a cloud of fast-moving nano e-penetrators, NePs in the jargon of the Marine technicians who'd grown them.

The Entruder was the software that constituted the EWC-9's principle payload, and was a neologism drawn from *electronic intruder*, or e-intruder, a term that had already been applied to a whole range of AI-driven electronic monitoring, warfare, and subversion software. Marines had won past engagements with the Xul by slipping complex, artificially intelligent software into the equivalent of Xul operating systems, piggybacking the software into Xul ships or fortresses by using RF leakage—exactly like the radio noise emanating now from the asteroid field ahead.

Chesty had done this sort of work at Starwall, burrowing like a self-aware computer virus into the Xul system, picking up and transmitting data on the Xul presence in that system, and ascertaining that the Xul forces there, tens of thousands of light-years from human space, knew about the captured *Argos*. In fact, a great deal of Chesty—including everything he'd learned in his penetration of the Xul ship at Starwall—had been copied and packed into the Entruder software.

The Marine programmers back in Skybase had named the Entruder package, by ancient tradition, after a hero of the Corps. Where Chesty had been named for Chesty Puller, the Entruder was named *Evans*, for Evans Fordyce Carlson, three-time winner of the Navy Cross, and the creator and leader of the legendary Carlson's Raiders of WWII.

Spacecraft like the EWC-9 *Argus*, and AI software payloads like Evans, had been vital components in warfare for centuries. In fact, it could be argued that they were the remote descendents of twentieth-century computer viruses and primitive atmospheric craft like the EA-6B Prowler and even earlier electronic eavesdropping aircraft. There were military theorists—in fact there'd been military theorists for many centuries—who insisted that *real* war had little to do with armies or ships, which they considered superfluous. It was, these armchair strategists insisted, the electronic engagement in the opening nanoseconds of any battle that determined winners and losers, the outcome predicated on which side gained more elint—electronic intelligence—in the collision, and which one better defended its own electronic trenches.

Warhurst didn't agree. There would always, he was convinced, be a need for someone—a basic infantryman or Marine rifleman—to go in and take the high ground away from the enemy.

Evans
Aquila Space
1254 hrs GMT

From Evans' point of view, he was on board the *Argus* spacecraft, resident within a heavily shielded and protected central processor, but with secondary nodes on board the Ontos and the widely scattered fighters. Redundancy was key, here. If things went wrong with the e-penetration attempt, one, at least, of the dispersed network nodes could receive what data had been collected and, with luck, get it back through the Stargate to Puller 659.

Somewhere up ahead, several thousand individual nano-probes, hurtled through space at some hundreds of kilometers per second. In the first seconds of free flight, the NeP probes, each one a few centimeters long and as slender as a human hair, had released an extremely fine, gossamer net that encircled its body. The net served both to receive RF signals from the objective, and to maintain a connection with Evans through tightly focused, highly directional microwave beams. Each probe selected a radio-frequency source and began to home on it, using the local magnetic field to minutely adjust its course.

Most missed their selected targets. Their velocities were too high, the energies they could bring to bear on course correction minute. But a lucky few found the source of radio emanations squarely within the cone of space available to them. And they struck.

The flash of kinetic energy released by the impact served as power source, charging the molecule-sized components of each NeP thread. These burrowed deep into the surface of the target, then began tasting the material in which they were imbedded.

The nanopenetrators had been programmed to accept a wide variety of materials, including the self-repairing hull composites of a Xul starship. In this case, the raw materials were those of a typical H-class chondritic asteroid, consisting of approximately twenty-three percent iron, ferrous sulfide, iron oxides, and nickel, with the rest comprised of silicates such as olivine and pyroxene, and an aluminosilicate of magnesium, iron, and calcium called feldspar.

The twentieth-century mathematician John von Neumann had described a visionary system whereby a suitably programmed robot might land on an asteroid and, using available materials, construct an exact replica of itself. Those two would build more replicas . . . and more . . . and still more . . . until there were enough replicators that the programming could shift production over to something else, such as refined metals packaged for shipping back to Earth. These von Neumann machines, as they were called, were an early concept in the evolution of nanotechnology, for they showed how asteroidal nanufactories might be grown in the Solar System's asteroid belt or Oort Cloud.

A similar process was under way now, as the nano probe began recruiting molecules and even individual atoms from the surrounding matrix—iron and iron oxides, nickel, iron sulfides, and magnesium for metal, calcium, potassium, carbon, sulfur, and silica for other materials. Much of a chondrite's substance was, in fact, a kind of clay called a hydrated silicate, which contained a high percentage of water and organic materials.

Swiftly—the mining, refining, and assembly processes took place *very* quickly on a molecular scale—the thread of nanomaterial injected into the asteroid's surface began growing in two directions—*up*, creating a new sheet of gossamer webwork on the surface of the asteroid in order to establish a microwave link with the distant *Argus* spacecraft, and *down*, sending a vast and complex web of threads, each finer than a human hair, down into the rock's deeper structure. The threads, navigating now by sensing heat in the substrate around them, delved deeper and deeper until finally one thread made contact with, not asteroidal rock, but something else . . . a ceramic shell housing a bundle of fiber-optic cables carrying pulses of laser light.

Several hundred NePs had impacted on that one, relatively nearby asteroid. Within a few minutes, fast-burrowing roots of nanoassembler threads began encountering one another, exchanging data, interconnecting their networks, and rerouting their joint explorations inward. Each probe had no intelligence of its own beyond the bare minimum required to carry out its mission, but was still loosely linked to Evans by microwave.

Evans was highly intelligent, with all the technical and background data acquired from centuries of intermittent contact with Xul networks, with more substantial exchanges with the alien N'mah originally encountered at the Sirius Stargate, and with extensive studies and reverse-engineering of artifacts left behind by the Builders half a million years ago, from the surfaces of Earth's Moon and Mars to the ruins on Chiron, Hathor, and elsewhere.

A blob of assemblers gathered around the ceramic conduit containing bundles of fiber-optic cable, delving, probing, sampling. Patterns were noted—fluctuations in frequency, in amplitude, in spin. Data streamed back to Evans, who began comparing them to the AI's extensive technic and linguistic files.

The electronic system here was *not* Xul. That much was clear from the start. Indeed, attempts to probe the alien network using Xul-style signals were effectively and immediately blocked. In biological terms, the electronic network within the asteroid possessed a complex and well-adjusted set of anti-Xul "antibodies," which appeared to be designed expressly to counter electronic incursions by the Xul.

Knowing this, Evans was able to focus on *non*-Xul electronic strategies; there still were a daunting number of possibilities available, but at least the field was reduced somewhat. Where humans used binary logic as a means of encoding data, and the Xul used a trinary system, this alien network appeared to use another form of numeric code entirely.

Evans needed to establish just what the mathematical key to this code might be before he could begin to make some sense of the streams of alien data. He tried and discarded a number of possibilities—the ratios of prime numbers to one another . . . the intervals between oddly-even numbers, even numbers that, when one was divided by another, produced even numbers . . . even a numerical ordering of the hydrogen emission lines resident within the spectrum of the local star.

It was definitely a brute-force method to cracking the code, trying one method after another. Evans' one advantage was that he was *fast*, working on a molecular scale and with very tiny energies.

And ten minutes into the attempt, as more and more nanothreads wormed their way into the vast and tangled electronic network beneath the asteroid's surface, he found the key.

It was Fibonacci numbers and Phi.

One plus one equals two. Add the 2 to the 1 and get 3. Add the 3 to the 2 and get 5. Each number added to the preceding number gives the next number in the series, creating an ongoing string of numbers: 1, 1, 2, 3, 5, 8, 13, 21 and so on to infinity in a never-ending series.

A curious fact about this series is that if you divide any Fibonacci number by the next number after it, you get a value quite close to, but never quite equaling, the transcendental 0.618034 . . . , *Phi*, the so-called "Golden Mean" that seems miraculously to appear everywhere in the universe—in the curves and spirals inherent in pine cones and sea shells and spiral galaxies, within biological ratios and the arrangements of flower petals and leaves growing around a stem, and even within the proportions of the human body.

The frequencies of the photon packets traveling through the alien fiber-optic network could be expressed as ratios between the first few thousand numbers in the Fibonacci series. The first level of the code had been cracked.

After that, still working by a kind of well-educated trial-and-error, Evans began to translate signal ratios into layer upon layer of nested patterns. By now, nanothreads were sampling thousands of different sources of electrical and photonic signals, providing an avalanche of data that would have taken merely human signals analysts centuries just to separate and describe.

It took Evans about three hours.

And then the humans on board the Ontos had their first good look at one of the aliens.

Although, at that point they couldn't really tell *what* it was. . . .

21

UCS Hermes
Stargate
Puller 695 System
1740 hrs GMT

"What the *hell* is that?" General Alexander wanted to know.

"The intelligence analysts are still going over it," Cara told him. "They're especially trying to see if there are any other ways to make this data fit together into meaningful patterns. But these particular images appear to be intended as cels in a visual record of some sort.

"We think these are landscapes. . . ."

Alexander was studying the first of the images sent back from Aquila Space by Recon Sword, watching them unfold in his mind. "Landscapes?" he said. "Looks more like the deep ocean."

The scene was otherworldly . . . but it was tough to tell whether that was due to the environment or an alien *perception* of that environment. Reds, violets, and blues predominated. Whatever Alexander was seeing, it was murky, with vague and uncertain shapes just visible in the background. In fact, his first impression was that he was looking at a series of abstract paintings. After clicking through several dozen of them, though, he began to recognize patterns to the background and in the color.

"So . . . this is a single cel in some kind of animation?"

"Yes, sir. Project a number of these in rapid succession, and you would have the sensation of movement. We have recovered some fifty thousand of these so far, enough for half an hour of video, if projected at twenty-four frames per second. However, so far most appear to be of different sequences. In other words, they're not all part of the same 'movie,' or, if they are, they represent widely different scenes, different places, within a single sequence."

Alexander could only imagine the computing power necessary to sort through the incredible mountain of data recovered from the alien network so far. And this represented only the barest beginning.

"What the hell is this?" He'd brought up a new scene. Again, it was a murky blend of violets and blues, but with an intensely bright patch of green at the center. Something like a cloud of purple smoke appeared to rise from the light. Nearby, illuminated by the bright patch, was a forest of brilliant scarlet tubes, each sprouting a mass of purple-red feathers.

"We are still analyzing those," Cara told him.

"Yeah . . . but, these tubes. Could they be the aliens? Or some kind of vegetation? Obviously, these things are *alive*. . . ."

"Possibly," Cara told him. "They actually resemble certain species of deep-sea worms living in Earth's oceans. That light could be thermo- or sonoluminescence from a deep-sea volcanic vent."

"I've simmed teleoperated excursions to deep-ocean vents," he said. There were companies in Earthring that for a fee let you piggyback your consciousness into robots probing the deep ocean trenches, or the poisonous murk of Venus. Alexander had taken a teleoperational excursion to the bottom of the Marianas Trench once, about five years before, and on another occasion had visited one of the deep-sea smoker vents near the Galapagos Islands. "I've seen benthic tube worms . . . and they can grow pretty big. How long are these?"

"Unknown. We have not yet established a scale for measurement within these images."

He nodded. The tube-worm things in the alien data might
be several meters long. Or, if the alien camera that recorded
them was small and this was a tight close-up shot, they could
represent organisms the size of human hairs. How could you
tell, without knowing the scale of what you were looking
at?

However large they were, these were indescribably beautiful, with glittering, deep violet highlights, and feathery
protrusions arrayed in delicate spiral patterns around the
mouth—if that's what those openings were. And were those
stalked eyes around the ends? Or organs of some other sense
entirely? Were they worms of some sort, analogues of the
tube-worms of Earth's oceanic deeps? Or were they some
sort of background vegetation?

How, Alexander wondered, *can we even begin to communicate with something when we're not even sure what it
is we're looking at in the first place?*

Historically, of course, the Marines were not intended to
be agents of first contact with new species. Their job was to
find the enemy and kill him.

As the ancient joke had it: "Join the Marines; travel to
exotic worlds; meet strange and exciting foreign peoples;
kill them."

And yet if Operation Gorgon was to succeed, the MIEF
was going to need to adopt the roles both of first-contact
team and diplomatic corps. So far, and not counting the Xul
themselves, or the apparently extinct Builders, the only other
sapient species encountered by Humankind in eight hundred
years of exploration beyond its home world was the N'mah.
It was self-evident that humanity would not be able to defeat
the Xul alone. Earth *had* to find allies out there among the
stars, however strange. . . .

He thought-clicked to another image and started. This
was obviously a life form of some sort—the eyes were the
giveaway—and a nightmare one at that. Alexander found
himself looking into the face, if that was what it could be
called, of something that might have been a terrestrial octopus, but with six black and gold eyes spaced around the
head, with multiplying branching tentacles, and with a

transparent body—he could clearly see what appeared to be internal organs, as if rendered in glass—that looked like nothing Alexander had ever seen in his life. A flatworm? An insect? He was actually having trouble seeing the thing as a whole, because his brain was not able to compare what he was seeing at all closely with the memories of life forms already in his mind.

Still, those six eyes seemed to be staring back at him with a cold, inner light and, to Alexander's mind, at least, there was something there . . . something aware, something intelligent. What, he wondered, could humans have in common with such nightmares?

He was reasonably certain, however, that this was an image of one of the aliens.

But whether it would prove to be an ally against the Xul, or something as implacably hostile as the Xul, remained to be seen.

Ontos 1, Recon Sword
Stargate
Aquila Space
1905 hrs GMT

"Recon Sword copies," Lieutenant Eden said out loud. "We'll see what we can do. Out."

Warhurst appreciated the fact that FTL radio allowed them to stay in touch with the MIEF, even though straight-line communications through the Stargate were impossible, and the fleet was now twelve hundred light-years away. Still, there was something to be said for *not* having the capability to talk to HQ instantaneously—like freedom from micromanagement. The good news here was that they were on their own.

The bad news, of course . . . was that they were on their own.

"So what's the word, Lieutenant?" Galena wanted to know. "When's the damned fleet comin' through, anyway?"

"Not just yet," Eden said. "They want us to follow up on all the data they've been getting."

"Meaning? . . ." Warhurst asked. He had a feeling he knew what the answer was going to be.

"Meaning we get our asses in gear and approach RFS Alpha for a closer look."

Radio Frequency Source Alpha was what they were calling that nearest asteroid, the one from which they'd been getting most of the data so far. With one exception, RFS Bravo, none of the other targets had been reached yet by the fast-expanding cloud of nano e-penetrators. Some were days away from their targets, in fact, even at 300 kps. Bravo, at an awkward angle relative to the gate, had been hit by only a single penetrator, and data from that source so far was miniscule.

But Alpha was proving to be an electronic treasure trove. Once Evans had cracked the code, torrents of data had been coming back over almost two hundred separate microwave channels, relayed back to Recon Sword, and then, via the QCC net, back to *Hermes* and the Fleet.

One of the early images from Alpha might actually have been of one of the aliens—something like an octopus head on a flatworm's body, but with odd extrusions and extensions that made little sense to human eyes, the whole rendered in what looked like transparent glass, internal organs and all.

Sitting down to have a meal with these guys must be a real treat, Warhurst thought. You'd be able to watch the whole process of digestion. . . .

"Alert," Chesty said, interrupting his bemused thoughts. "We are being electronically compromised."

"What?" Eden snapped. "How? I don't see anything on the interface. . . ."

"It would not show there," Chesty replied. "The penetration is extremely subtle, and I am aware of it only as a kind of echo of certain data. I believe the aliens may have multiple probes piggybacking in through our own microwave data channels."

"Shit!" Galena said. "Lieutenant? What do we do? *We're* supposed to be spying on *them*, not the other way around!"

"I . . . don't know." Eden sounded hesitant.

Warhurst scanned the various internal readouts. Whatever was peering into the Ontos' computer system wasn't tripping any of the safeguards against electronic sabotage. Chesty was right. The probe was extremely delicate, exquisitely sophisticated.

"Hey, turnabout's fair play, right?" Warhurst said. "Why not let them look?"

"Do you think that's wise, Gunnery Sergeant?" Eden replied. He was already using Chesty to shut down specific blocks of computer memory, seeking to slam the door shut. It looked to Warhurst, though, as though it was already too late. This thing was *fast*.

"Why not?" he said. "We're sterile, right? They didn't send us out here with any sensitive data on board, stuff like the coordinates of Earth, or the TO&E of the MIEF."

"No. Of course not. If there were Xul here . . ."

"Right. Nothing to tell the Xul where we're from if we get spotted and picked up." He didn't add that, if the scuttlebutt in the fleet was any indicator, the Xul already knew *exactly* where Earth was, thanks to the capture of the *Argo*. "These guys on Alpha aren't Xul. We came here to find aliens, right? We want to talk to them. So . . ."

"So we make it easy for them to exchange data with us," Eden said, completing the thought. "Still, I wasn't expecting to be announced quite this soon."

"They obviously have some pretty sophisticated computer shit over there," Warhurst said. "They must've seen what was happening when our NePs started hitting the surface of their asteroid, and figured out we were trying to communicate, or at least trying to find out about them. Now they're doing the same to us."

"Our orders allow us to exchange data with the aliens," Eden said, but slowly, as though he was still trying to figure things out. "But just basic stuff. This . . . this probe is going through everything we have!"

"And probably finding us as weird as we find them. Let's just keep moving toward Alpha, Lieutenant, but dead slow. See if they put out the welcome mat for us. . . ."

$e^{(i\pi)} + 1 = 0$
RFS Alpha
Aquila Space
1912 hrs GMT

In a large enough cosmos, all things are possible. Even unexpected potential congruencies between fundamentally
different statements of Reality.

The beings' name for themselves, their self-identifying
thought-symbol, would have been incomprehensible if spoken,
for it was not a word, but a mathematical relationship, an
equation, that to their minds spoke of the elegance, the perfection, and the essential unity of the cosmos. The $e^{(i\pi)} + 1 = 0$
were, above all else, mathematicians . . . minds that sought
to understand and describe the cosmos through the beauty
of abstract relationships.

They watched, now, through complex electronic senses,
as the odd little spacecraft approached, the ugly machine
unfolding in their collective minds not as something visible,
but as angles, surfaces, and curves, a manifold of continu-
ous and discrete structures and tensors. The beings watched
through a virtual reality created by their computer network;
they had already ascertained that the aliens, too, possessed
computer technology, and appeared to communicate with
one another by means of similar artificially contrived virtual worlds.

Their network was extensive, powerful, and worked very
quickly. Already they'd begun building up a model of the
alien intelligences. There were two, evidently, one identified
as "Chesty"—though the symbols for that identifier were
unintelligible as yet—and one, equally mysteriously, called
"Evans." Chesty appeared to inhabit the larger, more distant spacecraft, Evans the smaller, nearer ship, the craft
that had initiated contact in the first place.

The important thing, the supremely important balance of
the equation, was that the aliens were not the Enemy. And
if they were not the Enemy, they might be . . . what? Associ-
ates? Congruent mentalities?

The $e^{(i\pi)} + 1 = 0$ had thought themselves alone, utterly *alone, in an extremely large and violent universe. The thought of allies did not come easily to them.*

But they understood the concept of complementary interaction, and of the whole being greater than the sum of the component parts.

In a big enough universe, wholly independent sequences could sometimes combine, resulting in startling and unexpected convergence.

They would not engage the Trigger to destroy the newcomers . . . not yet. . . .

Ontos 1, Recon Sword
Stargate
Aquila Space
2119 hrs GMT

"Fifty meters," Warhurst said, reading off the dwindling numbers on his internal projection. "Thirty . . . twenty . . . fifteen . . . ten meters . . ."

The Ontos was slowly, almost grudgingly approaching the asteroid's surface, gentling down on carefully adjusted coughs from its gravitic drive. Outside, the asteroid's surface appeared harshly illuminated in white light, every shadow of each loose rock or fold in the landscape sharply etched into a surface of smooth gray dust. Landing legs, claws extended, splayed out, reaching for the surface. Through his mental window, linked to the craft's external cameras, Warhurst was aware of the Ontos' own shadow moving up to meet them as they descended.

"Five meters . . . three . . ."

Eden gave a final burst of power to the drive. "Okay. We're down. Cutting drive power . . . cutting AG."

Warhurst hadn't even felt the bump of landing. As Eden cut the artificial gravity, his stomach surged, the sensation almost that of free fall. This tiny drifting mountain did have a gravity field of its own—but at about one ten-thousandth of a G it wasn't enough to keep things nailed down or give a distinct feeling of up and down. Warhurst reached out and plucked a pen from a nearby rack and dropped it. The silver tube appeared to float in front of his eyes, and only very, very gradually did it begin to make its way toward the deck.

Warhurst turned his full attention to the view outside, enlarging the window with a thought. The surface looked like gray beach sand or coarse powder, the horizon startlingly close. The local sun, blue-white and intensely brilliant, hung just above the horizon. The asteroid's rotation was rapid enough that the sun's movement was clearly visible as it drifted toward the horizon.

"You sure this is the place, Lieutenant?" Galena asked. "Where's the welcoming committee?"

"This is where Chesty brought us," Eden replied.

"The alien signal is coming from that mound in the landscape some 20 meters in *that* direction," Chesty said, marking the indicated hillock with a green cursor in their minds. "And it appears to be opening up."

The three Marines watched for a long moment. Something like a door was indeed opening in the side of a hill . . . inviting.

"Well," Eden said. "Time to go earn our pay. Prepare for egress."

Ten minutes later, the Marines emerged, one by one, from the belly of the Ontos and began drifting across the surface toward the open door. There wasn't gravity enough to keep them on the surface, and a hard jump could have put them into orbit. Instead, they used their 660 armor's thruster packs, using gentle bursts to guide themselves forward.

As they neared the opening, the sun slid beneath the impossibly close horizon. Night closed in with startling swiftness; stars winked on, along with the flat band of zodiacal light stretching up from the spot where the sun had set.

Lights winked on within the entrance ahead.

"You sure this isn't a Xul trap, Chesty?" Warhurst asked the invisible but ever-present AI.

"If it is," Chesty's voice replied in his mind, "it is an uncommonly convoluted and opaque one. I have been exchanging data at an extremely high rate of speed for several hours now, and am beginning to understand the conventions these . . . beings use. True communication is as yet impossible, but

I can with some confidence tell you that these are not Xul. I
see no evidence that they intend us harm."

"So . . . what's inside the door?" Galena asked, braking to
a halt relative to the gray and dusty hillside. His jets stirred
up a cloud of powdery dust that hung suspended above the
surface, glowing in the light spilling from the entrance.

"Unknown," Chesty told them. "But we may learn more
if we enter."

UCS Hermes
Stargate, Puller 695 System
2140 hrs GMT

"The Marines are entering the opening now," Cara said.

"Very well," General Alexander said. He was going over
the ready list one final time, but at Cara's warning, he re-
opened the mental window to the feed from Recon Sword.
The transmission was coming from a camera mounted on
Lieutenant Eden's helmet. He could see the back of Garroway's M-660 armor just ahead as the Marine pulled himself
into the doorway.

He fought the temptation to tell the Marines to be careful. They didn't need micromanaging . . . and wouldn't appreciate the offer. He remained silent as the trio descended
deeper into the tumbling mountain.

Garroway stopped, and affixed a small, black box to a
rock wall—a comm relay that should keep the three in touch
despite the rock around them.

And then the signal began to fuzz and break up.

"Recon One," another voice said over the channel. "This
is Ops. We're losing your signal. Do you copy?"

Alexander heard a reply, but it was garbled and broken.

And then the image was gone, replaced by hissing
static.

Damn. . . .

A QCC link could send comm signals across twelve hundred light-years, from the Ontos to *Hermes*, in an eye-blink
. . . but the Marines in their armored suits were dependent
on conventional radio to get their data streams back to the

Ontos. The relays they were using *should* have kept them linked in no matter how deep into the asteroid they went. Evidently, something else was blocking the signal, most likely some sort of alien shielding technology.

And that might be accidental, or it might be the closing of a trap.

"Cara," Alexander snapped. "Open a channel to Admiral Taggart, please."

"Aye, aye, General."

Taggart must have been waiting for the call. His voice came back almost at once. "I'm here, Martin. Time to roll?"

"We've just lost contact with our scout team, Liam. I need the full fleet over there, ASAP."

"We've been monitoring the op here," Taggert replied. "The ship captains have all been brought on-line already, and we're ready to move."

"Let's do it, then."

"I've just given the order to proceed through the Gate."

Alexander had wanted to hold back on passing through the Gate until they were more certain of how they would be received, until contact with the aliens was established, but it was too late for that now.

They were committed, and Alexander was *not* going to abandon those men on the other side.

$e^{(i\pi)} + 1 = 0$
RFS Alpha
Aquila Space
2209 hrs GMT

Sensors imbedded within the access corridor kept the $e^{(i\pi)} + 1 = 0$ *apprised of where the three alien probes were as they descended from the surface. Communication, however, was not possible. While the* $e^{(i\pi)} + 1 = 0$ *could sense—the closest analog in terms of sensory input actually was* taste—*the internal communications of the three, there was as yet no way to derive meaning from them.*

Indeed, the watchers were having some difficulty now

determining whether the intruders were organic beings or if they were robotic extensions of some sort.

The intruding automatons shared characteristics of organic beings and machines. To $e^{(i\pi)} + 1 = 0$ senses, they appeared as interpenetrating patterns of n-dimensional solids and complex surfaces that were bound by complex tensors and their associated scalar fields, radiating heat and occasional bursts of heterodyned radio noise that may have been attempts at communication.

After several moments, the watchers monitoring the aliens' approach assumed they were autonomous probes, possibly robots, possibly engineered bioforms in protective armor and under the control of "Chesty" and "Evans," the alien intelligences in the ships still outside. Blocking the probes' radio links with Chesty had not incapacitated them, demonstrating that they were not teleoperated machines.

It was equally possible, however, that these three were biological constructs analogous to the $e^{(i\pi)} + 1 = 0$'s own sigma forms, life forms bioengineered eons ago to allow them to extend their reach into alien environments.

A major problem remained, now, in establishing communication with the beings, whatever they were. The $e^{(i\pi)} + 1 = 0$ could feel the flow and surge of internal virtual worlds riding some of the emitted RF noise—a clear point of similarity between the two distinct sequences. If there was to be communication, it might best be effected through a shared artificial reality.

But deriving common ground, even a virtual common ground, was going to be an incredibly complex and difficult task with the limited number of axioms that could be assumed. To build a valid model, the $e^{(i\pi)} + 1 = 0$ desperately needed more data.

Then, as the $e^{(i\pi)} + 1 = 0$ watchers continued to observe the three alien probes, other monitors raised an alarm.

The Translation Ring, orbiting slowly at the outer rim of the $e^{(i\pi)} + 1 = 0$ Collective, had just opened . . . and more alien tensors—ships, apparently, though the forms were difficult to integrate within $e^{(i\pi)} + 1 = 0$ concepts, were now coming through.

Recon Sword
RFS Alpha
Aquila Space
2210 hrs GMT

"Hold up, Marines," Eden said. "We've lost signal. I'm not reading Ops Control!"

Warhurst checked a readout. "The relays are functioning, sir," he said. "Must be some kind of shielding."

"Should we turn around and go back?" Galena wanted to know.

Eden considered this. "No. We're here to make contact. Let's keep going. But . . . watch yourselves."

The passageway was a cylindrical tunnel 3 meters wide plunging almost directly down into the heart of the asteroid. The gravity was so slight that the descent was easy, a matter of guiding themselves forward by pushing along the walls, or with short, tightly controlled bursts of gas from their jets. Warhurst was wondering when they would find an airlock. The entranceway had opened directly into this tunnel from the hard vacuum outside, and they were still in vacuum as they continued moving deeper.

And *deeper*. The rock was only about 12 kilometers across. How much deeper were they going to go?

And then, without warning, the tunnel opened into a large, a huge chamber, one with polished walls that shone in the Marines' suit lights. That chamber was filled with rank upon rank upon gleaming rank of polished-silver cylinders, each 3 meters long and 1 meter thick and with rounded endcaps, each imbedded in a tight-packed tangle of conduits and plumbing.

"My God," Warhurst said. "What the hell have we found? . . ."

System Outskirts
Aquila Space
2315 hrs GMT

The Xul sentry probe had waited, silent, unrecognized, for a

*long time . . . ever since the vicious series of actions result-
ing in the extermination of Species 3119.*

*The ancient Hunters of the Dawn knew this star system as
1901–002, the second system of Galactic Sector 1901, and
it possessed an inherent importance simply by being one of
those rare and far-scattered suns possessing a Gateway.*

*But System 1901–002 was important also because, once,
it had been part of Species 3119's small but troublesome
collective. The extermination of Species 3119 had not been
as serious a problem as the genocidal war against the Associative, half a million years ago, but it had still given We
Who Are cause for serious concern. Somehow, despite all of
the Xul's technological resources, Species 3119 had evolved
an extremely advanced and deadly technological base, one
capable of exploding stars.*

*Even the largest hunterships of the Xul could not with-
stand the flood of energy loosed by the destruction of a
sun.*

*Long debate had followed the final destruction of Species
3119. How had they managed to evolve such an advanced
technology without alerting those elements of the Xul galactic collective tasked with identifying threats to Xul survival? The question had become academic, of course, with
the destruction of the last stronghold of the bitterly suicidal
3119s . . . but there had remained a genuine concern that
other hold-outs might have escaped the notice of the giant
hunterships, might have survived to rebuild their culture,
their numbers, and their star-annihilating technologies.*

*And so Xul scout-probes had been seeded within each
of the star systems scattered across Sector 1901. Carefully
disguised as solitary lumps of carbonaceous rock and ices
a few kilometers across, orbiting in the cold, dark, outer
reaches of each system, these probes used almost no energy
and therefore were essentially undetectable. The sentient
mechanisms within each slept through the millennia, until
passive sensors on their surfaces registered activity within
certain narrow parameters.*

*Such activity was evident now in the probe orbiting two
light-hours from the local star.*

A *fleet*, a *very* large *fleet, was coming through the 1901–002 Gateway.*

As yet, the Xul sentience didn't have enough data to be able to identify the operators of that fleet. Possibly, the fleet's arrival represented the reemergence of Species 3119, after thousands of years of quiescence. Equally possibly, the fleet was that of another alien technic species, quite possibly of Species 2824, which had also caused unexpected difficulties for We Who Are in the recent past.

If it was Species 2824, their fleet's arrival was of particularly serious import, for that species originated in Sector 2420, ten to fifteen hundred light-years distant. They must be learning to use the gateway network, and that could have unfortunate repercussions for We Who Are.

Even more ominous was their presence here, in one of the ancient systems of Species 3119. The alien fleet's arrival suggested that they knew about the war with 3119, knew how close 3119 had come to stopping We Who Are . . . and might be looking for clues to the Weapon 3119 had employed.

Such . . . curiosity could not be permitted.

After recording the event, now two hours old, the Xul probe powered up, made a final internal check of all systems, then shimmered in a roil of twisting space/time, and was gone.

This time there could be no delay. An immediate and overwhelming response was absolutely necessary.

The supremacy, no, the very survival of We Who Are was at stake.

22

UCS Hermes
Stargate
Aquila Space
0945 hrs GMT

General Alexander hadn't gotten much sleep that night.

Not that abstract terms like *night* and *day* had much to do with the operation of a starship on deployment. By convenience and by tradition, 1MIEF operated on Greenwich Mean Time, but, in fact, all ship stations had to be fully manned at all times. Besides, ship captains, to say nothing of the MIEF commanders, Lieutenant General Alexander and Vice Admiral Taggart, were by definition *always* on duty, no matter what their actual state of consciousness.

He'd spent much of the night, so-called, monitoring the incoming tide of data transmitted first by Recon Sword, then by Marines of the 55th MARS off the *Samar* who had arrived some hours later. Currently, forty-five Marines of First Platoon, Alpha Company, were in the large subsurface chamber Recon Sword had discovered. The Marines, guided by intelligence and xenosophontologist personnel on board the *Hermes*, had spread out through the chamber, trying to gain an understanding of just what it was for.

The best guess so far was that each of those curious cylinders contained an alien held in suspended animation—an analogue of the old cybe-hibe capsules once used by the Corps on long, speed-of-light deployments between the stars centuries before. The conduits appeared to carry life-support fluids and power. While the alien technology was still difficult to understand, certain things—electrical pumps and fiber-optic cables, for example—were recognizable as such no matter how strange their outward appearance or form.

"I'm not sure," Alexander was telling one of the MIEF intelligence officers, "that poking holes in their equipment is the right way to get started with them. Especially if those cylinders represent some sort of suspended-animation canister. What if we kill someone inside?"

"That, General," Colonel Jen Willis replied, "won't happen. Nano microprobes are perfectly safe. And the data we get will tell us a great deal about alien physiology."

The technique was simple enough, Alexander knew. A tiny amount of specially programmed nano, consisting of nano-D and the raw materials for the probe itself, was placed on the surface of the device or container being sampled. The disassemblers ate a literally microscopic hole through the material. As soon as they detected a change in the material, the probe nano would insinuate itself through the hole, growing itself into a variety of sub-microscopic probes. If there was air or liquid inside the container, the probes would identify it and radio the results to the Marines outside. If there were electronics inside, the probes would trace and sample them, transmitting information on what types of signals, at what voltages, were being encountered. The whole probe process occurred at such a tiny scale, however, that even living organisms could be sampled without harming them. Doctors used similar means to diagnose illness, with patients who lacked their own internal nanosystems for some reason.

Still, Alexander was concerned. They as yet had no idea what they were dealing with, and the MIEF certainly could not afford to turn potential allies into enemies by a careless or clumsy misstep.

At the same time, they had to learn what they were dealing with. Continued probes of the alien computer network had amassed huge amounts of data, including more of the enigmatic cels that might be landscapes or portraits, but most of it was still unintelligible. If the xenosophontology department could come up with some clues to the nature of the aliens, the AIs might be able to work out clues to the language.

A few clues had been gleaned already.

"So . . . what was it you've named the aliens?" he asked Willis.

"'Eulers,'" she said, giving the name its Germanic pronunciation which sounded like "Oilers."

"And that was the name of . . . what did you say? A mathematician?"

"Yes, sir. Leonhard Euler. Eighteenth century . . . one of the greatest mathematicians of all time."

"Okay. But I still don't understand—"

"Whoever these people are," Willis explained, "they seem to incorporate a lot of pretty sophisticated mathematics into what they're doing. Our AI analyses were able to pick out basic number theory from their computer net pretty quickly, and give us an understanding of some of what they're saying. We were able to determine the electrical signals they use for a lot of their communications that way . . . zero, one, pi, e . . ."

"You told me earlier they use Fibonacci numbers as a means of encoding their computer data."

"Well . . . it's not that simple, but, essentially, yes sir. In fact, that gave us our first clue, when we figured out they were using the Fibonacci series and its relationship to phi as a means of encoding data. And one of the things we've picked up since is what appears to be a mathematical equation that they use to refer to themselves."

"Yes, e to the i times pi, plus one equals zero," Alexander said, reading the equation off of an open memory window. Math had never been his forte. "You told me. But I don't understand what that means."

Willis sighed. She'd explained all of this before. "Sir, the equation is significant because it very succinctly relates five of the most important, most basic of mathematical constants—e, the square root of minus one, pi, one, and zero—in a single brief, elegant statement. It also employs the mathematical notions of addition, multiplication, exponentiation, and equality. Are you with me, sir?"

"I think so. . . ."

"It's important to understand that these are not *human* concepts. The relationship of the radius of a circle to its circumference, the base of the natural logarithm, these are very special numbers that simply appear, all by themselves, in a whole host of mathematical operations. It's as though numbers like pi and *e* are built into the nature of the universe itself. In fact, some mathematical philosophers have used that equation to attempt to prove the existence of God."

"I see. And Euler? . . ."

"Came up with the equation, yes, sir. It's an identity derived from the Euler Formula. Or, I should say, he was the first *human* to derive it. Any mathematically competent species would do the same, sooner or later, because things like *e* are the same whether you're human or Xul or An or N'mah or whatever."

"So how do you know the aliens are using this as their name for themselves?"

"Guesswork, sir. But educated guesswork. The identity appears again and again within the data streams we've been receiving, and it appears to be a placeholder, a way of identifying something else. So maybe it's what they call their home planet . . . or maybe it's something else entirely, but the likeliest explanation is that they've adopted the term to mean themselves."

Alexander remembered having downloaded an e-pedia history, once, that had described how Thomas Young and Jean-François Champollion had first deciphered the Egyptian hieroglyphics and Demotic script found on the Rosetta Stone, a thousand years before. Champollion, in particular, had noticed that certain repeating collections of hieroglyphic symbols on the stone were enclosed in ovals, called cartouches, and that these seemed to correspond to certain names, like Ptolemy and Cleopatra, that appeared in the stone's parallel text in classical Greek. The names of rulers mentioned in the text had proven to be the key to unlocking the writing of ancient Egypt. Perhaps the AIs working on translating the alien data streams were employing a similar strategy.

Of course, translating the Rosetta Stone would have been child's play compared to this, working out the linguistic and conceptual symbolisms of the completely unknown language of a completely unknown alien species.

"An equation is a little hard to pronounce," he said, bemused.

"For us," Willis said. "But we don't yet know how they speak to one another. Maybe the mathematical term sounds to them like a single, short word would to us. Or their language might be nothing but equations and numerical relationships. And they might very well not have speech as we know it, with audible sounds. Maybe they use organic radio. Or fluctuating magnetic fields. Or changing colors or skin patterns. Or, hell, as a particular *smell*, if they communicate by means of odors.

"The fact is, sir, we don't know enough about their biology to even guess at what we're working with here. That's why we need to probe one of those capsules, very gently, very subtly. Until we do, we simply won't have enough information to go on, and all of the data we've recorded so far is just, for the most part, noise."

Alexander thought about it a moment more. "Okay," he said, but reluctantly. "But only one, and I want you to use the absolute least amount of intrusion possible. We're the guests, here, and uninvited guests at that. I don't want to blunder in and break up the furniture."

"Of course, General," Willis said. "That goes without saying."

When it came to understanding the alien, Alexander thought, *nothing* went without saying. "Just be damned careful," he said. "We're already fighting the Xul . . . and maybe the PanEuropeans as well, if the negotiations back on Earth break down. Let's not make these guys mad at us, too!"

"Nothing," Willis said, "can possibly go wrong."

But Alexander wasn't so sure. Beings that thought in terms of higher mathematics—for him that seemed to define the very term "alien."

And the more alien these beings were, the more opportunity there would be for something to go horribly wrong.

First Platoon, Alpha Company
RFS Alpha
Aquila Space
1010 hrs GMT

"Wait a second," Garroway said. "They want us to fucking *what*?"

Gunnery Sergeant Ramsey turned, looking at the array of cylinders gleaming, rank upon rank, into the surrounding darkness. "We're supposed to poke a hole in one of those things? I don't like it."

Sandre Kenyon held up the probe pack she'd just brought down from the surface. "They said the hole would be too small to cause any problem, Gunny."

"Yeah, but I don't like the idea of poking at stuff we don't understand."

"It's fucking crazy," Sergeant Chu said. "What if there's, I don't know, radiation inside those things? Or antimatter power plants?"

"That's a hell of a lot of antimatter generators," Garroway said, still looking at the rows of silently waiting cylinders. He could see several small, black shapes—platoon remote sensor drones—were patrolling among the cylinders, searching for anything out of the ordinary. "But that doesn't really make sense, power plants that small, and so many of them. They look more like the old cybe-hibe capsules, y'know?"

"That's what Master Sergeant Barrett said," Kenyon said. "That's why the whiz-boys want a sample of what's inside."

PFC Sandre Kenyon had arrived from the outside moments ago, bringing with her the sampling kit. Radio communication with the outside was still blocked, so the Marines had fallen back on the ancient expedient of using runners—or, in this case, *fliers*—to maintain communications with the ships of the MIEF.

"Do you know how to use that stuff, Private?" Ramsey asked her.

"Sure, Gunny. They gave me a download."

Ramsey hesitated. It felt to Garroway like he wasn't at all happy with this. "Okay. Do you want to do it, or do you want to uplink the data to one of us?"

"I can do it, Gunny." She tapped the side of her helmet. "They loaded some special software just now, to record what happens on a molecular level. The Master Sergeant wants me to hot-foot it back up there to upload the results as soon as the probe is complete."

Another long hesitation. "Very well, Marine. Go ahead." As she started to move toward the nearest of the cylinders, he stopped her with a gauntlet on her shoulder. "Wait one, Kenyon. The rest of you! Move back. Set up a globe perimeter, interlocking fields of fire. Chu, Takamura, Delgado, Doc . . . you four at the tunnel entrance. Put the remotes out at least 20 meters beyond the globe. We're going to do this by the book."

It took only a few moments for the Marines in the chamber to take up new positions, with Ramsey and Kenyon at the center. When each Marine signified that he or she was in position, Ramsey gave Kenyon the word. "Okay. Do it."

Garroway was floating behind one of the cylinders about 4 meters away. Though he was facing away from the two Marines, he was able to use his helmet optics to zoom in close, in effect looking over Sandre's shoulder as she approached the selected cylinder. The kit she'd brought down from the surface contained four probe units, each the size and shape of a bottle cap. Selecting one, she placed it against the cylinder, then touched its upper surface with the hard-wire e-contacts in the palm of her left glove. The device was activated by a mental trigger command, transmitted through the suit's electronics.

"Okay," Sandre said, removing her hand and maneuvering closer so that she could better see. "Probe activated. It looks like it's—"

Something like a bright, silver shaft, needle-thin but

meters long, speared from the back of Sandre's helmet. There was no sound, of course, in the vacuum of the chamber, but the effect was like that of a gunshot. The back of Sandre's helmet exploded outward in hurtling shards of metal, ceramic, and bone mingled with a shocking scarlet mist that swiftly froze into glittering pinpoints of ruby ice.

"*Sandre*!" Garroway screamed, turning sharply. Sandre's body tumbled backward, arms flung wide, her helmet a gory tangle of shredded composites and blood-ice.

"Belay that!" Ramsey snapped. "Hold your positions!"

But Sandre's body was tumbling past Garroway only a couple of meters away. Reaching out, he grabbed one of her combat harness straps and dragged her toward him. Gobbets of red and gray ice continued spinning across the chamber, disconcertingly, and Garroway struggled not to be sick.

As he pulled her close, he saw the circular, two-centimeter hole leaking freezing red mist that now punctured her helmet visor dead center. Most of the back of her helmet was gone.

"*Corpsman*!" he yelled over the company frequency. "*Corpsman front*!"

Doc Thorne was already on his way, however, jetting across from the tunnel mouth in a long, flat trajectory.

"Where the hell'd the fire come from?" Corporal Allison cried. He was pivoting nearby, the muzzle of the field-pulse rifle mounted on his right forearm seeking a target. Most of the Marines on the perimeter were turning now to face the dark corners of the chamber behind Sandre, a rough, curving surface of rock all but lost in the shadows 30 meters from the nearest side of the cylinder array. A dozen suit lights began searching the walls of the cavern in that direction, as remote drones closed in from every side, piercing the shadows with beams of glaring white light.

Garroway saw at once their mistake. They were assuming a sniper had drilled Sandre from behind as she worked at the cylinder . . . but he'd had the distinct impression that whatever had hit her had come from the cylinder, punching a two-centimeter entrance hole through her visor, and exploding outward from the back of her head in a classic exit wound. The way her body had tumbled heels-over-head *away* from the deadly cylinder seemed to support the idea.

"Wait!" he yelled. *"That's not—"*

"I got targets!" Corporal Allison yelled, and he fired his pulse rifle. White flame blossomed off the side of the cavern wall, 30 meters away.

Okay, you got it wrong, he thought, releasing Sandre's body into Doc Thorne's keeping. He raised his own pulse rifle, looking for a target. He knew the difference between an exit wound and an entrance wound, thanks to ballistics training in boot camp, but he also knew that a shaped-charge explosive round might reverse the picture, causing explosive damage on impact and firing a tightly focused needle of hot plasma out the other side. Everyone else seemed convinced that there was a shooter out there in the darkness. Anger surfaced through the numbness left by Sandre's shockingly sudden death, anger at himself for having jumped to the wrong conclusion.

There! His suit optics caught an awkward scramble of movement, though even under infrared it wasn't giving much of a signature. What the hell was that thing? . . .

His simulations of close-combat with Xul robots had accustomed him to tracking stealthy movement as hostile war machines emerged from the surrounding bulkheads. This didn't look like that, however. The thing looked like an immense spider . . . or possibly a crab, but with multiply branched legs spanning a good 3 meters.

But there was no time for analyses, no time for thought. He triggered his weapon and felt the sharp, visceral thrill of a solid hit as the spidery thing came apart in a messy splash of green and yellow liquid.

Other spider-shapes were moving across the cavern walls, now, the lights from the Marine armor and the drifting remotes casting weirdly shifting, nightmare shadows everywhere. Garroway used his suit optics to zoom in close on one, trying to understand what he was seeing. He could see some sort of harness on the thing, proof that it wasn't an animal. He had a moment's glimpse of six glittering silver beads arranged in a circle around what might have been the thing's face, three above, three below. Eyes? Or weapons? Xul combat machines possessed randomly scattered lenses across their egg-shaped bodies, some of them eyes, some of them beam weapons.

Shit! Maybe these things *were* Xul! He triggered his pulse rifle, and the spindle-limbed creature disintegrated in an eerily silent flash of blue-white energy.

It was distinctly odd, though. The spiders didn't appear to be carrying anything like weapons in those branching, clawed arms, and they *weren't* shooting back.

$e^{(i\pi)} + 1 = 0$
RFS Alpha
Aquila Space
1012 hrs GMT

Inequivalence!
  Perhaps the intruders were Enemy after all. They weren't of the usual design—oblate spheroids of complex topology, with beam weapons hidden inside—but they did appear to be autonomous machines of fairly high sentience, and they did possess potent beam weapons mounted to their exoskeletons.
  They also possessed the Enemy's predilections both for unthinking destruction and for a suicidal disregard for individual remote elements, using individual machines as tools, as expendable parts of the whole. The $e^{(i\pi)} + 1 = 0$ regarded their autonomous extensions, the Manipulators, both as part of the racial Set, and as pets.
  And the Enemy intruders were destroying those pets now as soon as they emerged into the cavern. The monitors transmitted a command, pulling the Manipulators back into the walls of the Third Chamber of Repose.
  At the same time, other monitors readied the Trigger.
  The Set of $e^{(i\pi)} + 1 = 0$ was under deliberate and deadly attack.

* * *

First Platoon, Alpha Company
RFS Alpha
Aquila Space
1014 hrs GMT

"*Cease fire! Cease fire! Cease fire!*" Ramsey, Garroway thought, had apparently come to the same conclusion. The spiders weren't shooting, weren't even armed.

Responding to training, the Marine platoon stopped shooting almost at once. There'd been five or six of the things on the cavern wall. At least four had been destroyed in the volley of fire, and the others were already vanishing into an almost invisible opening in the rock.

"Chu!" Ramsey snapped.

"Yeah, Gunny!"

"Get back to the surface. Give 'em your memory."

"Aye, aye, Gunnery Sergeant!"

"Doc! How is she?"

"Clinical," the corpsman replied. "Don't know if she'll be irrie . . ."

Clinically dead. Garroway felt a surge of grief at that. The thing was, nanomedicine could patch up almost anyone nowadays, unless they'd been vaporized—turned to smoke. Usually, irries—irretrievables—were smokers, with so much of the body burned away there wasn't enough for full-body forced cloning.

But there was another class of irrie that no Marine liked to think about. Sandre's head could be regrown easily enough, but her brain had been pulped and sprayed out the back of her head. The revived Sandre Kenyon would have none of the memories, experiences, or training of the original. In fact, she would be, in effect, a newborn baby, one who would have to learn to crawl, to toddle, to speak from the very beginning.

Sandre—the Sandre that Garroway had known and loved—was gone.

And the pain he felt now at that realization was almost unbearable, a sharp, burning despair that threatened to paralyze him.

"Garroway! Garroway! Snap out of it!"

He became aware of Ramsey shouting at him over the platoon channel. Doc Thorne was already following Chu out the tunnel entrance, with Sandre's body in tow. He hadn't even heard Ramsey give the order to take her out.

"Uh . . . yeah . . ."

"Square yourself away, Marine!" Ramsey said, the words hard and sharp-edged. "Eyes on your front! That goes for the rest of you devil dogs, too! Watch your fronts!"

Long, silent seconds passed. Garroway was gasping for breath, struggling to control his grief, his rage, his screaming thoughts. Damn it, damn it, damn it. He *knew* what he'd seen. He'd been right the first time.

"Hey . . . Gunny?"

"What is it, Garroway?"

"I don't think Sand—uh, Private Kenyon was shot. I don't think those spider-things on the wall were attacking us."

"I know," Ramsey said. He was floating next to the cylinder Sandre had been probing, examining the neat, round hole in its side. A thin rime of ice coated the tank's side. "If I didn't know better, I'd say this tank was holding something, a liquid, maybe, under incredible pressure. When she triggered the probe, the pressure broke loose, and what was inside hit her like a mass-driver cannon."

Garroway nodded inside his helmet. "It was a fucking *accident*!"

"Take it easy, Marine. It happens." He drifted back from the now-empty cylinder. "Okay, Marines, listen up! By the numbers, fall back to the tunnel entrance, then start back up, single file."

"What the hell?" Allison said. "We're retreating?"

"I think we've done enough damage here," Ramsey said. He was working at the release catch for the pulse rifle on his right arm. It flipped free, and the weapon drifted off. Catching it, he handed it to Vallida.

"What are you doing, Gunny?"

"Disarming. I'm going to stay here and see if those beasties come out of the walls again."

"Unarmed? You can't—"

"*Just get the fuck out of here!*" Ramsey shouted. Then, more quietly, "The rest of you get back to the surface. Upload what you've seen here. Garroway? Tell them what you think, what you told me. I'm going to see if they try to talk to me."

"Right, Gunny." Garroway felt stunned, and he felt an odd sense of déjà vu—not a repeat of something he'd felt before personally, but of a similar incident, one every Marine studied in downloaded sims in boot camp.

Centuries before, a group of Marines exploring the interior of the Sirius Stargate had gotten into a firefight with monstrous, aquatic beings. One of those Marines had been his many-times-great grandfather, one Corporal John Garroway.

Somehow, John Garroway had become separated from the rest of his unit, but with considerable presence of mind in a terrifying situation, he'd put up his weapon and allowed the aliens to take him. They'd started showing him movies, then teaching him their language.

And that had been Humankind's first modern contact with the N'mah, an amphibious species that had visited Earth in antiquity. The N'mah, or the Nommo, as they'd been known in prehistory, had first visited Earth around 6000 b.c.e. and quite possibly ensured the survival of the scattered and Xul-brutalized humans who had gone on to found ancient Sumeria.

Modern Marines were trained to kill, but they were also trained to use their heads, and to attempt communication with, to attempt to *understand* the unknown whenever possible.

That was what Gunny Ramsey was doing now.

"Gunny?" Garroway said. "You want me to stay with you?"

"Negative, Marine. Get to the surface." He was unshipping his flamer from his left forearm, now, letting the weapon drift toward the blast-charred rock wall of the cavern. He was completely unarmed, now. The question was, would the aliens understand that?

"If you don't hear from me again," he went on, "well . . . it'll be up to the general to figure out what happens next. But give me a few hours, at least."

"Aye, aye, Gunny." He started to go, then turned again. "Gunny?"

"What?"

"Semper fi." And then he was gone.

23

UCS Hermes
Stargate
Aquila Space
1132 hrs GMT

General Alexander was listening in on the debriefing of the Marines of the 55th MARS. They'd emerged from the asteroid habitat moments before, and were now on the surface, once again linked in with the MIEF computer net. In effect, Alexander was an invisible presence within the virtual room where Colonel Willis was carrying out the debriefing.

"And Gunnery Sergeant Ramsey is trying to establish contact alone?" Colonel Willis was asking one of the MARS Marines.

"Yes, sir," PFC Garroway replied. In the Corps, female officers were always accorded the courtesy of *sir.* "He wouldn't let me stay with him."

"I see," Willis said. "Okay, Private Garroway. You may go."

"Uh . . . sir?"

"Yes?"

"Have you heard anything about Private Kenyon? Are they going to be able to bring her back?"

"I . . . don't know, Garroway. But we'll keep you informed."

"Yes, sir." He hesitated.

"Something else, Marine?"

"Yes, sir. If you need people to go back in for the gunny, I want to volunteer."

"Thank you, private. Dismissed."

"Aye, aye, sir."

Alexander checked his internal timekeeper as Garroway vanished from the virtual compartment. Gunnery Sergeant Ramsey had been alone inside the alien habitat for over an hour, now. Damn it, how long did they need to wait before he sent in the whole MIEF assault force to bring the man out?

"General Alexander?"

"Yes, Colonel?" The two of them were alone now in the virtual debriefing room.

"You've been listening in?"

"Yes, I have."

"I . . . don't think the Marine boarding party came under attack."

"I know they didn't, Colonel. It was a horrible mistake. An accident." That much was clear from slow-motion playbacks of the data in the Marines' implant data storage, and through the recordings made by First Platoon's AI, Achilles.

"What the hell happened to that one Marine, though?" Willis asked.

"Kenyon? Apparently the contents of those cylinders inside the asteroid are under pressure . . . tremendous pressure. Achilles thinks something like 10 tons per square centimeter. Kenyon triggered that nanoprobe that began eating a microscopic hole into the cylinder, and the contents explosively decompressed through the hole." In fact, the pressure had propelled the bottle-cap-sized probe package affixed to the surface of the cylinder straight through Kenyon's visor and out the back of her head like a high-velocity kinetic-kill round.

In the stress of the moment, the Marines had assumed they were taking fire, and responded appropriately. The question now was whether the damage could be undone, at least insofar as human-Euler relations were concerned. There was little chance that the docs and meds would be able to bring Private Kenyon back. And a number of Eulers—if that's what the spidery crab-things were—had been killed as well.

Operation Gorgon was *not* off to a good start.

RFS Alpha
Aquila Space
1132 hrs GMT

Ramsey faced the alien.

He knew that what he was experiencing wasn't *real*, not in the usual sense. This was clearly a piece of virtual reality programming, an illusion unfolding within his mind, but it was as solid and as realistic as any training sim or virtual briefing session he'd ever encountered.

Achilles had found the door for him, picking up a thread of radio noise and following it into this simulated reality. Most of the platoon AI had vanished with the rest of the MARS Marines, but a small operational portion of the AI software remained resident within his armor and his implants, as much as could be supported by the available hardware. This version of Achilles was sharply truncated, its experience and memory limited to what Ramsey himself had on board.

He thought of the AI as Achilles$_2$, a subset of the larger program, and was grateful to have someone else with whom to talk. Not only that, but virtual reality was the AI's natural habitat. He would have been lost without the intelligent software's ability to interface with the alien signals.

"Is this their native environment?" he asked. "A representation of it, I mean?"

"It seems likely," Achilles$_2$ replied. "I cannot be certain that details such as color are correct, but the data is coming from the surrounding structure . . . from the asteroid-habitat itself. Their computer system is extremely sophisticated, almost invisible."

"Invisible?"

"The most advanced technology," Achilles$_2$ informed him with something that almost sounded like pride, "is that

which interfaces so smoothly with the user that he is unaware of its actions. The Eulers appear to *live* here."

It still seemed strange, naming an alien race after a long-
dead human mathematician. Especially since it was hard to
imagine anything more alien than this.

Ramsey was most aware of the being's . . . face; it had
what he assumed were eyes, six of them, so "face" was as
good a term as any. The eyes, three above, three below, encircled a clump of multi-branchiate tentacles, something
like the branches of a tree limb.

It reminded Ramsey rather strongly of an octopus, though
the tentacles were nothing like the tentacles sported by that
denizen of Earth's oceans. The body, however, was utterly
unlike anything Ramsey had ever seen before, a transparent to translucent gray mass, something like the body of a
huge, flattened worm or snake, but with six bulbous append-
ages that might be legs, each sprouting long and interweaving tentacles that faded away into the surrounding darkness.
The body itself appeared boneless and changed shape as he
watched, from long and thin to short and squat. And were
those three triangular extensions small wings, or large fins
. . . or something else entirely? He found himself fascinated
by what he assumed were the being's hearts, five of them
running in a line from just behind the head to deep within
that monstrous translucent body, pulsing in series, one after
the next.

He found he could only study the creature for a few moments before the sheer strangeness began to overwhelm him,
and he had to look away for a time. The surroundings weren't
that much better, though. He seemed to be standing underwater, very *deep* underwater. It was like being enmeshed
in liquid blackness. The only light came from the near distance, where something like a sphere of bubbles churned
and pulsated, seeming to emit a cool greenish light. Nearby,
a forest of scarlet feathers waved gently in the current.

In this sim, he noted, he wasn't wearing armor, but plain
black utilities. His boots were planted in viscous mud; he
could not feel the cold, the wet, or what must have been a
crushing pressure from the surrounding water. How many

kilometers of ocean, he wondered, looking up into blackness, were supposed to be piled up on top of him?

The alien continued to watch him. Nearby, he noted, were two of the spidery creatures the Marines had encountered in the chamber earlier, but there was no question in his mind that the tentacled being directly in front of him was the controlling intelligence here. There was something about its eyes, something radiating awareness, calm, and assurance. *Intelligence.*

The question was, how did the alien perceive him? As intelligent? Or as a computer-simulated icon within the alien computer net, a manifestation of software expressions that could be . . . anything?

He thought for a moment, and the alien watched him, its tentacles drifting and weaving with a current Ramsey could not feel. The Marines had been briefed before being deployed to this rock. The Eulers, the xenosophies thought, knew mathematics, even identified themselves by means of a math equation.

Okay. Ramsey wasn't a math wiz, but he knew a few things. Reaching up, he slapped his chest with his right hand, paused, then slapped twice. Then three times. Then five. Then seven. And eleven. Not a simple counting sequence, but counting in primes, whole numbers that could only be divided evenly by themselves or by one.

Wondering how long he should continue the sequence, he started slapping his chest to count out the number thirteen . . . but then he felt something like a series of light taps on his forehead . . . thirteen of them, as the Eulers picked up the sequence.

Good, he thought. *I couldn't have kept on slapping myself all day.*

The exchange of prime numbers, perhaps, had been a test . . . or maybe it was simply an Euler's way of saying a polite "hello." He waited. . . .

And then images began to form, unbidden, in Ramsey's mind. They were fragmentary, at first, and incomplete, but he sensed that the alien was uploading information to him, a very great deal of information, and at a staggering rate.

Language, of course. History. Strange images that Ramsey couldn't even grasp as they slipped past.

But he opened himself, and watched . . . and learned.

So . . . this was another marine race, an oceanic species like the N'mah, amphibious beings with a two-stage life cycle. N'mah juveniles were true amphibians, walking erect on more-or-less human legs but able to return to the sea. After perhaps forty to forty-five years, the juvenile forms lost their legs, grew considerably bigger, and never again emerged from the depths; they also seemed to lose much of the questing inventiveness of their young, preferring instead a quiet life of contemplation in warm, shallow, sunlit seas. In N'mah civilization, it had been the amphibious juveniles that had discovered dry land, tamed fire and stone, metal and electricity, and eventually built the ships that took them to the stars. Sometime around 6000 b.c.e., the juveniles had visited Earth, helping re-establish civilization in the Fertile Crescent after the Xul had wiped out the local An colonies. The N'mah had been remembered in myth as the Nommo.

The Eulers, he saw, were like the N'mah in the scope of the problems they were forced to overcome as an aquatic civilization. No fire, an understanding of chemistry limited by water and pressure, and not even the first glimmer of understanding concerning astronomy or cosmology.

And yet, given enough time, given billions of years, perhaps . . .

Ramsey wasn't sure how long it had taken. The thought-images flowing through his mind conveyed the sense of passing time, a lot of it, but he couldn't begin to put a meaningful figure to it. The Eulers learned, eventually, to use the intense heat found in the throats of volcanic vents to smelt metal, and they appeared to develop an advanced understanding of chemistry as well, especially the chemistries of sulfur, methane, and certain salts. It was in biology that they excelled, however, breeding new species, then altering the genome of the flora and fauna of the extreme depths to suit their needs.

The spider-things, he saw in a succession of images, had been created by the Eulers, who gave them extremely dextrous, three-fingered manipulators at the end of each of twelve jointed legs. They could swim as well as walk, using directed bursts of water to jet forward like armored squids, and they appeared unaffected by changes in pressure. Achilles$_2$ whispered to him an aside that certain terrestrial sea animals—sperm whales and seals, for example—could dive to extreme depths without being imploded by the pressures of the abyss. Somehow the spiders did the same trick in reverse, and it was through them that the Eulers, many ages ago, had discovered the ceiling of their watery world, and broken through to the land and skies beyond.

Through the spiders, which Achilles$_2$ dubbed "Manipulators" because of their obvious dexterity, the Eulers eventually reached the surface of their world. Ramsey saw pictures of that world unfold in his mind and was immediately reminded of Europa in the Sol System, the iced-over ocean world that was one of Jupiter's major satellites. The Euler home world, evidently, was similar, an icy moon kept liquid by tidal stresses as it circled its vast, gas-giant primary. Unlike Europa, this world possessed solid land, however, scattered across an ice-free equatorial zone.

For untold millions of years, Euler civilization grew both on the sea floor and in pressurized cities built on land, where an inborn propensity for mathematics led them, in time, to add astronomy to their growing repertoire of skills. Long before, in the cold dark of the benthic deep, they'd developed abstract mathematics to an astonishing degree—or so Achilles$_2$ suggested—but the full flowering of math and physics began when they first saw the stars.

Eventually, they and their Manipulator creations learned to leave their world entirely, traveling in immense ships filled with highly pressurized seawater.

By that time, the Euler-Manipulator partnership was a true symbiosis. Manipulators, in their rigid, jointed exoskeletons, were unaffected by extremes of heat or cold, by radiation, even by hard vacuum. By wearing a kind of body harness that provided methane-rich, sulfur-laden water under pressure to the respiratory spiracles along its sides, a Manipulator could work in open space for long

periods. Ramsey and the other Marines had seen several of
the Manipulators tasked with maintaining the pressurized
cylinders in the chamber they'd entered. He'd seen the res-
piration harness, though he hadn't realized then what he'd
been seeing.

Driven more by curiosity than by a need for living room,
Euler explorers had eventually left their original star system
and ventured to the planetary systems encircling other
nearby stars. If Ramsey was understanding the charts he
was being shown, they'd visited worlds across a swath of the
galactic starscape far larger than that now occupied by humankind. Among those stars they'd found ice-roofed ocean
worlds similar to home, and colonized many of them. At this
point in their history, they'd not possessed faster-than-light
travel. They hadn't needed it. The Eulers were immensely
long-lived and they took their civilization with them in immense city-ships.

But in time they'd encountered the Xul.

Ramsey easily recognized the characteristic lines of the
Xul huntships . . . the slender gold needles 2 kilometers
long, the even larger disks and flattened wedges, each the
hardware "body" of an electronic community dedicated to
Xul survival, and the utter extermination of any competing
species.

The war, Ramsey sensed, had been a long one. The Eulers
were not warlike; indeed, from what they were able to communicate through Achilles$_2$, they didn't even have a concept
for war. They learned, however, as the Xul began a bitter
and implacable campaign to eradicate each of the worlds
occupied by the Eulers.

With the Xul as teachers, however, the Eulers *had*
learned, and learned well. The Xul had bombarded their icy
worlds with high-velocity asteroids until whole oceans had
boiled away; the Eulers had learned how to reach down into
the Quantum Sea and adjust such basics of Reality as inertia, mass, and velocity, and bombarded the Xul huntships
with asteroids in return. The Xul had possessed overwhelming tactical superiority in their FTL ships. The Eulers had
worked out how to wrap space around their ship-habitats

and travel faster than light as well, using a system that, if Ramsey understood the animated schematics he was being shown, was identical to the Alcubierre Drive developed a few centuries ago by Humankind.

But the Xul kept coming, pounding world after world into crater-gouged ruin.

And then, if the images were to be believed, if he was understanding this right . . . the Eulers stopped the Xul.

And they did it by blowing up stars.

That, it seemed, was the secret of Aquila Space. Ramsey could see how they did it, too, as the Euler showed him another set of animated schematics. They would wait until an entire Xul battlefleet had entered a star system and begun hammering the local Euler colony. An Euler ship under their equivalent of Alcubierre Drive would elude the Xul fleet and dive into the local sun.

Every star, Ramsey knew, was poised in a delicate balance between its own radiation pressure, which threatened to tear the star apart, and its own gravity, which sought to pull it together. The Alcubierre Drive sharply warped space, compressing the space ahead of the ship, and attenuating it behind. Put enough of a warp into it, and that fast-moving bubble of distorted space actually compressed the tightly packed matter at the star's core. As the ship tunneled through the core of the star, more or less shielded from the awesome heat and pressure by the warp field around it, it triggered a wave of compression that shattered the balance between radiation and gravity. The core partially collapsed, then rebounded, hurtling outward.

Nova . . .

Ramsey watched the wave-front of white-hot plasma sweeping out through a star system, watched it catch the Xul fleet as it hung above the frozen moon of a gas giant, watched even those massive constructs soften, crumble, soften and melt, and finally vaporize in the intense blast of star-stuff. The blast savaged the moon as well, of course, turning it into a short-lived and massive comet as the ice vaporized in a long, brilliant tail, even as it stripped away much of the atmosphere from the gas giant primary.

As the wave-front continued to expand, everything in the system died.

Ramsey found himself breathing harder, his heart pounding. *My God, they destroyed themselves to kill the Xul.* But, then, perhaps they rationalized the exchange as a good trade, with the Euler colony doomed in either case. Would humankind have shown the same single-mindedness of purpose, he wondered?

"What can we show them in exchange?" he asked Achilles$_2$. "This guy just uploaded their whole damned history to me."

"I have been sending them animated schematics showing our ships in combat against the Xul," Achilles$_2$ replied. "I fear more detailed conversations must wait until we can work out a common language."

Right. The thing floating in front of him wouldn't speak, wouldn't be able to form words the way humans did, so communication wouldn't be a matter of just learning one another's language. Deep sea life forms . . . maybe they communicated via sonar, like whales and dolphins. Or through changes in color and patterning, like octopi and squids. Or by electrical fields. Or by sensing changes in pressure in the surrounding water. Or bioluminescence. Or through some other sense entirely.

"Can you tell him . . . tell him that we're sorry we damaged that tank?"

"*Sorry* is a rather advanced concept," Achilles$_2$ replied. "I do not have the required symbology. However . . . he . . . she, rather . . . has just showed me what those tanks are for."

"They're like cybe-hibe canisters," Ramsey said. "The Eulers are hibernating in those things."

"Not hibernating," Achilles$_2$ told him. "Not quite. Again, I lack adequate symbols for full understanding, but I believe the beings inside those tanks are alive and aware. They apparently share an extremely rich virtual world, within which they interact with one another as a viable culture."

Ramsey digested this. It made sense, in a way, rather brilliant sense, in fact. In creating asteroid habitats like this one, or starships crewed by Eulers, they could hollow out a mountain and fill it with water under high pressure—in effect taking a part of their seafloor world with them. Or, much simpler, much safer and more efficient, they could encapsulate each Euler in just enough pressurized seawater to keep him alive, pipe in nutrients and pipe out wastes . . . and free his mind to interact with his fellows in a virtual reality that could be as vast, as rich, and as varied as their computer network could allow.

And judging from the way this Euler was using a virtual reality sim to communicate with him, the alien computer net must allow a very great deal indeed.

"How advanced do you think the Eulers are, Achilles?" he asked. "How far ahead of us are they?"

"That question is meaningless, Gunnery Sergeant. The two cultures, Euler and human, are so different in so many ways, there are few benchmarks against which both may be measured. The evolution of their science and technology took considerably longer, and more effort, than did those of humankind. However, I estimate that the Eulers as an intelligent species have been in existence for something in excess of one hundred million years . . . and quite possibly much longer still."

"Jesus . . ." When the Eulers had first mastered the ocean depths of their homeworld, dinosaurs still stalked the Earth.

It was interesting, though, that the Xul had taken that long to notice the Eulers. The first appearance of the Xul with which humans were familiar had taken place half a million years ago, with the extinction of the commonality of advanced civilizations variously known as the Ancients or the Builders.

The fact that the Eulers hadn't encountered the Xul until a mere two thousand years ago—when the novae in this region of space had been deliberately triggered—strongly suggested a weakness in the way the Xul thought and acted.

That weakness had been suggested before, and it had to do with a kind of short-sightedness on the Xul's part when it came to understanding life. The Xul seemed to understand

and expect civilizations on worlds like Earth, worlds at a comfortable distance from the local sun, with liquid water and Earthlike climates.

But life, as was well known by now, was not constrained by concepts like *Earthlike*. Life had taken hold and thrived in myriad places—from deep-sea volcanic vents on Europa to the subsurface Martian permafrost to traces found in Oort-Cloud cometary nuclei. For eight centuries, human science had been redefining what the very word *life* meant; the search for life in a new solar system was no longer confined to the star's so-called habitable zone.

And what was true for life in general, it seemed, was also true for whole civilizations.

When the Xul had destroyed the interstellar empire of the An several thousand years ago, they'd overlooked one An colony—the satellite of a gas giant at Lalande 21185 far from the meager warmth of the system's red-dwarf primary. By chance, a few An and their human slaves had survived there, unnoticed by the marauding hunterships.

And the amphibious N'mah—a marine species, like the Eulers, with only a limited presence on solid land—had been overlooked as well. Eventually, the N'mah worlds had been discovered and destroyed, but the N'mah, too, had survived . . . by living inside the hollow structures of a Stargate, and, more recently, in asteroid habitats hollowed out for the purpose.

And now it seemed that the Eulers had long been overlooked by the Xul, apparently because their favored worlds were gas-giant satellites well outside the usual habitable zone of a given planetary system. Once the Xul had finally noticed the Euler worlds, the Eulers, evidently, had, like the N'mah, moved to hollowed-out asteroids.

Ramsey remembered how many RF targets had been detected in this star system alone, in the vast band of asteroids circling the local star. There might be some hundreds of inhabited planetoids lost among the hundreds of thousands of chunks of debris making up the asteroid belt.

He had so many questions. Surely the Xul could pick up radio frequency noise as readily as could human ships.

Weren't the Eulers afraid that their radio leakage would give them away?

Or were they unaware of it? They must know radio, since their virtual reality world seemed to be transmitted at radio wavelengths. Or, perhaps the Xul were oblivious to leakage at radio frequencies?

"Unknown," Achilles$_2$ said, reading his thoughts and stating the obvious. "There is reason to suspect that the Xul are so self-centered they don't notice relatively subtle effects like secondary radio transmission. But, ultimately, we simply don't know."

Ramsey stared at the nightmarish being floating in front of him. If the scale was accurate, the thing was almost 3 meters long, with easily twice the mass of a human, at least. He felt no fear now, however. The being—had Achilles$_2$ called it *she*?—appeared to be waiting.

Waiting for what?

Waiting, perhaps, for an apology.

Or, at the least, for some sign that the humans *wanted* an alliance. That might be self-evident, especially in the images of humans battling Xul that Achilles$_2$ was sending them—*the enemy of my enemy is my friend. . . .*

On the other hand, there was no way to guess what the Eulers were thinking, how they thought, how they connected with or even perceived aliens in the first place. These things were *different. . . .*

"Achilles? Can you create an animation of humans and Eulers working together? Maybe show them fighting the Xul?"

"I will try." A moment passed. "Done."

There was no response from the Euler. It hovered there in the darkness of a virtual sea, its tentacles waving gently in an unfelt current.

"Achilles . . . bring an image of the damaged cylinder into this simulation, would you?"

"Yes, Gunnery Sergeant."

A lone tank appeared in the shared simulation, upright, 3 meters tall, a meter thick. The 2-centimeter hole was clearly visible in the side.

At least the Euler crammed inside that thing would not have suffered. Literal explosive decompression as the contents blasted out into hard vacuum would have killed it instantly.

As instantly as it had killed Private Kenyon.

Ramsey moved forward in the simulation until he was standing directly beside the cylinder. Reaching out, he tapped it, just above the hole. Then he tapped himself on his own chest. Finally, he opened his arms wide, hands open, legs spread apart. Spread-eagle, he stood there for a long moment, hoping the symbols were clear.

He'd already pointedly divested himself of his weapons, and, in the sim he wasn't even wearing armor. There wasn't a lot else he could do to prove peaceful intent to these beings, except try for an empty-hand-means-no-weapon gesture. Hell, even that might not be understood by a being that had no hands.

How did one mime an empty tentacle?

If these beasties knew math, though, they must understand a one-to-one equivalence. He'd been the one in command when Kenyon had drilled into the tank. He was offering himself, one for one. . . .

The damaged tank vanished. Slowly, when nothing further happened, he lowered his arms.

"Did you take the tank out of the sim, Achilles?"

"No, Gunnery Sergeant. She did."

Communication.

He studied the impassive being for a moment. "Achilles? What makes you think that it's a *she*?"

"They have been transmitting a great deal of data, Gunnery Sergeant, more than what you have been experiencing for the past few moments. Some of that information includes data on their biology . . . which appears to be based on polyaromatic sulfonyl halides, by the way."

"I'll take your word for it."

"Do you see *this*?" Achilles$_2$ asked, putting a green cursor over a part of the alien's body, just below the octopoid head and between the front two tentacled protuberances. There, buried between the outer layers of transparent skin and the uppermost of the five pulsing hearts, was a dark, knobby shadow, like a bunch of grapes the size of Ramsey's fist.

"Yeah. . . ."

"In the Eulers, the male is a parasite living inside the larger female. Some species on Earth show similar adaptations."

Ramsey had heard of deep-sea angler fish that did that, and possibly for the same reason . . . to ensure that mates could find one another in the dark and cold of the benthic abyss.

"Gunnery Sergeant?"

"Yes?"

"I believe they are responding in the affirmative." Achilles$_2$ opened a new window in Ramsey's head. "They are retransmitting the animations I just sent them, showing humans and Eulers working together to fight the Xul."

The image was a crude animation, showing cartoon representations of a human and of an Euler on one side, a recognizable sketch of a Xul huntership on the other. Human and Euler moved up and down quickly and in unison for a moment, and the Xul ship broke into pieces and dissolved.

Thank God!. . .

"Gunnery Sergeant?"

"What is it, Achilles?"

"We now have a clear radio channel back to the fleet."

Excitement thrilled, pounding at Ramsey's awareness. "Excellent!"

"Perhaps not. According to FleetCom, the Stargate has just changed pathways . . . and a Xul fleet is coming through. A very *large* Xul fleet. . . ."

As Ramsey accessed the newly opened command channel, he heard the alert sounding as the Fleet went to battlestations.

24

UCS Hermes
Stargate
Aquila Space
1157 hrs GMT

Emerging from the tube-car transport from his office,
General Alexander entered the Ops Center, a large and
circular room given over primarily to communications
equipment and to the couches used by Ops personnel
when they linked in full-sim with the Fleet Command
Net. At a brisk walk, he threaded his way through the
couches, most of them occupied by men and women of
his command constellation, and lay down on the central
couch reserved for CO-MIEF2. CO-MIEF1, Admiral
Taggart, was already strapped to the couch next to his,
his face white and drawn as he wrestled with the fast-
deteriorating tactical situation.

As he lay down, contacts in the material connected with
his implant interfaces at wrists and palms and the back of
his head, snapping him instantly into a virtual world perfectly re-creating the view outside.

The eighty ships of 1MIEF hung suspended between the
icon representing RFS Alpha and the wedding-band hoop of
the system's stargate.

The Xul ships were still emerging from the Gate. He
counted five so far, four of the 1- to 2-kilometer-long needles
commonly referred to as hunterships, Types I and II, and

one of the larger, far more massive flattened spheres that Marine Intelligence called "Nightmares." Another Type I huntership was just emerging from the Gate, the gold-hued spire of its prow protruding from the grav-twisted emptiness at the Gate's center.

"Welcome to the show, General," Admiral Taggart's voice said in his mind. "Ain't we got fun?"

"Is this real time or time-lagged?" Alexander asked. The question was vital. The Stargate was twenty-five light-minutes away. What he was seeing now might be real-time, or it could be the tactical situation of almost half an hour ago, with the light they were seeing having taken that long to crawl across space to the MIEF.

"Real time," Taggart replied. He indicated four green icons encircling the Stargate, but well distant from the merging enemy fleet. "We have four patrol-picket ships posted around the Stargate—*Sentry*, *Defender*, *Patriot*, and *Watcher*. They're relaying their sensor data via QCC."

"Good." Patrol pickets were the smallest FTL-capable ships in the MIEF's inventory, snug little eight-man vessels massing 500 tons, not a whole lot bigger than an Ontos, but they could be customized with swap-out sensor pods and drone controls.

As he watched, a blue-white thread of light snapped out from the largest Xul ship, the saucer, and touched one of the pickets. There was a flare of light. . . .

"Damn," Taggart said. "That was *Watcher*. The others are taking evasive action."

The pickets, darting gnats to the ponderous Xul behemoths, jinked and shifted, making targeting them difficult. The Xul, however, after destroying *Watcher*, appeared to take no more notice of them. *Arrogant bastards*, Alexander thought. *They honestly don't care whether we see what they're doing or not.*

That, he thought, was the worst part about dealing with the Xul. The slow-paced tempo of their response to humans suggested that humans simply weren't that significant to them, insects to be swatted at leisure.

And, watching those huge ships sliding into the hard,

blue-white glare of the HD387136 system's sun, it was easy to believe that such was exactly the case.

Admiral Taggart, he saw, was already deploying the MIEF to strike the Xul ships before they could get organized. The fleet carriers *Chosin* and *Lejeune* were lining up for FTL runs into the near-Gate battlespace, where they could release their fighters, while the heavy guns, *Ishtar*, *Mars*, and *Chiron*, spread out in order to catch the enemy vessels in a three-way crossfire. Cruisers, destroyers, and frigates were scattering across the sky, arcing in on the Xul flotilla from every possible direction.

"You're trying for englobement?" he asked the admiral.

"That's the idea," Taggart told him. "If we can close in on them, englobe them up against the stargate before they can spread out, we might have a chance."

The Xul ships were still very close together. Alexander saw what Taggart was suggesting. Hit them now, before they dispersed, and the massive bulks of the Xul ships themselves might block some of their own fire.

"How close are you trying to get?"

"Fifty thousand kilometers," Taggart told him. "Any closer, and we won't be able to stand up to the big Xul guns."

The sixth huntership was all the way through the Gate, now. Were any more coming through? How long would they stay in place? The MIEF was accelerating now, preparatory to engaging their Alcubierre Drives for the short sprint in to the Gate.

"Cara," Alexander asked, curious. "Do we have a fix on where they're coming from?"

"Affirmative, General. The Gate has been retuned to the orbital resonances associated with Starwall."

Alexander had suspected as much. Starwall was the location of a major Xul node, and that was where Lieutenant Lee had picked up the intelligence that the Xul had learned of Earth after taking the *Argo*.

Starwall, then, would be the MIEF's first objective . . . *if* the enemy fleet now flowing into Aquila Space could be stopped.

As one, linked together by the FleetCom net, fifty-eight of the MIEF vessels blurred, streaking forward, leaving behind the carriers, the troop ships, and the noncombatant logistical vessels. FTL maneuvers across a scant twenty-five light-minutes, were touchy, requiring absolute precision and timing. In fact, AIs were at the helm of each of those vessels; no human touch at a control or thought-click could possibly be precise enough.

The Xul ships were beginning to accelerate, slowly, at first, but they were drawing away from the Gate. *Not* good. Ships in Alcubierre Drive could not see out or communicate; they might arrive to find the Xul fleet already behind them.

Minutes passed . . . and then the MIEF ships dropped out of FTL.

No battle plan, the ancient saying went, ever survives contact with the enemy. The englobement had *almost* succeeded . . . but the Xul ships had moved far enough in the intervening minutes that two of the hunterships were already outside the globe, and the others were *much* closer to the nearest MIEF ships than had been planned. The light cruiser *Shiva* had dropped into normal space less than 8,000 kilometers from one of the Xul needles, and came under immediate and devastating fire.

Among other high-tech magic, Xul weapons included linear accelerators that hurled microscopic black holes at the target. *Shiva* staggered under a barrage from the enemy warship, her structure crumpling as naked singularities the size of a human blood cell ripped through her hull and internal spaces. Such tiny black holes couldn't eat much matter in a single pass; the excess was bled off as fiercely radiating energy, much of it in the x-ray frequencies. In seconds, *Shiva* had been transformed into a drifting knot of white-hot wreckage.

But one of the Xul ships, a kilometer-long Type I, was crumpling as well. Alexander saw the huge vessel slew to one side and begin drifting helplessly, the long, slender blade of its structure beginning to collapse toward the aft end. Alexander pointed this out to Cara.

"I have just analyzed the paths of each of the MIEF vessels," Cara told him. "One, the path taken by the *Valkyrie*-class light cruiser *Judur*, intersected that Type I huntership while *Judur* was still under Alcubierre Drive."

"Interesting." He'd not thought about the possibility of what might happen if the warp bubble enclosing a ship under FTL passed through another ship. He knew there'd been some discussion of the idea among tactical planners, but that the practice was *not* recommended. The warp bubble tended to compress space ahead of the ship under drive, and extend space astern; he could see how that might badly chew up a ship that happened to be in the way. "Could that be adapted as a weapon?" he asked.

"Negative," Cara told him. "There have been numerous studies since the inception of a practical Alcubierre Drive. Essentially, there is no way to aim a vessel traveling under Drive, since it cannot see past the horizon of its own warp bubble. An actual hit would occur only by sheer, random chance."

"I see." In simplistic terms, hitting another ship while under FTL drive would be like hitting another bullet with a bullet of your own—fired with your eyes shut.

But sheer chance *did* happen in combat, especially when the combatants were as relatively close-packed as these. Chance or not, the *Judur* had just cut down the odds against the MIEF by a substantial margin.

"The *Judur* doesn't seem any the worse for wear," he commented, checking the telemetry on the cruiser.

"A ship within the Alcubierre warp bubble is effectively cut off from the rest of the universe," Cara reminded him.

"Damn, there's got to be a way we could use that," Alexander said.

The *Judur* was firing her main batteries now into the nearby Xul vessel, which continued to slowly crumple and deform. Xul hunterships possessed small black holes as the hearts of their power plants; serious damage to the ship could result in the black hole getting loose from its magnetic restraints and eating its way through the collapsing vessel.

Elsewhere, other MIEF warships were beginning to

engage the enemy now, ganging up four and five and six to one, where possible. *Chosin* and *Lejeune* were loosing streams of Skydragon fighters. As soon as all fighters were away, they would pull back out of the engagement area. Until that happened, however, they were vulnerable. *Chosin* lurched sharply as a micro-black hole passed through her bow, radiating fiercely.

Xul warships possessed electromagnetic screens powerful enough to twist aside charged particle beams and any solid object with enough ferrous material to grab hold of. Lasers, however, were unaffected by magnetic screens, and could punch holes in Xul warships *if* they were powerful enough.

Much research had gone into this aspect of space-borne weaponry. During the battle to save Earth 563 years ago, titanic high-energy laser arrays in solar orbit had been used as *very* long range artillery and had managed to disable the Xul hunter, opening up a way for Marines to get on board with their backpack nukes.

But Xul hulls were built up of composite adaptive materials as tough as diamond, and the ships themselves were so huge that most lasers small enough to be mounted on board a warship simply weren't powerful enough to punch through one-on-one. The three heavy battlecruisers *Ishtar*, *Chiron*, and *Mars*, however, were built around spinal-mount HEL weapons—the acronym stood for High-Energy Laser—each with an output of 10 million billion watts—1,000 terawatts, or 1 petawatt.

A 5 megawatt laser delivers the energy equivalent to the detonation of a kilogram of TNT. A spinal-mount HEL, then, firing in a tenth-second pulse, released 500 terawatts of power in a pulse equivalent to a 1 megaton nuclear explosion.

Not even the thick, tough skin of a huntership's hull could stand up to that much energy concentrated in one small spot. Xul ships repaired themselves swiftly—Marines had witnessed huge holes burned into a Xul warship's hull literally growing shut in the course of a few moments—but tactics had evolved to circumvent, or, rather, to overwhelm Xul technology. Where possible, the AIs controlling the aiming of shipboard weapons would focus *all* available weapons on the same spot, the first bursts opening up a hole in the target, and subsequent laser bursts or remote-guided warheads traveling into the target's interior, causing massive internal damage.

The other capital ships possessed lighter weapons, of course, but each still packed a significant punch. Light cruisers like the *Judur* and her Valkyrie sisters each possessed turret-mounted lasers with a 100TW output, roughly the energy released by a 20 kiloton nuke. Xul hunterships could generally shrug off 20KT pinpricks without much effort, but a concentration of such bursts could add up to significant damage. The main batteries of deity-class cruisers like the *Diana*, the *Kali* and the hastily repaired *Morrigan* could deliver pulses five times stronger, in the hundred-kiloton range.

Guided by the command net, then, the MIEF warships swarmed the far larger Xul vessels, blasting at their thick outer hulls with big-gun petawatt lasers, then following up with smaller but far more numerous laser weaponry to cause greater internal damage. When Xul magnetic shields collapsed, then, the way was open for swarms of smart missiles with megaton thermonuclear warheads, and the sharp, savage bursts of charged-particle weapons. The fighters darted in close, skimming the Xul hulls, slashing at hot craters with missiles and beams that could never have touched the carapaces of those giants, but which now wreaked searing damage within the enemy warships' interiors.

But even piling on at ten to one odds, it took *time* to reduce the armored mountain of a Xul huntership, and during that time the huntership could do serious damage in turn. Besides tightly focused plasma weapons like the one that had flashed *Watcher* into hot vapor, or the microsingularities fired at high velocities like the barrage that had destroyed the *Shiva*, the Xul possessed another weapon that Commonwealth science had not yet been able to get a handle on, either to duplicate it, or to defend against it. Somehow, the Xul could reach down into the Quantum Sea itself and change the basic metric of a tightly focused sphere of space. With this, they could grab random asteroids and impart high velocities to them, as when they bombarded planets, or they could grab a human starship and crush it into a gravitational singularity. The light cruiser *Skeggold* seemed to crumple and fold in upon herself in the invisible grip of the deadly weapon, then vanished in a burst of hard x-rays. Seconds later, the heavy cruiser *Hera*, 3,000 kilometers away, staggered and rolled under a titanic impact, then flared into nova brilliance as the micro-black hole that had been the *Skeggold* hurtled through the *Hera* at nearly half the speed of light.

Perhaps the most shocking aspect of the battle was how *quickly* it proceeded. Ten seconds after the general engagement had begun, eight MIEF ships had been destroyed, thirteen percent of the Commonwealth warships engaged so far, and *all* of the Xul monsters were still firing, even the doomed vessel that had been inadvertently rammed by the *Judur.*

The fighters were beginning to swarm through the battlespace, accompanied by clouds of USCVs—unmanned space combat vehicles mounting tactical nukes and nano-D warheads. The Xul ships *were* taking damage, a lot of it.

But the monsters were simply too strong. . . .

At this point in the battle, there was little Alexander, as commander of the Marine contingent, could do. Although the recon Marine element had already been deployed onto and around RFS Alpha, several hundred Marines were now in their SAP capsules and ready to deploy against the enemy with backpack nukes . . . but in this hellfire chaos of plasma beams and mass cannon blasts, of petawatt laser bursts and high velocity microsingularities, he would be throwing them away unless he had a clear target, a clear plan. That largest Xul ship, the squat, weapons-laden Nightmare, *might* be their command ship, but it was as yet unclear that the Xul even *had* command ships. The Xul were rarely encountered in groups—thank the gods—and the smallest of those needle-slim Type I hunterships was a match for the entire MIEF.

Gods! Another huntership was emerging from the Gate. He remembered the scans picked up by the Night Owl reconnaissance into the Starwall system. There were a *lot* of Xul ships over there. . . .

"Message from the Eulers, General," Cara told him, startling him out of his increasingly black thoughts.

"What?" He didn't even know communication had been opened with them.

"The message is in animated-simulation form, sir, but it seems to be a suggestion that we prepare to accelerate under Alcubierre Drive. They are preparing . . . it appears to be a small starship that they are going to fire into the system's sun, which apparently will trigger a nova. If we are prepared to enter Alcubierre Drive a few seconds before the wavefront of the exploding sun reaches us, we might escape, while the Xul ship is enveloped and destroyed."

So that was the source of the novae in this region of space, two thousand years ago—the Euler ultimate weapon.

But . . . no.

"Send a negative," he told Cara.

"Repeat, please?"

"Tell them no, damn it! We have a couple hundred fighters out there, and they can't travel FTL. And the Marines on Alpha. And the *Hermes*, too. They'd all be fried."

A moment passed. "The Eulers have sent an interrogative," Cara told him. I believe they are asking what you plan to do instead."

A very good question, Alexander thought. *I wish I had a good answer. . . .*

The battle was going to be over, with 1MIEF wiped out of the sky, if someone didn't come up with something damned fast. . . .

RFS Alpha
Aquila Space
1215 hrs GMT

Garroway stood on the bleak and dusty gray surface of the asteroid, looking up. The Marines of the 55th MARS were queued up to board a *Brigid*-class shuttle, which would ferry them back to the *Samar*, which was stationed a few thousand kilometers off of the asteroid RFS Alpha, along with other troopships, with the hospital ship *Barton*, and with other non-combatants like the supply vessels.

The light from the battle at the Stargate had not yet reached the Euler planetoid, but a window open to the platoon channel was showing a scaled-down running commentary, showing lists of the ships engaged, of the damage they were taking, of the orders being issued to them.

It looked like one hell of a fight.

"Jesus," Corporal Chu said. "We're *losing*!"

"When are they going to put *us* into the fight?" Sergeant Ernesto Delgado wondered.

"I don't think there's a hell of a lot we could do if we were there," Takamura pointed out. "Shit! They just nailed the *Osiris*!"

Marine training had emphasized the use of SAP capsules to deliver Marines to the interior of large enemy vessels, where they could cause considerable mayhem, up to and including planting nuclear charges deep in the target vessel. That training was based on the experience of multiple encounters with Xul ships, but the most recent of those encounters had still been over five hundred years ago. Would such old tactics even work nowadays? The Xul weren't supposed to be very innovative, but still, they must do *something* besides sitting around waiting for another threat species to show up. . . .

Whole starships were being wiped away out there. What chance did individual Marines possess in that hellish combat environment?

"Hey, guys!" Ran Allison called, pointing. "What the hell is *that*?"

Garroway turned, looking up. That was an oddly shaped vehicle of some sort, dust-gray, like the asteroid's surface, and looking something like a smoothed and somewhat elongated asteroid itself, an egg shape in clay squeezed and misshapen under a giant's hand. Garroway's helmet display gave a readout on the thing—20 meters long, with an estimated mass of 35 tons. It was rising above the asteroid's horizon.

"That is an Euler spacecraft which has just emerged from a tunnel complex on the other side of this asteroid," Achilles told him. "Specifically, it is a craft they refer to as a 'trigger.' It creates a powerful warp bubble similar to that of a ship under Alcubierre Drive." There was a hesitation, as though the AI didn't quite understand, or quite *believe* the information it was passing along. "If the information I am receiving is accurately translated, the Eulers use devices like this to induce a nova in a star."

"Jesus, Mary, and Joseph," PFC Emilio Santiago said.

"What," Chu said. "They're going to blow up their star?" He indicated the blue-white beacon of HD387136 hanging low above the asteroid's impossibly near horizon. "*That* star?"

"Unknown," Achilles told them. "The Eulers have suggested using the device to blow up the local sun. General Alexander has refused, however. Too many MIEF vessels operating now do not have FTL capability, and would be caught and destroyed by the blast. We do not yet know if they intend to comply with General Alexander's wishes."

"I wonder what the chain of command is where aliens are concerned?" Master Sergeant Barrett wondered aloud.

"Not our business," Lieutenant Kaia Jones, the platoon CO, said. "Keep in line. Get on board the shuttle."

But Garroway couldn't help thinking that it damn well *was* their business, if the aliens were about to flash them all into cinders in the light of an exploding sun. . . .

UCS Hermes
Stargate
Aquila Space
1220 hrs GMT

The battle was going badly. Ten MIEF ships had been destroyed already, and three others were badly damaged. The fighters—Marine squadrons off the *Chosin* and the *Lejeune*—were pressing home their attack at point-blank range, and two of the Xul craft, one Type I and one Type II, appeared to be crippled, but the MIEF could not keep sustaining casualties at this rate.

There was a possibility, though. Definitely a long shot, but better than watching the entire MIEF being chewed to pieces. He shifted his attention to the Euler trigger, as Cara called it, which had just emerged from RFS Alpha.

"Admiral Taggart? I suggest that it's time to go over to the offensive."

"What the hell are you talking about?" Taggart growled in his mind. "We're not holding them as it is!"

"Old Marine maxim," Alexander replied. "When things get desperate, attack. Cara? Connect with the Eulers. See if they can use that trigger against the *Xul* star, the one on the other side of the Gate."

There was a pause, maddening as the battle continued to swirl in front of the stargate. The Xul Type I rammed by *Judur* finally collapsed in upon itself, devoured by the black hole running wild at its core. Nuclear blasts from fighter-launched missiles were savaging two more hunterships . . . but the much larger Nightmare-class hunter appeared virtually untouched. For several minutes, now, *Mars*, *Chiron*, and *Ishtar* had been concentrating their heavy lasers on the largest Xul vessel, but the damage inflicted so far appeared minimal. The Nightmare had returned fire, however, and *Chiron* had been badly hurt.

"General?" Cara said. "There is a problem. If I understand the transmission correctly, the Eulers cannot control the nova trigger once it passes through a stargate."

"Damn . . ."

"However, Gunnery Sergeant Ramsey is still inside RFS Alpha, and has been monitoring our conversation with the Euler. He says that the nova trigger might take a human pilot . . . and he has volunteered."

"Ramsey has been in communication with the Eulers?"

"Yes, sir. He appears to have exchanged a substantial amount of data with them. We are still evaluating most of what he has passed on to us."

Alexander thought for a moment. "Okay . . . let's try that.

But I don't want Ramsey at the controls. I want him brought back safe so the xenosoph people can download everything he's learned in there. Am I clear?"

"Yes, General."

Alexander checked the swarming icons around the Euler asteroid. There were a number of Marines in open space, preparing to board a shuttle.

"Ask Ramsey to find out how difficult piloting that thing should be."

"Gunnery Sergeant Ramsey says he has already discussed this with his . . . hosts. He says a simple program could be downloaded to a Marine's implant hardware that would give him full control of the trigger."

"Let me ask this. This . . . trigger makes a star explode. Does the trigger get destroyed too?"

"That is unclear, General. The trigger is, in effect, a small starship under Alcubierre Drive. The warp bubble triggers the nova. The ship *might* be safe inside that bubble but . . . there are numerous unknowns."

Unknowns? About diving a tiny one-man ship into a star? Imagine that.

"Okay. Cara, put out a request for volunteers among the 55th MARS Marines still on the asteroid."

"Yes, General."

"And Admiral Taggart? Start rounding up your ships. We're taking 1MIEF through that Gate!"

RFS Alpha
Aquila Space
1234 hrs GMT

In the last few moments, the light from the battle had reached the Euler planetoid. There wasn't much to see . . . a delicate twinkling against the stars, but Garrison knew that each momentary pinpoint of light was another nuclear detonation, or a dying ship.

And then the request for volunteers came through.

"They want a volunteer to do *what*?" Master Sergeant Barrett said.

"Someone to pilot the alien ship," Lieutenant Jones said. "That volunteer will steer the ship through the Gate, then engage the Alcubierre Drive and take it through the star on the other side. That should trigger the star into going nova."

"Yeah, Lieutenant, but what's the point?" Delaslo said. "How does that help us?"

"The MIEF is preparing to break through the Gate, through to Starwall Space. That's eighteen thousand light-years away from here, in toward the galactic core. When they do so, the Xul ships should follow them. On the other side, the flight of the Euler trigger ship will be carefully timed, so that our fleet can withdraw just before the wave-front from the exploding star reaches them."

Several people started talking at once. Garroway thought for a second, then thought-clicked a signal, the electronic equivalent of raising his hand. "Lieutenant?"

"What is it, Garroway?"

"I volunteer, sir."

"I volunteer, sir," Sergeant Chu said, an instant behind Garroway.

"No, I do," Shari Colver said. "I volunteer!" And then everyone was clamoring for attention.

"Silence!" Jones rasped. "As you were, all of you! Private Garroway . . . you know this could be a one-way flight?"

"Yes, sir."

"Why do you want to do it?"

He was wondering that himself. Part of him was still in shock after Sandre's abrupt death, and he knew that when the shock wore off the grieving would begin. He wasn't looking forward to that.

But was grief enough for him to risk suicide?

He didn't think that was the reason . . . not all of it, anyway.

But he did know that if nothing was done, every Marine in the MIEF would be killed when the Xul finally over-whelmed the hard-pressed fleet, him included.

And these Marines were his family, his *new* family. He couldn't let one of them go instead.

"Sir," he said carefully. He wasn't going to mention

Sandre; somehow he knew that that would get him turned down for sure. "Marines go back a long way in my family. Ever hear of 'Sands of Mars' Garroway?"

"You're related to *him*?"

"Yes, sir. And a few others, Marines who fought the Xul later on. It's only fair that I finish what they started, right?"

"That," Jones told him, "is a load of crap. But I don't have time to argue. Report to Master Sergeant Barrett for a download. You've got about three minutes to learn how to pilot an alien starship!"

"Aye, aye, sir!"

He was jubilant as he sought out the master sergeant. There were some wild stories about Garroway Marines . . . like the one about Sands of Mars Garroway capturing a detachment of French soldiers at Cydonia by dropping aluminum cans of contraband beer on them from a small cargo hopper. In the all-but-vacuum thinness of the Martian atmosphere as it was back then, long before the planet's terraforming had begun, the falling beer cans had exploded like tiny bombs, coating French optics and suit visors with a sticky, boiling, freezing mess that convinced them they were under attack by weaponry far more deadly than beer.

And now he was about to dive a starship into a sun eighteen thousand light-years away . . . a fitting way, he thought, to continue the family saga.

Besides, then he wouldn't have to think about Sandre.

25

RFS Alpha
Cygni Space
1244 hrs GMT

The side of the Euler ship cycled open as Garroway and the other Marines approached it, and one of the gray crab-creatures scrambled out, all jointed legs and weaving antennae.

Now that he wasn't trying to kill one, Garroway was able to get an interested close-up look. The creature—what had they called it? The Manipulator was naked to space except for black strips of some obviously artificial material running around each side of the thing's flat, round body—devices, he gathered, for circulating water and chemicals through its respiratory system. What he'd at first taken for a swollen part of the creature's carapace, on closer inspection proved to be a kind of strap-on backpack, presumably its life-support system.

"So why doesn't *that* thing fly the ship?" Chu wanted to know. "Why does Garry have to go?"

"The word is that the Manipulators don't think all that well on their own," Barrett replied. "By themselves, they're maybe as smart as, I don't know, a smart dog? They have to be linked with one of the Eulers to, ah, reach their full potential. And the Eulers say they can't maintain that link through the Gate."

"They don't have QCC?" Colver said. "Hey, maybe their science isn't as hot as everyone's been saying."

"Technology doesn't necessarily go in a straight line," Garroway said. As the moment approached, he was trying not to think about it, and he welcomed the chance to talk about something else. "We only figured out FTL communication after studying the hardware left on Mars by the Builders, and even that took us a few centuries before we could pull it off, right?"

The Euler ship was resting on the asteroid's surface, now, the entrance a wide, very flat strip open in the hull. Garroway leaned over and looked in.

"Shit," he said. The ship had not been designed with humans in mind.

For a moment, Garroway wasn't sure he was going to be able to do it. The cockpit, if that's what you could call it, was less than a meter tall, high enough to accommodate a Manipulator with its life-support backpack, but it was going to be a *very* tight squeeze for a human in combat armor.

"You sure you want to go through with this, Marine?" Barrett asked.

"Yes, Master Sergeant." There was no backing out now. "Maybe you guys can pick me up and kind of feed me in there?"

"Okay, Marines. All together. . . ."

Manhandling Garroway into a prone position and sliding him forward into the flat opening required finesse but not a lot of strength, not in RFS Alpha's weak gravitational field. Garroway weighed only a few hundred grams, here, though he and his 660-armor together still massed almost 200 kilos. He'd already unshipped his weapons, equipment pouches, backpack, and everything else he could unhook and discard.

Once, as a teenager, he'd gone caving with some friends in Arkansas—the real thing, not a remote sim. Sliding forward on his belly through the mud, squeezing absolutely flat between the painfully narrow gap between floor and ceiling, and always the chittering fear in the back of his mind that he was about to find himself stuck, unable to move forward or back—this experience was like that.

The inside of the cockpit was not smooth, but folded into wrinkles and swellings and depressions above and below, as though designed to mold to the actual carapace of a Manipulator.

But as the others pushed him forward, he felt the surfaces above and below relax, slightly, almost as though the ship itself were alive, adapting itself to this alien shape.

"Okay, Garroway," Barrett told him. "You're all the way in. Check your software."

Closing his eyes, he thought-clicked on a mental icon, a new icon downloaded into his implant hardware only a few moments ago. He felt a small, inner thrill as current flowed, and a display swam into view against his mental landscape.

He hadn't had time to practice with it yet, but the advantage, the whole point of downloaded training was that you didn't need to practice to create and reinforce new synaptic links. The links were there . . . though you often needed to practice just to get the feel of the new skill.

That sort of thing had been honed by the Marines through almost seven centuries of work with cerebral implant technology. Some of the skills required of Marines—firing a forearm-mounted pulse rifle while moving, for example, or kicking off with your 660's jump jets and skimming across a hundred meters of open ground in a single bound—those were not natural acts. Without download training, they would require months of intensive training and practice; instead, the skill set was downloaded in a few seconds, and the recruit spent a day or so practicing with it, getting it nailed down solid.

So he knew what mental buttons to push. He just wished he could have some time with a hammer to be sure the knowledge was in good and tight.

"Okay, Garroway," Barrett's voice said in his mind. "How's it feel?"

"Okay, Master Sergeant. Not much room in here." He wiggled a bit. "I think the space is closing around my suit."

"Yeah. The word is the ship is alive." He chuckled. "Your call sign is *Jonah*."

"Does that mean something?"

"Swallowed by a big fish?"

The reference meant nothing. "Sorry. . . ."

"Never mind. Old Judeo-Christian religious reference. The hatch is closing."

He couldn't move his helmet to see, but he was aware of a new and deeper darkness. He let his AI connect with the alien vessel's external sensors, and was enveloped in a sim of surrounding space. He could see stars, and the gray, pocked terrain of the planetoid beneath him.

"You still hear me okay?"

"Yeah, Master Sergeant."

"Okay, son. I'm passing you over to the lieutenant. She's in direct link with *Hermes* Ops."

"Hello, Garroway," Jones' voice said. "How is it in there?"

"Snug, sir."

"Okay. Just sit tight. We're waiting for the right tactical moment before you get the go, okay?"

"Aye, aye, sir."

Sit tight. Well, *lie* tight. There wasn't a lot else he could do right now.

Curious, he did pull down an e-pedia entry on "Jonah." Garroway was, at least nominally, neopagan, and had never read the Old Testament, or the story of the Biblical prophet swallowed by a "great fish." The story wasn't exactly comforting, or particularly appropriate. The prophet Jonah, as near as he could tell, had been swallowed by the fish because he'd been disobedient to God.

He wasn't being disobedient. Quite the contrary. He was allowing the bioengineered fish to swallow him out of what he perceived as his duty to his brother and sister Marines.

The tightly enclosed space grumbled and fluttered around him, settling into an even tighter embrace. He ignored the claustrophobic sensations—he'd not felt *those* since that one, abortive time in that cave ten years ago—and instead opened a tacsit feed.

The battle at the stargate was still raging strong . . . and *not* going well for the good guys.

UCS Hermes
Stargate
Aquila Space
1248 hrs GMT

"Okay," Taggart said, grim. "There's our opening!"

Alexander could see the moment as it shaped itself. The MIEF ships had slowly moved past the Xul ships, abandoning their englobement technique and placing themselves—most of them, anyway, between the Xul ships and the stargate.

"I see it," he said.

"You do know, I trust, that this is going to leave *us* 'way out on a limb'. . . ."

"And the Marine fighters, too," Alexander replied. "But if this thing works, we wouldn't survive on the other side."

"Yeah. The question is how long we survive on *this* side. The Xul may not care if the rest of the fleet goes through. They may decide to stay here and stomp on us."

"It's all we have, Liam. Let's do it."

Taggart gave the mental command, putting the MIEF in motion. At the same time, Alexander issued a command of his own, ordering Jonah to commence his run.

Mars and *Ishtar* leaped forward, under high acceleration, with the injured *Chiron* lagging along after. Their spinal-mount main batteries were pointed uselessly ahead at the center of the gate, but their turret-mounted secondaries lashed out in all directions, slashing and shearing through the nearest Xul hunterships.

The trio of planet-class battlecruisers was followed by the other MIEF capitol ships—all save the *Hermes*, which lacked the Alcubierre Drive, and the fleet carriers *Chosin* and *Lejeune*, which would remain on this side of the gate with their fighters. Those three hung back, then began accelerating clear of the battlespace. The hope, of course, was that the Xul warships would ignore them, focusing instead on the greater threat of what the larger MIEF flotilla might do on the other side, at Starwall.

Following in cone formation, the rest of the redeploying MIEF fleet accelerated toward the gate, the cone's apex at the three battlecruisers. The formation was ragged and incomplete; three destroyers and a light cruiser were left behind, helplessly adrift, sections of their hulls white-hot from the tunneling of enemy weapons, clouds of debris adrift around them.

A final check. The Gate's tuning was still set to Starwall. In Alexander's mind, the two flotillas pulled apart from each other, three ships and a cloud of fighters staying behind, the other thirty-seven surviving ships of the MIEF battlefleet moving toward the Gate under their gravitics, faster . . . still faster . . . and faster still before plunging through.

And *Hermes*, *Chosin*, and *Lejeune*, attended by their attendant fighters and remote combat drones, remained alone.

"Okay, everyone," Taggart said over the Net. "Now we see if this is going to work!"

The Xul ships didn't react at first to the sudden exodus, and for a horrible moment, Alexander thought that the enemy force was going to ignore it entirely, to stay instead and continue pounding the ships remaining in Aquila Space. There were five Xul vessels in all—the Nightmare-class monster, a larger Type II, and three Type I's. All five showed some indication of the pounding they'd been taking, at least, and the Type II and one Type I showed serious damage.

All five were definitely still in the fight, however. *Hermes* shuddered as a string of five microsingularities snapped through her hull, tunneling through in an instant in searing blasts of x-radiation. Alarms sounded in his head. One of the four *Atlas*-class tugs mounted on *Hermes*' hull had been badly hit, her power plant off-line, her gravitics drives down. Damage reports were flooding back. *Hermes* was venting atmosphere, radiation levels were climbing. At least two hundred of her crew and passengers were dead already.

And it was going to get worse.

"I think . . ." Taggart said, somewhat tentatively. "I think they're starting to go for it."

The Nightmare Xul ship was definitely moving toward

the Gate, now, following the vanished MIEF. Two . . . no, all three of the Xul Type I hunterships were following as well, one of them limping well behind the others.

The Type II, though, clearly was not joining the others. It was outbound from the Gate, closing in the *Hermes*.

"All ships, focus on that Type II," Taggart ordered. "Take him down!"

Hundred-terawatt lasers snapped out from turrets mounted on *Hermes'* hull, and the equivalent of 20-kiloton nukes sparkled across the Type II's hull. The Xul hull material was so thick and strong that those blasts had little effect overall. Still, in places the gunners and AI directors were able to concentrate on gaps in that charred armor, and when the laser fire burned into the vessel's dark interior, bursts of gas, of broken hull fragments and other debris spewed into space like tiny geyser plumes. Alexander could see sullen, interior glows here and there through gaps in the outer shell, as portions of the interior structure became molten under the barrage.

Again, microsingularities lashed out from the enemy vessel, striking the *Hermes* and passing clean through. Damage-control parties were overstretched as it was, using nanotech repair robots to patch the holes and stem the loss of internal atmosphere.

"Why haven't they used their force weapon?" Alexander asked Cara. *That* was the deadly signature of the Xul hunterships—that seemingly magical means of reaching out and crumpling a target vessel into a tiny black hole. The Type II was definitely in range, now, for that weapon. . . .

"Analyses of the timing of past uses of the weapon suggests that there are constraints in power usage or availability," Cara told him. "They may need a sizeable recharge time."

"I'm glad there are *some* constraints to those things," Alexander said, watching the monster's approach. *Hermes'* laser batteries continued slashing into the thing, but were having little obvious effect. "You don't have hard figures for us, do you?"

"I am sorry, General, but no."

"We'll keep pounding the bastard," Taggart said. "Maybe we've damaged the weapon already. Or maybe we can kill them before they get it working again."

"Gods willing," Alexander said. "Right now, I think they're trying to *ram* us! . . ."

But Taggart had already given another command, and the *Hermes* was pulling back as fast as the straining gravitics of her three remaining tugs could move her. Both of the carriers had pulled well off to the side, and were adding their volleys to the firepower now playing across the Xul ship's hull. The Xul ignored them, following the limping *Hermes*.

"Is Jonah on the way?" he asked.

"Affirmative," Cara told him. "He departed the Euler planetoid three minutes, five seconds ago, just before the MIEF went through the Gate."

Then we just need to hold on a little longer. . . .

Jonah
Cygni Space/Starwall Space
1252 hrs GMT

Garroway waited in an absolute blackness.

Three minutes before, the order had come through and Jones had passed it on. *"You're clear to launch! Good luck!"* He'd thought-clicked a command, and the ship, propelled by something similar to the gravitics drive used by the Commonwealth, had slid up and forward into the night, the planetoid falling away and vanishing astern in seconds. In open space, he gave the necessary commands, followed by a final thought-click . . . and the universe winked out.

From the Euler planetoid, Garroway needed to fly a two-legged path, the first leg to line himself up squarely with the stargate, so that the ring was facing him full-on, and the second leg, to bring him to his jump-off point. He would not attempt to thread the gate's eye under drive, because no one knew if that would work. Technically, the ship was not in normal space while under Alcubierre Drive, but enclosed within its own tiny, pocket universe; whether that pocket universe would be affected by the gravitational twisting at the center of the gate, whether it would pass through to Starwall or be destroyed or not be affected at all, no one knew.

Jonah would go through the gate at sublight speeds.

The actual timing of the maneuver would be handled by Achilles$_2$, a subset of the platoon AI traveling with him, since as soon as he switched on the drive he'd be cut off from the rest of the platoon.

Minutes dragged past, and Garroway waited them out in the enveloping and absolute dark. This first jump—moving fifteen light-minutes at five times the speed of light—would take 3 minutes. During that time, he was completely cut off from everything except what was already in his head—the downloaded flight-control program, and the waiting, reassuring presence of Achilles$_2$.

He remembered when Sandre had taught him how to switch his platoon AI off, and wondered how he could *ever* have contemplated such a thing. Achilles$_2$ was a part of him, an *important* part, and right now he was damned glad he was there.

And then the stars were back. If Achilles$_2$ had gotten the timing right, the trigger ship had just shifted across fifteen light-minutes.

"Do you see the gate?" Garroway asked the AI. All he could see were stars—one, the system's primary, a dazzlingly brilliant blue-white pinpoint off to his left and slightly behind.

"I have the navigational telemetry," Achilles$_2$ told him. A green curser marked an otherwise empty bit of sky. "The gate is there, range eleven light-minutes."

"Okay, send a signal. 'Waypoint Alpha reached, okay.'"

"Transmitting." They would get the word back at the planetoid in fifteen minutes, after he was long gone.

Using his mind, Garroway gentled the trigger ship into a new orientation. Controlling the thing was much like controlling his own body, a sense of nudging himself *that* way, and having the body turn in response. A targeting crosshair thrown up against his visual field showed the precise aim point of the ship. When that intersected with the green cursor, he thought-clicked again, and, again, the universe winked out.

The timing needed to be excruciatingly precise. Two minutes, twelve seconds at five times the speed of light would take him eleven light-minutes. But at that velocity, if the timing was off by a hundredth of a second, he would over- or under-shoot by 15,000 kilometers—a distance considerably greater than the diameter of the Earth. $Achilles_2$, he knew, was working at the nanosecond level. If the AI missed by a nanosecond, he would only overshoot by . . . what? He pulled down the figures. One and a half meters.

No human mind could hope for that degree of precision.

The universe winked back into existence. The stargate was there, hanging in space dead ahead, a golden ring with a thread-slender rim. Nearby, off to starboard and below at this orientation, was the UCS *Hermes*. Farther off were the carriers *Lejeune* and *Chosin*.

To port and high was the vast, slender blade of a Xul huntership, needle-slim forward, swelling at the stern into bulging protuberances and sponsons a hundred meters long.

The Xul ship was hurt, and badly. Vast craters showed in that geometrically patterned surface, and the hull was enveloped in a silvery mist, part debris, part clouds of nano-D and remote drones. Nuclear explosions flashed and flickered, like the popping of strobes, along the damaged hull surface, as the *Hermes* slashed at it with barrage after barrage of nuke-tipped missiles and 100-terawatt laser blasts.

But *Hermes* was injured as well. The double rim-to-rim-saucer of the former Skybase had been repeatedly hit by Xul singularity weapons, and portions of its dark gray hull showed a thick scattering of puckered craters and had been blackened by searing temperatures. As he watched, blue lightning played across the *Hermes*' hull, blasting away a cloud of fragments.

"Private Garroway," a voice said in his head. "Welcome to Hell. This is General Alexander."

"Yes, sir!" Garroway responded, surprised. What the hell was a *general* doing talking to *him*?

"We're all counting on you, son," Alexander said. "The rest of the fleet's gone through the Gate, as planned, and most of the Xul with them. We're all of us counting on you now to carry out your mission."

"I won't let you down, sir."

"I know you won't. Listen up, now. On the other side, you'll make contact with Captain Michael Angi. He's the skipper of the *Mars*, and he'll be . . . uh!"

The transmission was briefly interrupted, as another Xul barrage struck home.

"*Hermes*? Are you there?"

"We're here, Garroway. Okay, the skipper of the *Mars* is coordinating the operation on that side. If the *Mars* has already been destroyed, your contact will be Captain Gerald Baumgartner, of the *Ishtar*."

"Right, sir."

"Better get a move on, son. They're waiting on you, but they won't be able to hold out for long."

Garroway engaged the craft's gravitic drive, and watched the Gate loom huge across his view forward. "On my way, General."

"Godspeed, son. And semper fi."

"Semper—"

But before he completed the farewell, the alien starship snapped through the gate interface.

His view forward blurred sharply, then suddenly sprang back into sharp relief. The thin, background scattering stars of Aquila Space was gone, replaced by a wall of mottled night and light.

The panorama was breathtaking, and magnificent. It was like looking at a towering cliff, hundreds of meters high—but instead of rock the cliff face was made of stars, of millions, of *billions* of stars massed and piled high and thronging deep, a wall of blazing stars interlaced through with the snaking tendrils of black, obscuring dust clouds, and with the shining radiant clouds and delicately hued sheets of reflective nebulae, their tattered edges gilded by starlight.

Billions of stars, the majority red or orange in hue, the

massed suns of the central bulge of the spiral galaxy that was the Milky Way.

"Private Garroway," Achilles$_2$ said. "We need to adjust course."

Shaking himself, Garroway tore his gaze away from that incredible starfield vista, and looked instead for the local star. He knew it should be *that* way, since part of his mission download had included data brought back from Marine recon flights into this space.

And there it was . . . a mottled, red-orange disk easily three times larger in apparent size than Sol appeared from Earth, its light stopped down by the alien vessel's optics—or by Achilles$_2$—to keep his eyeballs from frying. Garroway nudged, and the alien trigger ship responded, swinging to bring the crosshairs over the star.

"Jonah, this is *Mars*," sounded in his mind. "Do you copy?"

"I hear you, sir." He shifted his attention around to the other side, where brilliant flashes of light were sparkling in the distance, off to one side of the Gate. The *Mars* was quite close—several kilometers, her scarred hull clearly visible by the ruddy glow of the local star. The other ships of the MIEF were scattered across the sky, attempting to avoid the relentless approach of some *twenty* Xul hunterships of various shapes and sizes. Twelve light-seconds away, sunward, his sensors showed a large, stationary complex of some sort . . . obviously a large Xul orbital fortress. More Xul ships were emerging from it as he watched.

"Okay," Captain Angi's voice said. "We have you on lidar. Your range to the local sun is now seven point one-three light-minutes. The flight profile calls for you to go through at five *c* . . . so that puts the detonation at one point four two six minutes, that's one minute, twenty-five point five six seconds. If all goes well, the star blows and the wave-front reaches us seven minutes and eight seconds after that . . . so call it eight and a half minutes after you engage your drive. We will time our maneuver from that moment."

"Right, Captain," Garroway replied. All of this had been downloaded to him already, but the confirmation—being certain that everyone was operating on the same wave-length—was vital.

"With luck, you'll pass through the star and emerge on the other side. Just keep your drive on long enough to clear the radiation front, and you should be okay."

He could hear the unbelief in Angi's mental voice. The guy was whistling in the dark. Or he was convinced that Garroway was on a suicide run, and lying to spare Garroway's feelings.

"I was told to hold my speed at five *c* and to stay in warp for an hour after I hit the core," Garroway said. "That will put me five light-hours from the star, which should be plenty of space."

There was no reply at first. More Xul Type I's and Type II's were converging rapidly on the MIEF squadron, and the *Mars* had just taken a savage burst of particle-beam fire. The battlecruiser lurched, rolling heavily to starboard, already slewing to port to return fire with her main gun.

"You'd better get going," Angi told him. "Good luck, Marine. God go with you!"

"You, too," Garroway said. "Looks like you may need Him more than me."

He checked his targeting cursor, which was centered perfectly on the red-orange globe of the local star. "Are we set, Achilles?"

"All systems on-line," the AI said. "Ready at your command. . . ."

He gave the thought-click order, and the universe—MIEF fleet, Xul attackers, red-orange star, and that incredible background vista of star clouds all blinked out of existence. . . .

26

Jonah
Cygni Space/Starwall Space
1258 hrs GMT

Garroway took careful note of the time—1258 hours, nine seconds. From the instant Achilles$_2$ engaged the Alcubierre Drive to the center of the star, the flight time should be one minute, twenty-five seconds. An abstract part of his mind wondered about acceleration; did a ship under this alien version of the Alcubierre Drive leap instantly to 5c? Or, as with human ships, did it take a few minutes to build up to speed from a standing start?

Then he realized that the flight profile called for a *mean* velocity of five times the speed of light. It might well take seconds or even as much as a minute to build up to speed, but if so, Achilles$_2$ would take the craft up to *more* than 5c in order to compensate for the lost time at lower speeds. He started to set the problem up—a simple enough bit of calculus—then decided it really didn't matter. He didn't know enough about the trigger ship's capabilities. Gods willing, Achilles$_2$ did. If he didn't, they were *all* in a lot of trouble.

He wondered what the star's name was. No one had told him. But then, Starwall Space was supposed to be eighteen thousand light-years away from Sol. You wouldn't even be able to see this star from Earth, save as a part of the misty backdrop of the Milky Way, somewhere in the constellation of Sagittarius.

The data he possessed did say that the star was a Type K0 IV giant, with a diameter of about three times that of Earth's sun—make it 4, no, 4.2 million kilometers. That would be . . . he ran a quick calc, and blinked with surprise. Fourteen light-seconds. That was big. . . .

And at $5c$, it would take his trigger ship just under three whole seconds to pass all the way through the star. Somehow, when they'd told him he would be flying faster than light through the heart of a star, he'd thought he would be in and out so fast he wouldn't even notice. He'd had no idea it would take that long to make the passage.

Thirty seconds to go. . . .

He *did* wish he could see out. There was no sensation of movement or acceleration whatsoever, and not a glimmer of light from the outside. Considering where he was about to go, this was a *good* thing, he knew. If that glimmer was able to reach him, by the time the trigger ship hit the star's photosphere the energy would be enough to vaporize the ship.

Ten seconds.

He wondered if he would feel the star's gravity. No . . . gravitational effects should be shunted aside by the warp bubble as well. According to the experts, he ought to be so completely cocooned in that bubble that he would feel nothing at all . . . in another five . . . four . . . three . . . two . . .

In fact it felt like hitting a brick wall. He felt a violent shock, so hard the interior of his armor instantly embraced him in something like a thick, gelatinous foam to take up some of the impact.

And the shock continued, dragging on for what seemed like an eternity, and which in fact lasted less than three seconds.

Garroway was unconscious by the time he emerged from the star. . . .

* * *

UCS Hermes
Stargate
Aquila Space
1259 hrs GMT

"Okay," Alexander said, as his internal clock flickered past 1259 and thirty-four seconds. "Time."

A QCC message flashed over from the *Mars* had given them the word. Garroway had switched to Alcubierre Drive at 1258:09 and vanished; at 1259:34 he should have reached the center of the target star. As the seconds continued ticking, Garroway would be hurtling out the other side, and the star should be rebounding in upon itself after the hyper-*c* shockwave of the passing warp bubble tunneling through its heart.

A second clock was now counting down from seven minutes, eight seconds. That was how long the wave-front would take to reach the stargate from the detonating star.

The problem was, they were operating in unknown territory, here. The passage of the warp bubble should trigger a nova, yes. The Eulers had done this sort of thing at least five times before in their past. But the explosion probably—emphasis on *probably*—wouldn't be instantaneous. Theory said the wave of compressing, then expanding space within the star's core would create a massive shockwave that would force the star to begin collapsing upon itself. At some point, the star's mass would rebound, hurtling outward as a titanic explosion . . . but just how long would that take? Several seconds? A minute? Hell . . . a week?

They didn't have a week, of course. The Xul Type II was still bearing down upon them. *Hermes* shuddered under another direct hit.

"Tug Four is gone," Taggart said. "We're more adrift now than under power."

Alexander was studying the tactical situation. The Xul ship was still 500 kilometers away, almost directly between the Gate and the retreating *Hermes*. The *Hermes* was accelerating outbound from the Gate, but slowly, *slowly*, as enemy fire continued to rake her.

"Just how hard up are we?" he asked Taggart.

"Why do you want to know?"

"Look, it may be a bit late, but something just occurred to me. The blast from that nova is going to hit the other side of that gate just seven minutes from now. Do we want to be here when it does?"

"Oh, my God. . . ."

"I suggest, Admiral, that we find a way to put some lateral acceleration on this thing, see if we can nudge ourselves out of the line of fire. . . ."

"You're right." A pause. "Damn."

"What?"

"General, I don't think we're going to make it."

"Can we translate?"

"I was just checking that. The quantum tap converters are junk. We barely have enough battery and capacitor power right now to keep firing."

"Can we change the Gate's tuning?" If the stargate was open to another region of space—back to Puller 659, for instance—the Gate would effectively be closed when the energy from the exploding star reached it.

"No go. Navigation says they think the Xul are overriding our signals somehow. They tried to connect, and couldn't. We signaled both *Lejeune* and *Chosin*, and they couldn't get through, either."

"They may have locked the Gate open, so that if our people come back through, they know they arrive here."

"Good possibility."

No one had any idea what would happen when the star blew on the other side of the Gate. The immediate effect would be light and hard radiation, a very great deal of both. Traveling at the speed of light, they would hit the Gate seven minutes and a few seconds after the star exploded.

The second effect would actually be worse. Heavier particles and white-hot plasma would be following that initial wave front, lagging behind by about twenty minutes. Finally, the main body of stellar debris—a fast-expanding shell of intensely hot plasma—might take a day to reach the Gate. The light and radiation of the first front, though, would be

more than enough to cause a great deal of hurt if it was able
to pass through the open Gate.

"We may still have one chance," Alexander said. "Let's
try something. . . ."

UCS Mars
Stargate
Starwall Space
1306 hrs GMT

Captain Angi checked his time readout. "Okay, everyone,"
he said over the FleetNet. "Heads up, now. If that Marine
did his job, the star should have blown and the wave-front
ought to be on its way. We have thirty more seconds to go."

The battle continued to flash and flame around them as
the Xul ships closed in. Commanding the flotilla, Angi had
directed all surviving ships to align themselves in a particular direction, aimed at the stars. Navigational officers
on every ship in the fleet had their full attention focused
on the local star, which continued to burn peacefully in the
distance.

Strange to think that, if all had gone as planned, the star
was already destroyed, already a blazing nova.

The light just hadn't reached them yet.

Fifteen seconds.

For this to work, they couldn't just slip into Alcubierre
Drive at the seven minutes, eight seconds mark. No one
knew just how long it would take for the star's core to rebound and detonate, and, evidently, the Eulers hadn't been
able to explain that part.

That meant that human eyes and AI senses would be
studying the star intently, and the word would not be given
until *some* sign of instability was detected.

How long that would be was anybody's guess.

The UCS *Alcyone* was gone, crushed from existence by
the unseen fist of a Xul force weapon. The *Hera* and the
Salamone both were drifting, helpless wrecks. Other ships
were taking hellish damage.

This could *not* go on much longer. . . .

"Ares? Give me a count, please."

Ares was the *Mars*' shipboard AI, and Angi's personal assistant. "Five seconds," the AI murmured in his thoughts. "Four . . . three . . . two . . . one . . . mark. And counting. Plus two . . . plus three . . . plus four . . ."

"Never mind the second-by-second rundown," he told the AI. "Is everyone ready to go at the word?"

"All ships, all stations, report ready, Captain."

"Okay. Commence acceleration, but gravitics only. Ten gravities."

"Accelerating, ten gravities. Aye, aye."

But not all of the survivors of 1MIEF could manage ten gravities. The destroyer *Ganga* was barely able to make two. Two of the Valkyries, *Skuld* and *Radgrid*, were close in against a Xul Type II, pounding away at the monster at point-blank range. Either they didn't get the word, or their drives were dead. They weren't moving.

Angi stared into the sullen image of the star. *Do something, damn it*, he thought. *Do some—*

"Spectral shift in the star!" a voice called over the Net. "Going to blue! . . ."

"It's going!"

"All commands," Angi yelled. *"Execute! Execute! Execute!"*

And in rapid succession, the MIEF warships began winking out of existence.

UCS Hermes
Stargate
Aquila Space
1306 hrs GMT

"Captain Angi just gave the execute order," Taggart said.

"Here it comes, then," Garroway said. "How are we doing?"

"Not good, but we're moving. . . ."

Hermes massed some two million tons, the carrier *Lejeune* just over 87,000 tons, but the carrier's gravitics were still in good shape and she packed a hell of a lot of thrust.

Admiral Forsythe, the *Lejeune*'s skipper, had brought the carrier up to *Hermes*' massive flank, pressed her blunt nose up against the hull, and begun pushing, hard.

They'd only had time for a couple of minutes of thrust, and the Xul ship appeared to be trying to target the carrier now deliberately . . . but the vast bulk of the *Hermes* was moving out of a direct line with the stargate's lumen.

This might all be for nothing, Garroway thought, lying in the Ops couch and waiting for death as the Xul ship fired a final volley, or death as a star exploded through the Gate. One of the minor mysteries of the Gate was that light and other radiation did not normally pass through the central opening. That was why you couldn't signal through an open gateway with radio, or look through from one side to see an entirely different starscape on the other. The physics boys were still arguing about that one; the favored theory was that the gate was open in tiny, discrete instants of time. Why that would block visible light and not a slow-moving star-ship, though, was not translatable into something approaching standard Anglic.

The face of the Stargate, the space within the rim, was starting to glow.

Maybe it just took a *lot* of light. . . .

The Gate's face grew brighter, taking on the aspect of a shining, flat disk. *Hermes* and *Lejeune* were *almost* out of the shaft of light emerging from the Gate, now, almost but not quite. Damage control reported radiation levels rising in the illuminated portion of the ship.

The Xul Type II was still squarely in front of the Gate, one side of its hull sharply illuminated now by the rapidly increasing glare, the other half in utterly black shadow.

"Make to the *Lejeune*!" Alexander told Cara. "Give us more thrust!"

"Captain Forsythe reports he is at one hundred twenty percent power now. His power tap feed is threatening to overload."

"Tell him it won't matter if we can't get the hell out of the way!"

"Yes, sir."

Lejeune's thrust increased. Alexander could actually feel a slight shudder passing through the couch beneath his back, a kind of steady, building thrum as the carrier served as an immense tug, maneuvering the Goliath *Hermes* aside.

"We're clear, General. . . ."

"Thank God!"

The Xul vessel had stopped firing, had stopped accelerating, and now was drifting in that hellfire glare.

Probes still within the shaft of light from the stargate reported soaring radiation levels . . . and then, in rapid succession, they died.

"Make to *Samar*," Alexander said after a long, exhausted moment. "Tell them . . . tell them PFC Garroway has successfully completed his mission."

Cygni Space/Starwall Space
1307 hrs GMT

Nova light flooded circumambient space.

Type IV giant stars do not, as a rule, possess planetary systems, and this one was no exception. It did possess a fair amount of asteroidal debris, and the commune of intelligence known as We Who Are, millennia before, had used that material to build one of their primary nodes.

Circling the star at various distances were no fewer than three hundred fortress-like structures, each the size of a small moon. Thousands of ships of all types, including many not yet seen and catalogued by human observers, were moored at docking bays, or orbiting in the star's somber red light . . . some being readied for patrol, some undergoing a periodic refit and updating, some being constructed out of the available local raw materials.

And, of course, there was the stargate itself.

The Lords Who Are of this region of space had long been considering what to do about the troublesome life form known as Species 2824, and its originating system, 2420–544. Some, indeed, had moved at a most unseemly haste in their urgency to do something about the offending life form. The recent return of a galactic picket with word that one of the aliens' sublight ships had been taken, patterned, and destroyed, had accelerated that haste.

Perhaps that urgency was even justified. Species 2824 had proven to be unexpectedly resourceful. Evidently, they had allied with another troublesome species—designated 3990— and learned that species' techniques for destroying stars.

The battle with the intruding fleet had been raging for some time out near the system's stargate, and victory had been assured when, suddenly, shockingly, the entire enemy battlefleet had vanished.

No matter. It could only be a delaying maneuver. The aliens were cut off from the stargate, and could easily be pursued by hunterships. It would take only a few moments for the hunterships to come to full power and engage their drives. They would overtake the fleeing enemy ships in seconds, matching vectors.

And then . . .

But there was no "and then." One by one, in-laying stations and nodal structures had been overtaken by the fast-expanding wave of raw, horrific light racing out from the central star. Sensors overloaded and burned out. Radiation soared. Electromagnetic flux burned through circuitry.

The minds of We Who Are once had been organic, but existed now as nested electromagnetic patterns within the circuitry of their ships, their base fortresses, their planet-wide cities. As circuitry melted, those minds were destroyed.

The leaders of the Xul commune, the Lords Who Are, died as the hardware supporting them overloaded, then melted, then vaporized. As they died, the metamind of which they all were composite parts, the metamind that gave shape and purpose to the local will of We Who Are, died. Some individual fragments, lone hunterships or far-outlying bases and outposts survived . . . but only for a short while. Fast on the heels of the dying star's light came the more massive, deadlier onslaught of high-energy particles.

And not a single Xul huntership saw the danger in time to save itself.

Not a single one of We Who Are within the Starwall node survived. . . .

Jonah
Cygni Space/Starwall Space
1835 hrs GMT

This, Garroway thought muzzily, *is not good. I still can't see out, and it's been over six hours. Either I'm still going FTL, or the whole damned ship is dead.*

Either way . . . not good. . . .

He was just now clawing his way back to consciousness. His internal timepiece showed how much time had elapsed since his passage through the core of the star.

He felt . . . terrible, broken and bruised throughout his body, and he felt like he was suffering from an excruciating case of sunburn.

His stomach twisted, then heaved. His internal nano was damping down the nausea, but the treatment so far was only partially successful.

Medical sensors were reporting . . . no. He couldn't have absorbed *that* much radiation. . . .

"Achilles? Achilles, are you there?"

"I am here."

"What the hell is going on? Why haven't we dropped out of Drive?"

"Evidence suggests that we have, Private Garroway. The radiation sensors in your combat armor show an extremely high flux."

"Shit. Did that leak through from the nova, somehow? . . ."

"Nothing *leaked*, as you put it, while we were within the star. However, we did encounter some . . . turbulence during the passage. Many of the ship's systems were damaged or otherwise incapacitated. The Alcubierre Drive appears to have cut out only about ten minutes after our passage."

"Then . . . we got caught in the blast?"

"Affirmative. We were fifty light-minutes from the star by that time, however, so damage was relatively minimal. At least, we were not vaporized immediately. Radiation levels were high. We are also continuing to sustain radiation damage from the stellar background."

"Pardon?"

"The galactic core is an extremely active region, with over-all high levels of particulate radiation. Lieutenant Lee was badly burned after an exposure of about forty minutes."

"Forty minutes. And I've been out here for . . ."

"Five hours, nineteen minutes."

Nausea clawed at him. This time, his internal nano couldn't handle the surge, and he was achingly, desperately sick inside his armor.

A long time after, he sipped water from the helmet input valve near his mouth.

"How . . . long do I have?"

His suit monitors reported hard vacuum around him. Well . . . of course. He'd been in vacuum when they'd shoved him inside. He tried to rub his eyes, and was frustrated when his gauntlet bumped against the side of his helmet. He wasn't thinking very well.

Garroway was seriously tempted to open his helmet. Explosive decompression would kill him pretty quick—a rush of air from his lungs, a sharp pain as he gasped for breath. A moment or two of pain and cold and growing numbness . . .

The thought of slowly baking to death in hard radiation was not nearly so pleasant. In his mind's eye, he could imagine the blistering, the sloughing skin. His internal nano would fight to keep his organ systems going, though. He might linger . . . how long?

Achilles$_2$ had not responded right away. Maybe the AI was balancing the psychological harm the news might impart. Hell, he *knew* he was going to die. . . .

"There's no way to be sure," Achilles told him. "The dosage you've received already *is* fatal, and you're picking up more rads with each passing moment. Without intervention, and depending on the efficiency of your medinano at handling things like organ system shut-down and internal hemorrhage, I estimate you will survive between twenty-four and thirty-six hours."

A day to a day and a half of agony. He already hurt, and he knew the pain would get worse.

Better to crack his helmet while he still could, while he still had some strength.

"What did you mean by 'intervention?'"

"There remains the very real possibility of rescue," Achilles₂ told him. "Do you think your comrades will give up on you without even trying to find you?"

"No," he said. Marines never abandoned their own. "No, but what chance is there of them finding us?"

The MIEF flotilla on this side of the stargate was poised to enter Alcubierre Drive just before the wave-front hit them. If all went according to plan, the Xul ships would have been overwhelmed and destroyed before they could pursue. The MIEF ships would have retired to a safe distance, outside of the star's primary blast radius, then would have begun searching along our projected line of flight. They would not leave you.

"Yeah . . . but if what you say is right, we lost our drive fifty light-minutes out from the star. We were supposed to stay under Drive until we were over five times farther out. This is a very tiny ship. They'll never . . . never . . ." He stopped, overwhelmed once again by savage nausea. He began vomiting, and when there was nothing left to come up he continued retching again and again and again. He lay there, wondering if that was the end of it, and then he began vomiting again . . . this time blood.

His helmet systems drained much of the mess, keeping him from drowning, but he wore a mask of foul slime, and the pain was nearly unbearable. He was so weak that each breath was a struggle. The stench . . . the stench alone made him long for death.

"Even . . . if they find us . . ." he said at last. "I'm an irrie."

"Not true, Private. What is it you humans like to say . . . 'where there's life, there's hope'? The medical facilities aboard the *Samar* are quite good. The facilities on the *Barton* are even better. Radiation poisoning is well understood. There are nanomedical techniques that—"

"They're not fucking going to find us, damn it! We are a *very* small grain of sand lost in a very large ocean." He paused, gasping for a moment for his next breath. When he had strength again, he added, "Take over, Achilles. If they

do find us, they'll want a complete download of all of this. I'm cracking my helmet."

"I recommend that you do nothing, Private."

"Who are you to give me orders?"

"I believe there is a genuine chance that help might come. It is my duty to preserve your life, if possible."

"Fuck you. . . ."

He reached for the lever on the side of his neck coupling that would release the helmet lock, but he couldn't move his arm.

"Achilles? Is that you?"

"I have overridden your armor's power systems, Private. Help *is* on the way."

He struggled for a moment, trying to move his leaden right arm, without success.

There was another way. He brought to mind a particular mental code, the code that would let him switch Achilles off. He wasn't entirely sure it would work. The code Sandre had taught him essentially caused the AI to overlook him without realizing he couldn't be seen, but that was for when Achilles was running in the hardware of a platoon of a hundred or so Marines. If there was just one Marine, and the AI was resident inside his internal hardware, what would happen?

He thought-clicked the code.

"Achilles?"

There was no response. Garroway tried moving his arm. It moved, sliding heavily across the surface of the Euler ship's cockpit deck. His glove hit the side of his helmet, and he fumbled for a moment, trying to find the lever.

He thought about Sandre.

He thought about the Corps. . . .

Ontos 7
Aquila Space
1842 hrs GMT

"*Got* him!" Warhurst cried. "Haul him in, gently!"

Gunnery Sergeant Warhurst, armor clad, was clinging to the flame-scoured hull of the Euler triggership with one

hand and both legs, his other hand gripping the line extending from the Ontos cargo deck.

The long, desperate search had paid off. Every ship in the
MIEF had been looking for him, including *Samar, Chosin,
Lejeune,* two wings of aerospace fighters, and fifty human-
piloted Euler triggerships that had come across just as soon
as it had been verified that the stargate was still operating.
The smaller ships couldn't search for long in the hellishly
high radiation fields here, but they'd contributed . . . mostly
by patrolling along the blast front to make sure there were
no surviving Xul in the system.

It had been Gunnery Sergeant Ramsey, back at RFS
Alpha, who'd suggested using clouds of NeP probes, firing
them at high velocity along the projected line of Garroway's
flight path out from the star. There was no radio signal to
track, and the Euler triggership's infrared signature was lost
in the far greater heat-glare of the exploding star.

But by chance alone, some few of those millions of nano
e-penetrators, their antenna-nets flung wide, had passed
through the shadow cast by the triggership, detected the
faintest fall-off of light from the star, and homed on the
source.

One had struck the triggership's hull, and transmitted
back to the *Mars* the triggership's hull composition and its
location.

Moments later, *Mars* and *Lejeune* were closing on the
spot, far deeper into the deadly white blossom of the exploding star than anyone had guessed.

Ontos 7 had been back on board the *Lejeune.* Warhurst,
Eden, and Galena had emerged from the battered carrier's
launch bay to make the actual capture.

The Euler triggership was too large to winch into the
Ontos' cargo bay. Instead, Warhurst had emerged with a
tow cable and used a nanolock to fuse it to the tiny vessel's
hull.

"The controls aren't working," he said after a moment's
trying to link with the triggership's AI. "It won't respond to
the codes. I'll have to melt through the hull." He brought his
fist down on the hull, hard, several times. "Hey, in there!" he

called on the assigned frequency. "Garroway! Do you hear me? We're going to get you out!"

There was no response, which could mean that Garroway's radio was out. Or, judging from the look of that hull, and the levels of background radiation, it could mean—

No. Don't think about that.

Warhurst had been Garroway's DI. He still thought of the kid as one of *his* Marines.

He could feel the mad tingle, the burn of the radiation. The nova was an intensely brilliant blaze of light that blotted out one entire half of the universe, and turned his visor opaque every time he twisted in that direction. He'd learned to keep his back to the star. Even then, the reflection off the triggership's hull was so bright he could scarcely see anything at all.

He pulled a squeeze tube from a thigh pouch and began squeezing the contents out onto the Euler vessel's hull.

"Warhurst?" Eden's voice said from inside the Ontos. "You've got five minutes."

"I know, I know." The Ontos' magnetic screens provided some shielding, at least, from particulate radiation. Out here, there was nothing but his armor. He knew he was being badly burned, but he tried not to think about that. His 660-armor was deflecting the worst of the hard stuff, especially the heavier particles, but he only had another five minutes or so out here before he started suffering physical effects—nausea and vomiting, sloughing skin, weakness, bleeding. . . .

No matter what, it would be medical cybe-hibe and nano-reconstruction on board the *Barton* for him, no question. . . .

But that was a small enough price to pay, if he could bring Garroway with him.

The paste outlined a rectangle 2 meters long and a meter wide. He pulled a nanocharge release from another pouch, stuck it in the paste, and pulled his hand away. "Fire in the hole."

There was no actual fire, of course. The nano was nano-D, designed to eat quickly through various composites. A quick test had already verified that it worked on Euler ship hulls.

Something like white talcum exploded from the strip, and the hull section floated free, opening up the craft's interior. There was no need for his armor lights. The dying sun behind him illuminated the interior clearly. Reaching in, he grabbed Garroway's arm.

"Garroway? You okay?"

At first there was no reaction, and he thought—

Garroway moved. He couldn't turn his helmet, but Warhurst could see movement behind the vomit smeared visor. The Marine's hand reached out and grabbed Warhurst's wrist, weak . . . but alive. *Alive.*

"I've got him, people," Warhurst said. "I'm bringing him in. . . ."

Epilogue

UCS Barton
Cygni Space
0915 hrs GMT

"Garroway? How you feeling, son?"

Garroway opened his eyes, trying to focus. There was a tall man standing next to him. A tall man in a Marine dress uniform.

"Terrible," he replied. He managed to focus on the apparition's rank tabs, and his eyes opened wider. "Uh . . . terrible, *sir*!" He tried to sit up, and failed. He was pinned to the bed by a labyrinth of tubes, conduits, and data feeds.

"At ease, at ease," the apparition said. "I'm General Alexander. They told me they were bringing you out of medical cybe-hibe this morning. I wanted to stop by and see you."

"Uh, yes, sir." He blinked. The last thing he remembered . . .

"You have every right to feel terrible. I gather they've been practically regrowing you from scratch. Right now, I think you have more medical nano inside you than you have cells, snipping out the bad bits and weaving together the good!"

"I . . . was going to kill myself. I was trying to kill myself. . . ."

"I know. Your platoon AI told us all about it." Alexander folded his arms. "I suppose I should chew you a new one for trying to destroy government property. But under the circumstances, you had every right. I'm just glad you didn't carry it through."

"I tried, sir. I really did. But I couldn't find the catch on my helmet."

He grinned. "Yeah. I heard, Achilles said when you shut him out, he couldn't freeze your arm actuators any longer, but he *could* still overload the sensory feedback circuits in the sleeve of your armor. Not lock them, but feed extra energy through them, burn them out. You thought you were reaching for the release lever, but you couldn't control the arm of your 660 well enough to find it."

"I . . . know. I kept hitting my helmet, scraping at the side. Couldn't figure why I couldn't hit it. Such a simple thing. Then . . . then I heard a thump on the ship's hull. I thought God was knocking."

"Almost," Alexander said, nodding. "Gunnery Sergeant Warhurst. Now Staff Sergeant Warhurst, by the way. He's in the next compartment over, next to yours. You'll be able to thank him in person in a day or two, I'm told."

"'Next compartment?' Where are we, anyway, sir?"

"You're on board the medical ship *Barton*. You've been a long time healing. So has he, though he wasn't nearly as burned to a crisp as you were!"

"How . . . long?"

"About a month. It's now 15 January, in this, the Year of our Corps 1103."

"A month! And . . . did it work? The mission, I mean."

"Perfectly. Complete success. You followed your mission profile down to the letter, the star blew, and as near as we can tell, every Xul in the system was vaporized." His face showed a sudden sadness. "We lost a lot of ships before it was all over. A *lot* of people. But most of the MIEF came through."

"So . . . what happens now, sir?"

"Operation Gorgon continues. We rest, we refit. We make up our losses, both in men and ships. And we plan where to hit the Xul next."

"We have a weapon that can kick 'em right where it hurts, General."

"And allies," Alexander added. "Damned if I know how we're going to incorporate them into a *Marine* unit, but we have allies. The Eulers, definitely. And maybe some others as well."

"Uh, where are we now, anyway? Back at Earth? Or at Puller 659?"

"Actually, we're in Aquila Space, though we have pickets rotating out at Starwall, watching for the Xul. We've been in contact with Earth, though, with QCC . . . and with Aurore, too, and there's been some ship traffic back and forth. You'll be interested to know that we might have some unexpected reinforcements coming through the Gate soon. The PEs are joining us. The *Rommel* and some of the other ships at Puller have already come through. I guess the PanEuropeans were rather impressed by your little escapade at Starwall. Or . . ." He shrugged. "Maybe they just don't want us to have the technology for blowing up stars all to ourselves. The politics of this are going to be damned interesting."

"Shit, sir. Who the hell needs them? We can take on the Xul ourselves!"

Alexander grinned. "That's the spirit, Marine." Bending over, he clapped Garroway's shoulder, then reached into a belt pouch. "Oh, by the way. I've got something for you here. . . ."

He pulled out two felt-covered gray cases, and opened them one after another, then set them on the pillow by Garroway's head. Garroway turned his head, trying to focus on them.

"The Purple Heart," Alexander said. "And the Medal of Honor. There'll be a formal ceremony later, when you're recovered, but I wanted to be the one to let you know."

"I . . . I don't know what to say, sir."

Alexander shrugged. "What is there to say? You earned them both."

"But it wasn't just me, sir. I was just stupid enough to volunteer."

"You're right, of course. But, well . . . you and I both know it's not about medals."

"No, sir."

He gestured at the Medal of Honor, gold star gleaming beneath a blue silk ribbon, a design a millennium old. "I did some checking. I gather you're not the first Garroway to win that little blue ribbon."

"No, sir." Sands of Mars Garroway had won the coveted award some eight centuries before.

Tradition.

Duty.

Brotherhood.

"General?"

"Yeah?"

"Thanks for coming after me. For looking for me. I . . . I guess I kind of lost faith out there. I didn't think you would find me."

"Hey, Marines never leave their own behind. *Never.*"

"I . . . know."

"Semper fi," Alexander told him. "Semper fi, *Marine.*"